Kerryl's eyes grew wide and he felt Dalli's sticky hand clutching his as the first of the Thirty-six Flowers at last approached: sixteen matched allosaurs, their horrendous talons gilded a sparkling gold. Seventeen feet high, the terrible yellow and gold carnosaurs marched stiffly forward on their two enormous hind legs, their massive tails held straight behind them in delicate counterbalance. Their frightful heads darted from side to side as their glittering yellow eyes moved unnervingly over the ranks of recoiling spectators, while their two small forearms with three hook-like talons twitched in excitement.

An enormous garland of blue and white blossoms from the moonfruit tree had been fixed around the rear of each bony skull; a thick lei of the same meaty blossoms had been draped around the animals' brutish necks to dangle against their glossy round bellies. On the top of each head sat a small Jairaben drover in bright red breeches and silver tunic, apparently imperturbable as he directed the progress of his fearsome charge with judicious taps from a silver swagger stick.

Dalli's small damp hand tightened around Kerryl's as the hot fetid breath of first one allosaurus and then another wafted down and over them. Snuffling and belching, the great monsters marched past the Tandryl-Kundórrs and on to the reviewing stand, where the cold black eyes of the Most Immaculate Ultim of Aberdown now glittered with a dreamy pleasure.

BEN BOVA PRESENTS

THE THIRTEENTH MAJESTRAL

HAYFORD PEIRCE

TOR

A TOM DOHERTY ASSOCIATES BOOK
NEW YORK

Pour La Belle Douchka, la joie de ma vie, enfin

THE THIRTEENTH MAJESTRAL

Copyright © 1989 by Hayford Peirce Living Trust

A TOR Book
Published by Tom Doherty Associates, Inc.
49 West 24 Street
New York, NY 10010

Cover design by Carol Russo

ISBN: 0-812-54892-2   Can. ISBN: 0-812-54893-0

Library of Congress Catalog Card Number: 88-51632

First edition: May 1989

PRINTED IN THE UNITED STATES OF AMERICA

0 9 8 7 6 5 4 3 2 1

PROLOGUE

At the urgent summons of Lord Blaibeck of Phaëtan, Majestral Doyaine, the prisoner had been brought to the Crystal Tower atop the Adamantine Overlook in the hours before dawn on the nineteenth day of Hespheros in the year 28,395 FIP. Here the paralyzed outworlder, a certain Lulmö Häistön of the planet Ambrose, had been examined under mindflow by the twelve Palatines who comprised the Colloquy of the Duze Majestrals.

Interrogation had quickly identified him as being in actuality one Kerryl Ryson of the obscure planet of Stohlson's Redemption in the equally obscure Diobastan Cluster on the far side of the galaxy. Now Kerryl Ryson stood rigidly between a guard of four nervous leperons in a distant corner of the octagonal room, his features cast into heavy shadows by a beam of harsh yellow light as he silently awaited his fate.

For only the second time since their initial Colloquy twenty years before, all twelve of the current majestrals were physically present at the Adamantine Outlook. Lord Blaibeck of Phaëtan, the Majestral Doyaine, could be seen shimmering in a dozen translucent colors somewhere within the highest point of the glittering crystalline structure that filled most of the airy tower chamber; below him his eleven peers were scattered in haphazard fashion throughout the same semi-transparent construct.

Uneasily fingering his long narrow chin, Blaibeck nervously whistled a few shrill bars from "The March

of Vainglorious Yellow," one of the invaluable perqui-
sites accruing to the victors of the Tinctorian Games.
The eleven other majestrals, five men and six women,
scowled darkly at their Doyaine and his churlish whistling. None of them were at ease encased here in the
bowels of the peculiar crystalline contrivance which
Blaibeck had provided in lieu of straightforward chairs.
To Blaibeck this curious artifact might well represent a
sublime expression of the crystal-growers' art; to his
fellow majestrals its disconcerting semi-insubstan-
tiality and unpredictable propensity for suddenly rotating its startled occupants along of three axes only
exacerbated the emotional discomfort already engendered by the convocation of this extraordinary gather-
ing.

"Are we decided then, Citrine, what must be done
with this disruptive outworlder?" demanded Lady
Laizon of Baurauban, Majestral of Tebbiwez, in the
language native to the planet. The captive, almost
totally paralyzed by the neuronic grapples wielded by
his leperon guards, could only roll his eyes in the
direction of her voice. In addition to Versal, Kerryl
Ryson spoke three other languages fluently and had a
smattering of a dozen more; but that of the majestrals
was to him merely a babble of meaningless sound. "He
has now answered our questions; the danger is plain. Is
there any further reason for prolonging this Colloquy?
Already it has deprived me of many invaluable hours of
contemplation of The Four Ripple Conundrum."

The Majestral Doyaine tugged at the heavy amulet
of beaten gold in the form of a prancing chamois that
dangled against his thick yellow chemise and sighed
heavily. Once again his eyes were drawn reluctantly to
the far corner of the chamber where pallid leperons in
red kirtles, yellow breeches, and glossy black boots
maintained their neuronic grapples upon the outworld
prisoner, their pale blue eyes flickering nervously. "We
are agreed that his very existence represents the most
fearful risk our planet has faced in over a million

years," said Blaibeck. "Surely there can be no doubt as to the outcome?"

"But according to what we have just heard," protested the Majestral of Saverhol, Lord Cundee of Cockaloupe, in a voice in which hysteria clearly lurked, "there *is* no way by which we *can* implement his deletion!" He darted an uneasy glance at the silent captive. "He is totally impervious to anything we can—"

"Nonsense!" interrupted Lord Zeeder of Mistane, Majestral of Dreymon, the zoïtie adjudicated second in the most recent Games and hence denominated Lofty Damson. "Spoken like a very Mouse!" Lord Zedder glared at Lord Cundee through the opaque crystal of Lord Blaibeck's outlandish furniture with all the ferocity of his clan's zoïdion, the Tassavian Devil.

"If it's insults—" flared Cundee, but was quickly overridden by Damson's longtime ally, Worthy Cadmium's Lord Gaugrich of Greenwood.

"What Damson intends to convey is that means of deletion exist which are so ancient and so seldom employed as to have fallen into total abeyance among genteel folk such as the Palatines. They are known only to the rude outworlders."

"You mean: we must *physically* kill this man?" Lord Cundee of Cockaloupe rocked back in astonishment.

"What else do you suggest?"

"But—*how*?" Lady Taum-Shu of Cobbset, Majestral of Neavre, leaned forward and fixed her sharp gray eyes on Gaugrich. "You personally then, Gaugrich, will affix your fingers about his throat and—"

The skeletal-thin majestral representing the Zoïtie of Curf paled in dismay. "*I*, dear Dove? I merely—"

"So I imagined!" Lady Taum-Shu's slight frame twisted about in her semi-transparent enclosure as she let her scornful gaze fall in turn on each of her fellow majestrals. "We speak of killing. Who among us has had practical experience of this novelty? You, Bold

Ebon? Wilting Lilac, Illusive Jasper, Valued Turquoise, speak up! Perhaps you, Towering Vermillion?"

"Fah!" interjected Bold Ebon, Lord Mesmer of Frotz, Majestral of Gollimaul. His tiny black eyes glittered in his round, florid face, his voice was heavy with sardonicism. "Let us first review our respective positions. Here in the central fastness of the Crystal Tower stands the outworlder some twenty thousand light-years from home; he is hemmed in on all sides by determined and ferocious leperons, totally immobilized by neuronic grapples." Lord Mesmer gestured derisively. "And which of us quails in trepidation before the other: this utterly helpless captive, or those twelve mighty rulers, the dauntless Duze Majestrals?"*

A babble of protesting voices instantly arose.

Only Kerryl Ryson's eyes, a lustrous green tinted with bright flecks of gold, were capable of movement; they glittered with thwarted rage and naked hatred as they flickered back and forth between the grim and frightened faces of those who sat to decide his personal fate, and that of his distant home of Stohlson's Redemption . . .

---

*A few scholarly eccentrics perversely maintained that the word *duze* had once signified the number twelve in some long-forgotten language. The majority of authorities, however, citing its present connotation of "stately or weighty deliberation," traced its roots to *doojden* or *doosten*, which in the ancient language of the Naracooti in southern Biloela was generally translated as "unrelenting authoritativeness."

PART ONE

CHAPTER 1

Who was Stohlson, what was his Redemption?
No one knows.

Humanity had spread across the galaxy, its birth-
place largely forgotten. It had mutated, changed, and
adapted. A million bizarre societies flourished; as many
more religions, cults, and sects proclaimed their univer-
sality. Only the most inaccessible and sparsely popu-
lated planets were immune to the blandishments,
threats, and entreaties of the hordes of messiahs, re-
deemers, evangelists, and cranks who roamed the cosmos seeking converts.

At some time in the distant past the adherents of
one such sect had perhaps sought to colonize the fourth
planet of a harsh blue sun on the edge of the Diobastan
Cluster, itself a distant grouping of recently formed
stars at the far end of the galaxy's spiral arm. If so, no
trace now remained of their works or their doctrines,
unless it was in the tantalizing name bequeathed to the
hot violent world which ten-year-old Kerryl Ryson
knew as home.

The Languid Endeavor, a heavily laden motor
barge of a hundred and sixty feet with a four-foot draft,
drifted ghost-iike through the dark gloom of the Great
Dismal Forest in the spring of 28,373 FIP.* Cargo was

---

*More formally: The 28,373rd Flowering of the Indomi-
table Perpetuality, a touchstone of universal convenience
acceded to by a slender majority of the delegates from
112,714 worlds at the Conclave of Mulhaut in the year
1,637,231 OFR (Old Fallacious Reckoning).

stacked high: a single tightly secured consignment of prime seven-year-old goldenose logs; three piles of lesser grade goldenose cut into roughly-shaped planks; six towering stacks of gobbleweed and fingerleaf boards; two hundred sacks of goldenose shavings.

A small red cabin with an angular blue smokestack sat athwart the bow a few inches above the placid current of the Sleepyhead River; here lived the ship's master with his three Cherryskin wives from Rupert's Diversion; the remaining deck space had been given over to two makeshift communities of circular lintwool tents. Nine of the tents were a cheerful orange with dark blue trim; within them were quartered the hundred and seven members of the Tandryl-Kundórrs. The other three tents were a sedate brown and maroon; here could be found the forty-four members of the small neighboring clan of Coober-Weezlers from Hunter's Hill, twenty-three miles to the east of Strichum's Wood.

Inside the largest of the orange and blue tents a fair-haired woman knelt on a blue velour cushion beside an impatient ten-year-old boy while she entwined a thick crown of aromatic whitebird flowers around the glossy brown tresses of his shoulder-length hair.

"But, Mother, must I *really* marry this awful girl from the Coober-Weezlers? Everyone will make mock of me with a name like Ryson-Weezler."

"*I* won't laugh at you," Kerryl's mother promised solemnly.

"Why can't she marry one of my brothers, Alvo, or Vartum, or Luslem?"

"They already have far more than enough wives of their own."

"But this one has red hair and freckles."

"Red hair can be most attractive."

"Yellow eyes and a squint!"

"She's only seven: ample time for a squint to subside."

"But I have to go and live with *them*, the Coo-ber-Weezlers!" wailed Kerryl Ryson. "In Hairy Goblin Wood, away from *you*! I'll never see you again in my entire life!" Unable to keep back tears, he threw himself miserably into the comfort of his mother's arms.

Elaina Ryson-Greenfern pulled his face against her shoulder to prevent him from seeing the grief that misted her own green eyes. "We'll see each other," she promised. "It simply won't be as often."

"But it's *you* I love, not this awful girl with freckles and a squint! Why can't I marry *you*?"

Elaina Ryson-Greenfern smiled wanly. "I fear that your father might raise practical objections, not to speak of the theological impediments posed by the Archimandrite of Ost."

"But *why* do I have to get married?"

"Because it is written in the Sixteenth Verse of the Second Chapter of the Seventh Enchiridion: 'It is better a thousand times to marry than a single time to mortify the flesh.'"

"I wish someone would tell me what *that* means," muttered Kerryl Ryson sullenly into the soft warmth of his mother's neck.

"Perhaps the Archimandrite will find the time to explain."

By imperceptible degrees *The Languid Endeavor* drifted out of the cool green sanctuary of the conifer forest and into the sullen damp heat and fetid stink of the Miasmic Swamp. The water became a turgid brown; the great fingerleaf trees that shaded the river gave way to sinister dark green clumps of stiletto pine surrounded by gossamerweed, Hoffdinger's singing cabbage, and sawtoothed devilgrass; glistening yellow hemispheres of noxious gases bubbled up and burst noisily to foul the air with the sour reek of sulfur and corruption; the quiet chirps of gigantic brachiosaurs browsing peacefully in the forest on goldenose gave way to a frenzy of shrieks, howls, and gibbering as the denizens of the Miasmic Swamp unremittingly tore each other to bloody shreds.

"Look, a brawny!" cried Dalli Weezler as the motor barge moved slowly through a shallow glade of bright purple marshberry. Kerryl dashed to the prow of *The Languid Endeavor* just as the massive arch of the animal's back rose ponderously out of the murky waters to starboard. Dalli Weezler squealed with delighted horror.

Myopic brown eyes blinked at the passing ship from either side of a tiny gray head appended like an afterthought to the end of a long rubbery neck; a single broad nostril flared between its two bulbous eyes; the beast moved slowly forward. The three Cherryskin females of the ship's company made ready to launch explosive noise-makers to fend off the forty-ton monster. Still half submerged in the reeking waters, the brontosaurus opened its delicate little mouth and yawned daintily. A moment later it had scrambled out of the water and into a thick clump of weedy green tanglewort. It lowered its head and began to eat. *The Languid Endeavor* passed on.

As the placid herbosaur was left behind, Kerryl quickly scrambled to the top of a high stack of gobbleweed planks for a last glimpse of the gigantic beast. "Have you ever seen a brawny before?" asked the freckle-faced seven-year-old as she infuriatingly clambered up to join him, her pale yellow eyes leering at Kerryl with their disquieting squint. "I didn't know they lived here in the swamp."

Angrily he turned his back to her. "Of course I have," he lied resolutely, "they're all around Strichum's Wood, thousands and thousands of them. Sometimes they fight with the reachers for the goldenose." He paused and took a deep breath. "And every one of them is prettier than you!"

Dalli Weezler's richly freckled face flushed an

angry red. "Just for that I won't tell you what trick Yonas Pionk the wiggleroot farmer once played on the Jairaben's tyran."

"I don't *want* to know."

"Good: I'm not going to tell you in any case."

Kerryl Ryson stared furiously into the passing swamp. Far away against the pale haze of the horizon he could now discern the faint outline of Mount Vomity. A thick plume of brownish-red smoke drifted lazily from its summit to smudge the hazy sky. His fists tightened in fury. "Why do you want to marry *me*?" he cried, half choked with anguish.

"*I* don't want to marry you! You think *I* want to make babies who'll have nasty green eyes like a sandy-finned slime-slider? Ugh!"

"No worry! I'll never make a baby with you!"

"Ha! My father will make you!"

"I'm not old enough, stupid!"

Dalli Weezler laughed knowingly. "Someday you will be, though. *Then* you'll have to!"

"I thought you said you didn't like green eyes," muttered Kerryl.

"I don't mind them; it's my mother who says they look like sandy-finned slime-sliders."

Kerryl Ryson shook his head incomprehendingly. "Then why does she want you to marry me?"

"*She* doesn't want me to. It's Father: he's discovered a thicket of goldenose on our freehold at Hollo's Junction that no one is working. *Your* father wants it all for his silly old mill."

Kerry considered this information morosely. Without goldenose, he knew, the Blue Finger Mill and the Tandryl-Kundórrs would hardly have prospered as they had in the two centuries since their founding by the clan's progenitor, the legendary Hollis Sasso. The rich odor of fragrant goldenose shavings was so much a part of life that on his infrequent trips away from home he was constantly amazed at how wrong the rest of the world smelled. Like the delicious odor of baking bread, the aroma of well-aged goldenose was both evocative and tantalizing. Little wonder that everyone on the planet, even the heathen Jairaben, sought to buy all the goldenose that Blue Finger Mill could produce!

Even Kerryl's father, Jeord Greenfern-Ryson, the font of all wisdom, was unable to satisfactorily explain why choice commercial-grade goldenose could only be milled from those towering conifers of the Great Dismal Forest which had first been stripped of their tender lower branches by the insatiable appetites of the herds of giant long-necked reachers that marched endlessly back and forth through the silent woods. Why was the nature of the goldenose tree so radically changed by this ruthless pruning of the lower sixty feet of branches? Could the flow of thick orange sap to the open wounds combine with unknown substances transmitted by the reachers to alter the goldenose?

Nobody knew.

Only one thing was known with absolute certainty by the inhabitants of Blue Finger Mill: the welfare of one hundred and seven Tandryl-Kundórrs was inexorably linked to the strange symbiosis that existed between goldenose and brachiosaur.

And this horrid redheaded girl's father was the owner of a thicket of goldenose . . . "And so *we* have to get married! That's not fair!" cried Kerryl Ryson.

"Life is never fair," replied Dalli Weezler triumphantly. "That's what *my* father says."

"Mine too." Kerryl took a hesitant step closer. "I've seen *lots* of brawnies, but never a tyran. They're big and *horrible*!" Reluctantly he raised his eyes to Dalli's. "What *did* the wiggleroot farmer do to the tyran?"

The air grew drier, the dank vegetation of the Miasmic Swamp slowly gave way to the bare brown riverbanks of Deadman's Desert. The flatness of the swamp became first rolling badlands, then a vast irregular desert with here and there an outcropping of some gigantic butte or mesa. The single smoking crater of Mount Vomity fell slowly behind them, replaced by a dozen others. Pale ocher shrubs and twisted yellow and brown cacti struggled for survival at the sides of the great lava flows that spread across the desert from the shattered craters of the volcanos that day after day stretched across the entire horizon.

From where they sat high atop their perch of gobbleweed planks Kerryl and Dalli breathlessly watched small bands of tusked wartdevils bounding tirelessly across the barren wastes in mysterious pursuit of the monstrously armored triceratops and stegosaurs. Towering duckbills identified as scarlet howlers strutted ponderously along the riverbanks on hind legs as large as goldenose trunks, their heads bristling with the strange bony crests through which they emitted loud bugling sounds, their long red tails swishing restlessly. Noxious fumes from the intermittently active volcanos and fissures in the arid desert drifted slowly upwards to a roiling sky of murky brown in which the harsh blue sun catalogued as Haiera 4CT3 was little more than a diffused luminosity.

How, wondered Kerryl Ryson, could so many enormous beasts eke out a living on the inhospitable wastes of this burning desert? Only by eating each other, he decided with a shudder, as he listened to the distant roars of bloodlust and anguish borne to the barge by the dry desert winds.

When evening fell the three Cherryskin women from Rupert's Diversion were assigned to all-night vigils, armed now with linger-flame lances, neuronic disrupters, and metabolic grenades. As the three gaunt women ceaselessly paced the deck flesh-chilling howls and shrieks rent the cool night air. The cloud-choked sky glowed red, orange, and yellow above the smoldering summits of the desert's active volcanos, and the wasteland's somber daytime colors of dull ochers, browns, and russets had now become the eerie blue and green glow of fierce radioactivity. Gigantic silhouettes of the deepest black moved out of the inky shadows to stalk back and forth against the shimmering luminescence in search of prey. Twice a nearby splash in the Sleepyhead River followed by horrific moans and screams jolted Kerryl from already uneasy sleep and into the protective arms of his mother, where he listened to the ghastly sounds apparently following *The Languid Endeavor* throughout the night. In the morning when he went on deck nothing was to be seen.

Three days passed, then four. At the end of the fifth day of passage through Deadman's Desert the murky brown and red clouds began to thin and the pitiless blue sun around which revolved Stohlson's Redemption once again shone through. The endless ridge of smoking volcanos gradually fell behind the barge, and the barren furrows and lava flows gave way to a low range of hills covered with coarse green beggar's thistle.

Gray and white clouds laced with pink began to drift slowly across a pallid blue sky; the beggar's thistle became a vast savanna of gently waving knuckle grass, so-called for the small yellow kernel resembling a man's clenched fist which waved on the end of each blue-green stalk. Great herds of browsing herbosaurs, iguanodons, valdosaurs, boneheads, and nodosaurs, moved placidly through the shoulder-high grass, apparently oblivious of the silent passage of *The Languid Endeavor* and the menacing silhouettes of the occasional predatory carnosaurs stalking them warily from a distance.

At last a faint dark shadow appeared across the far horizon: enormous black storm clouds battering against the peaks of the range of craggy mountains known as the Straggletooth.

Kerryl Ryson sat glumly on the tall pile of gobbleweed planks, beset by a variety of emotions, sullenly ignoring the infuriating presence of the girl Dalli Weezler. On the far side of the misty Straggletooth Mountains, he knew, was the great city of Tyhor; here would be found the wonders of the Spring Festival of which he had been told all his life; here also was the Archimandrite of Ost who would rip him away from all his family by enslaving him for the rest of his life to this small redheaded pest beside him. He uttered a deep sigh from the very bottom of his soul, and despairingly watched the Straggletooth Mountains draw nearer.

CHAPTER 2

The city of Tyhor was situated on the broad alluvial delta formed by the junction of the Sleepyhead River and the Kneedeep Ocean. The heavy moisture of the damp sea breezes was trapped by the massive barrier of the jagged mountains at the foot of the delta; by noontime churning black thunderheads hid the barren peaks of the Straggletooths. Regularly every midafternoon, while sheet lightning flickered eerily across the city, torrents of warm rain fell to feed the innumerable streams and rivulets that veined the fertile delta.

In centuries past thousands of farmers and herders had once tended their freeholds on three sides of the city; as adherents of the Jairaben sect had invested the delta and Tyhor in ever-increasing numbers, the small holdings had gradually been consolidated into larger and more efficient units and their original owners displaced. Now, as *The Languid Endeavor* unloaded its cargo at the Eggemoggin Docks, a single great agricultural holding spread across the Hanchu Delta, the property of the Jairaben lords in their enormous keep at Pandow in the foothills of the Straggletooth Mountains.

The delta's dark fertile soil easily fed the three hundred thousand artisans, tradesmen, and laborers who comprised the city's population, but it remained primarily suited to agriculture, for it was soft and marshy. None of the steeply pitched wooden structures that jostled each other in the narrow twisting streets of Tyhor were more than two stories high, and in consequence the constantly growing city was expanding relentlessly across the delta.

In spite of the innumerable hostelries, inns, and hotels for which Tyhor was renowned, all available lodging for the duration of the Spring Festival had long since been spoken for. Now the thirteen tents of the Tandryl-Kundórrs and Coober-Weezlers, struck earlier in the day to permit the unloading of *The Languid Endeavor*, were being hastily reerected by the two clans on the open deck space leased from the master of the barge for the following fortnight.

"But when do we go to the Festival?" asked Kerryl, impatiently tugging at his mother's arm as they watched the final stack of goldenose planks being swung off the barge under the direction of a tiny Jairaben overseer wearing a suit of soft green leather.

Elaina Ryson-Greenfern smiled and ran her hand through Kerryl's curly brown hair. "Surely you don't think the entire clan has come all this distance just to attend a celebration of animal husbandmen?" she teased. "Your marriage is—"

The barge quivered to the sudden shock of a mighty clap of thunder, louder than any of those that had exploded over the city in the course of the afternoon's storm. Elaina's hand tightened convulsively on the shoulder of her son.

"Look!" cried Kerryl, pointing up to the sky, his eyes wide. "Just there! Coming through the clouds: a starship!"

All eyes aboard *The Languid Endeavor* were raised to the gleaming white cylinder of the starship as it sank silently with aching slowness across the tumultuous black clouds. Kerryl's breath caught in his chest at the ship's beauty and size. Its line of descent was on the far side of the city, making it impossible to precisely judge its dimensions, but he knew that it had to be enormous, far bigger than the barge on which he stood, or even the huge wooden warehouses and sheds that loomed over them at quayside.

Suddenly he gasped.

A dazzling red and orange flash had totally enveloped the milky white cylinder so that now only a giant fireball drifted slowly to earth. A collective murmur of horror whispered across the city of Tyhor. Then to Kerryl's wonder the fireball abruptly vanished, revealing the undamaged pristine white of the starcraft against the deep purple shadows of the Straggletooth Mountains. As his breath caught in his throat, the starship was engulfed a few heartbeats later by the same terrible flash. Simultaneously the blast of a mighty klaxon enveloped the city like the wail of a god-sized foghorn, followed by a second blaring of the same hideous sound and then a third. As the third and fourth flashes of red and orange fire washed imperviously over the falling spacecraft, it at last became apparent that these were measures somehow attendant upon the landing of the ship. His mouth open in awe, Kerryl stood motionless beside his mother until at last the ship sank from sight behind the bulk of a timber shed and its frightful wails abruptly ceased, leaving a vast eerie silence over the city of Tyhor.

"The starship!" cried Kerryl, suddenly released from his spell, as he raced across the deck to tug at his father's elbow. "Did you see the starship? Where did it come from? Why is it—"

Jeord Greenfern-Ryson could only shake his head in silent wonder. Unexpectedly it was the tiny Jairaben foreman on the dock beside them who broke the silence, his eyes still turned upwards. "The Most Immaculate Ultim of Aberdown, it is," he murmured softly, "come personally to witness the miracle of the March of the Thirty-six Flowers."

"Father, Father," demanded Kerryl, dancing on the tips of his toes with excitement at this further revelation of the wonders of the Spring Festival, "how can flowers march?"

"That I admit I don't yet know," admitted Jeord Greenfern-Ryson. "But perhaps—just perhaps—if we have the time we'll stroll by the Festival and find out."

In spite of the solemn ecclesiastical purposes for which the two clans had come to Tyhor, their initial audience with their spiritual leader, the Archimandrite of Ost, had been fixed for the seventeenth day of Germinal—the day after the official conclusion of the Spring Festival.

"Ten days of Festival; and *then* the marriage," noted Kerryl's eldest brother Alvo Ryson-Slendoddi with deep satisfaction. "Followed, of course, by the obligatory nine days of merriment to celebrate the holy nuptials." He tousled Kerryl's long curly hair, then shook him affectionately by the shoulders. "Our doddering old father's not such a fool as one may suppose, young Kerryl, at least when it comes to arranging the calendar. Those of us who weary of unremitting labor at Strichum's Wood—which is to say, all of us—owe you our gratitude. Here then, young voluptuary: a prenuptial offering from your kinsmen to let you profit from your last carefree days of freedom before flinging yourself heedlessly into the arms of your object of misplaced passion." With a sardonic grin, Alvo Ryson-Slendoddi pressed a soft leather purse into Kerryl's hand and leapt down from the barge to join his own two wives amidst the noisy crowd of brightly clad Tandryl-Kundórrs and Coober-Weezlers now gathered on the quay.

Kerryl tore open the purse. Inside were forty golden seqqinos. Added together they made four seqqims: a fortune!

"Four seqqims!" marveled Dalli Weezler as they pressed through the dense crowd that surged along the

Bluewater Esplanade. "You're rich! What are you going to do with it all?"

"I don't know. I've never been to the Festival before; how would I know what to spend it on? Let's look around."

"You don't think our parents will be angry if—"

Kerryl turned his green eyes to her in puzzled indignation. "How could they be angry with *us*? *We're* not the ones who have gone astray: *they* are! Look, a Cherryskin dumpling barrow! Let's have a yellowberry dumpling!"

"And an angelwing sausage!"

"And a sizzling-tingletongue!"

"And a—" The girl's excited words were lost as the children dashed into the tumultuous crowd.

For three thousand years now the broad curve of the Bluewater Esplanade in the Witherhome district of Tyhor had annually been given over to the needs of the Spring Festival. On one side of the sweeping tree-lined boulevard the soft swells of the Kneedeep Ocean lapped gently against the pink sands of Desperation Beach. On the other the majestic range of the distant Straggletooth Mountains dominated the skyline. All traffic had been diverted from the thoroughfare for the duration of the Festival; now every inch of space beneath the esplanade's towering canopy of flaming dragonbreath trees was jammed by the half million Festival-goers drawn from all over the continent of Woolywobber by the four hundred brightly painted wooden booths and carnival attractions.

Gone now were the lotteries, gaming shops, and bordellos that had animated the Festivals of a distant past, along with booths dispensing mind-benders and hallucinogens from a thousand planets across the cosmos. Gone as well were the brutal trials to the death between man and beast, or occasionally man and man; gone too were the raucous cries of the dozens of competing preachers and evangelists who had sought to win converts by the promise of eternal hellfire or by the more worldly enticements of green-flame spicewine and the hot embrace of unclad women.

All of these ungodly vestiges of the paynim had been swept away when the Hanchu Delta had come beneath the ecclesiastical sway of the Jairaben; but not even the dourest Jairaben lords of the Pandow Keep dared entirely stifle the addiction of the lusty and fun-loving Tyhonese to their Spring Festival.

Instead of women, drugs, and religion, the colorfully painted booths now purveyed all manner of candies, dumplings and baked meats, spiced fish and pickled fruits. The carcasses of gently roasting browsers turned on spits over glowing coals, dripping with piquant sauces; a hundred varieties of ale and beer were drawn from a thousand wooden kegs; makeshift dance floors and ballrooms shook to the pounding of hops, reels, mazurkas, quadrilles; fifty competing airs from the energetic bands of the dance halls and taverns clashed with the recorded music that blared from the carnival rides at the broad clearing of Oceanview Park in the middle of the esplanade. But even without the music there was never respite from din, for all along the mile-long concourse barkers, hawkers, and fortune-tellers shouted the merits of their trinkets, knick-knacks, souvenirs, cheeses, linens, amulets, predictions, philters, and talismans.

The Jairaben had always been keen tallymen; now they relaxed their tenets sufficiently to mount a great multi-colored Wheel of Fortune. Manned by youthful and jaunty Jairaben acolytes under the suspicious eye of a senior official, the wheel turned slowly to solemn music at the corner of a strategic intersection. Thwarted elsewhere in their quest for games of chance, a milling crowd gathered to choose that colored sector which proffered the hope of wealth, success, and happiness; their coins were taken in by the Jairaben; the wheel spun furiously to the air of a lilting tarantella, came slowly to a halt. The lucky winner was accorded his spoils: a squalling piglet and a week's remission from the wages of venial sin; the disgruntled losers were exhorted to purchase another chance.

In the brief annual freedom from normal constraints of the Spring Festival lovers embraced openly, inebriates stumbled drunkenly through the crowds, heretics defiantly proclaimed their message. Jairaben aediles and city beadles alike turned a blind eye . . .

"Look," said Kerryl, licking a last sticky patch of drizzle cream from the back of his hand. "See that booth over there? An herbalist."

"Idiot," giggled Dalli. "Notice the detailed anatomical emblem over the entrance; even to a Tandryl-Kundórr it must be evident that those are love potions and blood thickeners the woman is selling. Are you sure that this is what you really want? Or need? Remember: we're not even married yet!"

"Idiot yourself!" Kerryl felt himself flushing hotly. "Remember what you told me about Yonas Pionk the wiggleroot farmer and the jape he played upon the Jairaben's tyran? Where do you think this wiggleroot farmer got *his* chuzzleneck?"

"Is chuzzleneck a love potion too? I didn't know that." The redheaded girl sniffed disdainfully. "We Coober-Weezlers are *never* obliged to resort to aphrodisiacs."

CHAPTER 3

The association of Jairaben and dinosaur stretched so far into the legendary past that its roots had long since become mythological. The most ancient and sacred records preserved in the Pandow Keep purported to reveal that Holton Jairaben, the chieftain of an obscure clan in the desolate Ashland Marshes, had received a visitation from the messiah Durster sometime in excess of fifty thousand years before. The hetman and his followers were enjoined by Durster to devote themselves to the veneration and domestication of those great beasts that roamed the Woolywobber Continent—or suffer an eternal torment of allosaurs devouring their ever-regenerating entrails. Few except the actual adherents to the Jairaben sect gave much credence to this colorful account, but none would deny that for hundreds of centuries now the cleverest minds and most intuitive stockbreeders of a dynamic Jairaben clan had pursued their baroque goal with singleminded fanaticism.

In honor of the high presence of the Most Immaculate Ultim of Aberdown, the March of the Thirty-six Flowers was to be the culmination of this year's Spring Festival. The site chosen was Bezzlerunners Road on the eastern side of the city, a broad avenue that led to Tyhor from the great husbandry stables of the Jairaben in the Salvation Hills just below the Pandow Keep.

Here half a million Tyhonese and Demptionists from all over the continent had gathered in the early hours of a warm summer's morning. A few hundred yards to the seaward side of Bezzlerunners Road the rays of the rising sun glinted brightly on the gigantic white spacecraft stretched out across the tumbledown and seldom used Woolywobber Interstellar Landing Facility. Speculating noisily as to the purport of the enigmatic spaceship, the cheerful Festival-goers breakfasted heartily on thick steaming sausages, crusty loaves, and cold foamy ale sold by a multitude of vendors. The crowd swirled and re-formed, held in check by a heavy red rope on either side of the boulevard—as well as the surly presence every four paces of brightly costumed city beadles and Jairaben carabineers wielding twelve-foot staffs of hardened agatewood.

Not far from where Bezzlerunners Road crossed the dank waters of the New Canal an additional squadron of beadles and carabineers now formed a tight cordon around a large reviewing stand of glistening goldenose draped with silver and red bunting. Here sat the two hundred highest and most lordly dignitaries of the Jairaben, come down from the Pandow Keep for the March of the Thirty-six Flowers. In the center of the front row, his glistening copper-colored face protected from the cruel rays of Haiera 4CT3 by a broad purple parasol, the Most Immaculate Ultim of Aberdown chatted easily with the Jairaben grandees, a crystal goblet of light blue wine sparkling in his hand.

Fifty yards distant, on the other side of Bezzlerunners Road and within easy view of the exalted offworlder, stood the hundred and fifty-one members of the clans of Tandryl-Kundórr and Coober-Weezler who had fought by irresistible determination to the forefront of the tightly packed crowd. Among the garments of green, purple, and blue favored by the native Tyhonese, the uplanders from the Great Dismal Forest were easily distinguishable by their costumes of yellow, mauve, and lavender, and by their elaborate headdresses of broad red hats topped by fluffy white plumes.

A sudden fanfare of trumpets and horns stilled the impatient mutter of the crowd. Far down the road to their left, against the mighty silhouette of the Straggletooth Mountains, distant movement could now be discerned. In the front row of the reviewing stand the gleaming copper face of the Most Immaculate Ultim of Aberdown turned with half a million others to peer into the clear morning sunshine. Another flourish of trumpets, and a hoarse roar went up: the March of the Thirty-six Flowers had at last begun.

No sooner had the Tandryl-Kundórrs and Coober-Weezlers squeezed into place in the hot sun than Kerryl and Dalli had wriggled away from the grips of their parents' hands and snaked off through the legs of their tightly packed relatives to the edge of Bezzlerunners Road. Here they immediately darted under the rope barrier, to be herded back by a sullen green-clad Jairaben carabineer with an impatient rap of his agatewood staff. As he ruefully rubbed his elbow, Kerryl heard a number of his kinsmen muttering angrily at the Jairaben's officiousness. Kerryl shrugged, then turned his eyes along the parade route.

The throaty roar of the crowd along the road grew gradually louder as the procession neared, then fell off abruptly into awed silence as the parade came into full view. Kerryl's eyes grew wide and he felt Dalli's sticky hand clutching his as the first of the Thirty-six Flowers at last approached: sixteen matched allosaurs, their horrendous talons gilded a sparkling gold. Seventeen feet high, the terrible yellow and green carnosaurs marched stiffly forward on two enormous hind legs, their massive tails held straight behind them in delicate counterbalance. Their frightful heads darted from side to side as their glittering yellow eyes moved unnervingly over the ranks of recoiling spectators, while their two small forearms with three hook-like talons twitched in excitement.

An enormous garland of blue and white blossoms from the moonfruit tree had been fixed around the rear of each bony skull; a thick lei of the same meaty blossoms had been draped around the animals' brutish necks to dangle against their glossy round bellies. On the top of each head, nearly lost in the depths of the colorful floral bower, sat a small Jairaben drover in bright red breeches and silver tunic, apparently imperturbable as he directed the progress of his fearsome charge with judicious taps from a silver swagger stick.

Dalli's small damp hand tightened around Kerryl's as the hot fetid breath of first one allosaurus and then another wafted down and over them. Snuffling and belching, the great monsters marched past the Tandryl-Kundórrs and on to the Jairabens' reviewing stand, where the cold black eyes of the Most Immaculate Ultim of Aberdown now glittered with a dreamy pleasure.

Ten thousand generations of selective breeding had reaped a certain success in domesticating the disparate dinosaurs of Stohlson's Redemption; but not to the point where the wary Jairaben would permit their carnosaurs to mingle promiscuously with their placid herbivores. At a discreet distance from the terrifying allosaurs came a small marching band of six green-clad Jairaben acolytes blowing lustily into varnished duckbill bugles. Following the band was another grouping of carnosaurs, the only slightly less fearsome ceratosaurs, trailed by twenty-four waddling spiny dimetrodons, three herrerasaurs, a dozen mottled red macrodontophions, and a team of eight small green picrodons snapping and snarling as they pulled an elaborate black and silver chariot in which a single Jairaben loftily acknowledged the acclaim of the crowds. Each beast had been elaborately adorned with a colorful flowered garland and lei appropriate to its genus—though only the Jairaben themselves were capable of fully appreciating each pattern's subtle distinctions.

"But where are the tyrans?" whispered Kerryl as the last of the seventeen varieties* of carnivores trailed past the reviewing stand and a large marching band of green-clad carabineers strode past, their ornate silver horns playing the sprightly air "If Only My Girl Had a Tail like Yours!"

"I don't know," admitted Dalli, biting a knuckle to hide her vexation. "Are you sure that those first ones weren't—"

"You may be right," admitted Kerryl glumly. "But I thought they were only allosaurs. Maybe I should have tried it on one of them: they look almost the same as—"

"Look! A brawny!"

Kerryl looked up to see the first of the ponderous brontosaurs shuffling slowly down the road, their great serpent-like necks swinging back and forth across Bezzlerunners Road as their tiny brown eyes peered myopically into the crowd. Two disdainful Jairaben stood in waist-high howdahs swathed with flowers strapped to the top of the animal's arched back; a smaller drover directed the beast from his position at the top of its neck. So great was their length that it seemed to Kerryl as if the twenty-four enormous beasts would never finish passing before him. And how, he wondered, did they keep their great mottled tails balanced so rigidly in place behind them without ever brushing the ground?

At last the gigantic brown brontosaurs were succeeded by a waddling procession of spiny stegosaurs, followed by a dozen plodding iguanodons. An hour

---

*The other twelve species were: zanclodon, megalosaurus, erectopus, dilophosaurus, torvosaurus, ceratosaurus, spinosaurus, alectosaurus, itemirus, erlikosaurus, rapator, and arctosaurus.

passed, and then another, as the sun grew higher in the sky and the remaining fourteen species* of herbivores marched slowly down Bezzlerunners Road. The last of the great brachiosaurs, serpent-necked beasts even longer and heavier than the giant brontosaurs, marched by with their thirty-foot tails waving behind them, reached the reviewing stand, and moved slowly into the distance. Bezzlerunners Road stood empty except for the enormous piles of steaming dung deposited by the parade of monsters.

Kerryl was at a loss to understand why the heads of the august occupants of the reviewing stand were still turned expectantly in the direction of the breeding pens: there was nothing to be seen. Or was there? The green-clad carabineer just to Kerryl's left brusquely pushed the straining crowd back with his staff. Kerryl peered around the leg of a stout Coober-Weezler matron. Yes, there *was* movement at the far end of Bezzlerunners Road.

A soft murmur arose from the most distant spectators: not their earlier boisterous cheering, but an involuntary exclamation of awe mingled with fear. Ten minutes later Kerryl could feel his resolve wavering and his legs quivering as the majestic tyrant kings marched regally into view. Twenty feet high and forty feet long, ten of the terrible biped carnosaurs tramped forward in a wedge-shaped formation: a single leading beast, followed by two others, with three behind them and another four in the rear. Jairaben drovers nearly hidden in yellow and red flowers were perched on each of the terrifying heads, their brown faces agleam with perspiration as they sought to control their fearsome charges with nothing more than a flexible crop. Six-inch fangs flashed as the tyrant kings' horrific mouths gaped in snarls that instantly silenced the uneasy murmur of the

---

*These were: protoceratops, muttaburrasaurus, hadrosaurus, lambeosaurus, bonehead, acanthopholis, triceratops, homalocephale, titanosaurus, duckbill, diplodocus, euoplocephalus, paleosaurus, and ceratopsian.

awestruck crowd. Kerryl shrank back between his future clansmen's legs: suppose that one of those terrible muzzles above the two absurd forelegs dangling from the massive chest should reach down and pluck him out from the crowd? He could be swallowed in a single gulp!

"Well? Are you going to do it, are you going to do it?" whispered Dalli Weezler urgently. "Hurry up, now's the chance!"

"They're awfully close . . ."

"You *said* you would!"

Kerryl's throat tightened: why had he ever vowed in a burst of vainglory to repeat the glorious exploit of the legendary Yonas Pionk? How could he now back out?

The first of the tyrant kings was just strutting past.

As he reluctantly pulled forth the apparatus concealed beneath his bright yellow jacket a fleeting thought occurred to him: why had he not thought to ask what had happened to Yonas Pionk *after* he had fired his load of chuzzleneck?

Kerryl Ryson sighed and thrust his way back between the legs of the clan Weezler; the fetid brown bulk of the tyrant king loomed just above him. With no further reflection he lifted the tube to his mouth and blew with all his force.

The fragile vial of triple-concentrated chuzzleneck shattered against the massive jowls of the six-foot-long head. Instantly a tenuous pink cloud enveloped the head of the strutting beast and the startled Jairaben drover perched on the rear of its bony skull. The tyrant king's nostrils flared, and an enormous red and black tongue flickered within its cage of horrific fangs.

The monster sneezed once. And marched on.

Kerryl stared after it in dismay, the blowgun still held to his lips. Nothing at all had happened.

The glittering yellow eyes of Dalli Weezler turned to him in reproach. Kerryl scowled angrily. "*You're* the one who told me that chuzzle—"

The hand of a Jairaben carabineer clamped pain-

fully around his upper arm just as the phalanx of ten
snarling tyrant kings reached the reviewing stand.
Vainly Kerryl tried to wriggle free, the blowgun still
clenched in his hand. An angry red face scowled down
at him and the pressure on his arm increased. As he
struggled furiously to break away, Kerryl's heightened
senses were keenly aware of the sudden protesting
rumble from his uncomprehending clansmen, of the
tight press of their bodies against him. He caught a brief
glimpse of Dalli Weezler's gleaming yellow eyes fixed
on him in bewilderment, and then they vanished
behind the forest of legs.

And as the carabineer jerked him brutally out of
the crowd into Bezzlerunners Road he saw the lead
tyrannosaurus suddenly misstep, lurch, and sneeze
enormously. A moment later the beast had staggered
out of formation, shaken now by a whole series of
monumental sneezes. Twenty feet above the ground the
terrified drover clung grimly to the monster's neck as its
head whipped spasmodically up and down. The astonished spectators fell totally silent as the great beast
staggered erratically across the road to loom directly
above the Jairaben notables in the reviewing stand.

In the front row of the stand the Jairaben's guest of
honor, the Most Immaculate Ultim of Aberdown,
stared up in sudden horror as the terrible muzzle of the
uncontrollable tyrant king towered above him and its
great jaws opened. Two rows of glittering teeth as long
as a man's hand stretched wide and suddenly veered
downwards as if to pluck him from the crowd. The
Immaculate Ultim shrank low in his seat and uttered a
stifled croak of dismay.

The massive jaws neared, the hot fetid breath of
the carnosaur engulfed the offworlder. Numbly the
Immaculate Ultim watched the terrible mouth approach. The monster shuddered, the pink and black
tongue quivered tremulously within its mouth, and
then with a hideous cry of torment from deep in the
monster's throat a thick steaming mass of unspeakable

corruption was regurgitated from the beast's vast maw, instantly covering the unfortunate visitor to the March of the Thirty-six Flowers. Two hundred grandees of the Jairaben scattered wildly in abject confusion. The anguished scream of the Most Immaculate Ultim of Aberdown was abruptly blotted out as he disappeared from view beneath the noxious mixture of half-digested meats and seething digestive juices still pouring forth from the great mouth of the retching tyrant king.

CHAPTER 4

One of the carabineer's bony hands had clamped painfully upon the tangled mass of Kerryl's long brown hair; the other was trying to grasp his throat. A bare wrist passed in front of Kerryl's mouth; he fastened his teeth upon it and bit with savage force. At the same time a long arm draped with the yellow and lavender cloth of the Tandryl-Kundórrs closed around the carabineer's neck from behind and began to tighten. A moment later the hand fell away from Kerryl's hair and both the carabineer and Kerryl submerged in the turmoil of the furious clansmen.

A great hoot of raucous laughter from those thousands of Tyhonese in view of the reviewing stand greeted the reappearance of the offworld grandee as his semi-conscious form was pulled by nauseated Jairaben lords and carabineers from the stinking mound of the tyrant king's half-digested breakfast. Nor was the Most Immaculate Ultim of Aberdown the only notable so besmirched. Incoherent bellows of fury and outrage issued from the two dozen high Jairaben who had at least partially shared his fate. All about the reviewing stand beadles and carabineers milled and shouted in dismayed confusion.

Baffled as to the means of enforcing some appropriate admonition upon the now-receding tyrant king, an angry sergeant of carabineers noted the growing disturbance among the spectators across the road. His lips tightened: one of his men had just been pulled into the midst of a howling mob of obviously savage foreign-

ers. He raised a whistle to his lips. A moment later a
squad of incensed carabineers had leapt into the turmoil, their long agatewood staffs rising and falling with
agonizing thuds.

The Tandryl-Kundórrs and Coober-Weezlers were
sinewy foresters and muscular mill workers, no strang-
ers to vigorous physical effort; at the sight of their
women and children being inexplicably attacked by the
paynim forces of the godless Jairaben they fought back
with a will. Agatewood staffs were seized from outnum-
bered troopers and fiercely wielded. Bloodied and
unconscious carabineers were passed from hand to
hand and ejected disdainfully into the great piles of
steaming dinosaur droppings which mottled Bezzlerunners Road. Reinforcements from the semi-hys-
terical cordon of beadles and troopers around the
reviewing stand beat their way into the screaming
crowd with an assortment of ivory nightsticks, leather
truncheons, and agatewood billies.

Somehow in the chaos Kerryl found himself
thrown up by the eddying mob against his father. Jeord
Greenfern-Ryson was busy disengaging the hands of a
red-faced Tyhonese beadle from the neck of a future
Coober-Weezler kinswoman. As Kerryl stood by indecisively, an inarticulate cry of triumph rang out behind
him and scalding agony suddenly shot through him as
both his ears were grabbed and viciously twisted. "To
me, lads!" cried a bloody-faced carabineer in a shred-
ded green uniform, "to me! I've caught the lizard spawn
who poisoned our lovely tyran!" A moment later
Kerryl felt himself being pulled painfully out of the
midst of his clansmen by his ears and hair.

"Father!" he screamed, dangling helplessly in the
iron grip of the grim carabineer. Jeord Greenfern-
Ryson struggled for an instant to free himself from the
simultaneous attack of two municipal beadles, then
turned and fought his way through the savage confusion. His enormous brown hands fixed about the neck
of the frantically retreating carabineer. His arms quiv-

ered and cords of muscle stood out on the sides of his neck. Kerryl heard a dreadful snapping sound and the carabineer suddenly sagged, his head lolling against his shoulder at a peculiar angle. An instant later a black leather truncheon wielded by an infuriated beadle smashed against the side of Jeord Greenfern-Ryson's head.

One hundred and forty-two Tandryl-Kundórrs and Coober-Weezlers had been herded roughly into the Hall of Durster's Judgement by grim Jairaben carabineers wielding neuronic disrupters. Of the nine other clansmen who had stepped down from *The Languid Endeavor* onto the Eggemoggin Docks with such jaunty anticipation earlier in the day three lay lifeless on Bezzlerunners Road and the other six were even now being hunted through the streets of Tyhor with utter relentlessness.

High on the lustrous marble wall at the far end of the great echoing chamber seven furious Jairaben stood in long green robes behind a semi-circular balcony. The senior Jairaben among them gestured and Jeord Greenfern-Ryson was separated from his kinsmen by four carabineers and roughly jerked three paces forward. His head was swathed in a bloody bandage and he stumbled uncertainly. A moment later a trembling Kerryl Ryson was pulled from his mother's arms and dragged forward to stand beside his shackled father. He stood shaking with fear, defiance, and dazed horror at the ghastly consequences of his heedless gesture. Beseechingly Kerryl turned his gaze to his father's bloody face. He found in the glazed eyes nothing but a dull animal incomprehension: it was obvious that only the support of the enormous carabineer on either side kept his father from crumbling to the floor.

Kerryl wrenched his eyes away as they welled up with tears. His beloved father, beaten and bloodied, unconscious on his feet—because of him!

Miserably, he raised his eyes to the heavy stone

balcony above. There, in an elaborately carved chair of darkened fingerleaf set to one side of the seven standing Jairaben, his eyes met those of the offworlder, the Most Immaculate Ultim of Aberdown. The muscles of Kerryl's face twitched. Already the corrosive digestive juices in which the offworlder had been immersed had taken an unexpected toll: a large tuft of thick black curls had fallen away from his massive head, leaving a disconcerting patch of mottled coppery skin just above his left ear; and even as the Immaculate Ultim stared stonily down at Kerryl a second clump of ringlets fell suddenly to his shoulder. A terrible chill gripped Kerryl's already shaking body. He knew that his father and clan could expect no mercy from that pitiless judge. As for himself . . .

"This is an affair of unparalleled and unprecedented gravity," declared the Jairaben Advocary General in a quavering voice. "In the midst of our most joyful ceremony, the culmination of centuries of striving, our honored guest the Most Immaculate Ultim of Aberdown has been subjected to brutal attack and inconceivable insult. A loyal and blameless member of the Bugler's Own Carabineers has been wantonly murdered. An entire tribe of notorious troublemakers and outlaws, cynically taking advantage of the hospitality and freedom unstintingly offered them, has risen up against the people of Tyhor in armed rebellion. Fortyseven of the city's beadles and our own carabineers are even now physically incapacitated."

The Advocary General scowled. "To obviate all prospect of future insurrections of such a nature, we are obliged to make a stern example for any other savage tribe of Woolywobber who might be tempted to take advantage of our own unworldly loving kindness." He directed a bony finger at the lolling head of Jeord Greenfern-Ryson. "There stands the murderer of our most cherished servant, the titular leader of this villainous tribe." The finger moved on to Kerryl Ryson. "There beside him, equally unrepentant, stands his devil's spawn, himself responsible for the incomprehensible attack upon our inoffensive tyrant king and His Exaltedness the Immaculate Ultim of Aberdown." The Advocary General now encompassed the restless mass of scowling and defiant Tandryl-Kundórrs and Coober-Weezlers with a disdainful gesture. "Behind these two stands the rest of this accursed tribe, a clan whose truculence and savagery have been known to us for some two centuries now, ever since their insensate and unprovoked mutilation upon the person of the inoffensive Mordunt AlleKary of sainted memory." The Advocary General turned his somber gaze to the three gaunt Jairaben who flanked him on either side. "How say you all?"

The seven green-robed Jairaben now huddled together while the black eyes of the offworlder flickered between their deliberations and the softly muttering crowd of prisoners below. At last the Advocary General returned to the rail and directed his gaze downward to Kerryl Ryson. "The Seventeenth Book of Durster's Witness enjoins us to be merciful, even unto our most pitiless enemies. In spite of the enormity of his offense, it has been put to us that the tender years of the boy in question should predispose us to clemency. His life, therefore, shall be spared, at least for the present time." A great echoing gasp from the Tandryl-Kundórrs filled the lofty chamber. The Advocary General ignored it. "He shall therefore be taken into the keep, where he will be given the duties of probationary acolyte and instructed in the Seamless Way of Durster. He will be inculcated with decorum and correct attitudes. It may be that even the soul of so blasphemous a sinner as this can yet be saved. Upon the attainment of his majority, we shall then take up the question of the final disposition of his fate."

Kerryl's eyes turned to his father in helpless dismay, while an icy trembling shook his body. Taken away by the Jairaben? To be their slave for the rest of his life? His eyes blurred. If this was his fate for puffing a small pink cloud of chuzzleneck at an overbearing tyrannosaurus, what then was to be the lot of his father, who had snapped the neck of a Jairaben carabineer?

The Advocary General leaned forward. "As to the paynim warlord Jeord Greenfern-Ryson, he is condemned to execution at the end of these proceedings. The other members of his—"

"The fetish!" cried a hoarse female voice from within the seething mass of prisoners on the floor of the Hall of Durster's Judgement, "we must have the fetish!" In spite of the menace of the carabineers' neuronic disrupters, a hundred Tandryl-Kundórrs suddenly surged forward, their goal the sacred fetish that lay strapped to the skin beneath the jacket of the doomed uplander.

A dozen unwary carabineers fell before their single-minded fury, but before the uplanders could attain their semi-conscious hetman another two dozen troopers had stepped forth from the shadows of the hall and impartially subjected all those caught up in the melee to the terrible lash of their neuronic disrupters. Shrieking in unspeakable agony, clansmen and carabineers alike fell in a single writhing mass to the stone floor, their limbs and bodies twitching and jerking spasmodically.

Two large carabineers were needed to restrain a screaming Kerryl Ryson from running to the aid of his mother, but the leader of the clan, Jeord Greenfern-Ryson, remained oblivious to the whole incident as he lolled torpidly against his escorts.

As the hellish screams echoed through the Hall of Durster's Judgement the Advocary General turned away in profound disgust and made ready to depart the balcony. His guest the Immaculate Ultim of Aberdown stopped him with a gesture and beckoned him close. Even as he struggled against the grip of the two Jairaben troopers Kerryl could see the copper-skinned face of the offworlder hovering over the Jairaben's shoulder and his thick lips moving earnestly.

The Advocary General's eyes widened, but then returned to the ghastly spectacle below. His mouth tightened and he nodded curtly. A moment later he and his fellow Jairaben had vanished from the balcony, leaving only the Immaculate Ultim of Aberdown leaning over the edge, peering down at the hundred and fifty tortured and shrieking beings with grim satisfaction.

CHAPTER 5

The following morning, while a shackled Kerryl Ryson hobbled slowly about in the muck of the brachiosaur stables at the foot of the Pandow Keep, a small portal swung open high in the side of the enormous white spacecraft and the Immaculate Ultim of Aberdown stepped into view. Most of his remaining black hair had now fallen from his head, and his naked skull glittered in the early morning sunlight. He gestured imperiously and a second, larger, hatch opened. From this a broad ramp descended to the cracked concrete surface of Tyhor's landing field. The Immaculate Ultim moved back into the dark shadow of his own small portal, squinting impatiently into the sun.

Ten minutes later three large drab vehicles came slowly down Bezzlerunners Road from the Pandow Keep and approached the starship. Heavily armed Jairaben carabineers in full body armor jumped down from the vehicles to watch stonily as one hundred and forty-six tightly shackled uplanders still wearing the tatters of their gay yellow and lavender costumes stumbled painfully out into the shadow of the spacecraft. There they stood waiting in total silence until in a grotesque parody of the previous day's March of the Thirty-six Flowers a small procession of dinosaurs marched out of the purple shadows of the Salvation Hills at the base of the Straggletooth Mountains and onto the landing field.

Their bodies still tormented by the effects of the neuronic disrupters, the Tandryl-Kundórrs and

Coober-Weezlers watched with apathetic eyes as the great beasts were marched by their Jairaben drovers up the ramp and into the darkness of the spacecraft. Two yellow and green allosaurs led the way, followed by four mottled spinosaurs with orange sails on their backs, then two enormous gray brachiosaurs, their tiny eyes blinking down from a height as great as that of a four-story building. All were swallowed up by the vastness of the cylindrical white starship.

At last, prancing and snarling, their great brown-and green-striped tails quivering rigidly behind them, came a pair of the ruling carnosaurs of the planet, the baleful tyrant kings. The upland prisoners muttered softly among themselves and fell back deeper into the shadows of the spacecraft. The smaller of the two tyrans was prodded by her drover until she reluctantly mounted the ramp and disappeared into the maw of the ship; the larger male was left to stomp in disgruntled fury, his glittering red eyes turning with increasing attention to the group of nervous prisoners.

The sun rose higher in a cloudless sky. At last a shiny green vehicle appeared in the distance. It approached and drew near the spacecraft's loading ramp. Down from the car stepped six Jairaben dignitaries; in their midst was the shambling figure of Jeord Greenfern-Ryson, the bandage around his head stained the dark brown of dried blood. A defiant roar went up from the ranks of the Tandryl-Kundórrs and the cordon of guards lifted their disrupters meaningfully; if he heard or saw his clansmen, Kerryl's father gave no sign of it.

Down from the spacecraft came the Immaculate Ultim with stately tread. A hooded cloak of shimmering silver material protected his head from the late morning sun. At his appearance the tyrant king snorted loudly and pawed the cracked concrete with his enormous talons. The Immaculate Ultim glanced up at the towering beast with a wry smile and approached the waiting Jairaben. They conferred softly with him for a moment, then regained their vehicle and drove away. The offworld grandee was left standing in the harsh sunlight, his hand placed as if by solicitous concern on the brawny forearm of Jeord Greenfern-Ryson.

The Immaculate Ultim gestured at the troopers who surrounded the Tandryl-Kundórrs; their grips tightened on their disrupters. A sudden hushed silence fell across the spacefield, broken only by the snuffling of the monstrous biped. The Immaculate Ultim nodded with satisfaction at the troopers' precautions. Leaving Jeord Greenfern-Ryson standing inertly by himself in the dazzle of the sunlight, he ponderously made his way back to the open portal high in the side of the space-craft. There he stood motionlessly, his eyes fixed on the apathetic prisoner below, his pale blue boots on a level with the horrific head of the angrily growling tyrant king. He raised a finger and waggled it at the drover who sat upon the monster's head.

The wiry Jairaben drover leaned forward and tapped the tyrant king smartly with his crop. The great beast snarled, then took a step forward. Someone among the Tandryl-Kundórrs screamed in horrified comprehension, and then another. Jeord Greenfern-Ryson shuffled aimlessly backwards, his glazed eyes fixed obliviously on the looming peaks of the Straggletooth Mountains. He stumbled and began to fall: his back was mercifully turned as the six-inch daggers of the tyrant king's hideous mouth snapped shut around his torso and instantly shattered his spine.

The drover let his gigantic charge finish gulping down his mangled prey, then easily turned the partially sated beast and directed him smartly into the bowels of the ship.

Trembling, weeping, and howling abysmally, what had been the once-proud clan of Tandryl-Kundórr allowed themselves to be prodded up the ramp and into the starship. Immeasurably more than just their het-man Jeord Greenfern-Ryson had been irrecoverably lost; with him had disappeared the clan's two-hundred-year-old sacred fetish. Without it they were little more than the beasts in the swamps.

An hour later the hatches swung shut, the starship lifted smoothly out of the profound indentation that its weight had made in the field's concrete, and like a glowing fireball vanished upwards into the roiling black clouds that hung over the city of Tyhor.

PART TWO

CHAPTER 6

The Jairaben were meticulous tallymen: on the anniversary of Kerryl's first year of captivity in the Pandow Keep, he was summoned from his morning drudgery on the walls of Lake Bliss. A gaunt Jairaben who might have been one of the seven that had stood in judgement of the Tandryl-Kundórrs in the Hall of Durster led him silently past the third of a mile of walls and ramparts that held back the millions of gallons of seawater in which the keep's long-necked ocean monsters frolicked. Above the top of the wall loomed the vast structure of the Jairaben's ancient fortress and the forbidding outline of the Straggletooth Mountains.

Halfway along the lake they came to a narrow, cobblestoned courtyard which led to the Jairaben's sprawling dinosaur stables. Built into the outer wall of the courtyard was a low stone building; before its door stood two armed carabineers. From the building's flat roof a spidery metal tower soared high against the bright morning sky.

Inside the building Kerryl followed the Jairaben along twisting narrow corridors until they came to a heavy metal door. Beyond this was a large, brightly lighted workshop overlooking the broad Hanchu Delta. Through its heavily barred windows Kerryl caught a brief glimpse of the great fields and parklands in which the Jairaben's herds of dinosaurs grazed and battled.

A moment later he had been directed by another Jairaben to a heavy wooden chair, where he was immobilized by thick leather straps around his arms and calves. A cacophony of screams and roars from a dozen species of dinosaurs echoed through the underground complex of the Salvation Hills; the sounds suggested the most gruesome tortures, and Kerryl was shamefully unable to prevent his legs from trembling uncontrollably.

The workshop's technician approached. Kerryl watched with apprehension, then relief, and finally with barely concealed rage as the short, stout Jairaben knelt before him and ran a small glowing instrument around the dull metal band that encircled each of his ankles. Kerryl's nostrils had long since become accustomed to the keep's pervasive stink of dinosaur; but he had never grown accustomed to the ever-greater constriction of the two loathsome anklets that had been clamped around his legs just moments after being pulled screaming from the Hall of Durster's Judgement.

Now for a few tantalizing instants he stretched his feet in luxurious freedom, heedless of the chafed red skin around his ankles. A moment later the Jairaben snapped a pair of larger bands into place and activated them with yet another instrument from his workbench.

"Lest you forget, my haughty uplander," intoned the gaunt Jairaben who had led Kerryl to the coding room. He gestured at the technician, who fastened one of Kerryl's discarded bands around a stout ironwood post that stood behind a transparent screen on the far side of the room. The coder returned to his bench and bent over an instrument.

Kerryl flinched at the sharp crack of explosives as the metal band vanished in a puff of greasy smoke. With a harsh clatter, the length of ironwood toppled to the paving-stone floor, leaving jagged splinters protruding from its severed base.

"That," declared the Jairaben, "could have as easily been your ankle. You will continue to bear that in mind." He gestured at the instruments on the bench. "The range of our equipment is as infinite as the power and mercy of Durster the All-Inclusive. Nowhere in the universe could you hope to flee."

The straps were removed from Kerryl's wrists and calves. The coder made an entry in an enormous ledger. "A larger size will be fitted a year from today?"

"Such is the case," confirmed the senior Jairaben.

"A pleasant change from banding spiny sawbacks and dyspeptic tyrant kings," sighed the technician. "This particular savage is still too scrawny to stomp me into the dust if he takes a dislike to his band."

Kerryl returned glumly to his post at the base of the immense aquarium that housed the keep's seventy-three semi-domesticated plesiosaurs. Tears of rage and frustration welled up in his eyes as he retrieved his fragment of diplodocus gristle and blindly resumed his mindless task of meticulously polishing the great planks of goldenose that supported the inner lining of the immense tank.

Two thousand youthful probationers and apprentice acolytes lived within the walls of the sprawling Pandow Keep, he knew, but less than a dozen were stigmatized by the metal rings that denoted abject serfdom. The bands had been contrived thousands of years before as a precautionary measure to be fixed to the legs of each of the keep's thousands of dinosaurs; two Jairaben stood duty in the metal tower above the outer walls monitoring the behavior of the great beasts in the parklands and training fields below. At the least sign of trouble the animals' feet could be instantly blown from their legs.

Now the same cruel bands assured Kerryl's earnest attentiveness to the rigorous strictures of his Jairaben masters. Absolutely convinced of their efficacy, the Jairaben were surprisingly liberal in leaving him free to wander at will throughout the enormous structure that had been built over a hundred generations on the Salvation Hills hard against the Straggletooth Mountains. But let Kerryl set foot outside the keep's irregular perimeter and somewhere a hidden registering device would blast his feet away.

Which, he wondered as he listlessly scrubbed the polished wood, of his Jairaben captors was the most hateful?

Tholeen Narse, Advocary General, who had sold his family into slavery, and murdered his father?

Tooli Vaxto, Revered Edificationist, who, for Kerryl's failure to correctly aspirate the Nineteen Unpronounceable Syllables of the Bride of Durster, had scourged his naked back with branches of powderwort until it bled?

Daunton Doozel, Probationary Second-Grade and Food Master for Kerryl's table in the refectory, who had stirred a handful of goldenose sawdust into his bowl of breakfast mush?

Hamble Tarton the Exalted, overseer of the Mochkon Memorial Breeding Pens, who had crushed his face into a pile of stegosaurus dung for failure to curtsy with sufficient alacrity?

Or—

"You, down there!" cried the thick and hateful voice of Aladeen the Allsoul, known to his resentful charges as Alldumb the Allosaur. "You, the uplands savage! Where have you disappeared to? Up here with you, then, where we have means to keep you from shirking!"

"Yes, your lordship," muttered Kerryl, and beneath the stony gaze of the Jairaben overseer began to climb the shaky metal scaffolding with as much indolence as he dared while the probationers nearest him on the rigging looked up from their tedious work on the walls of goldenose and waggled their heads in mute sympathy. Six generations of Tandryl-Kundórrs, he knew, had labored to produce these thick goldenose planks that now glittered so brilliantly in the late morning sun. And for what? he asked himself furiously. To retain a bunch of mindless monsters!

For centuries the Jairaben had dreamed of breeding a domesticated plesiosaur high in their mountain keep, instead of being constrained to make the tedious descent to the shallow pens of the Kneedeep Ocean. A deep basin had therefore been hacked out of the Salvation Hills at the base of the keep and fresh salt water pumped up through miles of mighty pipes from the shores of Tyhor. Each succeeding basin had eventually been deemed insufficient to their needs, and at last a single sinuous lake had been fashioned from the half dozen smaller ones.

Some of the basins had been set at different levels in the hills; now gigantic retaining walls were needed to bridge the different elevations. Initial attempts to build them from a translucent material that would permit the Jairaben to stroll at leisure along the base of the tank and gaze within at their frolicking monsters had proved unsuccessful. Now the millions of tons of the lake's water were held back in part by mighty walls of goldenose reinforced by great stone and wooden buttresses.

Kerryl reached the top of the scaffolding and for a moment stood looking down into the artificial lake in which the long sinuous necks of twenty or thirty graceful plesiosaurs could be seen cutting smoothly through the clear green water. Even these beasts of the seas had families of their own, thought Kerryl wistfully as he watched two recently born cubs gamboling with their mother in a quiet inlet between two arms of the rocky hills. As for himself, he had absolutely nothing— even though by the simple process of abject elimination he was now the eleven-year-old titular hetman of the clan of Tandryl-Kundórr!

Kerryl felt his heart pounding in his chest. He had not even the secret fetish of the Tandryl-Kundórrs which had been worn concealed about his father's person. For a dozen generations, ever since the engendering of the clan by the legendary Hollis Sasso, the fetish had encompassed the total mana of the Tandryl-

Kundórrs. Now it had vanished into the maw of the same beast that had murdered his luckless father. Without it the entire clan was intrinsically non-existent, and even his own existence would be considered moot by the more orthodox of the clan's elders. If he, Kerryl Ryson, hetman of the Tandryl-Kundórrs by sole right of survival, failed to replace the sacred talisman in a manner satisfactory to Great Darv, then the clan itself would have come to an inglorious end . . .

Kerryl was jolted from his sad introspection by a sharp buffet upon the shoulder from Alldumb the Allosaur that nearly knocked him from the spidery scaffolding. "Where have you been hiding?" cried the Jairaben, dealing him another blow on his upper arm. "How did you hope to escape my vigilance?"

"But, your lordship: I was summoned by his exalted lordship! You yourself saw him call me. You—"

"What! You dare to tell me lies such as this? Your insolence knows no bounds! And that piece of golden-rub you surreptitiously clutch: it is obviously defective! Did you think thereby to mar the luster of my walls, even scratch them?" A third blow, this to the head, sent Kerryl reeling back against the lake's thick retaining wall. Head spinning, he shied back as the long stalk of a plesiosaur's neck rose from the water and its gleaming brown eyes fixed him curiously from its small gray head. A hundred razor-sharp teeth in the reptile's mouth glittered in the morning sun.

"You're more than just an upland savage, you're an active saboteur of the Pandow Keep!" cried the furious Jairaben. "You should have been fed to the flowers, like your murderous father! Quick, then, down to stores to procure another golden-rub! Already you have forfeited the rest of today's meals by your idleness and recalcitrance. Make haste or you shall forfeit tomorrow's as well!"

"Yes, your lordship," said Kerryl in a tight voice as he edged away from the wall and the waving stalk of the reptile's neck. The golden flecks in his green eyes flashed with rage.

"What!" cried Alldumb the Allosaur, falling back a step in horror. "You attempt to ensorcel me with the Malignant Eye of Malodorous Darv?"

"No, your lordship! I—"

But in an excess of fury and fear, Alldumb the Allosaur had stepped forward and grasped Kerryl by the arms. He pivoted, and with hysterical strength flung the boy over the wall and down into the tepid waters of Lake Bliss.

Kerryl gasped with shock at the sudden impact. Salt water flooded his lungs, and he began to choke painfully. As he struggled to the surface he felt himself nudged sharply. He splashed frantically in terror as the small gray head of one of the great reptiles prodded him indecisively back and forth. Razor-like teeth that could shred him to pieces in an instant flashed inches from his face. Without conscious thought, Kerryl threw his arms around the beast's long sinuous neck. As the startled beast reared high above the surface, Kerryl desperately wrapped his legs around the twisting neck.

The plesiosaur bucked and jumped, its four long fins pounding the water, its bony head twisting frantically as its mouth tried to snap shut on the boy clinging just beneath its chin. Terrified as never before in his life, Kerryl held on to the beast's powerful neck as it lashed back and forth, not daring to lift his eyes to the horrific mouth he knew was only inches away.

As if from a great distance, he heard shouts and curses, and then the enraged reptile had plunged deep to the bottom of the murky lake. There it turned and gamboled as it tried frantically to dislodge Kerryl, whose grip grew steadily weaker as his lungs grew desperate for air. He could feel the harsh buffeting of the beast's chin against his shoulder, and a terrible pressure building up in his chest. Yellow and red spots danced across his vision. The grip of his fingers on the beast's slippery neck began to loosen, and he felt himself sliding down the length of its neck. With what little consciousness still remained he knew that in a few moments the terrible fangs of the furious plesiosaur would be tearing at his flesh. He dug his bony knees frantically into the dinosaur's neck.

The awful constriction about his chest was suddenly relieved, and blinding sunlight dazzled him as the beast broke from the water and leapt high in the air. Even as Kerryl's tortured lungs gasped for breath, the reptile's neck snapped forward like a great whip and he felt himself flying helplessly through the air. When he landed in the water, he knew, the enraged beast would—

He saw the splash of foam, the glint of sunlight on water, the sudden gray of rock. An instant later he was smashed into unconsciousness against the unyielding rock of the Salvation Hills.

CHAPTER 7

As one painful day succeeded another in the probationers' stark infirmary, Kerryl had ample time to reflect upon the grisly and soul-satisfying vengeance he would someday inflict upon the Jairaben and all their works. A vengeance to dwarf the legendary humiliation which the grandsire of all the Tandryl-Kundórrs had once wrought upon the imperious Jairaben . . .

But when his own bloody fantasies grew increasingly repetitious, Kerryl's mind always came back to the story he had wheedled from his father so many times, the story of Hollis Sasso and Mordunt AlleKary and the origin of the clan's sacred fetish . . .

Two hundred and nine years earlier a Jairaben purchasing agent from the Pandow Keep in Tyhor had made his way slowly along the unpaved track that wound through the Painted Hills and Deadman's Desert until disappearing into the gloom of the Great Dismal Forest. Accompanied on his six-wheeled articulated wagon by two armed acolytes and two probationary drovers, Mordunt AlleKary eventually came to Strichum's Wood and the small clearing of Tomdoddy's Mill.

The blue and yellow wagon was towed by a matched pair of those leathery-skinned omnivores denominated Haydrick's green resolutes by the Jairaben and wryly called lop-tails by the rest of the continent's population. A wiry brown Jairaben drover was perched monkey-like upon the neck of each of the heavy-bellied beasts, directing its progress by a constant prodding of its long bony muzzle with a flexible green switch. Snarling and belching, the dryptosaurs advanced awkwardly, their meaty rear legs churning ponderously, the small forelegs high on the chest encircled by black leather harness. The last six feet of their heavy tails had been excised to prevent them from lashing the occupants of the Jairaben wagon. Their beady yellow eyes glistened malevolently in the dappled sunlight. The drovers wielded their switches; reluctantly the lop-tails turned into the timber yard of Tomdoddy's Mill.

Here the youthful Hollis Sasso had recently settled with seventeen indentured workers, an ancient and infertile aunt, and two younger brothers as the result of an angry disputation with the elders of the Kundórr-Bobent clan. Already the dilapidated buildings ceded him by the former owners of Tomdoddy's Mill had been freshly varnished and the rubbish of a dozen generations thrown into the river. But the ceremonial fetish box cached above the lintel of the principal dwelling place was empty, and would remain so until Hollis Sasso had engendered the beginnings of his own clan.

Snapping and barking in a frenzy of rage, the settlement's dozen brown and yellow dogs raced forth to engage the noisome and alien invaders. As always, Stout Lurcher, Hollis Sasso's prime hunter, was in the lead. Quivering with fury, the dogs pranced about the feet of the advancing lop-tails, furtively nipping at their mottled green flesh.

For all their ungainly bulk, the dryptosaurs were deceptively swift. In a flash an enormous rear paw had crushed the yelping Stout Lurcher to the dust of the lumberyard. Before the startled inhabitants of Tomdoddy's Mill could react, Stout Lurcher had been lifted howling to the maw of the lop-tail, where with a ghastly gnashing of yellow teeth he was savagely ripped in half. An eerie silence ensued in which the only sounds were the rattling advance of the Jairaben wagon and the bestial grunts of the reptile as it swallowed the remains of Hollis Sasso's favorite dog.

The six-wheeled wagon came to a halt beside the mill and Mordunt AlleKary the Jairaben stepped down with precise movements while his two bodyguards stood clutching their muskets grimly. Like the drovers perched upon the reptiles' necks, the Jairaben was thin and wiry, with a wizened brown face and scrawny arms that dangled to his knees. His robe was a sullen blue, the fluffy plume in his headpiece a pale mauve.

Hollis Sasso stepped forth from the mill to meet the Jairaben while the rest of his settlement lurked silently in the shadows. "Your lizard has destroyed my companion," he pointed out with ominous calm.

"An impediment upon the public thoroughfare," replied Mordunt AlleKary indifferently. "Moreover, beasts of the canine genus have specifically been adjudicated impure by the Advocary General; this should be well known even to the idolatrous paynim of the Great Dismal Forest. And finally, Haydrick's green resolute is by no means a lizard."

Hollis Sasso pursed his lips. "Interesting theological strictures, to be debated at leisure at some future time. How then may the idolatrous paynim of Strichum's Wood serve his lordship the Jairaben?"

"Your shipments of goldenose have lately become dilatory; the quality deficient; the charge excessive. I have come to set matters aright."

"I see. The previous owners of Tomdoddy's Mill may have been remiss in certain essential respects. As the new proprietor, I am ready to consider all constructive suggestions."

"The keep is now engaged upon a project of some amplitude. Production of goldenose must be trebled, shipments made fortnightly. Grading and selection must be rigorously ameliorated: henceforth nothing less than triple-grained, seven-year-old, double-dipped goldenose will be accepted."

"All of this is possible," agreed Hollis Sasso,

"especially if payment is effectuated in advance by
irrevocable draft upon the Fisherman's Bank of Tyhor.
But before we begin to marshal our resources, I imagine
that you also foresee a substantial readjustment of the
honorarium?"

"That is so. In view of the fact that the keep will
now be purchasing at least six times your present
production, and foresees a minimum of thirty years of
endeavor, a reasonable charge would henceforth appear
to be one hundred seqqims the shipment rather than
the present exorbitant two hundred and forty."

Hollis Sasso considered the tops of the fingerleaf
trees swaying softly in the light breeze, the grim muzzles of the two twelve-foot-tall dryptosaurs. "An interesting concept. It will have to be carefully weighed.
Already I foresee certain difficulties." He gestured at
the mill behind him. "Perhaps your lordship would
care to inspect the baths and emulsifiers in which the
goldenose is initially immersed? This, of course, is the
process by which the otherwise mundane and useless
wood of the goldenose is miraculously transformed
into an unparalleled marvel of beauty and utility. The
goldenose tree itself you will know to be found in ample
quantities in Strichum's Wood and other thickets of the
Great Dismal Forest. Nor is there any shortage of
reachers to strip them of their branches. It is in the
essential processing of the raw logs that I discern the
primary obstacle to augmenting production. The elev-
en precious agents and constituents which compose the
baths, a proprietary formula devised over many generations by the previous owners of Tomdoddy's Mill, are
exceedingly limited in their availability, and correspondingly expensive."

Hollis Sasso led the way into the stripping room,
and while the Jairaben's four drovers and guards
looked on curiously from a discreet distance gestured
broadly at the first of the baths. "Notice! Your lordship
will readily observe how the stripped logs must be held
entirely submerged in the emulsifying agent. Here they

must remain for at least six full days." He leaned forward over the bath and made a gentle stirring motion with his hand, then pursed his lips thoughtfully. "I fear that the present mixture may be slightly too cool to bring out the maximum intensity of the desired triple-grain. Would your lordship perhaps care to favor me with his own expert assessment?"

Mordunt AlleKary stepped forward with haughty dignity to dip a long bony finger into the murky brown liquid in which lay the great lengths of goldenose. He stirred his finger back and forth in the viscous mixture, then removed it and fastidiously shook it dry. "Quite definitely a degree or so too cool," he declared judiciously. "How then will you readjust it?"

"I will give certain orders to my workmen; they will see to it. It is a tedious business. Would you care to join me for a mug of ale in the cool of the fingerleafs?"

"Only if during its brewing the ale has been consecrated by the appropriate ritual of the seven yellow stones and the three gray feathers."

"I fear that such is not the case."

"Then a jug of cool spring water must suit my needs."

"As your lordship wishes."

Hollis Sasso and the Jairaben sat in the shade of an ancient fingerleaf as the fierce noontime sun beat down. A savory aroma of six-pot stew emanating from the settlement's communal kitchen mingled with the pervasive odor of curing goldenose. A dozen chastened dogs crouched whimpering in the shadows while the Jairaben's drovers tended to the needs of the wagon's snuffling green monsters. Hollis Sasso poured himself another mug of frothy brown ale and with the aid of a pointed stick began an elaborate calculation in the warm dust at his feet. "Three hundred and twenty-five seqqims," he murmured absently. "We will let this figure represent the revised price per shipment—"

Mordunt AlleKary leaned forward to remonstrate and uttered a sharp gasp of dismay. "My finger," he cried, holding the quivering digit beneath Hollis Sasso's nose, "it has become blue!"

The hetman of the yet-unengendered clan inspected it closely. "Peculiar! A very bright blue indeed! It is tingling now, and beginning to feel warm, as if invested by a thousand fire ants?"

"Yes. Yes!"

"This is hard to credit." Hollis Sasso shook his head in bewilderment. "It gives every appearance of being Maramot's Malediction. But this is engendered by a single means. Surely his lordship would not have been so foolhardy as to have introduced his finger into the goldenose emulsifying agent?"

The Jairaben's wizened brown face was now a sickly beige. "But you asked me to assay the temperature!" he croaked tremulously, unable to tear his eyes away from the horrid spectacle of his bright blue finger.

"Only by passing your hand above the surface!" Hollis Sasso sat back in his chair, a finger tapping pensively upon the side of his nose. "I fear that given the altered circumstances we shall now have to conclude our agreement with rather less ceremony than I had intended. Soon your lordship's hand will be blue, and then the arm. As soon as the tint reaches the chest, of course—"

"What?" gasped Mordunt AlleKary in horror. "You mean—"

"I fear so. Still, we will do our best to give your remains a dignified burial following the customs of the country, though you are not of our own faith. Now then," he added briskly, "let me call for pen and paper to seal our bargain while your arm is yet functioning."

"But— Is there nothing to be done?" bleated the trembling Jairaben, his eyes wide with terror.

Hollis Sasso stroked his chin. "Perhaps, perhaps. I have heard of certain possible remedies and alleviations. But all in good time. I fear that my powers of concentration are not what they used to be: I am no longer capable of dealing with more than one matter at a time. Has the tingling reached the middle of your palm yet? Let me know when it does. Ah! Here is the contract prepared by my tallyman. Hum! Four hundred seqqims per shipment! Surely he has erred: had we not agreed upon four hundred and fifty? No matter, four hundred seqqims it shall be!" Hollis Sasso dipped the pen into a vial of green ink tendered by his tallyman and affixed his signature to the document with a lordly flourish. "And now your own, your lordship, after which we will consider what steps might be most efficacious in halting the relentless progression of Maramot's Malediction."

The document was duly signed and witnessed, the perspiring Jairaben led tottering to the smoky communal kitchen of Tomdoddy's Mill. Here the womenfolk of the settlement had nearly finished their preparation of six-pot stew. An ancient crone in a shapeless black shawl hunched over a great goldenose chopping block, deftly shredding cabbages with an enormous iron cleaver.

"Your hand, good Jairaben," ordered Hollis Sasso, "that my aunt might examine it."

"Ha!" muttered the crone as she poked at the livid blue finger. "Another few moments and the poisons would have passed irrevocably into the hand. Good fortune smiles upon you, young paynim. Affix his hand well then," she commanded, and before the aghast Mordunt AlleKary could protest or his horrified body-guard intervene the trembling hand had been immobilized upon the smooth yellow surface of the chopping block. The great cleaver flashed once, and with a meaty thwack! the infected blue index finger bounced high in the air.

"Fortunate that we have a kettle of oil on the boil for deep-fried snipsnap greens," grumbled the crone. "Bring the paynim creature here and let us cauterize the stump. But I won't answer for what it may do for the taste of my snipsnap greens!"

CHAPTER 8

The dormitories and refectories that served the Jairaben probationers were in the middle levels of the great keep, below the larger, though equally spartan, quarters of the senior Jairaben, and above the complex of workshops and kitchens that served the twelve thousand inhabitants of the keep. A thousand junior probationers slept side by side in a dim and cavernous dormitory whose narrow window embrasures overlooked the western end of Lake Bliss.

Twisting staircases of bare stone wound down through the lower levels to the stables at the very bottom of the keep, passing at times through the naked rock of the Straggletooth Mountains. Two levels below the probationers' refectory were the sprawling quarters of the Seventh Legion of Carabineers. Here large raucous soldiers in green uniforms could occasionally be glimpsed from the stairs as they tramped noisily along their stone corridors.

The explosive bands chafing painfully against the raw skin of his ankles, Kerryl limped slowly down the stairs as the first pale light of morning marginally brightened the gloomy passageways. Already he had spent a weary hour with the other probationers in the Conclave of Seriality as they shouted their devotion to Durster and read another chapter of the endless liturgy that had accreted over countless millennia. Now he was descending to the very lowest level of the keep, there to procure yet another chunk of golden-rub. For seven months now, ever since leaving the infirmary, he had been polishing the outer walls of the plesiosaurs' tank —would this hateful task never end?

Hobbling silently at the heels of a dozen chattering probationers, he passed through the levels given over to the Jairaben's soldiers and then down into the endless series of workrooms and ateliers that maintained the keep. In the deep shadows of a wide corridor he saw a shaft of bright yellow light spilling out from a workshop. Two solar-paneled delivery wagons stood by its broad doors. Even the passing glimpse from the stairwell was enough to reveal to Kerryl's practiced eye the glint of triple-grained, seven-year-old, double-dipped goldenose.

He slept badly that night, tormented once again by the vivid sights and sounds of Blue Finger Mill and his boisterous, loving family. The following morning, with no clear reason in mind for his actions, he dashed ahead of his fellow probationers as they filed sedately away from their tedious devotions in the Conclave of Seriality.

As quickly as his leg would permit, he ran down the stairway until he came to the level on which he had seen the goldenose. A quick glance around the landing showed that he was unobserved. He stepped out into the inky shadows and moved silently down the corridor until he could peer through the open doors of the carpentry shop.

Here a handful of artisans were already at work on what appeared to be the frames of a hundred or more peculiarly structured chairs. The logs of triple-grained goldenose he had seen the day before were stacked in a shadowy bay; nearer to hand were planks and pieces of seasoned goldenose, all of them gleaming with the characteristic sheen and richness that unmistakably denoted Blue Finger Mill.

Kerryl felt himself trembling with the same helpless rage that had gripped his body throughout the night as he tossed on his narrow cot. With all of his family and clan enslaved on some distant world, who was now the overlord of what had once been Kerryl's home?

The wild beasts of the forest? No, for who worked the mill? Who sent the treated goldenose logs downriver on the quiet barges? Those same Jairaben murderers who had seethed with jealous greed ever since their defeat at the hands of Hollis Sasso?

He took a step nearer the open door and risked a quick glance into the shop. There before him, his broad back unmistakable, was Alldumb the Allosaur, the overseer who had thrown him to the plesiosaurs. With a sharp intake of breath Kerryl ducked back into the corridor.

When he had eventually been discharged from the keep's primitive infirmary, his left leg trailing at an awkward angle and his right arm in a cast, he had learned soon enough that Alldumb the Allosaur had been relieved of his duties at Lake Bliss for gross dereliction of duty. Disruption of the plesiosaurs' training by permitting unauthorized personnel to gain access to the lake was a fault of enormous gravity; Alldumb the Allosaur had henceforth been banished to the tedium of the inner ateliers.

Pain from his shattered kneecap stabbed him with every step as he hobbled back to the staircase. The unexpected sight of Alldumb the Allosaur had effectively answered the question he had posed himself eight months before: no doubt at all existed in his mind as to which of the numerous Jairaben was fractionally more detestable than the rest—and most deserving of whatever vengeance he could inflict.

A whispered table-time conversation with one of the thirteen other probationers shackled with explosive leg bands informed Kerryl that Alldumb the Allosaur was now overseer for the production of furniture. A week later Kerryl made the acquaintance of an apprentice actually employed in the workshop. Now he learned that the workshop was engaged in the fabrication of one hundred and twenty-eight chairs for the forthcoming Feast of the Arboreal Epiphany. The peculiar design that had caught Kerryl's attention was easily explained: the seat of each chair was being constructed to mimic the contours of an enormous bird's nest.

As he endlessly scoured the goldenose planks that held back the waters of Lake Bliss, Kerryl had much to occupy his mind besides the constant throbbing of his leg. The chairs were being crafted entirely of the rarest of all woods: triple-grained, forty-year-old, double-dipped goldenose. They would be taken to Gammahanny Hall shortly before the arrival of the hundred and twenty-eight Jairaben lords gathered together for the annual celebration of Durster's miraculous appearance in the nest of the cloverbirds in the distant forests of Bizum.

Kerryl rubbed his chin pensively with his piece of hard gristle wrested from the ninth vertebra of a Plewwer's diplodocus. The most fearful secret of the Tandryl-Kundórr, so terrible that in every generation it was whispered but once from father to son, had suddenly come back to Kerryl as he gazed into the workshop of the Pandow Keep. He shook his head in wry surmise. Could it possibly be true what his father had confided about the impact of a neuronic disrupter upon—

"You there! The one-legged savage! Why are you shirking?"

With a sigh Kerryl returned to work.

Three weeks remained before the Feast of the Arboreal Epiphany. The frames of the hundred and twenty-eight chairs had been completed; their upholstering in red, yellow, and black damask in the shape of a soft, downy nest was well underway. Alldumb the Allosaur stormed and cursed as he goaded his team of

artisans and apprentices to completion; even his fellow
Jairaben found his comportment increasingly intol-
erable.

So much Kerryl had learned from apparently
casual conversation with Jarveton Aarl, the apprentice
from the shop. Now Kerryl moved stealthily through
the darkness of the sleeping keep. Past the thousand
exhausted probationers in their tiny cots; past the
drowsing Jairaben monitors in their chambers at the
end of the vast dormitory.

Up three flights of dim staircases to the level of the
Conclave of Seriality, then haltingly along a totally
black corridor, guided only by his hand against the
wall. Finally a faint light ahead: a staircase landing.
Down the steps on tiptoes, his bare feet silent on the
cool stone, his knee throbbing painfully, his heart
racing wildly in his chest as he approached the private
quarters of the Seventh Legion of Carabineers.

Kerryl peered cautiously around the corner of the
thick stone wall. The hallway luminifers were dim
yellow. A young private in the green uniform of the
carabineers slouched half asleep against a distant wall,
his head nodding upon his chest. Beside him the two
broad doors were firmly shut. His eyes appeared closed.

Kerryl raced silently out of the shadows, across the
landing, and into the darkness of the staircase. Four
steps down and he was out of sight of the guard. He
fumbled beneath his nightgown and brought forth the
two small blocks of wood he had surreptitiously fashioned in one of the keep's repair shops. A stout metal
hook had been screwed into each block, their backs
coated with a thick layer of bonding agent prepared by
the month-long boiling of the skulls of a hundred
duckbill buglers.

Now Kerryl smeared each block of wood with the
catalyzing agent, a greasy extract derived from the gall
bladder of Hawkabee's gibbering landroller. A moment
later the two pieces of wood were welded immovably to

the walls on each side of the smooth stone stairs and a length of wire stretched taut between the two hooks.

Kerryl inched back up the staircase and raised his head. The guard was still nodding drowsily at his post. Kerryl reached beneath his nightshirt and lifted a slim tube to his lips. He blew, and a dried lentil hit the guard just below the right eye.

The carabineer twitched and shook himself into partial wakefulness. Eyebrows knit, he scowled in bewilderment. Kerryl retreated silently down the staircase to the next landing and around the corner. He moaned softly, and then a second time. He lay listening for an endless moment, then heard the soft steps of the guard as he moved cautiously away from his post. He moaned a third time.

"Who's there?" whispered the guard. He stepped into the staircase. A moment later Kerryl flinched as the carabineer crashed noisily down the steep stone steps. A choked scream was cut short as he smashed heavily against the far wall. The feeble light of the landing was enough to show Kerryl what he wanted. He darted out from the shadows and pulled the small neuronic disrupter from the flaccid hand of the stunned guard. An instant later the twelve-year-old uplander from the Great Dismal Forest had vanished silently down the staircase into the depths of the Pandow Keep.

Four days before the banquet the hundred and twenty-eight completed chairs were taken from the workshop and carefully stored in an anteroom to the Gammahanny Hall while final adornments and embellishments were made to the banqueting room. It was to this anteroom that Kerryl came three nights later. In his hand was the stolen disrupter, which for seventeen tension-filled days now had lain concealed in a hole hastily dug beneath a puckerberry bush on the far end of the plesiosaurs' lake.

Narrow leaded windows were set in deep stone

embrasures of the anteroom. Outside, the two brilliant
moons of Stohlson's Redemption hung in a starry sky,
and a pale blue light washed the room. Kerryl moved
swiftly through the anteroom's deep shadows, bathing
each of the broad chairs with the invisible beams of the
neuronic disrupter.

If only he could be wielding this fearful weapon
against a hundred and twenty-eight living Jairaben
instead of these idiotic chairs! he growled as he moved
from grotesque nest to nest. But that, of course, would
be suicidal: the wrath of the Jairaben would be terrible
indeed. Up to this point his luck had held: the carabineers had apparently decided to protect their own, and
no word of the disrupter's disappearance seemed to
have reached the rest of the keep.

And now, if only the disrupter worked as his father
had once told him . . .

A great gong struck three doleful beats; the hundred and twenty-eight Jairaben dignitaries convened
from all across the continent of Woolywobber filed
slowly out of the Hall of Durster's Judgement. A dozen
acolytes marched solemnly before them, fanning the air
with ritual motions of their freshly cut branches of
bright green thornapple. The broad doors to the
Gammahanny Hall were flung open and the Jairaben
marched through.

At the head of the procession, the Most Fragrant
and Reverend Apotheosis suddenly leapt in sprightly
fashion high into the air. Now he jumped to the left,
now to the right, all in the random pattern of a great
crested tree frog leaping from branch to branch. His
loose-limbed capering eventually brought him to the
far end of the banqueting hall. Here he chirped melodi-
ously in the manner of the white-faced belly-thumper
while his exalted brethren silently took their places
around the long narrow table.

A hundred and twenty-eight footmen drew back a
hundred and twenty-eight upholstered goldenose chairs

in the shape of cloverbird nests. A hundred and twenty-eight Jairaben lords positioned themselves above the chairs.

"And thus do we heed thy words, O Durster!" proclaimed the Most Fragrant and Reverend Apotheosis as he wiggled his scrawny haunches in solemn imitation of the mud-churning cloverbird. "Thus do we commit our souls unto the fullness of thy nest!"

"Praise be unto Durster!" echoed the Jairaben dignitaries, as in a single swift movement all one hundred and twenty-eight of the continent's most reverend fragrances dropped heavily into the plush red, yellow, and black upholstery of their nests.

For a single precarious moment the upholstered seats yielded to their weight; then, with a tortured moan of disrupted molecules, the chairs disintegrated beneath the startled Jairaben and deposited them heavily upon the hard stone floor. As they lay with limbs asprawl, aghast at this sign of implacable disdain vouchsafed them by Durster, a million crystalline pieces of shattered goldenose from Blue Finger Mill glittered in the light of the great chandeliers.

CHAPTER 9

Two high points marked the next six years of Kerryl's drab existence among the Jairaben.

The first was the day he watched surreptitiously from a shuttered window while the Most Fragrant and Reverend Apotheosis personally directed the hanging of the three Jairaben who supervised the output of goldenose wood from Blue Finger Mill. While their gaunt forms still dangled from a ramshackle scaffold of gibberwood deep in the shadows of one of the keep's small inner courtyards, Alldumb the Allosaur was led forth from a side door. He was shackled to a post and his bare back flogged red with powderwort branches.

When he was released the following week from the medical center the once imperious Alldumb the Allosaur shakily took up his new duties as an apprentice in manure maintenance in the lower brachiosaur stables.

The second memorable occasion was the day Kerryl was allowed to venture into the city of Tyhor in official pursuit of his duties to the Pandow Keep.

"But mark!" warned the senior coder as he activated the newly affixed anklets. "The boundaries are Bezzlerunners Road to the west, Sleepyhead River to the east, and Bluewater Esplanade to the south. Wiggle your longest toe so much as an inch beyond those limits and your foot will be instantly detached from your leg."

Kerryl nodded. "To hear is to obey, your most revered lordship," he murmured with barely concealed sardonicism. He was now a curly haired, hard-muscled youth fully as tall as most of the gangling Jairaben, and far broader through the shoulders. His left leg still dragged noticeably when he walked, and his right arm was held at an awkward angle, permanent reminders of his brief encounter with the plesiosaurs of Lake Bliss.

He had just marked his eighteenth birthday: three years remained before the Advocary General would make a decision as to his permanent fate. Would he be judged to have mastered Jairaben decorum and theology with sufficient sincerity to be allowed into their exalted ranks? Or would he be expelled from their company in the most permanent of fashions?

Kerryl curtsied to the keep's senior coder, hard put to keep from snorting loudly in derision. With all the resources of Tyhor now at his command, long before the three years had passed he would have found his own means of quitting these unspeakable paynim!

It had been easy enough to move surreptitiously through the Pandow Keep, where the stern but guileless Jairaben had little reason to expect furtive prowling; it was far more difficult than he had foreseen to obtain the same freedom of movement within the city of Tyhor. Now he discovered that more than just explosive anklets penned him within the keep's walls; for those few gates allowing egress from the keep were zealously guarded by elite members of the carabineers.

More, his infrequent trips to Tyhor were always made in the company of his Jairaben masters or their dour ladies. Usually it was to accompany the engineers and artisans who maintained the keep on their expeditions for parts and materials. Occasionally he was summoned by a Jairaben lady to carry her packages or to stand behind her as a supplementary footman in the city's fashionable restaurants or tearooms. The opportunity of finding someone capable of striking the anklets from his legs was non-existent. Nor were his

chances of striking out on his own helped by his
costume: a short blue robe, bare legs, and sandusker-
leather sandals that only emphasized the two deadly
bands around his ankles.

Time passed. In the nine years since the bands had
first been snapped around his own ankles, Kerryl had
enumerated seventeen others who had suffered the
same cruel restraint. Of those reaching the age of
majority, six had been elevated to the ranks of the
Jairaben. Eight others had suddenly vanished from the
keep forever, their names never again mentioned. Of
the seventeen, but three remained.

Kerryl discussed the situation in frantic whispers
over a period of months with one of the remaining
three, a sly-faced probationer from Whispering Sands.
Sanjo Milobaq had originally entered the keep as an
ordinary probationer. In his third year he had organized a surreptitious race in the duckbill training compound between a Nastom's nasty and a great waddling
hooter. Halfway through the race the Nastom's nasty
had suddenly paused, first to eat its apprentice jockey,
then the great waddling hooter. The great waddling
hooter was the solitary offspring of four hundred and
sixty-one generations of sustained crossbreeding; explosive anklets were attached to Sanjo Milobaq's legs
until he should reach his majority and could be defini-
tively judged. Now he fretted about the outcome, and
vowed he would depart the keep forever.

Through sources judged to be trustworthy, Sanjo
Milobaq acquired the name of an electronics technician in Tyhor who was, he swore, capable of nullifying
the activating code within the explosive bands.

"Why should he do this?" demanded Kerryl skeptically, desperate to believe in the existence of such
altruism, but unable to actually do so. "If the Jairaben
found out, they would feed him to the allosaurs."

"His brother was unjustly executed by the
Jairaben; this is a measure of his vengeance."

Twenty-two months still remained until the day of

Kerryl's majority and ultimate judgement; life among the Jairaben had inclined him to wariness. Sanjo Milobaq's fateful day in the Hall of Durster's Judgement was now but five months away; he was inclined to haste.

Four days later in the heart of Tyhor, still unable to persuade Kerryl to join him in his desperate venture, Sanjo Milobaq suddenly pushed his Jairaben overlord into the path of a twelve-wheeled truck and dashed off through the noontime crowds.

Whether or not Sanjo Milobaq ever found his vengeful technician, Kerryl never learned. But three months later he stood to the side of a Jairaben dowager in a Tyhonese tearoom, carefully stirring a lump of crystallized honey into her bowl of Centralia tea.

"I *do* wish you wouldn't inflict the presence of your beastly criminal upon us," complained her companion. "It was only a short while ago that I was informed how the Lady Pollak was dining on the terrace of the Sweetwater Tavern—the one that overlooks the river, you know—when a young man sitting in a passing boat quite literally exploded beneath her very eyes. Her appetite was quite, *quite* devastated." She cast a hard look at Kerryl. "I do hope that your own young man will choose a more convenient occasion on which to blow himself to pieces."

A name that was never far from Kerryl's thoughts was that of the Immaculate Ultim of Aberdown, the offworld grandee who had been the victim of the tyrant king's dramatic, if mistimed, regurgitation, then become the murderer of Kerryl's father and enslaver of his clan. First in Kerryl's mind was the immediate need of escaping the Pandow Keep; next was the overriding obsession of his life: to inflict a just retribution upon this evil demon and to restore whatever remained of his family and clan to their rightful lands in the Great Dismal Forest.

For at least seventy-five years now the Immaculate

Ultim had been an occasional, though erratic, visitor to the world of Stohlson's Redemption for the purpose of acquiring dinosaurs. So much was common gossip. A number of probationers or apprentices had been present in the keep during his previous visits, and Kerryl had no great difficulty in determining that the nobleman's home was on the planet Qymset at the far end of the Diobastan Cluster.

Every night during the endless years of his captivity, Kerryl's eyes turned to the flickering stars that sparkled in the thick atmosphere as he pondered bitter thoughts of vengeance. But as one long year of serfdom slowly became another, he at last began to ask himself with increasing desperation just how he would ever succeed in escaping his captors of the Pandow Keep, much less in reaching distant Qymset . . .

As always, whenever confronted by this bitter question, he could see but a single indisputable answer.

Stohlson's Redemption was far removed from the lanes of interstellar commerce that linked the seven hundred inhabited worlds of the Diobastan Cluster. As the eleventh year of his enslavement began, Kerryl had seen but seven ships settle slowly over the landing field on Bezzlerunners Road. The last had been nearly two years before; not since the modification of his anklets to permit him movement within Tyhor had a spacecraft landed. Inwardly he raged, and screamed imprecations at all the paynim gods of the Jairaben pantheon who had subjected him to such agony. Outwardly he composed his features into the dour set of all good Jairaben, and grimly waited.

Three days before the Feast of Arboreal Epiphany, in the year 28,383 FIP, Kerryl stood morosely in the serving pantry of the Gammahanny Hall, languidly polishing the keep's formal silverware. Might it not be better, he wondered dispiritedly, to disinter his buried neuronic disrupter, and in a final gesture of glorious defiance use it to rearrange the neurons of the one hundred and twenty-eight feasting Jairaben as they

celebrated the apotheosis of Durster the Egg-hatcher?
That at least—

A tremendous sonic boom rattled the dishes on the
heavy wooden shelves. With leaping heart Kerryl raced
with the other probationers to the nearest window.
High above the glittering expanse of the Kneedeep
Ocean he spied a tiny red dot. It grew rapidly larger as it
fell towards the sprawling city of Tyhor.

"To work, then!" cried the scullery chief. "Do you
think that holy Durster had need of such outlandish
contrivances as spaceships to spread his miraculous
word? If not Durster, then why such scallywags as
yourselves? To work, I say!"

His features impassive, Kerryl stolidly applied his
cloth to an ornate fruit bowl. He had seen enough of the
enormous spherical starship to come to an irrevocable
decision. A mere six and a half months remained
before he was destined to be led to the Hall of Durster's
Judgement to learn the final reckoning of his fate. For
the sake of his entire clan, he would have to be on that
great red ship when it rose from the landing field on
Bezzlerunners Road.

But how was he to escape from the keep?

And how was he to prevent the Jairaben's explosive
bands from blowing him to bloody bits at his first step
to the far side of Bezzlerunners Road?

His lips drew back in the harsh rictus of desperation. Still concealed at the far end of the plesiosaurs'
lake was his neuronic disrupter. Twelve thousand heathen souls were gathered here in the Pandow Keep. He
would visit upon each and every one of them all the
torments of the damned in order to reach that ship, the
only conceivable hope for himself and the Tandryl-
Kundórrs.

The following morning Kerryl reported for work in
the keep's brewery on the seventh level, his mind an
agony of indecision. How long would the starship linger
in Tyhor? When should he—

"You, the uplander." Like a suddenly recurring

nightmare, the dreadful face of Alldumb the Allosaur unexpectedly glared at him from behind a vat of fermenting grain.

"Your lordship?"

"You will come with me."

"Most willingly, your most revered lordship, except that my duties constrain me to remain—"

"He has now been attached to the brewery," interrupted the assistant brewmaster. "You will do the bidding of the exalted Allsoul. The present brew cannot be consecrated by the ceremony of the seven yellow stones and three gray feathers owing to a deficiency of supplies. You will accompany him to procure a fresh supply of stones from town." He turned his haughty countenance to Alldumb the Allosaur. "Make haste, then, Allsoul. Do not dawdle upon the way; keep well away from the heathen Contractionites; do not let stones of an inferior quality be foisted upon you; do not stop to dally with the wenches of the Graceful Fancy."

Scowling ferociously, Alldumb the Allosaur stalked angrily down through the myriad levels of the keep with Kerryl at his heels. In an enormous garage jammed with trucks and wagons they came to a small blue van by which stood three youthful apprentices from the brewery. Alldumb the Allosaur gestured to Kerryl, and he joined the apprentices upon the bare metal floor in the rear of the van. The Jairaben climbed into the cab, and to Kerryl's unspeakable excitement the van moved slowly out of the keep's profound gloom and into the early morning sunlight beyond its massive walls. Far ahead, through the van's windshield, he could see the massive red sphere of the starship against the pale blue sky. Kerryl could feel his heart thumping in his chest.

"Where are we going?" he asked the nearest apprentice.

"To Joitah Myner's Brewery Supplies on Old Postkettle Street. He is acclaimed for maintaining the finest selection of yellow stones in all of Woolywobber."

The dull red globe of the starship loomed against the horizon and the conversation of the apprentices became animated.

"The Contractionites!" exclaimed one. "Can you imagine such effrontery?"

Another shook his head. "Inconceivable insolence! Setting down here in front of the very keep to spread their infamous doctrine!"

"But how can we permit this?" marveled the third. "Why does not the Most Fragrant and Reverend Apotheosis bid them be instantly gone?"

"Notice those concavities about the girth of the ship: within are blasters powerful enough to level a city."

"But Miraculous Durster! Surely *he* would protect—"

"Of course. Nonetheless, the exalted Apotheosis and the Advocary General have decided it best to offer the paynim no grounds for provocation."

"Excuse my abysmal ignorance," murmured Kerryl. "But what are the Contractionites?"

The Contractionites who manned the *Divine Providence* had come to solicit the help of the inhabitants of Stohlson's Redemption, for they knew with a terrible certainty that the universe was rapidly shrinking and that a ghastly doom awaited. Only by joining in the construction of a great psionic prayer wheel on the planet Fafarall could the peoples of the cosmos be able to reverse the remorseless contraction which even now was squeezing the borders of the universe inward.

Such was the message that Contractionism had come to deliver in the heart of the Jairaben stronghold on the Hanchu Delta on Stohlson's Redemption.

The Contractionites' starship receded into the distance as the van made its way into the crowded streets of Tyhor. Kerryl continued to stare longingly through the rear window long after it had vanished from sight. At least he was now outside the walls of the Pandow Keep. But how could he make his way across the deadly barrier of Bezzlerunners Road to plead for asylum aboard the starship?

Tormented by this unanswerable question, Kerryl paid little heed to the angry muttering of Alldumb the Allosaur as he brought the Jairaben van to a sudden halt.

"Look!" cried an apprentice. "It's the Contractionites!"

CHAPTER 10

Kerryl peered through the windshield, eager to see these strange beings from beyond the stars. The van had come to the ancient open-air fruit and vegetable market on the Gurgly Canal. To all sides were its great airy sheds bulging with wooden crates of lush yellow and green produce. Kerryl saw that the van's progress had been blocked by a small procession making its way slowly between the delivery trucks that already clogged the area.

A glittering blue sphere twice the size of the Jairaben's van floated in the air, just above the heads of six grinning children and a stout, red-faced adult. The sphere sparkled with gold and silver flashes like tiny lightning bolts, and seemed to Kerryl's wondering eyes to be pulsing to some regular beat. The children and their benevolently smiling mentor were dressed in robes of the purest white and wore glistening round helmets of bright green upon their heads. A hundred or more workers from the produce market clustered about the Contractionites, pointing in wonder at the floating blue sphere and shouting good-natured comments.

"Disgusting," muttered Alldumb the Allosaur. "Where are the beadles when they are needed? Where are the carabin—"

He broke off as it became evident that the flashing sphere was rapidly dwindling in upon itself. As the sparks of gold and silver flashed faster and faster, the glowing ball shrank in size until it was no larger than

the van. A loud humming noise filled the truck, and
Kerryl inexplicably felt himself in the grip of some vast
dread. Uneasily, he watched the white-clad children
point up to the ever-dwindling sphere, now no larger
than a glittering beachball. Their eyes and mouths were
stretched wide with fear and apprehension.

The ball grew smaller still, while the sense of dread
that oppressed Kerryl grew commensurately greater.
He strained forward in dismay as the sphere continued
to dwindle. The sound of frenzied shouting came from
the street. He felt the blood pounding in his temples.

"No!" cried one of the van's apprentices in suppli-
cation as the ball shrank even more. "Oh, don't!"

Now the ball was only a pinpoint of flickering
brilliance. And then it vanished.

A vast clap of mournful thunder rolled across
Tyhor.

Kerryl was damp and trembling, in the grip of a
desolation he hadn't experienced since the Jairaben
soldiers had pulled him away from his father and
family in the Hall of Durster's Judgement.

"Ultrasonics," muttered Alldumb the Allosaur, his
face distorted with fury. "They've dared to use ultrasonics on the Children of Durster!" His shoulders
quivered and he stabbed blindly at the acceleration
button.

The van leapt forward.

Kerryl stood rooted in horror as two of the white-
robed children were smashed back into the stunned
crowd and the red-faced adult vanished beneath the
front of the van.

A moment later one of Kerryl's powerful hands
had seized the Jairaben by the throat and the other had
wrenched his fingers from the accelerator. Weaving
erratically, the van came to a halt in the midst of the
terrified crowd.

Hands pulled at Kerryl's arms, and as if from a
great distance he heard gasps and shouts. His fingers
tightened about the Jairaben's throat and he squeezed

with all the fury that ten long years of accumulated rage could engender.

"You've killed him!"

"I have?" Kerryl let the inert form of the Jairaben slump against the steering wheel. He stared down at his hands with curiosity and mild euphoria. Could they really have killed Alldumb the Allosaur? His euphoria became a fierce exaltation.

"You've killed him," repeated the apprentice, retreating in horrified awe. For an instant Kerryl stood locked in indecision; a thousand conflicting thoughts raced through his mind. Suddenly he saw what had to be done; he brushed past the trembling apprentices and stepped out into the mob of screaming Tyhonese.

Anonymous hands tugged tentatively at his bright blue robe as he pushed his way to the front of the van. He ignored them.

"Murderer!" cried a voice from the crowd. "Jairaben monster!"

"Murderer, I am!" shouted Kerryl, his gold-flecked eyes glittering brilliantly as he stared unblinkingly at the seething mob of brawny produce workers. "But only of this single animal, and no others!" He reached through the open window of the van and gripped Alldumb the Allosaur's lank brown hair. The lolling head was pulled into view. "Here is the sole murderer, this Jairaben lizard!"

The crowd's noise gradually abated as they pressed closer to the van. With a harsh grunt of disgust, Kerryl released the lifeless head and pushed his way to a knot of Tyhonese who were huddled around the six Contractionite children. Four of the pale blond children were wailing loudly as they gaped in horror at their two companions lying in the roadway. Their white robes were spotted with blood. Three brawny porters from the market had just succeeded in pulling the body of the adult Contractionite from beneath the blue Jairaben van.

"He's still breathing," murmured a flower seller in

astonishment as she stared down at the fat man's battered features.

"The children," whispered Kerryl harshly, gesturing at the two small figures.

"Not dead yet," replied a man who knelt beside them. "But without medical—"

"Yes, clearly they need medical aid." Kerryl's eyes met those of a broad-shouldered porter in a pale green smock who stood just behind the Contractionite children. He returned Kerryl's examination with massive composure. "Can you drive?" demanded Kerryl.

The produce worker inclined his head a fraction.

Kerryl gestured at the three pale apprentices still huddled in the van. "Clear out the Jairaben riffraff, then load the Contractionites. We'll need four more of you to attend to the injured on the way."

"The way to where?"

"To their ship, where else? The Contractionites will certainly want to care for their own people."

The porter considered Kerryl for a moment longer, then bunched his massive shoulders and bent to pick up the unconscious Contractionite. "What about the dead meat?" He glanced meaningfully at the head of the Jairaben dangling inertly through the window.

"We'll take him with us. Perhaps the Contractionites will know what to do with it: his carcass isn't worth being fed to the Jairaben dinosaurs."

CHAPTER 11

The van moved swiftly through the twisting streets of Tyhor as Rarifugo Meuws, the taciturn porter from the produce market, maneuvered deftly through the heavy traffic, unmindful of the groans and murmurs of the Contractionites stretched out behind him and the body of the dead Jairaben on the floor beside him. His thoughtful brown eyes darted back and forth from the road to Kerryl, but he made no comment as he watched the youth strip the long gray robe and floppy brown boots from the lifeless body of Alldumb the Allosaur and use them to replace his own short blue robe and plain sandals.

As the explosive bands around his ankles disappeared into the boots Kerryl sighed plaintively. If only their awful deadliness could be made to vanish so easily!

And if only they could get to the spaceport faster!

An endless time later the great red globe of the Contractionites' interstellar spacecraft could be glimpsed occasionally above the low wooden buildings of the city's perimeter. As the van at last turned into Bezzlerunners Road, Kerryl felt his heart pounding violently in his chest.

Far to his right, almost at the base of the starship, he could see the run-down buildings of the spacefield. On the other side of the highway, a few hundred yards before the entrance to the field, was a thick cluster of dark green and purple oaks. Kerryl laid his hand on the driver's muscular forearm. "Slowly, now, slowly. Stop!"

"Stop? We're nearly there!"

"Please! Just there by the trees."

Kerryl jumped down from the van into Bezzlerunners Road with a ghastly half smile twisting his features. "Those rings you saw around my ankles: they'll explode if I try to turn off from Bezzlerunners Road."

"Ah! Best you remain here, then. What should I do now?"

"Take the Contractionites to the ship." He nodded at the Jairaben's body huddled on the floor. "Explain the circumstances to whoever is in charge. Ask him to meet me as soon as possible: I have something urgent to communicate to him. I'll be here in the thicket of oak."

"And if he doesn't want to meet you?"

Kerryl tried to keep a tremor from his voice. "Then tell him that by his inaction my life is forfeit; you might ask him to say a Contractionite prayer for my soul."

Rarifugo Meuws' thoughtful gaze moved slowly from the gigantic spacecraft to the trembling youth, from the distant fortress of the Pandow Keep glittering in the morning sunlight to the lifeless body that lay at his own booted feet. He nodded somberly. "Be sure that I will tell him."

An hour passed.

Another.

Kerryl tried to sit patiently, impassively, deep in the inky shade of the oaks, but as the minutes passed his thoughts whirled and his spirits sank ever lower. A constant stream of traffic moved past him on the highway, speeding back and forth between the keep and Tyhor. Above him he could see the sun climbing high in the sky. What could possibly be taking Rarifugo Meuws so long? Surely by now the keep must have been informed! The hunt would be on for a renegade murderer! Even now the Advocary General might be in the coding room, commanding the technicians to—

He jumped to his feet as the dark blue van suddenly appeared from behind the spaceport's building and approached Bezzlerunners Road at a maddeningly deliberate pace. Heart pounding against his ribs, Kerryl watched it approach his clump of trees.

Why wasn't it slowing down?

Wasn't it going to stop?

At the last possible moment the van slued from the road and drew into the shadows. A short, muscular figure in a severe white uniform stepped down from the passenger's side and stood blinking in the harsh sunlight. A ceremonial scabbard of intricate design glittered against his left thigh. Kerryl limped forth from the shadows and curtsied formally. "Your lordship," he murmured softly in the Versal he had studied for so many tedious years in the Pandow Keep.

The Contractionite appraised him somberly, his lips pursed. He was in early middle age, with a thick, fleshy nose and a shiny freckled scalp that glistened in the sunlight. Curly red hair flecked with gray barely concealed long, pointed ears. His eyes were a startling pale blue.

"Your lordship is the captain?"

"Sergeant-at-Arms BuDeever. What do you want with his dignity my captain?"

Kerryl struggled to articulate his desires in this unfamiliar language. "Freedom, your lordship. Asylum. Awayness from here." He gestured at Tyhor, the Straggletooth Mountains, the flat Hanchu Delta, the harsh blue sun of Haiera 4CT3. "Awayness from the men who have fed my father to their animals and made me their slave."

"Fed him to their animals, did they?" A glint of animation lit the Contractionite's blue eyes. "What kind of animal?"

"A tyrant king," said Kerryl shortly. He stooped to roll down the tops of the Jairaben's boots. He gestured at the dull metal bands that circled his ankles. "If I step to the other side of the road, my feet will be blown off. I would therefore ask your lordship to remove these bands. Then I would ask him to let me join their lordships the Contractionites aboard their ship."

"Not lordships, boy, just Contractionites, for we are all lords on the road to the One True Center." He tapped his lips with the end of a stubby finger. "What is your religion, lad?"

Kerryl hesitated. "I am not a Jairaben; I am merely their slave. For ten years now I have been taught the supremacy of Durster the Egg-Hatcher. But still I believe in Great Darv."

"I am not familiar with Great Darv, but no matter: there are many paths to the One True Center." Sergeant BuDeever ran his hand through his grizzled hair. "We are always ready to accept a stout-hearted lad who is willing—and able!—to take up arms in defense of family and the Two Great Certainties. But in your own particular case, I fear, a more difficult path leads to the *Divine Providence*."

"The *Divine Providence*, your lordship?"

The Contractionite gestured at the great red spacecraft on the other side of Bezzlerunners Road. "Our ship is the *Divine Providence*. The driver of the van has told your story, lad, most forcefully. Without your intervention, the fate of our missionaries could well have been far worse; it now seems that all three of them will be saved. As sergeant-at-arms, I am eager to welcome you aboard. But . . ."

Kerryl's heart sank. "But . . . ?"

Sergeant BuDeever pointed to the anklets that banded Kerryl's legs. "We have no means of removing those terrible contrivances, at least here in this clump of woods, surrounded by savage heathens. If I tried, I would most certainly blow your legs from your body." He tugged awkwardly at his lower lip. "Moreover, I have been instructed by his dignity my captain to inform you that we can in no way encourage civil strife or insurrection; we may defend ourselves vigorously, but only if directly attacked."

"But you *were* attacked!"

"By a single madman. And thanks to your efforts, that madman has paid with his life. But his dignity my captain fears that even this might have been too definitive a gesture on your part: it may well jeopardize our entire mission to this world. He fears that in actuality you may be nothing more than a common criminal: certainly the Jairaben will be quick to describe you as such. We dare intervene no further." Sergeant BuDeever sighed unhappily. "To be honest with you, lad, his dignity my captain feels that this unfortunate incident may actually be nothing but a cunning provocation designed by the Jairaben to discredit our presence in Tyhor."

"But that's monstrous!"

The sergeant-at-arms pursed his lips in tacit agreement. "I told his dignity my captain, 'It's hard to overlook a corpse, such as the one that's resting in the van.' But as his dignity my captain pointed out in reply, what is one heathen life when the fate of the entire universe is at stake?"

Kerryl shook his head in appalled dismay. "I don't understand that reasoning at all."

"No matter, lad, nor do I. Theology I find best left to the theologians. Hrmph!" He drew himself up. "If you can devise some way of nullifying those bands and getting to the *Divine Providence* by your own means, I, for one, shall welcome you aboard. But for his dignity my captain to grant his approval, you will have to tender concrete evidence of your sincerity and devout good intentions."

"But I don't know *how* to remove the bands!" shouted Kerryl in anguish as he watched his life slip away in the course of this brief conversation. "If I knew that, I would already be aboard your ship!"

The sergeant-at-arms bent to run a finger cautiously around a band. "Hrmph! Tell me what you know about them." When Kerryl had finished, he rubbed his palm across the top of his shiny scalp. "It sounds as if the Jairaben devils have a central transmitter in the keep, with relays here along the plain and in the city. My sole suggestion is that you find a means of nullifying their transmitter, and possibly their relays."

"But the entire coding room is locked and under guard! I'd have to shoot my way in and then—"

"—destroy the transmitter." Sergeant BuDeever shook his head in somber appreciation of the task that lay before the paynim youth. "I must return to the ship now: his dignity my captain will be waiting for my report. My thoughts will be with you, lad."

"You're extremely kind to return me to the keep," murmured Kerryl as the van neared the Salvation Hills. "It will be your life as well as mine, if the Jairaben catch me."

Rarifugo Meuws' lips twitched in grim amusement. "Then they'll have to step lively: my passage has been booked for three weeks now on a grain barge to New South Anvilhead. It sails today at three."

"Is there room on the barge for a van?"

"Such as this one? More than likely."

"Then take it," said Kerryl urgently as he came to a decision of terrible finality. "Leave me at the gates, take the van, and flee for your life!"

Rarifugo Meuws looked at him speculatively. "Here are the gates, lad. Are you sure you won't accompany me back to the barge?"

"Later, perhaps," said Kerryl with a sickly smile. "But first I have something to attend to at the keep."

CHAPTER 12

Fearful of being entrapped by devilish Jairaben machinations, the captain of the *Divine Providence* had dealt decisively with the incriminating evidence of Alldumb the Allosaur by consigning his body to the reaction chambers of the ship's engine room. Now Kerryl's one-time Jairaben tormentor was nothing more than scattered molecules.

Kerryl tugged the long gray robe of the dead Jairaben around his slim hips as he strode with officious mien through one of the three broad service entrances that broached the walls of the Pandow Keep. The eyes of the four carabineer guards were on the blue van as it turned and moved rapidly down the road that led back to Tyhor.

Kerryl released his breath in a soft gust of relief as he entered the keep's courtyard without challenge, then glanced quickly to either side. Just to his right were the great stone and goldenose bulwarks that held the plesiosaurs' lake. Some hundreds of yards further away, barely visible beyond an outcropping of the mountain, he could see the spidery metal tower that rose from the roof of the coding room.

· Heart racing, Kerryl tried to minimize his easily recognizable limp as he strode across the courtyard, then through an echoing depot where workers grappled with the dozens of tons of fresh produce delivered that morning for the keep's kitchens. Exiting on the far side, he ducked into one of the innumerable twisting staircases that led to the upper levels. Three minutes later he emerged on the service level just below the refectory and turned immediately down a long, low corridor that led to the far end of the keep. In the five interminable minutes it took to reach its end, he encountered several dozen Jairaben and apprentices, but aside from an occasional puzzled half frown, none of them took any apparent notice of him.

A broad stone staircase took him down two levels. From there he used a freight elevator to descend to a subterranean storage area. Threading his way through bulky crates of machinery, he came to a small metal door. On the other side was a flight of narrow stairs. Kerryl limped awkwardly up a single steep flight in Alldumb the Allosaur's soft leather boots. On the dark landing a narrow metal door was secured by a heavy bolt. Kerryl pulled it back and slowly pushed the door open a fraction of an inch.

Bright sunlight pierced the landing. He peered cautiously through the tiny opening. Nothing but thick weeds and the gently waving tops of the trees growing on the slopes below could be seen. Kerryl drew a deep breath. No one else appeared to be about. He slipped through the door and across the knee-deep vegetation to the cover of a dark green thicket of butterbird bushes. There he plunged into deep shadows and crouched motionlessly.

Here in this small glade at the far end of the vast Jairaben Keep he could look out from the shadows of the butterbird bush upon the sides of the great Jairaben structures climbing the mountain behind. And here too was the far end of Lake Bliss, dug deep into the surrounding mountains. Kerryl caught a sudden glimpse of a long graceful neck gliding past a dozen yards above and inexplicably felt a moment's sharp regret for what he was about to do.

His lips tightened. The great monsters in the tank would tear his flesh to ribbons in an instant if they could; already he bore the lifelong scars of his single encounter with them. No, there would be no misplaced pity for the Jairaben's grotesque pets.

Even as he eyed the sleek beauty of the plesiosaurs, his hands were scrabbling frantically in the hard dirt around the roots of the butterbird bush. What had that Contractionite sergeant-at-arms told him that his dignity my captain of the *Divine Providence* would demand from the suspected Jairaben provocateur?

Concrete evidence of his sincerity and devout good intentions?

Kerryl smiled grimly as his fingers at last encountered the grimy piece of plastic wrapping he had been seeking. The golden specks of his brilliant green eyes gleamed in the sunlight as he pulled the neuronic disrupter from its wrapping.

He hoped that his dignity my captain had his eyes turned toward the Pandow Keep.

The irregular shoreline of Lake Bliss stretched five hundred and eighty-two yards along the western base of the Jairaben Keep, while its broadest arm was more than two hundred yards wide. Because it followed the contours of the stony mountains its depth varied, but Kerryl had been told that to maintain its giant plesiosaurs it was generally more than a hundred and twenty feet deep.

A billion gallons of seawater, Kerryl repeated to himself as he hurried down the passageway that led to the carabineers' sleeping quarters, a *billion* gallons! Enough to prove the sincerity of his intentions to anyone!

The seven bronze bells that announced the midday meal had tolled mournfully through the keep as he made his way back through its tortuous passages. All those carabineers not on active duty would now be gathered at their opulent private mess between the two main refectories.

Or so he devoutly hoped. For ten years of surreptitious exploration of the Pandow Keep told him that the single emplacement from which he would have any chance of success would be one of the windows in the quarters of the Jairaben's private army.

Ahead were the broad doors that opened to the quarters of the Seventh Legion of Carabineers. Kerryl paused to tighten his grip on the weapon concealed beneath his robe, then limped forward.

A single guard stood blocking the open entrance. Beyond him Kerryl could see that the large foyer was empty. The guard eyed Kerryl without interest. A moment later the carabineer screamed in agony as his body was lashed by the beams of the neuronic disrupter. Kerryl seized the carabineer's writhing body and manhandled it to the stairway at the end of the landing. He pushed, and the guard fell forward. The screams abruptly stopped. Kerryl turned and ran into the quarters of the Seventh Legion of Carabineers.

He paused in the large, gloomy foyer, momentarily disoriented, then caught a glimpse of bright sunlight through a window to his right. He whirled and hobbled down a short passageway, the disrupter held before him. The passageway ended in a narrow window embrasure which overlooked the broad Hanchu Delta. Kerryl climbed into the deep embrasure and jerked open the leaded window. Heart beating wildly, he twisted his head to the left to peer through.

Yes! This was a part of the keep whose construction had followed the contours of one of the mountainside's numerous outcroppings: from here he could look down on the outer walls of the plesiosaurs' lake just where it faced the inner walls of the stables' coding room. The spidery watch tower that surveyed the Jairaben's thousands of banded dinosaurs glittered in the noontime sun. Except for two carabineers standing guard in front of the entrance to the coding room the courtyard was deserted.

Kerryl drew a deep breath of hot summer air, and raised the neuronic disrupter. From where he crouched in the narrow embrasure, the distance to his target was at least a hundred yards. Only now had it occurred to him to wonder if the disrupter would function at such a distance . . .

Were those shouts he heard somewhere outside the carabineers' barracks?

How much time did he have left?

Kerryl gulped convulsively, and his finger tightened on the trigger.

Invisible beams from the neuronic disrupter washed against the glistening surface of the enormous planks of goldenose. As slowly as he dared, Kerryl played the beam painstakingly from top to bottom of the fifteen-yard-high section of wall that held the lake's flexible lining. The pistol grew heavier in his grip, and he braced both elbows against the embrasure's stony base for a steadier grip.

The shouts outside in the hallway were growing louder.

Kerryl looked down in despair at the massive walls gleaming in the sunlight. Nothing at all about the goldenose seemed to have changed. His eyes returned to the disrupter in his hands. Was it even *functioning*? Could the blast that had crippled the carabineer at the door have been its final flickering charge after eight long years of neglect?

Slowly he moved its sights up and down the seemingly impervious goldenose wall. Was that a humming noise emanating from the gun? And was it beginning to feel warm in his grip?

"What are *you* doing here?"

Startled, Kerryl nearly lost his grip on the disrupter. He whirled around, finger still on the trigger. The carabineer lieutenant who stood at the end of the passageway leapt high in the air as his body's neurons were tortured by the terrible power of the disrupter. He fell to the floor, his limbs twitching in horrid spasms.

Kerryl tried to shut his mind to the agonized

screams of the carabineer as he swung the sights of the disrupter back to its target at the base of the plesiosaurs' lake.

It would *have* to give! he told himself desperately. And *now*! Otherwise his lifespan could be measured in seconds. Hadn't the chairs at the Feast of the Arboreal Epiphany broken apart like so much shattered glass after being barely caressed by a few fleeting seconds of the disrupter's power? Why hadn't the unthinkable pressure of the millions of tons of barely restrained water—

A flash of brilliant crystal suddenly sparkled in the sunlight, and then another. Along a broad vertical strip of wall the glowing orange and red tones of the polished goldenose were rapidly losing their creamy luster. The wood glittered and sparkled as one crystal after another flaked away and tinkled down to the courtyard.

More shouts behind him . . .

Kerryl whirled and fired blindly—just as he caught a glimpse of a sudden jet of water lance across the courtyard, as straight and unyielding as a steel bar. Exulting fiercely, he sprayed the beams of his disrupter across the bodies of the three carabineers who stood bewildered in the middle of the passageway.

Even as they began to scream in torment, Kerryl turned away in jubilation to watch first one chunk of sparkling wall give way, and then another. Water gushed through, at first in a dozen wildly spraying laser-like beams, then in two great jets as thick as a man's body. One arched high above the walls of the keep, finally falling in a great curve to the parklands below. The other roared straight across the courtyard to batter against the thick stone walls of the ancient stables.

Now the remaining planks in the goldenose wall trembled and shuddered. With the sound of a million pieces of cloth being simultaneously ripped, the wall suddenly vanished and a torrent of water thirty feet high exploded into the courtyard. A deafening roar filled Kerryl's ears, and in the flickering of an eye the courtyard and its buildings had disappeared in a maelstrom of raging spray and foam. As Kerryl stood transfixed, the base of the transmitting tower was engulfed and the entire structure began to quiver. A moment later it toppled slowly into the seething cauldron of furiously churning water and was lost to sight.

With a tortured shriek that shook the entire keep another portion of the wall gave way. Awestruck, Kerryl watched as the sleek gray forms of two of the Jairaben's cherished plesiosaurs were caught up in the raging waters and were swept majestically past to vanish far below.

At last he pulled himself away from the window and limped rapidly down the passageway. The four carabineers shrieked their agony unheard against the thunder of the waters. Kerryl stepped gingerly around them and moved warily through the foyer, the disrupter gripped tightly in both hands. He peered through the door. The landing and stairway were empty.

Kerryl turned down the staircase towards the dull roar of thunder, his face grim with determination. No man-made construct in the world could resist the fearful pounding of a million tons of water. Already the coding room and all its contents must have vanished forever. He glanced down at his booted feet with a bleak half smile. They seemed to be still attached to his legs.

He came to a window that opened onto the Hanchu Delta. An ever-broadening river was roaring across the once-placid landscape of the delta. Mighty trees were being carried along by the raging torrent, and a thousand terrified dinosaurs galloped frantically in all directions. Even from here Kerryl could see the upright necks of four plesiosaurs as they struggled to retain their balance in their inexorable passage across the Jairaben's farmland to the distant sea.

Kerryl's tortured smile faded as he raised the pistol higher and turned away from the window. The way was clear before him; just beyond the flooding waters he could see the great red sphere of the Lingerlight Contractionites beckoning. Like the relentless sweep of the plesiosaurs to the sea, nothing at all was going to stop his own march to the sanctuary of the *Divine Providence.*

PART THREE

CHAPTER 13

The paynim inhabitants of Widderfurshire in the canteen of Dullings on the planet Pyp worshiped the aromatic contents of a ten-thousand-year-old stockpot. The same ancient cauldron, large enough to simmer an average-sized stegosaurus, had now bubbled uninterruptedly for more than a hundred centuries over a ring of bright blue flames in the catacombs of the Temple of the Thrice-Blessed Belly.

Every tenth day, each of the sect's adherents brought to the holy site a certain prescribed ingredient concomitant with the worshiper's age, sex, and status. This was ceremoniously stirred into the savory concoction by one of the three white-clad priests who attended the pot with enormous wooden paddles. At the end of the day's lengthy rites the Widderfurshians were vouchsafed a ladleful of the rich brown soup to carry home in intricately adorned golden containers. A ritual spoonful was thereupon incorporated into each of the next ten days' meals.

It was only from other members of the ship's Constabulary Corps that Kerryl learned of this palpable absurdity, for upon his incorporation into the Contractionites he had been immediately assigned to the personal stewardship of Sergeant-at-Arms BuDeever. In the ten months since the *Divine Providence*'s hasty departure from Stohlson's Redemption Kerryl had spent the entire time confined to the cramped quarters of the ship's armed forces in the company of Sergeant BuDeever and the other hardy advocates of Muscular Contractionism.

Unseen by Kerryl, the three great ships of the Contractionites, the *Divine Providence*, the *Divine Intervention*, and the *Divine Salvation*, were moving through the Diobastan Cluster in a complex mathematical pattern designed to bring their message to each of the cluster's seven hundred inhabited worlds over the course of the next three centuries. Goudie Azavery, the *Divine Providence*'s ranking theologian and dialectician, was far from pleased with this lackadaisical pace set by the main computer on Lingerlight. For according to his personal calculations, the universe would have shrunk by nearly thirty percent before all the worlds of even this single cluster had been visited . . .

This was far from being Kerryl Ryson's chief concern. For soon after his breathless arrival aboard the *Divine Providence*, his boots full of water, a neuronic disrupter in his hand, and a half-mad grin on his face, Kerryl had confirmed what he had always suspected during his years at the Pandow Keep: that he did not possess a talent for theological subtleties.

Even under the exasperated goading of Sergeant BuDeever he was obstinately unable to commit to memory whether it was everything within the known universe, his own body included, that was now contracting at an equal rate; or if, in fact, it was merely the physical borders of the universe that were relentlessly shrinking inward, eventually to compress all of the cosmos' trillions of stars and sentient beings into a single primal mass in its fiery center.

The prevention of this catastrophe Kerryl understood to be the central tenet of the Contractionites' doctrine. Their more immediate goal, he learned, was the construction of a continent-sized psionic prayer wheel on the barren planet Fafarall, which, according to their star charts, was located in the precise geospacial center of the universe.

By channeling the concerted will of trillions upon

trillions of committed Contractionites through this psionic focusing device, the inexorable contraction of the cosmos would eventually be arrested; with further prodigies of devotion, it would someday be reversed.

Three practical obstacles remained to be surmounted in the pursuit of this lofty goal: the conversion of trillions of sentient beings to Contractionism; the solicitation of billions of credits; and the subsequent construction of the gigantic prayer wheel, whose actual physical design still remained nebulous.

These were goals with which Kerryl supposed he had the profoundest sympathy; but since even the gloomiest prognostication of Dialectician Azavery relegated the final death throes of the universe to some four thousand years in the future, Kerryl's attention eventually lapsed to more prosaic concerns.

Chief among them for the first ten months of passage aboard the *Divine Providence* had been the intensive and peculiarly specialized physical training administered by Sergeant-at-Arms BuDeever. The Coven of Dreamers and Planners on Lingerlight were universally men and women of peace and goodwill, their only goal the physical salvation of the cosmos and its inhabitants. They would have been horrified to learn of the recondite lore that Sergeant BuDeever taught his charges. But Lingerlight was two thousand and seventy-four light-years distant, and the Constabulary Corps had more than nine hundred starry-eyed innocents committed to its protection.

"I've seen some terrible rascals and scallywags find the One True Center in the course of my training," said Sergeant BuDeever, "but never before have I been entrusted with a strong-arm who single-handedly demolishes a fortress, invests the countryside with a thousand ravening monsters, and drowns ten thousand godless heathen, may the Bountiful Flowering preserve their paynim souls, all in the course of an hour's work."

"My sergeant exaggerates," replied Kerryl in the vernacular of Versal spoken aboard the *Divine Provi-*

dence, and his face darkened at the memory. He sincerely hoped he hadn't caused the death of ten thousand human beings, even of soulless Jairaben. *But*— "They shouldn't have fed my father to their beasts!" he blurted. "Nor put their bands about my legs!"

"Spoken like a true son of BuDeever's Bersagglers!" guffawed Sergeant BuDeever with a lusty slap on the back. "If *I'd* been forced to keep a desperado like you under my charge, I'd have had a *dozen* bands about your legs—and anywhere else I could fit one!" He gestured for Kerryl and a muscular recruit from their last planetfall of Lander's Glory to move closer to him on the thin matting that covered the metal floor of his tiny gymnasium deep in the bowels of the *Divine Providence*. "Now, then, here's a wile I unexpectedly learned from the doorkeeper of a pleasure house on Sunaway. Charming woman: a mustache as long as your arm and twice as thick. Let's suppose, now, that you have a man coming at you from either side, knife in hand: this is what you do . . ."

The overriding concern, never forgotten in the years in which Kerryl Ryson grew to full manhood aboard the *Divine Providence*, was his quest for the planet Qymset. Here he would take a dispassionate vengeance upon the murderous Immaculate Ultim of Aberdown and his beast, and liberate his family and clan. His years among the Jairaben had made him a practical student of human nature: he supposed that in all likelihood the exalted ultim and his tyrant king would resist his intentions. It seemed best to prepare himself for a wide variety of contingencies.

The ship's doctors had treated the ancient disabilities of his arm and knee to the best of their ability; his movements now were fluid and supple, his limp barely discernible. Even after his initial formal training with the Constabulary Corps was finished, he continued to exercise incessantly in the gymnasium, and spent long and painful hours sporting with Sergeant BuDeever. His shoulders broadened and his body grew ropy with muscle.

At the successful conclusion of his third engagement with hecklers and provocateurs on planetfalls to which the *Divine Providence* hoped to bring its message of salvation, Ryson was made a squadron leader. He began the study of ancient manuals on the advanced employment of small arms, unarmed combat, military tactics and strategy, guerrilla warfare, terrorism, and counterinsurgency. The following year he snapped his sergeant's arm, clavicle, and seven ribs in the course of an exercise; from his cot in sick bay Sergeant BuDeever winced in pain and elevated him to corporal-chef. Ryson celebrated the promotion by spending an additional hour that evening hurling his two concealed leg knives unerringly into a six-inch target from every unlikely position he could contrive.

Slowly, erratically, in a pattern discernible only to the ship's central computer, the *Divine Providence* moved across the Diobastan Cluster in the direction of the tantalizingly elusive Qymset. Ryson impatiently paced the surfaces of a dozen bizarre worlds while keeping a wary eye on the white-robed innocents of the Contractionites as they moved fearlessly through the cities and countrysides in quest of converts and funds, their flashing blue spheres contracting and vanishing, their hidden emotional augmentors playing upon the fears and lusts of the local heathen.

From a distance he observed the curious rites and peculiar rituals that the misguided folk of a hundred different sects saw fit to practice. He shook his head in amazed disbelief: how could so many apparently sensible and intelligent beings delude themselves with teachings that were so manifestly absurd? Even more peculiar: how could Great Darv—to Ryson's sure knowledge the one true God—have apparently failed to manifest Himself throughout the rest of the cluster?

As he sparred in the gymnasium with a multitentacled machine that attacked him with four padded hands, Ryson asked himself what effect the visits of the Contractionites would ultimately have upon the peoples of the Diobastan Cluster. How, in fact, could the Contractionites ever hope to proselytize all the scattered billions of just this one small cluster?

"Why don't you—I mean, we—just try to convert Eldif the Equitable?" he grunted breathlessly as he successfully parried a triple-pronged attack directed at his face, groin, and ankles. "She's the Suzerain, isn't she? Then she could *order* everyone to find the One True Center and contribute a hundred VS* apiece. And then we could move on to the next cluster."

Sergeant BuDeever stared incredulously. "What? A hardhead like you actually believes that Eldif the Equitable rules the cluster?"

"She *says* she does. Who am I to deny it?"

"Many's the lass on many a world I've tried to convince I'm young and handsome. But even with the evidence before them, not all of them choose to believe me."

"*That* I can believe," grinned Ryson, and found himself suddenly knocked sprawling by a tremendous blow to the end of his nose from the relentless machine. He lay blinking on the gymnasium floor, colored spots dancing across his field of vision while he pondered the older man's words.

All he really knew of Eldif the Equitable was that on the planet Bir a score of light-years away from Stohlson's Redemption she reigned as Imperatrice Absolute of the Aeonian Galaxy and Holy Suzerain of the Diobastan Cluster. Her claim to the rest of the galaxy could probably be dismissed as ceremonial braggadocio, for even Ryson knew that a thousand other petty despots and rulers throughout the stars made the same grandiose claim.

---

*Valuta Standard: the official currency of Bir, and hence, in theory, of the Diobastan Cluster.

But what of the Diobastan Cluster?

Sergeant BuDeever was a keen student of intragalactic politics. From his mess-table monologues Ryson had learned that the entire galaxy was rife with open jealousies, keen animosities, incessant provocations, and constant trumpetings of ultimatums from one planet to another.

What was surprising, he reflected as he climbed groggily to his feet and shuffled unsteadily off to the showers, was how little actual violence and bloodshed ever transpired. For here in the Diobastan Cluster alone a hundred worlds or more must be capable of totally annihilating a rival planet or system by any of a dozen terrifying means. And yet it never seemed to quite happen . . .

Because of the vast distances between inhabited worlds, which rendered interstellar warfare impractical?

Because of the moral restraints imposed by the teachings of the thousands of cults and sects that seemed to spread across the cluster like a growth of mushrooms?

Because of the inherently peaceful nature of mankind?

Ryson grunted derisively as he stepped under the stinging water. Far easier to believe that the uneasy peace that embraced the Diobastan Cluster was due to the imperial fiat of Eldif the Equitable and the cautionary presence throughout the cluster of her sleek orange ships of the line.

He gingerly prodded the tip of his puffy nose. Long painful years among the Jairaben had taught him that while Might didn't necessarily make Right, it could most certainly constrain the weak to obey the whims of the more powerful.

CHAPTER 14

Whatever lay behind the millennia-long peace that encompassed the Diobastan Cluster, the actual writ of the all-powerful Eldif the Equitable stopped well short of the surface of her supposedly subject planets. The security and welfare of the inhabitants of each individual world were strictly a local concern; this was the primary reason for the thick cluster of blasters that girdled the waist of the *Divine Providence*.

In Ryson's third year aboard ship, the Contractionites' great red sphere dropped out of space to alight upon the island of Deliverance on the world of Azure, a bare twelve light-years from the goal Ryson so fervently sought, the planet Qymset. A small blue world circling a dull orange sun, Azure was little more than a single vast ocean. High in the northern hemisphere was its single land mass, an irregular island too small to be dignified as a continent.

Seven thousand years earlier, at the time of its initial colonization by a solitary spacecraft of pioneers, the island of Deliverance had been densely covered with a thick evergreen forest in which a rich and varied indigenous wildlife flourished. The settlers had fled to Azure to escape the bitter persecution they suffered on the planet Bójolly for their religious beliefs.

Free at last to worship as they pleased, the Azurians had joyfully unpacked their living gods, a six-thousand-year-old colony of giant green insects somewhat akin to termites. A temple was consecrated around the towering mound of thrice-digested cellulose in which the insects made their home, and the first of the succulent logs from the inexhaustible richness of the continent-wide forest was reverently offered up to the chitinous green gods . . .

Now, seventy centuries later, the island of Deliverance was totally denuded and its native wildlife long since exterminated. A handful of Azurians scratched a primitive living in the occasional oases that miraculously survived in the single great desert that covered the island. A bare two thousand others had retreated with their gods to the interior of a half-buried Remnant on the northeast coast of Deliverance.

It was here that the *Divine Providence*'s instruments had detected the presence of human life and cautiously set down in the blasted wastelands just beyond the Remnant. Its eager missionaries had departed the ship in the joyful hope of adding the few meager voices of even this miserable settlement to the mighty tide of righteousness that would eventually turn back the relentless contraction of the universe.

The missionaries crossed the sparse fields of scrawny yellow crops that maintained a precarious foothold around the glossy hemisphere of the Remnant and entered through a small, heavily fortified door set in a massive stone wall. Inside, they had barely begun to expound their message of Contractionism before they were cast into shackles and taken before the Council of Nouk for judgement.

Soon a message came back to the *Divine Providence*, along with the severed head of one the ship's seven-year-old children. The head appeared to have been snipped off, as if by a giant mandible. The remaining members of the outlanders' company would be returned, said the message, upon the timely delivery of one million tons of prime cellulose.

"Savages," stated Sergeant BuDeever with barely concealed satisfaction, for more than seven years had passed since his forces had last been called upon for any action more vigorous than dispersing a few militant atheists and hecklers. Here, after long years of painful inactivity, was an officially sanctioned opportunity for BuDeever's Bersagglers to knock together paynim heads in the glorious service of the One True Center.

"But how can they even consider taking our people hostage?" demanded Ryson in astonishment. "Can't they see the blasters aboard the ship? We can melt them down to slag in an instant."

"A Remnant, melted to slag? Remnants are impervious to anything we've ever invented." The sergeant-at-arms stared in dismay at his corporal's peculiar ignorance. "Don't you have a Remnant on . . . well, wherever it is you're from?"

"If we do, I never heard of it."

"Hrmph!"

The vast and enigmatic Remnants were all that remained of what the Diobastan Cluster called the Deliverers, an unknown race of beings who in the distant past had apparently been masters of the galaxy. To most of the rest of humanity they were more prosaically known as the Engineers. But wherever their monstrously outsized artifacts had been found, cults and religions incorporating their brooding presence had quickly arisen.

One such sect had come into being on the southern continent of the obscure planet Bir in the northwest quadrant of the Diobastan Cluster. The vanished race of god-like beings who had left the Remnant were denominated by them the Deliverers. A few centuries later, in the course of a bloody struggle for the accession to a minor throne, a distant ancestor of the present Eldif the Equitable had sought to legitimize her lofty aspirations by allying herself with the Deliverers' priests and having herself anointed spiritual heir and holy spokesman for these mighty gods. The bargain had proved a judicious one, for the descendants of that alliance had now ruled Bir and its nearby systems for more than two thousand years.

"If they're impervious to everything we can do to

them, then how do we rescue our people?" asked Ryson as he strapped a throwing knife to the inside of each calf.

Sergeant BuDeever snorted. "They only *think* they're impervious; they've been savages for so long they've forgotten that the only parts of the Remnants that can resist a blaster are those that were actually built by the Engineers themselves."

Ryson lifted his eyes to the armory's viewscreen on which the stupendous half globe of the Remnant gleamed dully in the late afternoon sun and nodded in comprehension. "All that stonework along the front: that was added by the Azurians."

The sergeant-at-arms grinned with malevolent relish. "They bricked up the hole the Engineers left and made it their own little entranceway. And now they think their bricks will protect them from Sergeant BuDeever and his little band of merry cutthroats."

The enormous stone archway that showed on the screen was large enough to have once permitted the passage of the *Divine Providence* itself. But in spite of its size, it was little more than a minor blemish in the seamless pale blue walls of the largest artifact in the known universe. All around the stonework that filled the half circle of the archway, the Deliverers' great hemisphere rose smoothly out of the Azurians' ragged farmland to fade from view in wispy white clouds three-quarters of a mile overhead.

The Remnant here on Deliverance was apparently identical in every way to the seven hundred and sixty-four other spheres so far discovered throughout the galaxy. The Engineers' reason for building these immense spheres remained as mysterious today as when the first Remnant had been found on the frozen planet Crystal three million years before. In all the time since that epic discovery not a single artifact of any kind had ever been uncovered in any of the two great hemispheres that composed each of the spheres. Many of the Remnants were now deep in the planetary crust, discernible only by deep-radar, and it had been easy enough for comparative geologists to estimate that approximately two hundred million years had passed since their creation.

It was speculated that an even greater number were still awaiting discovery beneath the mountains and oceans of the galaxy's rapidly evolving planets, for the vanished race of Engineers had truly merited their name: their mysterious creations were seemingly impervious to even the mightiest forces of nature. Indestructible, inalterable, and ageless, the Remnants were a terrifying reminder to those who reflected upon them that for all of Man's present preeminence in the galaxy, far mightier species than he might even now be lurking in ambush around the next turning in the celestial road . . .

Battle armor in place and weapons secured, two full squadrons of Sergeant BuDeever's Constabulary Corps left the ship just after sunset. Two armored hovercraft shot suddenly out of the side of the ship away from the Remnant and moments later had vanished into the silent wastes of the barren desert.

Just before midnight the hovercraft returned, this time approaching the looming mass of the gigantic Remnant from its rear. Just as they reached the great circular structure the craft commanded by Sergeant BuDeever veered away to the right, that commanded by Ryson to the left. They swept around the base of the giant hemisphere and thirty seconds later rendezvoused in front of its imposing stone archway.

Now the great blasters of the *Divine Providence* drilled six neat holes through the stonework at six different levels. Thrusters screaming, the two hovercraft wobbled a hundred yards into the starry sky, then shot forward through the uppermost hole.

Inside they were blanketed by total blackness. Six great flares were launched by each craft. Below him Ryson suddenly saw elaborate stone ramparts on either side of the now shattered entranceway. A hundred shadowy figures, garishly lit in the painful glare of the flares, crouched on the ramparts in ambush. Ryson's squad bathed them with neuronic disrupters while the other craft launched a thousand small missiles in every direction. A clear, odorless gas began to fill the hemisphere.

On Deliverance the Engineers' great floor that split the Remnants into two equal hemispheres had long since disappeared beneath the rubbish of generations of Azurians. The two hovercraft dropped down nearly to ground level, then raced across the ragged landscape toward a group of stone buildings that clustered around a ragged cone some sixty yards high. Missiles continued to streak forward to burst against the walls of the village. Ryson could see dark figures staggering jerkily between the buildings and collapsing to the ground.

The Azurians' chitinous gods seemed perversely animated by the same gas that was stupefying their human worshipers. The outlines of the giant cone grew blurred with the frantic movement of millions of fist-sized insects. The voice of Sergeant BuDeever rasped in Ryson's headset. Moments later, incendiaries shot forward to burst in great orange blossoms against the cone. The gods vanished into the flames.

At the base of the hive was a two-story building, larger and of more carefully dressed stone than the rest of the village. Ryson led his squad up its broad steps past the sprawled forms of eight guards dressed in leather. Inside, they found all seven members of the Council of Nouk huddled together, their faces hidden behind grotesque green masks in the shape of giant insects.

Further into the building they found another room, tightly closed and nearly airless. Here were the *Divine Providence*'s sixteen remaining Contractionites, most of them only half affected by the slowly seeping gas. Antidote was hurriedly sprayed into their bloodstreams, and they were loaded aboard the two hovercraft.

The armored craft moved away from the now silent village. The rest of the battle squad, harshly illuminated by the flickering orange flames that still chewed at the insect colony's great cone, moved systematically from hovel to hovel. Bodies were sprawled everywhere. Ryson moved rapidly among them, shining a powerful light on their faces. The females, as well as the boys up to the age of early puberty, were administered the antidote. The rest of the males were left to die without regaining consciousness.

Forty minutes later the *Divine Providence* lifted silently into space.

"Why did we kill all those people?" asked Ryson a little shakily, secretly appalled at the slaughter of the Azurian savages.

"Justice," replied Sergeant BuDeever. "They killed one of ours, and threatened the others."

"I see. In that case, why didn't we kill them all?"

"We had to leave someone to bear the message."

"Message? What message is that?"

The sergeant-at-arms poured himself a tumbler of clear blue wine. "That when our children are abroad upon their divine task, working for the salvation of all, their persons are inviolate. This must be made clear to the entire galaxy."

Ryson looked down to his hands that had so recently lifted a hundred children out of the long black shadows of death, leaving behind a hundred others who were hardly older. "What do you suppose will become of the women and children?" he asked.

"Oh, they'll survive," said Sergeant BuDeever with total confidence. "And when we return in twenty years or so, perhaps this time they'll be ready to accept our offer of salvation."

"And that's justice?"

"That's justice, lad."

CHAPTER 15

But justice, Kerryl began to feel, could be a curiously elusive commodity, as half a decade passed aboard the *Divine Providence* and he seemed no further along in his own search for justice than when he had been a slave at the Pandow Keep.

The planet Qymset was where he hoped to exact that bitter justice that had been his remorseless goal for so many years. But in the long sleepless nights that had sporadically tormented him ever since his rescue from the Jairaben, he often wondered hopelessly if he would ever find his way to that distant world and what awaited him there: the Immaculate Ultim of Aberdown, his tyrant king, and whatever remained of the Tandryl-Kundórrs.

And now the great arc of its glittering surface filled the upper quadrant of Ryson's viewscreen . . .

"Are you certain that this is the right planet, lad?" asked Sergeant BuDeever dubiously as he peered at the screen.

"So far as I know there's only one Qymset," said Ryson, his face pale, his initial exhilaration slowly giving way to a terrible emptiness.

"Looks like nothing but ice and snow to me. These dinosaurs of yours—would they be cold-weather beasts?"

"I don't know. I don't think so . . ." Ryson swung around, the curious golden specks in his green eyes blazing. "But they *have* to be!" he shouted. "The man was the Immaculate Ultim of Aberdown, a grandee of

111

Qymset! That's what everybody said! It was no secret! Everybody knew it!"

"Hrmph! Anything's possible, I suppose. His dignity my captain and the five senior dialecticians are in the observatory. Maybe they'll see something about Qymset that we don't . . ."

A variety of instruments revealed a single small settlement not far from the planet's equator, but buried far beneath the snow that covered the world's single land mass. Ryson began to prepare his battle gear. The Contractionite elders had belatedly rediscovered caution after the catastrophe with the insect-worshipers of Azure: no longer would the first wave of missionaries be allowed to stroll heedlessly into a closed environment such as the Remnant on Azure or the underground city here on Qymset.

The *Divine Providence* settled slowly into the icy landscape a hundred miles from the settlement, a vast cloud of mist engulfing the ship as its superheated surface sank deep into the ice. Communications were established with the governing body of the underground community of Wiswaygo, and an advance party consisting of the two oldest, hence most expendable, of the dialecticians set forth in the ship's pinnace. Accompanying them were Sergeant-at-Arms BuDeever, Corporal Ryson, and eight more constables in hastily donned civilian clothes.

Homing in on a signal transmitted by the Wiswaygans, the pinnace flew slowly across the featureless landscape in a howling snowstorm. Eventually its instruments showed a great white mound ahead. Another Remnant of the long-departed Deliverers? wondered Ryson.

A primitive but effective series of airlocks opened before the pinnace and the small craft came to rest in a surprisingly small and badly lighted hangar. Two dozen Wiswaygans in bright orange costumes stared in frank curiosity as the delegation climbed down from the pinnace. Laden with concealed weapons, Ryson and four other constables accompanied the two dialecticians. Sergeant BuDeever remained aboard with the rest of his squad, ready to instantly activate a variety of heavier armaments.

A Wiswaygan stepped forward, his hands held high above his head. "Welcome," he proclaimed in barely comprehensible Versal. "Very, very welcome. You are the first visitors to Wiswaygo in three hundred and ninety-seven years."

What meager hope had sustained Ryson since his first sight of the icy globe of Qymset on the viewscreen drained away. Numbly he followed the others down through a series of ramps and elevators until they came to the city of Wiswaygo nine hundred feet beneath the howling white surface.

Here lived twelve thousand people, the population of the Jairaben's Pandow Keep, in a series of claustrophobic man-made caverns. Several thousand of them now crowded eagerly around their offworld visitors in a small public square more suitable for accommodating hundreds. Ryson shivered in spite of the heating unit in the battle suit he wore beneath his long white robe. Only a meager heat and dim orange lighting were supplied by ancient devices that tapped deep into the planet's molten inner core, and he wondered if they could be slowly failing. "This can't be the place," Ryson muttered glumly in his throat transmitter to Sergeant BuDeever. "It's cold enough down here to freeze the Kneedeep Ocean."

The Contractionites were led to an inner chamber of hard concrete benches and roughly processed gray walls, and unstintingly offered the hospitality of the Wiswaygans. To Ryson, all their platters of cold gray food and chilly flagons of cloudy liquids tasted unremittingly of barely processed yeast. His eyes wandered to the three long icicles that had formed on the walls beneath the room's ventilation units.

"Why have you honored us with your presence?"

asked the senior Wiswaygan when he saw that his
shivering visitors could make no further pretence of
swallowing their delicacies.

"For the salvation of the very universe," replied
one of the elderly dialecticians between chattering
teeth, and made a concise summary of the
Contractionites' doctrine.

"Extremely interesting," muttered the senior
Wiswaygan, "and most provocative. But before I reply,
let me summon our community's senior physicist.
Yes," he said sadly sometime later, "it is just as I
feared: our theological positions are clearly diametri-
cally opposed."

"How do you mean?" asked a dialectician, his lips
a pale blue.

"The simple laws of physics tell us that the contraction of the universe will unavoidably raise the heat level
of the entire cosmos."

"That is true," conceded the Contractionite. "Beginning about three thousand years from now, we may
expect to succumb to the heat-death of the universe. In
actuality it is nothing more than our ashes that shall be
compressed to a single tiny ball in the moments of final
contraction."

"Ahhh!" The senior Wiswaygan smiled wistfully.
"If only I could be there to experience that glorious
moment!"

"But—"

The senior Wiswaygan brushed away a small icicle
that now depended from the tip of his mustache.
"Strange," he mused, "very strange indeed. Tell me
this: when your souls migrate at the end of their
corporeal existence, is it not to an eternal paradise of
searing and cleansing heat, one in which the soul is but
a glorious wisp of purest flame darting amongst the
all-enveloping incandescence of the Everlasting Fire?"

The Contractionite dialectician pursed his lips.
"This is surely a most unorthodox doctrine?"

"Is it?" asked the senior Wiswaygan, genuinely

startled. "We on Qymset have always considered this to be universal truth."

Another hour of argument was unable to reconcile the wildly disparate points of view. "If your psionic prayer wheel could only be used to speed *up* the contraction of the universe," summarized the senior Wiswaygan at last, "then we would most certainly join our efforts to yours."

"I fear that such would be counted a very great heresy by my theological superiors," replied the dialectician sadly.

"A pity. Your goals being what they are, then, I fear that I cannot in all conscience permit you to proselytize among us."

The dialectician blew vigorously on the ends of his numbed fingers. "I feel certain that my superiors will see the undeniable merits of your argument. May I now wish all of your souls eternal flames." He nodded to the others in his group, and they began to totter from the chamber on unsteady legs.

Ryson drew the senior Wiswaygan aside. "Before we leave, we are anxious to make the acquaintance of a certain one of your notables, the Immaculate Ultim of Aberdown," he murmured. "Is this possible?"

The senior Wiswaygan stared in bewilderment. "I fear that you are some three hundred and ninety-three years too late in your request."

Ryson's brain felt as numbed by the bone-chilling cold as his ears and nose. Could he have heard right? "Three hundred and ninety-three years?"

"How could we forget it? The Immaculate Ultim of Aberdown is the name of the last visitor to set foot on Qymset. His name is honored among us: was he not the Third Concubine of the Suzerain Eliandro on the great planet of Bir? His great-grandniece would be today's actual ruler of the galaxy, the exalted Eldif the Equitable."

CHAPTER 16

Electronic libraries had been unknown to Ryson on Stohlson's Redemption; it took him three weeks to master the primitive library aboard the *Divine Providence*. At last he was equipped to do what he now realized he should have done years ago: search the library for all references to Qymset. They were meager in the extreme, and told Ryson nothing beyond what he had already learned. There was no mention under Qymset of the Immaculate Ultim of Aberdown, of dinosaurs, or of the Suzerain Eliandro of Bir.

With a scowl, he tapped out instructions to search for Bir, the Suzerain Eliandro, the Immaculate Ultim of Aberdown, and, for no reason in particular, Eldif the Equitable. He spent the next six days scrolling through the mass of material the library presented. At the end of that time he voiced his determination to visit the Palace of Mercy and Justice in the Gray Spinster Mountains.

Sergeant BuDeever snorted disdainfully at such a fanciful notion. "So you believe that a machine can dispense absolute justice or absolute mercy? I thought I'd trained you better than that, lad."

"What else should I do, then?" demanded Ryson belligerently. "The man I'm searching for is apparently four hundred years old and once appeared on Qymset: that's all I know."

"What makes you think it's the same man? There are worlds where people live two or even three hundred years, but I've never heard of four."

"The holograms the Wiswaygan showed me on

Qymset: he was a little younger, but it was the same man." Ryson's lips tightened bleakly. "It's a face I'll never forget."

"And you say he called himself the Third Concubine of the Suzerain Eliandro? Easy to say when you're buried on Qymset beneath a mile of snow, a hundred light-years from Bir. Who's to know the difference?" Sergeant BuDeever scratched his fleshy nose. "What was he doing on Qymset, anyway?"

"His ship set down to make emergency repairs. While his crew was attending to that, he paid a royal visit to the Wiswaygans."

"So they really don't know if he was the Immaculate Ultim of Aberdown or not . . . What does the library say about this royal immaculate?"

Ryson scowled. "There *is* an Aberdown on Bir. It's the royal execution shed, for discarded lovers of the reigning suzerain. But the library has never heard of a so-called immaculate ultim."

Sergeant BuDeever guffawed in appreciation. "Hah! So our lad has a sense of humor! And you think the justice machine on Bir can tell you where to find him?"

"I've got to try," said Ryson doggedly. "It's supposed to have the biggest data bank in the cluster, maybe in the entire galaxy; how hard will it be to trace a man who's more than four hundred years old?"

"He'll have had lots of practice at covering his tracks."

"There must be *some* connection between him and the planet Bir. And if there is, the machine should find it."

"And you're going to ask it to dispense absolute justice? I'd be careful if I were you, my lad: I've heard some funny tales about this machine and its notion of justice and mercy."

"I don't know about mercy," said Ryson between clenched teeth, "but justice is justice, and that's all I'll ask for."

Sergeant BuDeever shook his head skeptically.

"There's but one kind of justice in this sad universe, lad: and that's the kind you administer yourself at the end of your bayonet."

By the time the *Divine Providence* came to Bir, Sergeant BuDeever had been blown to pieces in a skirmish with the Imperial Flower Judges on the planet Dandeleoni and Ryson promoted to his post. He continued to work out religiously in the gymnasium and small-arms firing range. Without being able to articulate his reasons, he knew that he was close to the fateful encounter with the man he had hunted so long. Whenever, wherever they finally met, Ryson would be prepared . . .

The Contractionites' reasons for visiting Bir were twofold: a general overhaul of the ship; and a resumption of their century-long campaign to add the Imperatrice Absolute of the Aeonian Galaxy and Holy Suzerain of the Diobastan Cluster to the lists of their faith. Her Imperial Majesty Eldif the Equitable was now well into her two hundred and forty-first year, and presumably ripe for comforting words of salvation. Just how far her imperial sway actually extended beyond her own small solar system, and how much her conversion would aid the cause of Contractionism, were questions that the ship's dialecticians left for their seniors on Lingerlight to ponder.

Three days after the ship had been lowered into the dock facilities of the Devadory Shipyards on the outskirts of Green Gully, Ryson drew his accumulated salary of eleven years of constabulary service and converted it into 12,768 VS at the Seafarers and Cottagers Bank of Luster. An hour later he had purchased a ticket on the Gorban & Green Gully monorail and was skimming rapidly across the checkerboard fields that ringed the planet's capital. Far behind him, he could see the vast yellow palace of the aged Eldif the Equitable sprawling across a rocky promontory that thrust into the storm-tossed Majestic Ocean. Ahead, the Gray Spinster Mountains were a barely perceptible line against a pale yellow sky.

Ryson stepped down from the car just as evening was falling. Gorban had once been nothing more than a lonely frontier post. Now a small city of innkeepers and souvenir merchants had arisen here in the bleakness of the Gray Spinsters to attend to the needs of the thousands of pilgrims who came in search of justice or mercy. As befit a site devoted to the eternal verities, Gorban had been reconstructed along severely classical lines: its creamy conical buildings all tapered to a rigorously proportioned green roof in the graceful shape of an empress lily. This broad leaf, Ryson learned from a brochure procured from the Office of Tourism, symbolized the headpiece donned by Elenora of the Woods just before rendering her epic judgement upon the Whirligigs of Prestabol on this very site nine centuries before.

Ryson sauntered slowly through Gorban's hilly streets, thoughtfully appraising the throngs of exotically dressed visitors from all over the cluster as well as the numerous hostelries and inns. He wondered if Eldif the Equitable had purchased all of the local real estate before decreeing the construction of her psionic justice machine in the mountains just behind town, for the imperatrice was said to have the soul of an accountant. He fingered the 12,764 VS in his pocket uneasily. The Holy Suzerain's justice was notoriously expensive, for the proceeds were reputedly needed to maintain her legendary seraglio. Ryson eyed the black crags of the Gray Spinster Mountains which loomed against the starry sky. How much absolute justice could the fruits of eleven years of unstinting labor purchase?

Ryson rose and bathed in the early dawn, but as he sat by a window in the inn's dining room waiting for breakfast he saw that already a steady procession of petitioners was making its way up the winding footpath that led to the Palace of Mercy and Justice. He spread a creamy layer of six-year-old cheese with dark green veins upon a chewy brown wafer. Twenty-one years he had waited for justice, he told himself: he could take an additional ten minutes to eat his breakfast at leisure.

By the time that Ryson had joined the other somber petitioners climbing the twisting path, the craggy summits of the Gray Spinster Mountains were a rosy pink in the rays of the morning sun. He passed an outcropping of the mountain, and the village of Gorban disappeared from view.

Five minutes later the path opened into a broad clearing at the base of a sheer gray cliff that rose vertically for thousands of feet into the sky. Fluffy white clouds scudded across its distant top, creating the disquieting illusion that the immense rock face was toppling forward to crush the ant-like figures at its base.

Seventeen small ivory booths, each in the shape of the ubiquitous cone, were placed at regular intervals across the clearing. Solemn guards in uniforms of glossy purple and yellow silently directed the petitioners to the end of a single line that snaked across the clearing. Ryson raised his eyebrows: he had conceived of the Palace of Mercy and Justice as being far more majestic in appearance than seventeen tiny booths with a green leaf on top. Dutifully, he joined the end of the line.

As he slowly shuffled forward he saw that most of the petitioners spent about ten minutes in the closed cones. Upon exiting, they were directed toward the looming rock face, to disappear from view beyond a dip in the clearing. Occasionally a disturbed-looking petitioner would reappear from the booth in a matter of minutes and hastily return the way he had come. For lack of funds? wondered Ryson. How much *did* justice cost?

Eventually his own turn came. He stepped forward to one of the center cones. Above its concealed door were discreet gold letters. FROM EACH ACCORDING TO HIS MEANS, read Ryson. TO EACH ACCORDING TO HIS ENTITLE-

MENT. The diaphragm slid open and he stepped into the cone's tiny compartment.

"Please be seated," said a sonorous voice in Versal from the cream-colored wall before him. "Then place your hands on the yellow screen on the counter before you." Ryson took his place in a chair and the diaphragm closed silently behind him. The glowing yellow screen felt faintly warm to his hands. "What is your desire," asked the voice, "mercy or justice?"

"Justice."

"Justice is invariably more difficult to adjudicate, and far more onerous to implement; it is correspondingly more expensive."

"A matter of no importance." Ryson wondered how the machine would have responded had he voiced a request for mercy.

"The petitioner clearly understands that whereas justice can always be eventually adjudicated, its actual implementation is occasionally beyond the means of even her exalted suzerainty, although her most diligent efforts will of course be exerted. In those rare cases, the imperatrice regrets to inform the petitioner that no reimbursement of honoraria tendered is possible: all adjudications are final, and without recourse. Is this clearly understood, and formally agreed to?"

"It is," said Ryson.

"Your assent has been recorded in our data bank. But whatever the outcome, you will be issued a handsomely framed certificate attesting to the adjudication officially delivered by the Palace of Mercy and Justice." The machine paused. "To expedite the judicial process, you must submit to a preliminary examination by psionic scanner, for your entire life, background, culture, and psychic aura must be evaluated and integrated before adjudication can proceed. All data garnered during the course of this process will be guarded in the strictest confidence, never be divulged, no matter what the circumstances. Is this also agreed to?"

Ryson hesitated. What were the dark spots and blemishes on his soul that he would wish to hide? The destruction of the Jairaben fortress on Stohlson's Redemption, with the probable loss of innumerable lives? Pah! What did a computer on Bir care about the just tribulations of an obscure colony of slavers on the far side of the cluster?

"I agree," he said.

"Then close your eyes, maintain your hands on the yellow screen, and concentrate on the bright spot of red light which you will apparently see in front of you. The process does not take long, and will in no way discomfort you."

It was true. Only a few seconds seemed to have passed before Ryson heard the voice again. "It is seldom that we receive a petitioner from Okalati; it appears to be a most interesting world. You may now open your eyes, and proceed to the adjudication of your request. The honorarium will be 643 VS, for such are your means in relation to your request."

Ryson counted out the required sum and deposited it in a slot which opened in the counter before him. Why had he feared that the fee would be beyond his means? Surely 643 VS out of the more than twelve thousand he possessed was a reasonable enough price for the assurance of absolute justice . . .

Something nagged at the edge of his mind. "Why do you say I'm from Okalati?" he asked as he rose to his feet.

But the diaphragm had already slid open behind him, and there was no reply.

Inexplicably uneasy, he let one of the somber guards in yellow and purple direct him down the sloping pavement toward the gigantic gray rock face before him. Why had the machine taken him to be from Okalati, a world he had never heard of? Was this the local name for Stohlson's Redemption? Could it be a world he had known by some other name as a trooper bringing the message of Contractionism to the Diobastan Cluster? What else could the machine have possibly meant?

Before him, two impassive guards stood motionless against the bare rock. As he approached, a triangular doorway slid open in the side of the cliff. Ryson stepped through the opening into a small square room of burnished stainless steel. Two other petitioners, a man and woman, stood before him, their faces puzzled. A moment later a door slid shut and Ryson felt himself dropping down into the heart of the Gray Spinster Mountains.

The elevator fell for three full minutes while Ryson's ears popped from the gradual change in pressure. It came to a sudden lurching halt and the door opened. Beyond was the vast semi-darkness of an enormous cavern cut from the living rock of the mountain. Flickering orange torches ringed its rough-hewn walls, unable to illuminate its distant ceiling. Faint, almost imperceptible wisps of orange, blue, and rose smoke drifted slowly through the void. An inexplicable feeling of immeasurable awe and trepidation suddenly gripped Ryson. After a moment he smiled grimly: who could recognize the use of emotional augmentors more clearly than a constable in the service of the Lingerlight Contractionites?

Three shadowy figures stepped out of the darkness, all of them women. One was tall, gaunt, and austere, the two others plump, rosy, and maternal, with eloquent brown eyes that spoke of infinite compassion and understanding.

"You," said the gaunt woman as she fixed Ryson with emotionless black eyes, "have come for justice. Follow me."

Ryson left the two petitioners who had opted for mercy and moved briskly after the angular figure through the drifting colors of the mist. A cold damp breeze blew against the back of his neck. For a hundred paces his boots echoed loudly on the uneven stone floor, and then were suddenly muted. He glanced down at his boots. Now the floor of the cave had tilted downwards, and handrails had appeared on either side of him. The floor was no longer the rough stone of the Gray Spinster Mountains, but a smooth, semi-translucent material that seemed to radiate a faint pale blue. Ryson looked to either side. The darkness was still all around him, but in the far distance he could see a few pale yellow cones of light clinging to towering walls. It was the same eternal material he had first seen on the planet Azure: miles beneath the surface of Bir, Eldif the Equitable had built her Palace of Mercy and Justice on the slightly askew floor of a Deliverers' Remnant.

He sensed the presence of a featureless dark mass looming before him. Ryson took another step forward, then halted, half dazzled by the sudden illumination of the gigantic white cone that now blocked his path. The angular female guide stood waiting beside a triangular opening in its base. Beyond her he saw a single gray chair in the center of an austere gray room. His attendant gestured him forward. "Be seated," she ordered. "And may you find the justice you seek." Before Ryson could reply, the opening had closed behind him.

After the chill of the gloomy cavern, the air here felt warm and dry. Ryson took his place in the chair and waited.

A voice seemed to speak within his mind. *You have come seeking justice. Justice you shall have. State the nature of your demand, vocalizing aloud: this will focus your thoughts more clearly.*

Ryson licked suddenly dry lips. "Twenty-one years ago my father was devoured alive by a beast set upon him by an offworld grandee who styled himself the Immaculate Ultim of Aberdown. He then embarked my mother, my brothers, my bride-to-be, all one hundred and forty-six members of my family and clan, upon his spaceship and flew them away to slavery. I know nothing more about this person, other than that three hundred and ninety-six years ago this same man spent a short spell on the planet Qymset, where he presented himself as being the Third Concubine to the Suzerain Eliandro."

What is the precise nature of the justice that you demand? Be specific.

"The return of my family and clan to Stohlson's Redemption. The restitution of our lands and property. A fitting chastisement for the person who calls himself the Immaculate Ultim of Aberdown."

Your case will now be considered. Close your eyes and concentrate on the yellow pentagon which you will see before you. Do not attempt to speak again.

For an interminable time Ryson sat uneasily while invisible mice seemed to scurry through the corridors of his mind. At last the voice spoke again.

You are a barely comprehensible clutter of discordant auras, contradictory impulses, and conflicting statements. Your life and background on Okalati are totally at variance with the statements you have vocalized.

"But—"

A single fact is clear: that you demand justice in the case of Dasgow van Hilder and the Three Negative Buoyancies. This will now be granted you, Ablin Whitherweather.

A disgusted grin crossed Ryson's face as he rose to his feet. He spoke coldly to the featureless room. "I am far from being the celebrated Ablin Whitherweather. I am, in fact, Kerryl Ryson!"

A harmless enough delusion, except when it comes in conflict with the Four Just Imperatives. Know then, Ablin Whitherweather, the justice you have demanded: for your heresy before the Grand Tribune of Warsee you are hereby sentenced to six months of labor in the service of the Excoriationists of Yellowjack.

Ryson shook his head in grim negation. "It has been an interesting experience, but I appear to have wasted my 643 VS after all. I wonder if you are not

actually in the pay of the Immaculate Ultim of
Aberdown. Now then, open the door, and I will be
upon my way." He turned expectantly to the far wall.

The barely visible triangle remained obstinately
shut. Instead, a slight hiss of air could now be heard
leaking into the room. Ryson looked around. A soft
pink mist was rising from concealed outlets in the floor.
He took an alarmed step backward, his hand moving
automatically to the throwing knife concealed beneath
his left shirt sleeve.

A moment later the mist had filled the room and
enveloped Ryson. A great peace engulfed him as he felt
himself slowly crumpling to the hard metal floor of the
Palace of Mercy and Justice.

CHAPTER 17

Ryson reflected wryly upon the extravagant amount of justice that could be obtained for a mere 643 VS as he was transported free of charge by an imperial ship of the line across sixty-three light-years of interstellar space. Admittedly, his accommodation was solitary confinement in the ship's brig, and the amenities correspondingly limited. But the food was surprisingly good, and served in unlimited quantities. Unable to exercise in the confines of his tiny cell, he sardonically noted that he was actually putting on weight, as if he were now a wealthy grandee on a pleasure cruise between the stars. And all for 643 VS! True, the rest of his twelve thousand VS had been removed from his pockets, along with his assorted weaponry, while he lay unconscious, but even here he had formal assurance of their restitution upon the completion of his six months of service on Yellowjack.

Six months of service, thought Ryson. That should be easy enough to serve. He smiled grimly. It would also give him ample leisure to reflect upon the retribution he would visit upon the perverse machine that had cost him half a year of his precious time . . .

Three weeks after lifting off from the naval fortress of Wrest on Bir, the imperial frigate *Determination* set down seventeen miles outside the town of Ferramonte's Landing on the planet Yellowjack.

Four stolid naval ratings under the command of

two supercilious officers fixed a metal band around his neck and shackles to his wrists and ankles.

"You realize that you are taking me into slavery," he protested to the scarlet-clad commandant.

"Surely not, dear fellow, her gracious suzerainty would never permit it."

Chains were attached, and he was led briskly to a square red van just outside the ship. The few seconds it took to move between the ship and the van were like stepping into a furnace. Ryson gasped as the awful heat enveloped him like a physical entity and the shimmering air seemed to suck the moisture from his body. He stumbled into the rear of the van, where the temperature approached two hundred degrees. "How long do you think I'll survive on a world like this?" he shouted furiously. "You're sending me to my death!"

"No concern of ours, I fear."

Ryson's chains were attached to rings in the bare steel walls. The door slammed behind him and the engine rumbled. He was on his way to the Yellowjack Labor Exchange & Bourse.

A heavily barred window permitted a view of the passing countryside. It was as harsh and desolate as anything Ryson had ever seen in the bleakness of Deadman's Desert on his long-ago voyage aboard *The Languid Endeavor.*

Craggy mountains and smoldering volcanos lay on the horizon of barren wastelands. Not a tree, a bush, or a blade of grass could be seen. Ryson rattled his chains plaintively. The band around his neck chafed painfully, reviving unpleasant memories of his years among the Jairaben. It appeared that his six months in the service of the Excoriationists of Yellowjack were going to be far more grim than he had counted on.

Even in the blazing heat of Yellowjack a little water managed to accumulate around the polar caps. The headwaters of the Lifesaver River collected deep underground, then ran for nine hundred miles through subterranean caverns and aquifers before suddenly bubbling to the surface in the southern reaches of the Central Highlands. A few miles further on, the highlands were abruptly sundered by the great abyss of the Bottomless Rift. A hundred miles long and three thousand feet deep, the immense fissure was less than a quarter-mile wide. Here the turbulent waters of the Lifesaver River tumbled into space and cascaded straight down towards the valley floor thousands of feet below.

The churning foam never reached the bottom. Dispersed and evaporated by the furnace-like gales that swept through the narrow rift, the dirty brown waters were only a heavy mist by the time they settled on the community of Ferramonte's Landing. Deep in the bottom of the harsh black shadows that darkened the Bottomless Rift for all but a few minutes at noontime, Ferramonte's Landing exulted in a cool, balmy climate that rarely exceeded one hundred and forty degrees.

The van conveying Ryson to the labor exchange and bourse came to a halt at the edge of the Bottomless Rift. Three enormously fat Excoriationists enthroned in bulky a-gravs that floated a constant fifteen inches above the ground shepherded him solicitously out of the broiling heat of the van. Ryson blinked in the sudden relative cool and darkness.

He was in an enormous concrete warehouse stacked to the ceiling with thousands of crates and cartons. He shook his head in bewilderment, then watched with barely concealed fury as the two naval officers who had brought him across the entire Diobastan Cluster on the whim of a psychopathic computer stepped down from the van's cab. Wordlessly the imperial officers joined Ryson in an immense freight elevator that dropped precipitously into the Bottomless Rift. The doors shut behind them and the elevator began to lurch down to the valley floor.

"I'll give you a last chance to reconsider," said Ryson through clenched teeth. "Take me away from here, and I'll reward you well."

The commandant and his flag-lieutenant glanced at him in astonishment, then hurriedly took a cautious step away.

Ryson glared at them, then turned his attention to the three native Excoriationists floating in their a-gravs. Both their clothing and their a-gravs dazzled the eye with an explosion of brilliant primary colors. All three were as fat as any man he had ever seen, with tiny eyes lost in folds of flesh, jowls that quivered and jiggled with the motions of the elevator. Their mouths were in constant motion as their chubby hands crammed them with sweetmeats and pastries from dispensers in the soft arms of their a-gravs, and great rivulets of sweat ran down their soft pink features. Strange, mused Ryson. On a world as fearfully hot as this one, he would have expected its inhabitants to be as lean and parched as a desert lizard . . .

The elevator shuddered to a halt in the middle of a vast warehouse that stretched for hundreds of yards to the left and right. Like the great entrepôt on the rim of the cliff, it was packed to the ceiling with crates of every foodstuff and luxury item that Ryson could imagine, as well as the most costly household machinery and articles of furniture. By their markings, the crates had been imported from all over the cluster. Automated machinery moved silently up and down the long corridors of goods at the direction of a single round Excoriationist floating near the distant ceiling. Ryson stumbled clumsily after the smoothly gliding a-gravs of his escorts, half blinded now by the heavy sweat that drenched him in the moisture-laden atmosphere, his shackles chafing almost intolerably against his damp flesh. But how, he wondered distractedly, could the inhabitants of such a barren wasteland afford to import such luxury from the stars?

The labor exchange and bourse was entered directly through a door at the far end of the warehouse. To Ryson's relief, here the temperature was almost tolerable. He was led to a small cubical where the most elaborate medical apparatus Ryson had ever seen hummed softly. It seemed to have been designed to handle patients attired in shackles and chains, for these caused no problems as an obese medical technician put Ryson through a complete examination. "Most exceptional," he enthused to the naval officers. "Your candidate is in quite exceptional health. It is my pleasure to certify him for a full six months." He signed his name to an attestation and blinked cheerfully at Ryson. "My own present contract is nearly at an end: I may well put in a bid myself!"

Now Ryson was conducted to a larger room where nine gaunt men and women in chains slumped apathetically in hard wooden chairs. The characteristic blue wattles of the natives of the planet Bresse dangled beneath their chins. They raised dull eyes at Ryson's appearance, then returned to their own somber speculations. "If you gentlemen will be patient for just a further moment," said a corpulent attendant to the naval commandant, "I will attend to your candidate's health insurance, social security card, and so forth." He led Ryson to a far corner of the room, where he was photographed in his chains and issued a labor permit, an identity badge, and a number of other cards which he scowled at in helpless fury.

"For the most vital part of all," said the Excoriationist, "I now summon the eminent divine, His Reverence the Diocesan Wystalorn."

A door opened, and the fattest Excoriationist Ryson had yet seen floated into the room. "Welcome, my children, to Yellowjack," murmured Diocesan Wystalorn to Ryson and the nine gaunt Bressians in sonorous Versal from the temperature-controlled comfort of his garish red and blue a-grav. "In just a moment it will be my pleasure to guide you to the somber embrace of the bosom of Hatrode, as fully participating adherents of Excoriationism. But first, my dear children, a few words concerning the austere nature of Hatrode and of his ineffable gift to mankind, Excoriationism, which you have all so selflessly elected to serve."

Great Darv, thought Ryson with a bitter groan of contempt, yet another false prophet! Could he never escape them?

The Excoriationist spoke of Hatrode and his prophet Cobbycol, of their creed of absolute asceticism. Of the malevolence of matter, and the insubstantiality of worldly possessions and pleasures. Of the necessity for absolute self-denial, self-abnegation, and self-sacrifice. Of the glorious laceration of the flesh in the name of the eternal Hatrode. "If I may venture an observation," interjected Ryson, "very little of what I have seen here on Yellowjack would tend to confirm the validity of your teachings. You and your fellow Excoriationists all seem, in fact, quite exceptionally merry and well fleshed."

"This is true," conceded the diocesan with a vast sigh, "for however lofty our intentions, in actual practice we occasionally find it difficult to fully live up to our high ideals." His a-grav moved smoothly forward. "But now let us attend to your spiritual rebirth, the most glorious moment of your lives!"

With the two curious naval officers in close attendance, Ryson and the nine wretched Bressians were herded into a tiled changing room where they were divested of their clothes. Totally naked except for their shackles, they now shuffled forward into the thick damp mist of what Ryson at first assumed to be a steam room. As a nauseous smell of sulfur and corruption assailed his nostrils he gradually made out through the clinging steam an irregular pool of viscous gray mud bubbling and heaving at his feet.

The voice of Diocesan Wystalorn drifted through

the mist. "Now you will be cleansed of all your worldly impurities by the holy Rituality of Surfeit."

Out of the mist a dozen Excoriationists in bright green battle suits moved forward in their silent a-gravs. Their booted feet effortlessly pushed the furiously struggling Ryson and the Bressians to the edge of the near-boiling mud, and then over.

Ryson gasped at the sudden blinding pain that lashed his entire body, and then even his head was thrust relentlessly beneath the surface. Burning mud seared his mouth and lungs, and he floundered frantically, the agony beyond bearing.

Just as he knew that he was on the verge of choking to death, he was lifted from the terrible cauldron and a moment later immersed in what seemed to his tortured body to be a bath of ice water. His heart pounded in shock, and his lungs filled with water. He spluttered and choked and splashed blindly in the freezing water, but at least the horrible agony of the boiling mud was being drawn away as the viscous gray slime was washed from his body.

Now he was suddenly pulled from the pool and a flagon of water pressed to his trembling hands. "Drink," urged a voice, "drink."

Ryson gulped convulsively, heedless of its ghastly taste. Moments later his stomach knotted in cramps and he fell to his knees, clutching his abdomen in agony.

"When the candidates have successfully passed the Trial of the Three Great Purgations," intoned the voice of Diocesan Wystalorn from somewhere in the swirling fog, "we shall then move on to the Ceremony of the Seven Whispering Lashes and the Fourteen Implacable Lusts. Rejoice, my children, for soon you shall be reborn as Excoriationists!"

Seven of the nine Bressians had survived the rigors of their conversion to Hatrodism. Quivering with shock and pain, they were urged forward to the raised auction block that stood in the middle of a pink sandstone rotunda. Their rapidly blistering skin was only partially hidden from view by their loosely-fitting gray overalls.

Two hundred garishly clad Excoriationists of both sexes milled noisily about the room in their a-gravs, all of them as grotesquely fat as the others Ryson had already encountered. Their chubby hands clutched frosty crystal glasses and silver plates piled high with elaborate pastries as they made further selections from the serving machines that floated deftly through the crowd. As the auctioneer began to chant in a singsong voice, few of the chattering Excoriationists raised their eyes from their plates to the auction block and its seven miserable Bressians. Bidding for the newly converted Hatrodians was desultory, but one by one they were eventually led away through the crowd to vanish from sight.

"Three weeks to a month," observed one of Ryson's guardians to the flag-lieutenant, shaking his head. "Hardly worth the trouble of conversion and drawing up a contract. A very poor consignment from Bresse indeed." His tiny eyes glittered as he considered Ryson. "But you, now, my lad: you're in the prime of life, husky, well fed. You'll easily fetch the full six months."

Ryson could only stare at him in numb anguish. His body hurt in places he had never before considered.

The last of the Bressians was led away, and now it was Ryson's turn to stumble gingerly forward on blistered feet that could barely support his weight. Nudged on by the neuronic disrupters in the hands of the imperial naval officers he mounted the auction block. In a sudden noisy surge of interest the Excoriationists crowded forward, their hands and cheeks smeared with rich yellow and pink creams from their pastries. Ryson blinked down at their great moon-like faces, then suddenly leapt forward in an uncontrollable paroxysm of rage to rattle his chains furiously in their startled faces, his lips drawn back in a hideous snarl.

The auctioneer beamed his approval at such indomitable high spirits, and while Ryson's arms were being shackled to an ornate iron post quickly began the auction.

Ryson sagged against the post while twenty minutes of spirited bidding ensued. With an anguished sigh he looked up to find that he had been sold to an Excoriationist who even among the others who crowded the exchange was notable for the enormity of his corpulence. His new master floated up onto the auction block and beamed at Ryson. Then he turned and carelessly spilled the contents of a small black purse on the auctioneer's broad desk.

"His Maigritude Lord Lustral of Lowlands has purchased your contract," whispered an attendant to Ryson in awed tones. "He is three times mayor of Ferramonte's Landing, as well as the sole proprietor of the Whimpering Virgin Mine."

Even in his present state of mind Ryson was dispassionately impressed by what was presumably the output of Lord Lustral's mine: seven perfect starfires glittering in all their hypnotic beauty, the rainbow-like spectrum of their self-generating rays filling the exchange with a swirling prism of colors. Even the smallest, Ryson knew, was worth more than the revenues from his parents' Blue Finger Mill for a century or more of work. Could it be here on Yellowjack that the most valuable commodity in the galaxy was mined? If so, no wonder that the deranged computer of the Palace of Mercy and Justice had dispatched a naval frigate to transport a single indentured laborer across the cluster . . .

"Only seven of them?" inquired the imperial commandant with studied indifference. "Oh, very well, I suppose it can't be helped." He bent forward to sign his name in triplicate on a thick sheaf of papers.

The mayor of Yellowjack, Lord Lustral of Lowlands, skimmed across the auction block in his glittering yellow a-grav to appraise his purchase.

"I now belong to you?" Ryson asked the grinning fat man. "I am a citizen of Yellowjack, and under its protection?"

"Your *contract* belongs to me," clarified his maigritude. "You are now a devout Excoriationist, a seeker after Hatrode, and a citizen of Yellowjack. You enjoy the full benefits of the ecclesiastical law of the Book of Hatrode, as well, of course, as coming under my personal aegis."

"I see." Ryson turned awkwardly and painfully to the two naval officers of her imperial suzerainty, who were about to step down from the auction block. His chains rattled softly against his dark blue overalls. "Did your lordships enjoy the sight of the starfires?"

"Immensely." The commandant glanced at his flag-lieutenant in puzzlement. "But why do you ask, my dear fellow?"

"Because I'm hoping that it's the last sight you'll ever see." Ryson drove an elbow with all the skill of Sergeant BuDeever's training straight into the Adam's apple of the startled flag-lieutenant, then stepped forward to loop the chains of his wrist shackles around the neck of the commandant. Ryson jerked upon the chains with all his strength, once, twice, a third time, and was rewarded with a sharp cracking sound. The commandant sagged heavily to the floor with the chains still around his neck, pulling Ryson down with him. A moment later Ryson was smothered beneath the flesh of a dozen howling Excoriationists.

CHAPTER 18

The terms of indenture among the starfire kings of Ferramonte's Landing were not precisely what Ryson had envisioned. There was no toiling in the infernos of the starfire mines that dotted the perpendicular sides of the Bottomless Rift, no backbreaking labor among the crops in the few green fields that clung to tenacious life in the moisture-laden air and deep blue shadows of Ferramonte's Landing.

For thanks to the chance discovery of starfires two centuries before, Yellowjack's tiny population of six thousand Excoriationists now lived lives of luxury that few of the planetary rulers of the galaxy could equal. Their marble palaces were dug deep into the walls of the Bottomless Rift, and from here they seldom set forth. The community's manual labor was attended to by the most sophisticated machinery the galaxy could provide, supervised by a small rotating cadre of Excoriationists in temperature-controlled suits.

Ryson himself now lived in one of the grandest of their palaces, in a bleak concrete room utterly devoid of furniture deep in the basement of the vast dwelling that Lord Lustral had built not far from his mine at the southern end of Ferramonte's Landing.

For three weeks Ryson had sprawled in his totally bare cubicle, naked except for the chains and shackles that clanked loosely upon his rapidly dwindling flesh. A single wall of the cubical was inch-thick seethru to permit his maigritude the pleasure of contemplating his charge at his leisure. Dim orange lights burned incessantly in both the corridor and the cell. Once a day an opening in the translucent wall dilated sufficiently to permit a serving machine to introduce a bowl of thin gruel and a flagon of sulfuric water.

For spiritual nourishment, Ryson had been provided a thick copy of the Book of Hatrode.

On the twenty-fourth day of his servitude, the immense form of the mayor of Ferramonte's Landing slid silently into view. To Ryson's bitter shame, he found his body cringing uncontrollably at the sight of the enormous Excoriationist.

What horrible new torment had he come to inflict today?

"How do you feel, my dear Kerryl?" asked his maigritude anxiously. "The blistering from last week's Rituality of Surfeit would appear nearly healed."

"Yes," conceded Ryson incautiously, unable to keep his eyes from the great white and red blotches that disfigured his entire body.

"As I feared: nearly healed, and yet the next Rituality is still some five days away! Yours is a constitution of quite astonishing resiliency. I shall speak to the bath-master about increasing the time of your next immersion by twenty-five seconds."

"Again?" cried Ryson, aghast. "You're going to immerse me in the mud again? But that's the third time! Have you no sense at all? You're going to kill me!"

"Kill you? Haven't you unstintingly offered your heartfelt services for a full six months? Haven't I purchased an indulgence from His Holiness Figourey IV, the Vicar of Hatrode? Aren't you obligated to fulfill my religious commitments for the full six months? Why in Hatrode's name should I want to kill you?"

"Then why are you torturing me like this?"

"Torturing you? Wherever do you derive such curious notions? It is seldom that I have seen a Hatrodian, even the strongest and most ardent of recent converts, commit himself so zealously to those practices of religious principle by which all our lives are guided." Lord Lustral of Lowlands smiled benignly.

"But you actively coerce me," cried Ryson in a passion. "You throw me into boiling mud until my skin burns away. You starve me. You poison me with your water. You keep me naked in chains."

"Merely to help you to resist the temptation of rich foods, spicy wines, and the approach of lewd women."

Ryson fell back limply, unable to continue the absurd dialogue. "I'm dying," he stated flatly.

"We have, in fact, remarked that overly zealous observance of our undoubtedly austere doctrines inevitably leads to malnutrition, chilblains, and untimely death," admitted the mayor judiciously. "It is a theological stumbling block which we have not yet resolved to our entire satisfaction . . ."

Ryson writhed in agonized delirium for the four days that followed the next Rituality of Surfeit. His skin was blistered far worse than before, and dimly he wondered how the Excoriationists considered it theoretically possible for him to survive for even another month. He stared dully at his trembling hands and emaciated legs. Unless he had evolved some plan of escape by the time they came to take him to the next Rituality, he knew he would never again have the strength. Painfully he reached for the Book of Hatrode. Perhaps there was something in its madness to inspire him.

"An interesting book, that," said a voice in clipped, precise Versal. "Do you find it of spiritual solace?"

Ryson looked up in wonder at the small dapper figure in a dark green suit who stood on the other side of the translucent wall peering at him through a hand-held recorder. "You're not a Yellowjacker," he managed to whisper through cracked lips. "Who are you?"

"Kalikari Stone, dear fellow, Baron Bodissey."

Ryson pulled himself painfully up until his still-burning back was against the rough concrete wall. "What are you doing *here*?"

"I am a cultural anthropologist and ethnologist, come to record the curious rites of the Excoriationists of Yellowjack."

"Their rites are indeed curious," agreed Ryson. He glanced cautiously down the dimly lit passageway that led to the elevator. His Maigritude Lord Lustral of Lowlands was nowhere in sight. Trembling with emotion, he began to struggle to his feet. "Quickly: release me from here, and I shall tell you just how curious are their rites."

Baron Bodissey raised a cautionary hand. "I fear that to interpose myself by even the most insignificant action into your unique situational matrix would run counter to the entire training of the ethical anthropologist, dear chap. A rigorously dispassionate non-involvement with one's subjects must be our scientific watchword."

"So you'll watch these savages murder me and not raise a hand to stop them?" shouted Ryson incredulously.

"*Murder* is a subjective and emotionally pejorative term which no reputable anthropologist would ever employ."

"I see," sighed Ryson, falling back painfully to the floor. His chains rattled softly. "How did you happen to come to Yellowjack?" he asked bitterly. "As an honored guest of the Imperial Navy?"

Baron Bodissey's bushy eyebrows rose behind the recorder that still masked his face. "Certainly not: in my own spaceyacht. Or, more precisely, that spaceyacht which is a part of my grant from the Historical Institute of Nautical Research on the planet Riverain."

"And you'll do nothing at all to save me from being tortured to death?"

"Much as I might personally like to do so, this would be contrary to every tenet I have ever learned as

an anthropologist." Baron Bodissey lowered the recorder and fixed Ryson with a pale blue eye. "Tell me,"
he whispered eagerly, "is there even the remotest
possibility that you might participate in the Ceremony
of the Blessed Ascension? It is one that has never been
recorded!"

"I know nothing of this ceremony. If it is particularly gruesome and painful, then no doubt it will
eventually be inflicted on me."

"I doubt if it can be painful for more than a single
brief instant." The baron's eyes glittered. "It is the
supreme expression of the religious zeal of the ultra-
devout Hatrodian: in an all-embracing demonstration
of his total contempt for the malevolence of matter, he
casts himself into the boiling waters of the Grand
Geyser!"

A voice cried indistinctly in the distance. "Ah! My
exalted host the mayor calls. Until our next meeting,
dear chap! And I do urge you to reflect upon the
Ceremony of the Blessed Ascension. If only it could be
recorded, immortality would be yours!"

CHAPTER 19

In the three days that remained before the next murderous Rituality of Surfeit, Ryson reflected deeply and keenly upon the Ceremony of the Blessed Ascension as it was set forth in the holy writings of the Excoriationists, the Book of Hatrode. His eyes widened at a passage in the Twenty-seventh Verse of the Nineteenth Chapter. Incredulous, he read it again, and then a third time.

Might it actually be possible? he asked himself, his heart suddenly racing at the absurdity of the thought that had just struck him and the wild hope that it held out.

Just how literal-minded *were* these madmen when it came to the interpretation of their holy book?

He raised the Book of Hatrode with a trembling hand. Even if it didn't work, he would only be exchanging the excruciating torments of an interminably lingering death for the comfort of a nearly instantaneous one . . .

His Maigritude Lord Lustral of Lowlands was accompanied by four Excoriationist beadles when he floated into view of Ryson's seethru wall three days later. Behind them, Ryson could see, was the slender form of the anthropologist Baron Bodissey, now recording events with three separate instruments.

"Garb yourself in your misery, my dear Kerryl," called the mayor of Ferramonte's Landing cheerfully, "and step forward, for it is the moment of the Rituality of Surfeit, Hatrode be praised!"

Ryson stood gaunt and naked in his cell, his matted hair and shaggy beard partially concealing the metal band that circled his neck. His chains rattled as he raised a hand. "A moment, your maigritude. Before proceeding to the Rituality of Surfeit, I first have need to take spiritual counsel with my mentor, Diocesan Wystalorn."

The mayor's great jowls quivered in astonishment. "But this is entirely irregular! Come, come, man, let us not tarry: the hot mud awaits!"

Ryson held up the Book of Hatrode. "Does not the Fourth Verse of the Seventh Chapter enjoin us to 'harken unto the voice of the penitent who would seek the words of him who brought him into my fold; if ye love me, do not gainsay his wishes'?"

The mayor cast a peevish look in the direction of Baron Bodissey and his host of sensitive recorders. "Oh, very well, then, if such is truly your wish."

"Praise Hatrode!" cried Diocesan Wystalorn twenty minutes later as he glided silently down the corridor in his red a-grav. "My dearest child," he murmured in sonorous tones, "why have you summoned me away from my numerous tasks?"

"For spiritual counsel, your most divine beatitude. I have reflected profoundly upon the Book of Hatrode and the message which it brings to us all." Ryson glanced down in disgust at his scarred and blistered body. "Under the guidance of His Maigritude Lord Lustral of Lowlands, I have grown increasingly weary of the materiality of my corporeal being. No longer is the Rituality of Surfeit a sufficient purgation of the overweening demands of my flesh." He raised a trembling hand. "I now invoke as my inalterable privilege as a Hatrodian the right to participate in the ultimate sanction against the ubiquitous malevolence of molecular matter: the Ceremony of the Blessed Ascension."

The enormous diocesan fell back in his a-grav in astonishment. "But this is today no more than a metaphor of ideal Hatrodian behavior: no one has actually participated in the Ceremony of the Blessed Ascension for well over three centuries!"

"All the more reason, then, to rededicate ourselves to its teachings in these degenerate days of abandon and laxity," said Ryson austerely.

The mayor of Ferramonte's Landing shook his great globular head in dismay as the implications of Ryson's request gradually became clear. "But you have three and a half months remaining on your contract!" he protested. He turned in appeal to Diocesan Wystalorn. "Surely the Ceremony of the Blessed Ascension must wait until the fulfillment of a legally constituted contract!"

The diocesan shook his head. "I fear not, your maigritude. The Book of Hatrode is clear on this point: the Blessed Ascension is the apotheosis of an Excoriationist's existence. It is his absolute and inalienable right, to be carried out by him at whatever moment he chooses."

The eyes of the six enormous Excoriationists and the tiny anthropologist turned to Ryson.

"I choose this very moment," he said without hesitation. "Let the ceremony proceed."

Ferramonte's Landing was a mere two hundred yards wide, but the town stretched for more than three and a half miles along the narrow bottom of the vertiginous rift. The Yellowjack Labor Exchange & Bourse was in the very center of town, the great palace of its mayor Lord Lustral at the southeast end of its single street. Two miles beyond the northwest side of town was the Grand Geyser.

Here the prophet Guyaume Smode had immolated himself in its superheated sulfuric waters on behalf of all mankind; here the arch-apostate Sinisterry Stone had cravenly turned away from the ultimate sacrifice and taken ship to Bir to open a sweetmeats shop on Green Gully Avenue.

Kerryl Ryson dragged his lacerated body painfully through the single narrow street of Ferramonte's Landing, naked except for his clanking chains. Following slowly in his steps was the baroque gold and silver a-grav of His Holiness Figourey IV, as well as those of Diocesan Wystalorn and the other six members of the Synod of Saints. The Book of Hatrode was clutched tightly to Ryson's chest.

By the time Ryson reached the edge of town, word of his extraordinary intent had spread throughout the community, for in his anguish the mayor of Ferramonte's Landing had appealed the decision of Diocesan Wystalorn to the Vicar of Hatrode and the full membership of the Synod of Saints. His desperate appeal had failed; now Ryson was surrounded by the gaily colored a-gravs of six thousand Excoriationists as they bobbed back and forth in the narrow confines of Ferramonte's Landing in the hope of glimpsing his holy person.

"Move back," cried Ryson hoarsely to the crowds, "move back! Do not interpose yourself in front of the exalted Baron Bodissey, for his anthropological recordings will be stored in the Historical Institute of Nautical Research itself!"

"How extraordinarily thoughtful of you," murmured Baron Bodissey as the nearest of the bulky a-gravs reluctantly fell back a few paces.

"I have always admired the scientist and his dispassionate pursuit of learning," gasped Ryson in the superheated air. "In my own modest way I myself have been a constant inquirer after knowledge. Your lordship's spacecraft, for instance, is which particular model?"

"Why, a PC Ranger."

"Ah! The virtues of classical simplicity."

"It is all that a simple scholar requires," replied the anthropologist with austere dignity.

"Of course, of course . . . You there," cried Ryson, "move back! Make way for the exalted scholar and anthropologist Baron Bodissey! The encryption, now: I wonder what marvel of intricacy a scholar of your universal erudition would engender."

"Once again, the keynote is simplicity. The keyword is nothing more than *starfire*."

"How extraordinarily ingenious!" marveled Ryson. He staggered a few yards further into the deep gloom that blanketed the Bottomless Rift. "Ah, I see we are already at the Grand Geyser! I wonder if I should cast myself in immediately, or if there is to be some sort of religious ceremony?"

"Without wishing to influence you in any way, I can only say that from the viewpoint of the Historical Institute—"

"I understand," murmured Ryson, tugging the anthropologist forward. "I'll try my best to make the ceremony as interesting as possible for you."

An expanse of steaming water some seventy yards across seethed and churned in the deep shadows of a broad natural basin. The superheated waters of the Grand Geyser had erupted just twenty minutes before: the next eruption would be in eleven minutes.

"Should I wait for the geyser to actually erupt," Ryson asked the Diocesan Wystalorn, "or should I cast myself in now to be ascended in blessed fashion by the subsequent explosion of water? I confess that I am eager to cast off this tyranny of materiality which imprisons me."

The diocesan conferred hastily with His Holiness Figourey IV and the rest of the Synod of Saints. "We think it more fitting to wait for the actual eruption," he said apologetically. "It should be no more than nine minutes from now."

"Very well," said Ryson. "Since there is time, let me prepare myself with a brief reading from the Book of Hatrode." He opened the thick volume which he had carried against his chest and raised his eyes to the turbulent crowd of Excoriationists who milled around the steaming waters. "My text," he cried hoarsely, "is the Twenty-seventh Verse of the Nineteenth Chapter of the Book of Hatrode. The prophet Smode has just immolated himself in this very geyser; the arch-apostate Sinisterry Stone has just fled in shame and disgrace. Harken, then, unto the words of the Divine Hatrode: 'Let him *cast* himself into the waters of the Grand Geyser, and thereby *cleanse* his soul for all *eternity* of the heavy burden of his *materiality*; but if he cast *not* himself into the waters, then let him cast the nearest *stone* into their boiling fury in his place; and thereupon let him *depart* forever from our holy community, no longer an Excoriationist, but now an out-cast *accursed* to the peoples of Yellowjack for the rest of his days!' "

"Hatrode be with you!" cried the crowd in frenzied union.

"Attend me then a single moment longer," shouted Ryson. "Here beside me stands the nearest Stone, who must now be cast into the waters of boiling fury, even as Hatrode enjoins us!" He raised a bony finger and pointed it squarely at the mildly quizzical Baron Bodissey.

"But that's only Baron Bodissey," protested Dioc-esan Wystalorn in bewilderment.

"Observe more closely," said Ryson, moving for-ward to pluck the baron's identity badge from his left sleeve. "Read the apostate's true name: Kalikari Stone, Baron Bodissey!"

A solemn hush fell over the community of Excoriationists as their twelve thousand eyes turned in sudden surmise to the astonished anthropologist.

Ryson removed one of the recorders from Baron Bodissey's suddenly nerveless fingers and passed it to the mayor of Ferramonte's Landing. "I am sure that the Historical Institute of Nautical Research would be uniquely honored if his maigritude would consent to record the final moments of their intrepid representative."

He turned his shackled hands to the stunned Vicar of Hatrode, His Holiness Figourey IV. "If you would remove these encumbrances and restore my personal possessions, then I shall not tarry upon my way, for as Hatrode so uncompromisingly tells us, 'Thereupon let him depart forever from our holy community.'"

"But . . . if they throw me in the water, that will *kill* me, you know!" suddenly observed Baron Bodissey plaintively.

"The geyser—it will be erupting in forty-five seconds!" cried a member of the Synod of Saints.

"So it will." Ryson turned to nod an affable farewell to the aghast Baron Bodissey, who was rapidly being divested of his clothes by the Synod of Saints. "Be reassured, my dear fellow: I shall do everything in my power to return your spaceyacht to its rightful owners, the Historical Institute of Nautical Research."

CHAPTER 20

Deep in the sparsely inhabited southwest quadrant of the Diobastan Cluster the *Skeptical Inquirer* drifted aimlessly between the stars. Eldif the Equitable and her Palace of Mercy and Justice were one hundred and seventy-four light-years behind: this was as far as Ryson could distance himself from their possible vengeance without venturing into the vast black gulf of the Homeless Abyss.

For the first two weeks of his precipitous flight from Yellowjack he had done little more than eat, sleep, and lie for long groggy hours in the ship's medical facilities. As the light-years passed and the last of the welts and blisters on his ravaged body gradually disappeared, his gaunt frame began to fill out. Finally he began a light regimen of exercises which daily grew more demanding. Slowly his muscle tone returned, the haggard stranger who had once so terrifyingly glowered from the mirror became again the familiar Kerryl Ryson.

In the seventh week he took his place before the controls of the ship's elaborate library and placed an index finger firmly on its activator. For nearly two months he had fled across the cluster in a half-blind panic; now it was time to resume the task to which he had devoted his life.

"Dinosaurs," he said aloud to the vast data bank of the Historical Institute of Nautical Research. "Tell me everything you know about dinosaurs."

* * *

"Earth," he muttered softly as he turned over the library's printout while absently chewing the meal which the *Skeptical Inquirer* had set before him, "Earth."

An insipid and uninspired name for a planet, he thought, but adequate enough for a mere footnote of a planet. For according to the ship's library, that was approximately its status: Earth was passingly referred to as being the only world in all the galaxy outside of Stohlson's Redemption on which more than a single species of those animals known as dinosaurs could be found. And even on Earth, it was only as captive beasts reputedly maintained in private reserves . . .

Ryson felt his pulse quickening as he pondered this scanty information and tried to reconcile it with what little he had learned about the Immaculate Ultim of Aberdown during his years at the Pandow Keep. A private reserve of dinosaurs . . .

He tugged at his lower lip for a moment, then moved across the small salon of the spacecraft to the controls at the front of the ship. "Earth," he said to the pilot, "the third planet of a star named Sol about halfway around the west rim of the galaxy. Check with the library for the coordinates, then tell me if we have the range to get there."

"We indeed have the range to get to Earth," replied the *Skeptical Inquirer* after a moment's pause, "but not the authorization. The library informs me that access to the entire system of the star Sol is forbidden to all private shipping. Measures have apparently been taken to enforce this edict, for no ship in the last three hundred and forty-seven thousand years is recorded to have breached this interdiction successfully. At least, none of them has ever been heard from again."

"How curious . . . But perhaps no one has actually *tried* to visit Earth during that time."

"This is possible; it seems unlikely. For further information you must refer to the library."

Ryson returned to the salon and sipped a glass of

wine from Baron Bodissey's ample cellar while the ship's data banks were searched for further information about Earth. Eventually he was presented with a single page of documentation.

Even considering its isolation halfway across the galaxy, information about the planet was remarkably scanty. If the Earthans still recalled the circumstances of their initial colonization of the planet, this was knowledge, like everything else about their world, which they kept zealously to themselves. Since no official record of its settlement existed, presumably it had been carried out in the very distant past. The world was warm, its surface mainly of water, its population small, its exports non-existent; indeed, its very existence was unknown except to an extremely limited number of specialists who knew only of its few captive specimens of exotic offworld animals from across the galaxy. Its natives had long proclaimed a fierce, if quixotic, independence; the rest of an indifferent galaxy had been willing enough to acquiesce and leave the bumptious rustics to wallow in their xenophobia.

"But how can I get there?" demanded Ryson, his curiosity increasingly piqued. "They can't be *completely* isolated!"

The library continued to search its vast collection of records. "Travel to any part of the solar system of which Earth is the third planet is strictly forbidden to all ships other than those specifically authorized by Earth," it repeated.

"*Are* there ships authorized to travel to Earth?"

"Yes. A small number of commercial packets are occasionally authorized to travel to Earth."

"Very well," sighed Ryson wearily. "List those ships on the screen, along with their planets of departure, their dates of departure, their dates of arrival, their fares, and all other information pertinent to transporting me in reasonable comfort to the planet Earth sometime within the next six months. You must rigorously exclude any itinerary which would take me to Bir, Yellowjack, or any other planets or systems which come under their direct or indirect sway or influence. Is that clear?"

"It is clear."

The encryption chosen by the late Kalikari Stone, Baron Bodissey, had consisted merely of the word *starfire*. Somewhat to Ryson's astonishment, this guileless keyword had been entirely sufficient for the *Skeptical Inquirer* to open its hatch to him on Yellowjack's burning spaceport and then to take him into space. Now he wondered how much further the anthropologist had entrusted the protection of his affairs to this single encryption . . .

"The keyword is *starfire*," he told the library. "Show me all of Baron Bodissey's financial records."

The screen before him immediately lit up with a statement of the luckless anthropologist's account at the Bank of Rigel in the Waterholt System. Ryson's eyebrows rose at the balance displayed: 32,473 VS, with an additional 79,837 VS in his savings account! Baron Bodissey had clearly been a man of independent means.

"What of the terms of his grant from the Historical Institute?"

The screen presented a lengthy document, which Ryson deciphered as being a guaranteed letter of credit on the Third Bank of Frugality in favor of Kalikari Stone, Baron Bodissey, in any amount up to 7,500 VS. Three hundred and seventy-three of these had already been drawn upon; there remained for the Baron's use 7,127 VS, a sum which represented the salary of a sergeant-at-arms aboard the *Divine Providence* for five and a quarter years.

Ryson leaned back in his seat and dialed for a glass of the '74 Rutherford Domain, Private Reserve, from the cellar. Never had he met anyone with the child-like innocence of the artless Baron Bodissey. Could it possibly be conceivable that . . . ?

He returned to the controls at the front of the *Skeptical Inquirer*. "At the rate of consumption of the past month, how much longer will the ship's supplies, including air, last?"

"By incorporating optimal recycling, approximately twelve thousand three hundred years, at which point certain trace elements essential to a human's well-being will be exhausted."

"Twelve thousand years. Ah . . . And the wine cellar?"

"The wine cellar is not susceptible to recycling. A consumption of one bottle per day will exhaust its supplies in seven years, three months, and twenty-two days."

Ryson looked down at the printout previously supplied by the library. "The planet Gys, in the Tribulation System of the Great White Cluster: if we now set course for Gys, how long will it take us to reach Gys?"

"Nine and a half weeks."

"And from Gys to the planet Phorophat Beta in the Frejax Minor System?"

"Another six and a half weeks."

Ryson raised the glass of '74 Rutherford to his lips and swirled the rich ruby liquid around the side of the goblet. The flowery bouquet reached out to envelop him. He sighed wistfully: never had he experienced the exhilaration of such tantalizing and evocative aromas. He now had unlimited food, and a cellar sufficient for the next seven years: were the possible benefits of going to Gys enough to outweigh four months in space?

He came to a decision. "Very well. Set course for Gys." He tilted the glass to his lips, then lowered it without tasting the wine. He was finally beginning to get the hang of dealing with the *idiot savant* hidden somewhere inside the *Skeptical Inquirer*. "And then *proceed* to Gys."

CHAPTER 21

The thousands of stars that made up the Diobastan Cluster gradually merged into a nebulous luminosity hanging across the cold black void of the Homeless Abyss. A month later they were little more than a glittering point of light far to the rear of the *Skeptical Inquirer*. Ryson moved ever deeper into the swarm of stars that made up the galaxy's Polapary Arm. At last the monitor displayed an amber circle around a faint blue dot of light: the system of Gys. Ryson set down his glass of '67 Fetzholm's Golden Delight and ran a hand through his thick brown curls.

If all was according to plan, he was on the tenuous trail of a man well over four hundred years old. As Sergeant BuDeever had once observed, a man of that age would have had ample time to learn how to cover his tracks. Ryson himself had already suffered the disastrous consequences of plunging heedlessly forward; in the future his watchword would be caution, and more caution. And in approaching a planet which had just conceivably systematically obliterated all unauthorized visitors for the last three hundred thousand years something more than ordinary caution was dictated.

He turned to the library. "How far can we stand off from Gys and yet remain in effective range of communications?"

"Two light-seconds. That is, fifty-seven planetary diameters, or approximately twice the distance between Gys and its moon."

"Very well," he told the ship. "Bring us to that point."

Eight days later the shining blue and white globe of Gys filled the viewscreen. Ryson took a deep breath. Now he would learn the value of his three months' crossing of the Homeless Abyss. "You have already prepared documents for me in the name of V. N. Gencia. Open a bank account in that name at the Drovers Bank of Commerce," he directed the library. "Then transfer into it whatever funds are available from Baron Bodissey's two accounts at the Bank of Rigel and his letter of credit on the Third Bank of Frugality."

"I will need proper authorization to transfer Baron Bodissey's assets."

"The authorization is *starfire*."

"I have opened your account," said the library twenty seconds later. "The Third Bank of Frugality has no branch on Gys. The Bank of Rigel in Hospitality refuses to transfer the assets of Baron Bodissey without proper authorization."

"*Starfire* is the authorization."

"That is not the authorization for the Bank of Rigel."

Ryson slouched deep into the salon's somber maroon settee. Had three months been totally wasted? What would a guileless anthropologist like Baron Bodissey choose as the keyword for his bank accounts? He sighed helplessly: the possibilities were infinite.

"Very well," he said at last, knowing that even Baron Bodissey's artlessness must have had a limit. "Tell me the keyword for Baron Bodissey's bank accounts."

"For this I need your authorization."

"The authorization is *starfire*."

"That is the authorization. The keyword is *allmymoney*."

As simple as that, marveled Ryson. "Transfer the

funds from Baron Bodissey's accounts to mine, that is to say, V. N. Gencia's. Use the proper keyword, *allmymoney*."

Two minutes later the library spoke again. "The transfers have now been effected."

Ryson shook his head in bemusement. He was now a wealthy man. Tonight he would broach a bottle of the wondrous '27 Horbangers Supreme to toast the late Baron Bodissey in a fitting manner.

Ryson's bank account had been opened in the city of Hospitality on the northern continent of Dosher, the planet's principal spaceport. Early the following day the *Skeptical Inquirer* set down on the hard red dirt of the field outside Faraway, a provincial capital in the southern hemisphere on the opposite side of the planet.

Seven hundred miles to the east of Faraway was the second reason for coming to Gys, a name extracted from the data banks of the Historical Institute: Meatmen Unlimited.

Ryson drew a deep breath of sweet air as he stepped down from the *Skeptical Inquirer*, then appreciatively filled his lungs with another. What a contrast to the faintly metallic recycled air he had been breathing for the last four months!

A pale orange sun hung in a cloudless sky of a crystalline blue deeper than Ryson had ever before seen. A soft warm breeze whispered against his ears. Except for the small gray terminal, and behind it the low silhouette of Faraway, a boundless prairie as flat as the landing field stretched out to infinitely distant horizons. Suddenly the breeze brought a tantalizing hint of an indefinable but achingly familiar scent to his nostrils. Ryson tried for a moment to identify the elusive odor, then with a faint shrug stepped confidently toward the terminal.

The documents prepared by the library identifying him as V. N. Gencia took him through the port's casual inspection without difficulty. He used his credit at the Drovers Bank of Commerce to post a surety of 250 VS, then moved deeper into the terminal to rent a small wheelless vehicle that apparently moved on a repulsion drive.

The clerk programmed it for him with the coordinates of Meatmen Unlimited. Ryson took his place on its cushioned settee and sat back to watch the vast, featureless prairie of southern Gys flow by at an even three hundred miles an hour. A few miles outside of Faraway the pampa's short brown stubble became a yellow sea of gently waving grass. An hour later a sudden wave of nostalgia and loneliness washed over him as he spotted a familiar sight: the long graceful necks and tails of a small cluster of brontosaurs browsing placidly in the knee-high grass. Ahead of him he saw another, larger, grouping against the horizon. As the minutes passed the size of the herds grew ever greater until the great brown beasts numbered in the thousands.

The vehicle came to a halt in the courtyard of a complex composed of immense red barns and shiny metal packing plants. The pungent odor of the Pandow Keep filled his nostrils, and he knew now what elusive odor he had scented at the spaceport.

Ryson presented himself to a harried clerk in a cluttered office as a journalist from Stohlson's Redemption. "I find myself by happenstance on Gys," he repeated a few minutes later to the director of sales. "I was told of your ranch, and my curiosity finally got the best of me. Tell me: did your original breeding stock really come from my own home planet?"

"My great-grandfather imported twenty-eight brawny embryos from Stohlson's Redemption one hundred and seventy-two years ago," said Javormooni Jastor. "He was convinced that given our unlimited plains and lack of natural predators they could be raised as meat animals, and perhaps also be sold to other planets for the same purpose."

"And was he correct?"

"Up to a point. Most of the population of Misum here in the southern hemisphere are now confirmed brawny-eaters. Those in the north, however . . ." He pursed his lips disdainfully. "Their superstition forbids them to eat any beast whose tail exceeds eleven feet in length. Such an appendage, says their Handbook of Wiqqerwaqqer, is an affront to the genie Qaqqam, and hence unclean. With this in mind, we have been breeding for a short-tailed brawny for over ninety-seven years, and now have but two feet to go."

"Your herds are enormous; you must also have enormous competition."

"None to my knowledge: it is a highly specialized field."

Ryson tugged at his chin. "Strange: I seem to have heard of a certain Immaculate Ultim of Aberdown who is reputed to be a major force in the field of dinosauria."

"If he is, it certainly isn't on Gys," said Javormooni Jastor with absolute conviction. "Nor on any of the seven neighboring systems in which we have experimental ranches. Dinosauria, of course, encompasses a far wider range than merely raising brawnies for the dining-room table."

Ryson shrugged. "How true. That is an exceptionally fine female brawny I see peeking at us from around the corner of her stall."

"Isn't she?" agreed Javormooni Jastor enthusiastically. "Would you care for a tour of our premises?"

"I would be greatly honored."

Ryson returned to the spaceport late the following afternoon, certain now of what he had already suspected: that his quarry the Immaculate Ultim of Aberdown had never set foot on Gys. A man whose taste ran to tyrant kings would scarcely be interested in even the largest herds of gentle brawnies.

His own encryption consisted of nineteen unintelligible words chosen at random from the library's unabridged dictionary of Middle Keutch, a language from the far side of the galaxy which had been extinct for three million years now. Ryson grunted the tortured consonants haltingly; the hatch opened and he stepped aboard the *Skeptical Inquirer*.

Six hours later his preparations were complete. He left the ship in the early hours of the morning while the small port facilities were utterly empty and walked beneath the starry sky of Gys until he came to a hostelry on the road to Faraway. Here he procured a room and slept peacefully until late in the morning.

After a leisurely bath he descended to the inn's flowered terrace and ordered an early lunch of the local gastronomic specialty: ground haunch of brawny shaped into a patty and grilled over hot embers, then served in a toasted bun with an accompaniment of piquant condiments and relishes. As Ryson stolidly chewed the last bite of this curious culinary conception, he glanced casually at his watch; a moment later he raised his eyes to watch the *Skeptical Inquirer* rise smoothly into the clear blue sky of Gys. The ship dwindled rapidly and was gone.

Ryson climbed somberly to his feet. His ship was now safely launched on a journey that would take it halfway around the galaxy to a parking orbit around the planet Brynt in the Capella system, a scant fifty light-years from the planet Earth.

He himself had nine full days to make his way by local transport from Faraway to the city of Hospitality in the northern hemisphere.

For on the tenth day the interstellar liner *Wanderer* would be calling at Hospitality for two hours before resuming its run to Phorophat Beta seven hundred light-years away. Two hundred and thirty-three VS from the account of V. N. Gencia at the Drovers Bank of Commerce, Ryson knew, would buy him passage.

His lips tightened at the thought.

At last he was on his way to Earth—and the Immaculate Ultim of Aberdown?

CHAPTER 22

Six and a half weeks later the *Wanderer* touched down at Cordeopolis on Phorophat Beta. To the authorities at the landing field Ryson presented a set of documents in the name of Lulmö Häistön of the planet Ambrose, occupation: dinosaur rancher. A visa was issued, and from the spaceport he took transport to a moderately priced hotel in the center of Cordeopolis. From there he strolled through the noontime crowds to a large travel agency on the Plaza of the Thirty-two Bleeding Martyrs.

"I am interested in procuring transport to Earth, a planet in the Sol System on the far rim of the galaxy."

"A moment, sir," replied the clerk, touching his keyboard. "You are in luck: the *Vagabond Princess* departs for Earth in no more than seventeen days." This confirmed what Ryson had already been informed of by the library aboard the *Skeptical Inquirer*. He tendered his VS card, but the clerk was staring with raised eyebrows at his viewscreen. "There seem to be a number of restrictions which pertain to passengers wishing to visit Earth, including the posting of a surety. First of all, I am instructed to inquire the motive for your visit."

"I am a commercial rancher on the planet Ambrose, raising dinosaurs for meat. Dinosaurs are large, warm-blooded animals of succulent flesh often attaining twenty tons in weight. Earth is renowned for the diversity of its dinosaurs: I am hopeful that by traveling to Earth I may establish relations which will be of mutual benefit to the Earthans and myself."

The agent entered Ryson's response. "This has been tentatively accepted by the spaceport computer which represents the *Vagabond Princess*. A ticket will be issued upon the satisfactory completion of an additional form, which I will now tender you. You must be forewarned, however, that after entering the Sol System the *Vagabond Princess* first stops at an outer planet. Here you will be more systematically examined by authorities from Earth. At their discretion, they will issue a visitor's visa; if not, you will be held in quarantine at your own expense until the first ship leaves the system. You will have no voice in your choice of ship or destination." The travel agent shook his head in perplexity. "A curious world: they don't appear to be overly concerned about developing a trade in tourism, do they?"

"No matter," said Ryson. "I'm not a tourist, I'm a businessman."

The *Vagabond Princess* plied a long erratic curve along the rim of the galaxy, setting down at seventeen planets before at last coming to the system of Sol. The voyage from Phorophat Beta was scheduled to take four and a half months. Ryson had long been accustomed to the spartan quarters of the *Divine Providence*; now, somewhat to his surprise, he had to acknowledge that he had become perhaps overly devoted to the pleasures purveyed by the kitchen and wine cellar of the *Skeptical Inquirer*. After a moment's further reflection he shrugged: surely the late Baron Bodissey could well afford a small recompense to the person who had introduced him at first hand to the mysteries of the Ceremony of the Blessed Ascension. Without further misgivings, Ryson engaged a second-class stateroom, while reserving a table in the first-class dining salon.

The ship was thirty-three hours late in setting

down at Cordeopolis. Ryson awaited its arrival with impatience, first in his hotel room, then at the spaceport. At last, just after midnight, the long blue and white form of the packet settled slowly to the ground. Three hours later Ryson completed the last formalities of embarkation and took his place in a line of two hundred sleepy passengers shuffling forward on the ramp to the forward hatch.

Ryson moved slowly forward. The shiny white wall of the ship neared. Inside he could see a brightly colored reception lounge and a cluster of ship's officers in glossy red uniforms greeting the embarking passengers. He tightened his grip on his small handbag and prepared to step through the hatchway.

The air thickened before him, as if he were pushing against an invisible barrier of water. It yielded to his pressure for a few reluctant inches, then grew increasingly dense. Ryson halted, puzzled. A security measure of some sort? A device to seal the ship's atmosphere against the microbes of Phorophat Beta? He raised a hand and jabbed a finger into the curiously viscous air.

With an impatient grunt, the man behind Ryson stepped around him and into the ship's reception lounge. He was quickly followed by another. Ryson shook his head in bafflement. Could he be imagining things? He moved a pace to his right, then stepped forward again. The same invisible barrier blocked his way. He turned his shoulder against it and pushed with all his force, as if struggling against the winds of a hurricane. Suddenly he looked up to see the ship's officers staring at him with open-mouthed astonishment.

"Are you all right, sir?" asked the purser, moving warily forward. Ryson nodded, and redoubled his efforts. An electric tingling ran through his body, his senses reeled, and his knees buckled beneath him. He was aware of his body falling helplessly against the soft cushion of the barrier, then rolling off it and down onto the loading ramp. As he sprawled across the carpeted ramp his head cleared with miraculous speed and his limbs regained their accustomed strength.

Two of the ship's officers solicitously raised him to his feet in the midst of a knot of curious passengers. Ryson could only smile wanly and shake himself like one of his father's dogs emerging from a water hole. "A passing moment of giddiness," he muttered apologetically. The red-clad officers considered him dubiously, then gestured for Ryson to accompany them into the ship. He retrieved his handbag and stepped tentatively forward, an officer to each side. The uniformed officers moved easily into the *Vagabond Princess*; once again Ryson was brought to a halt by the impenetrable viscosity. This time as his limbs began to tingle in warning he jumped quickly backwards.

"Is there some sort of force field across your entrance?" he asked. "Something triggered by my presence?"

"Force field? Of course not, sir. Are you *sure* that you're feeling all right?"

Rigid with tension, Ryson stared wildly through the open hatch at the wary ship's officers and the several dozen passengers who had now paused to watch. Was *this* the supposedly inconspicuous beginning of his journey to Earth? He raised a hand and hesitantly waggled it in front of his eyes. As it encountered the barrier his head swirled and his knees began to buckle. Ryson snatched his hand back as if from a fire; the sensations passed.

He was as frightened now as when he had helplessly watched the madmen of Ferramonte's Landing approach his cell to bear him away to the tortures of their boiling mud. More: for *that* at least he could understand. Sweat broke out on his forehead as he edged nervously away from the ship. "You may be right," he muttered, half-panicked. "Best that you leave without me." He turned and marched rapidly away from the liner that was to have taken him to Earth.

* * *

"You've missed your ship, sir?" repeated the travel agent.

"A sudden indisposition," said Ryson curtly. "But no matter. Book me passage on the next ship."

"Let me see, it was to . . . Earth? Mmph!" The clerk tapped his keyboard. "I fear, sir, that this time it will not be all that simple. The next ship scheduled to leave Cordeopolis for Earth is in . . . hmmm . . . approximately six and a half months."

"Impossible. Devise some other routing."

"Another routing . . . Yes . . . Here we have Charbedixe, a three-week trip from Phorophat Beta: the *Oakery* leaves for Charbedixe in just nine days. Four days after your arrival in Charbedixe we then have the *Meritorious Repose* leaving on an extended voyage along the West Rim with . . . yes . . . a stop at Earth!" The agent frowned at the viewscreen. "The *Meritorious Repose* is hardly the same class of accommodation as the gentleman engaged aboard the *Vagabond Princess*; moreover its time to Earth from Charbedixe is five and a quarter months."

Ryson scowled. "There is nothing swifter?"

"Not in my records."

"Very well: book my passage, from here to Charbedixe, and from Charbedixe to Earth."

One hundred and twenty-six days out of Charbedixe the *Meritorious Repose* dropped out of N-space for the eighteenth time since Ryson had come aboard. Ryson sighed with relief: his quarters here were as cramped as those of the *Divine Providence*, while the offerings of the ship's single mess hall were as unpalatable as those of the refectory at the Pandow Keep.

Nine of the ship's passengers were debarking here in Murr; grateful for the opportunity to stretch his legs, Ryson joined them in the cool night air to walk from their berth at the spaceport's cargo field to the distant passenger terminal.

Murr was a major commercial hub midway along

the Polapary Arm of the galaxy: even in the early hours of the morning its brightly lighted terminal bustled with activity. Those debarking on Murr were led away to complete their formalities; Ryson was shown into a sprawling transit lounge.

Here were restaurants, shops, and refreshment facilities, all of them open throughout the night. Six hours remained before the *Meritorious Repose* would lift off for its next destination. Ryson stepped into a restaurant advertising the cuisine of Old North Privverport and ate a leisurely meal. Afterwards he smoked a blue-worm cheroot from Medley, strolled to the baths where he luxuriated in a large steaming tub, then submitted to a long tingling electro-massage by a native of Whizz. Finally he had his hair and nails trimmed short. Still an hour and a half remained. He purchased an armload of randomly chosen magazines printed in Versal and settled himself in the corner of a small Packlander tavern. He ordered a steaming goblet of mulled toddy and idly flipped open the pages of *Galactic Report* magazine.

VAGABOND PRINCESS DISASTER—WHAT THE EXPERTS NOW SAY leapt out at him. Beneath the headline were holograms of the sleek blue and white ship floating in orbit, and of its uniformed captain, Commander of the Fleet A.J.P. Gorash. A cold chill of disbelief ran up Ryson's spine as he read the story.

Six weeks after leaving Phorophat Beta, so Ryson calculated, the *Vagabond Princess* had then left Antoria VI with nine hundred and forty-three passengers and crew. It was scheduled to put down at Gaylord three weeks later. When the ship was two days overdue an investigation was begun on both planets. Interstellar sounders of six neighboring systems clearly traced the ship's path through N-space from Antoria VI. With equal clarity they showed the *Vagabond Princess*'s N-wake disappearing suddenly and with brutal finality approximately halfway between Antoria VI and Gaylord. The greatest disaster to commercial shipping in seven and a half centuries was thereby confirmed. Its causes were utterly unknown.

Such was the opening paragraph's recapitulation of the three-month-old disaster. The second paragraph noted only what Ryson, and the rest of the galaxy, already knew: that no object, living or inert, once lost in N-space had ever been recovered.

His mouth dry, Ryson quickly skimmed the rest of the article, which was primarily a technical account of how a ship's N-wake left a characteristic disruption across N-space that could be infallibly tracked by sounders for as long as three weeks after the ship's passage. A flashing sidebar caught his eye; it explained how the development of sounders four hundred and twenty-two thousand years earlier had quickly led to the galaxy-wide extirpation of space piracy.

Ryson gathered up his magazines and returned somberly to the *Meritorious Repose*. Nine hundred and forty-three people gone, vanished forever into the mysteries of N-space! And except for the still unexplained circumstances of his own abortive attempt to board the *Vagabond Princess*, the casualty count would have been nine hundred and forty-four; he, Kerryl Ryson, would now be dead!

He shivered, and stepped through the hatch into the bare metal passageway of the *Meritorious Repose*. By the infinite grace of Great Darv, he had somehow avoided destruction by a margin so thin that a cold film of sweat now glazed his body at the thought.

Ryson leaned wearily against a bulkhead. An inauspicious beginning indeed!

What fresh catastrophes awaited him on Earth?

CHAPTER 23

The Theory of Four Equivalencies elaborated by Mestroh Jarka Jandrel seven hundred and thirty thousand years earlier had never been convincingly refuted; it stated dogmatically that no ship moving through N-space could be intercepted or infringed upon by any means whatsoever. Seven hundred and thirty thousand years of practical experience tended to confirm the theory. Ryson had consequently expected the *Meritorious Repose* to exit N-space at the farthest boundaries of the Sol System in order to submit to the inspection demanded by the pathologically suspicious Earthans.

But perhaps, he speculated gloomily as the *Meritorious Repose* swept smoothly past the frozen outer planets and gas giants of the system at faster-than-light speed, the Earthans had evolved a theory of their own, one which permitted them to destroy a ship while still in N-space. How else to explain their apparent indifference as the ship moved swiftly toward the interdicted planet Earth? The Earthans must be supremely sure of their system-wide defenses; would they also have unexpected defenses against purported dinosaur ranchers from the planet Ambrose?

"We will be exiting N-space in seven and a half minutes," came the tinny voice of the purser over the ship's information system. "All passengers and crew members should be ready to debark for inspection on Mars within the next three hours."

Ryson scowled at the list of items prohibited by the Earthans which the purser had handed him earlier. It extended to seven pages; among the articles enumerated were unirradiated fruits, vegetables, and hallucinogens; dental prosthetics; holograms or tracts of a religious or licentious nature; bombs or hand weapons of either fissionable or fusionable materials. Ryson snorted. It could be safely assumed that Earthans were not celebrated for their sense of humor or tolerance of other-world customs.

With a sigh he returned to his tiny cabin. There he removed the twin throwing knives from the inside of each calf, the stiletto from his right sleeve, the rapier-laser from his left sleeve, the miniature grenades from his armpits, the seven assorted systems for dispensing somnifants and poisons. Finally he took his two neuronic disrupters and holocaust laser from their concealment in his luggage. A race of paranoids capable of setting aside an entire planet in order to facilitate their landing procedures would be unlikely to regard so variegated an arsenal with toleration.

He carried his weapons to the nearest disposal chute and regretfully tossed them through; moments later they were nothing more than randomized atoms somewhere in the engine room. Ryson turned away and stumped down the corridor to the ship's tiny forward lounge. Whatever had to be done on Earth would now have to be accomplished solely by bare hands and his native wits.

Long Horizon was a fifty-mile-wide octagon of molecularly augmented agroconcrete set in the middle of the Great Southern Badlands. This was the port of entry for the Sol System. The *Meritorious Repose* took up orbit on the far side of the red, green, and white planet, and presently a naval tender came alongside bearing a pilot and three heavily armed subordinates. Ryson pursed his lips in uneasy speculation as he watched the four brown-skinned Earthans march imperiously through the airlock and onto the captain's deck, where they secured the door behind them. A

world which deemed a cross-galactic N-space captain
incapable—or untrustworthy—of berthing his own
command in the middle of ten thousand square miles
of desert was paranoid indeed!

The *Meritorious Repose* began to drift slowly
downward to the surface of Mars. Ryson stepped to a
corner of the lounge and peered curiously through a
small porthole; beneath scattered white clouds he saw
nothing more than endless green forests and prairies,
interspersed with occasional smaller deserts of arid
reds, browns, and oranges. The only tangible sign of
human activity was the tiny gray octagon of Long
Horizon.

The octagon of the landing field grew steadily
larger until its dull monotony filled the porthole; Ryson
returned to a seat and raised his eyes to the central
viewscreen which was showing the progress of their
descent. A nearly imperceptible line suddenly gaped
open, then rapidly widened to become a black circle.
The circle grew until its darkness engulfed the entire
screen. The *Meritorious Repose* dropped into the gap-
ing hole without slowing and continued downwards
until it came to a smooth halt three thousand feet
beneath the surface of Mars. Ryson rose to his feet and
strode briskly back to his quarters to collect his luggage;
the eyes of the Earthans were perhaps already upon
him: he was no longer Kerryl Ryson; he was now Lulmō
Häistön, rancher and dinosaur breeder of the planet
Ambrose.

"Lulmō Häistön!"

Kerryl Ryson stood impatiently among the forty-
seven other passengers and crew who had issued forth
from the *Meritorious Repose*. They were in a harshly
illuminated low-ceilinged room of raw concrete which
had the grace of a hastily constructed bomb shelter.
Ryson supposed that eyes and weapons were trained on
them from the numerous slots in the walls; he knew
from the second officer that the ship was encased in a

hundred yards of agroconcrete, held inert by damper beams which negated all chemical and nuclear reactions within their range.

"I'm Lulmö Häistön," he said, stepping forward, the provisional laissez-passer issued by the spaceport computer in Charbedixe in one hand, and identification card in the other. Two brown-skinned immigration officials in drab white uniforms eyed him speculatively from behind a counter set across a small cubicle. Behind them stood three obvious subordinates in sleeveless red kirtles, billowing yellow gloves, and long black boots. They were tall and ungainly, with pale, slack-jawed faces and faded blue eyes. Ryson's footsteps echoed across the bare floor, and he felt far less confident than the carefully contrived half smile on his lips indicated.

Ryson stepped into the cubicle. He lifted the identification card he had purchased surreptitiously for 475 VS from the third assistant attaché for Ambrose in a tavern in Cordeopolis. He touched it to his forehead and held it there with his thumb. The silver card glowed a brilliant pink, a photograph of Ryson emerged upon its surface, while a holographic image of his head simultaneously sprang into being in the air over the counter, three times larger than life.

The officials fell back in stupefaction.

"What is that?"

"My identicard. Such is our custom on Ambrose."

"Very well. Give it here, then, along with your laissez-passer."

Ryson handed over the two items; the holographic image winked out. The two officials conferred quietly; Ryson studied the three men who stood inattentively against the wall. Their eyes were dull and curiously unfocused, their hands and faces a uniform sallow white. More Earthans? he wondered. A subspecies native to Mars? Certainly there was nothing about them of the keenness and intensity that marked the faces of the two officials examining his credentials.

"You are a rancher on Ambrose?"

"Yes."

"Here to discuss dinosaurs?"

"Yes."

"A peculiar reason to travel twelve thousand light-years."

Ryson shrugged. "Dinosaurs are my livelihood."

"You have no other motive in coming to Earth?"

"None."

"Very well." The official fed his identicard and laissez-passer into a slot in the counter. "While they are being verified, we will consult our other records." He handed Ryson a small glass rod. "Wet this with the saliva on your tongue." Ryson did as he was told, returned the glistening rod. The official thrust it into a concealed opening in the counter.

"A gene scan?" asked Ryson curiously.

The official nodded curtly, clearly bored by Ryson.

Ryson shrugged, his confidence fully recovered. He had never in his life passed within fifteen thousand light-years of Earth. These paranoiacs would have to be magicians to have records of his—

A buzzer sounded. The official's eyes turned to a hidden viewscreen and grew wide. He looked up at Ryson in amazement, his mouth working. The other official was scrambling awkwardly to his feet. He jostled the three men in garish uniforms and shouted angrily. Ryson watched in horrified dismay as the three slack-faced guards produced manacles and lethal-looking handguns of unfamiliar design. The weapons were raised and directed at his chest. Ryson took a cautious step backward—into the beams of a concealed neuronic stunner. Every cell in his body seemed to become an individual entity, then to tingle, finally to explode in agony. Totally paralyzed, Ryson toppled rigidly towards the floor.

CHAPTER 24

The Adamantine Overlook nestled high on the craggy summit of Mount Vinewald's Horn in the Cantonne of Seanoy in the Overweal of Schuizze. The crystalline overlook, all lofty translucent towers and sparkling prisms glittering in the clear blue of the mountain skies, had long been the personal domain of the Zolotny-Daunders from whom sprang the present Lord Blaibeck of Phaëtan.

For thirty years now the quirky Blaibeck, Paramount Margrave of the primogenial line of Zolotny-Daunder, had been Majestral of the Zoïtie of Burgou, the clan whose sway encompassed the continent of Yuro from the Landers Ocean in the west to the peaks of the Aurolles in the east. Acceding late in life to the title of Paramount Margrave, the capricious Blaibeck had moved quickly to stamp his own whimsical imprint upon the ancient faery structure of the Adamantine Overlook.

Of the twenty-seven gleaming minarets and glistening spires that rose from the precipitous slopes of Mount Vinewald's Horn, the Crystal Tower was the loftiest and most gossamer-like. But to the keen indignation of his fellow majestrals, the freaky Blaibeck had contemptuously disfigured its lacy beauty. For twenty years now an enormous yellow mountain antelope stood grotesquely balanced by a single hoof upon the tower's highest point—a deri-

sive reminder to the other majestrals of the Burgous'
stunning triumphs in the two most recent Tinctorian
Games.

Twenty years earlier, in 28,375 FIP, the perennial-
ly lowly Burgous had unexpectedly emerged victorious
from the rigorous trials of the 61,643rd Games, the
ultimate determinant of social status for nearly a
million years now. As overall victor, the zoïtie had
been officially denominated Preeminent Citrine until
the next Games, two decades hence. No longer
was the Burgous' zoïdion, or symbolic totem, of a
dancing chamois linked to the humiliating color of
mouse-brown, the hue with which it had been in-
extricably bound for thirty thousand years of inep-
titude. As Preeminent Citrine, the Burgous now
held exclusive claim to lemon-yellow, the loftiest distinc-
tion to which the twelve competing zoïties might
aspire.

By immemorial tradition the principal residence
of the paramount margrave of the preeminent zoïtie
became the formal venue for the Duze Majestral's
biannual Colloquies. To the Adamantine Overlook
therefore had come the eleven peers of Lord Blaibeck
for the first of the Colloquy's gatherings. None of the
majestrals had been pleased to be reminded of the
Burgou clan's egregious triumph by the indecorous
addition of the yellow chamois to the top of the Crystal
Tower as though it were nothing more than an outsize
weathercock.

At the next scheduled Colloquy, six months later,
Lady Danzel of Appis, Majestral of Rondyl, had mani-
fested her smoldering resentment of the bumptious Blaibeck by breaking with ancient tradition and
attending the meeting only by holographic projection.
One by one her fellow majestrals followed suit,
so that by 28,380 only Blaibeck himself was left to
mount with surly pomp to the glitter of the Crystal
Tower.

Now, six weeks after the 61,644th Games* had confirmed the dominance of the Zoïtie of Burgou, a loud gong sounded throughout the Crystal Tower. It was followed by the materialization of the life-size hologram of Allden Janders the Intransmutable on the far side of the chamber. The Intransmutable was a small wizened figure perched stiffly in a subtly contoured chair of lustrous donjonwood. His insignia of office, an elaborate headdress of blue, yellow, and turquoise ribbons, balanced precariously on a wrinkled skull. His shriveled body was lost in a loosely fitting costume of dull white. Behind his donjonwood chair hung an intricate Heitzo tapestry of sumptuous reds, flashing orange, and muted browns.

The Intransmutable raised a finger and spoke briefly to the twelve men and women ensconced in Blaibeck's curious crystalline structure which took up so much of the room. In a far corner, guarded by four pale-faced leperons in red, yellow, and black, stood Kerryl Ryson.

Totally paralyzed except for his eyes, Ryson stared grimly at the Intransmutable, desperately seeking to glean some sense of what was being said. As he strove futilely to comprehend the unknown language, a thousand unanswerable questions swirled in his mind.

Who *were* these people? Brown-skinned Earthans, yes. But beyond that?

Why had he been paralyzed, then rendered unconscious, totally without warning?

Where was he now?

And what could this scrawny old man possibly be saying?

"None of you will recall the event, naturally," said Allden Janders in the language of Earth to the twelve majestrals, "but a single fact is a certainty: the creature before you is the same man who occasioned your last Colloquy during the final days of the Tinctorian

*The final adjudication of the 61,644th Games of 28,395:

RANK:	COLOR:	ZOÏTIE:	MAJESTRAL:	ZOÏDION:
1. Preeminent Citrine	Yellow	Burgou	Lord Blaibeck of Phaëtan	Chamois:
2. Lofty Damson	Purple	Dreymon	Lord Zeeder of Mistane	Tassavian Devil
3. Towering Vermilion	Red	Rondyl	Lady Danzel of Appis	Bog-Stalker Moose
4. Bold Ebon	Black	Gollimaul	Lord Mesmer of Frotz	Stegosaurus
5. Worthy Cadmium	Orange	Curf	Lord Gaugrich of Greenwood	Tree Tiger
6. Loyal Dove	Gray	Neavre	Lady Taum-Shu of Cobbset	Cougar
7. Valued Turquoise	Blue	Alifan	Lady Oänis of Syra	Downy Walrus
8. Faded Emerald	Green	Ingerton	Lady Natchen of Caldo	Screech Owl
9. Wilting Lilac	Lavender	Tebbiwez	Lady Laizon of Baurauban	Eagle
10. Melancholy Rust	Copper	Bandledoon	Lady Soldot of Quisk	Elephant
11. Illusive Jasper	Verdant	Preëpau	Lord Wishaw of Purlym	Singing Whale
12. Furtive Mouse	Brown	Saverhol	Lord Cundee of Cockaloupe	Hill Buffalo

Games six weeks ago. Observe this hologram, if you will."

The lights dimmed and a bright holographic image flashed into existence on the far side of the room. Ryson stared at it incomprehendingly: it represented a scudding gray sky, distant mountains, a barren spaceport. Presently a dot appeared against the stormy sky. It grew larger, took form, became a spaceship. Why did it seem somehow familiar? Ryson wondered. Long and cylindrical, blue and white: something about it recalled—

The *Vagabond Princess*, the ship that had vanished into N-space!

But what was the connection between this hologram of a vanished ship and his captivity in the hands of these mysterious Earthans?

Ryson watched with glittering green eyes as the ship settled to the ground. Ramps extended from its sleek blue and white flanks, a handful of passengers began to exit. Now the boarding ramp grew rapidly in size; the face of each debarking passenger became clear, his features distinct. Suddenly Ryson recognized the red-uniformed purser who had helped him to his feet at the spaceport in Cordeopolis. Now he stood at the open hatch, nodding cordially to the passengers as they filed by.

Ryson tried to frown, but his eyebrows were as solidly frozen as the rest of his body. *When* had this hologram been taken? And *where*?

He watched a passenger step out of the shadows of the hatch, exchange salutations with the ship's officer, move confidently down the ramp.

Ryson's mind reeled at the impact of the most stunning blow it had ever known:

The passenger walking away from the *Vagabond Princess*—a ship he had never boarded, a ship that had been lost in N-space—was unmistakably Kerryl Ryson!

PART FOUR

CHAPTER 25

Ryson nodded farewell to the purser aboard the *Vagabond Princess* and stepped onto the ramp that after one hundred and thirty-seven days in space would at last bring him to his goal: the planet Earth! He stood for a moment in the thin warm air of the Tibbitane Plateau, then walked briskly with the seven other debarking passengers to the ancient stone building on the edge of the field. It was long and low, with a black slate roof and narrow windows, and seemed as integral to the desolate landscape as the scudding gray clouds and the jagged gray and brown mountains that rimmed the horizon.

Inside the waiting room, Ryson set his handbag on the clammy flagstone floor and waited for his single suitcase to arrive from the ship. What precisely, he asked himself as he glanced curiously around the nearly deserted terminal, was his next step? He had in his pockets 2,500 TUE* which he had been obliged to purchase with his galactic VS at the immigration outpost on Mars, a suitcase full of clothes obtained on Gys, and no weapons at all. And in addition, a single burning vision: the bloated red face of the Immaculate Ultim of Aberdown.

The luggage arrived aboard a small glide-cart directed by another of the pale, melancholy creatures Ryson had observed on Mars. As they pushed forward

---

*Terrestrial Unit of Exchange, generally shortened to a simple U.

to designate their luggage, Ryson now saw that three of the other passengers were apparently Earthans, two brown-skinned men and an elderly lady, all of them attired entirely in glittering blue; wherever they had been on the *Vagabond Princess*, they had kept to their own company. Six pallid servants ambled forward to collect their bags; the group moved to a turquoise-blue aircar that hovered just outside the waiting room. It soared off into the gray sky, leaving Ryson and his fellows standing morosely by their luggage.

"Notice," exclaimed a native of Felic Faru triumphantly, pointing to his left. Ryson turned. On the far side of the somber waiting room stood a dark wooden counter with the faintly glowing word INFORMATION floating above it. The four visitors to Earth made their way across the room, where they found the information desk deserted and coated with dust. Ryson drummed his knuckles irritably upon the scarred wooden counter; a holographic Earthan materialized behind the counter. Black eyes glittered from a coppery-brown face; he wore a dull brown tunic and matching brown cap with broad visors above each ear.

"Welcome to Earth," said the image. "How may I be of service?"

Three impatient voices spoke simultaneously; two more images of the same Earthan flashed into existence, the identical expression of supercilious disdain on each coppery face.

"First, I need information," said Ryson to the nearest of the holograms, turning his back to the sudden babble of the other passengers. "Then I shall require transport and lodging."

The image stared at some distant point beyond Ryson's right shoulder. "Transport from the spaceport to the city of Agu-Agu leaves daily at eight in the morning. At Agu-Agu you will find transport to the rest of the planet. While waiting for tomorrow's conveyance to Agu-Agu, overnight lodging is available here at the spaceport for a nominal fee."

"Very well," said Ryson. He examined the Earthan thoughtfully. "Am I now speaking to an actual person, or to a computer-generated simulacrum?"

"The entire population of Earth is but twenty-four million Palatines; none are available for menial tasks. What you see before you is a simulacrum. Few outworlders notice. What information do you require?"

Ryson hesitated. Probably this information service was operated by the same paranoid Earthans responsible for the restrictions upon its visitors; undoubtedly their security services were even now monitoring this conversation. Finally he shrugged minutely. What, after all, did it really matter? He was Lulmö Häistön of Dunferlin Province, Ambrose—a dinosaur rancher with nothing to hide. "I am interested in dinosaurs; I wish to establish communication with those who are knowledgeable in this field."

The image hesitated perceptibly before replying. "Dinosaurs are archaic beasts, for which the data is paradoxically both scanty and extensive. Please be more explicit."

"I am a dinosaur breeder on the planet Ambrose. I raise, for commercial purposes, that species of beast called in Versal a brontosaurus. I would like to meet Earthans engaged in similar enterprises, or failing that, Earthans engaged in raising any kind of dinosaurs for any purpose whatsoever."

"Inhabitants of Earth should be referred to as Earthmen, or better yet, Terrans," instructed the simulacrum pedantically. "Citizens of Earth are known as Palatines, and are addressed by that honorific. Brontosaurus meat, as well as that of other dinosaurs, is unknown to Palatines as a foodstuff, and no beasts of that ilk are raised commercially."

"But for other reasons, perhaps."

"I will consult my records." Once again the hologram paused. "Only the Zoïtie of Gollimaul is associated in any way with the breeding of dinosaurs."

"I would like to speak with Palatine Zoïtie, then."

"Earth's Palatinate is divided into twelve clans, or septs, known as zoïties. Gollimaul is the zoïtie adjudicated, and hence denominated, at the last Games as Bold Ebon."

"I see," said Ryson, entirely baffled by this strange disquisition. "Then I would like to speak with whoever within the Zoïtie of Gollimaul is both knowledgeable about dinosaurs and actively engaged in raising them."

"This is impossible; this hypothetical person is clearly descriptive of Lord Mesmer of Frotz, Majestral of Gollimaul."

"Majestral of Gollimaul?"

"A majestral is titular head of his zoïtie, and one of Earth's Duze Majestrals. It is inconceivable that Lord Mesmer be importuned by a rancher from the other side of the galaxy."

"A *dinosaur* rancher," insisted Ryson. "If Lord Mesmer is, as you say, even slightly interested in dinosaurs, then he will be overwhelmingly interested in seeing me."

"Impossible."

"Where is he? I'll talk to him myself."

The matrix generating the simulacrum was evidently programmed to respond to any apparently reasonable question, for after another brief hesitation its copper-skinned image said, "Lord Mesmer is now at the Games, in the company of his immediate family and zoïtiemen."

"And where are the Games?"

"The Games are at Carayapundy, where they have been staged for 979,740 years."

"I see." Ryson reflected for a moment. "To recapitulate: there is lodging available here at the spaceport for the night; tomorrow morning there is transport from here to the city of Agu-Agu; in Agu-Agu I will find transport to Carayapundy, where the Games are now underway."

"All of that is correct." The hologram hesitated

once again. "But in Carayapundy you will not be permitted to importune Lord Mesmer."

"Nothing could be further from my thoughts," said Ryson blandly.

"It is well," said the simulacrum, and vanished.

The lodgings referred to by the information service were entered by an inconspicuous door at the far end of the waiting room. Ryson stepped into a pale drab room scarcely larger than his cabin aboard the *Vagabond Princess*. His three fellow passengers were already crowded before a tiny counter; behind it, apparently flesh and blood, officiated a long-faced creature with the same melancholy air as that of the other pallid Terrans Ryson had briefly encountered.

Currency passed across the counter; another sallow-faced Terran led the offworlders away. Ryson stepped forward. "A room for tonight, if you will, and dinner as well."

The clerk bowed obsequiously. "It shall be as your lordship requires. The tariff for both dinner and sleeping arrangements is 12 U; wine, spirits, and hallucinogens require supplementary fees."

Ryson counted out 12 U from the collection of bills and markers he had received on Mars.* "I have been informed that I am to address Terrans as Palatine. Does this apply equally to both male and female? You, for instance, are Palatine . . . ?"

The clerk's faded blue eyes widened. "Oh no, your lordship! None such as I may be addressed as Palatine! Palatine is to distinguish their highnesses the citizens, and no one else."

Ryson fingered his own tanned chin, while he

---

*The Palatines themselves used no money; the Terrestrial Unit of Exchange existed solely for trade with the outworlds and the convenience of the occasional visitor. The integrity of the TUE was backed by thirteen thousand flawless starfires held on deposit at the Bank of Rigel.

considered the brown- or coppery-skinned Terrans he had encountered, their white-skinned menials. "Those with brown skins are Terrans, and hence Palatines?" he ventured.

"Yes, your lordship, oh yes!" The clerk's head and shoulders bobbed in a frenzy of excitement, much like an overly affectionate dog Ryson now suddenly recalled from his distant youth at Blue Finger Mill.

"You yourself are not Terran, then?"

"Oh no, your lordship! Your humble servitor is Martian, as are all of us whose honor is to serve our highnesses."

"All of you with white skin are Martians?"

"All of us," sighed the clerk with a certain resigned pride. "We are known as leperons."

"And are all of you . . . leperons servitors to the Palatines?"

The hotel clerk fell back in astonishment. "What else could we do, except to serve our highnesses?"

"I see." Ryson regarded this abject creature with wary speculation as he remembered his own dark years of degradation in the fortress of the Jairaben, his own obsequiousness and carefully dissimulated hatred. Could the same unquenchable flame of fury and rebellion that had at last set him free be smoldering behind this slack-faced facade of utter subservience? Ryson's mouth twitched: impossible to tell. He glanced around the tiny foyer. The two of them were entirely alone; the servitor seemed disposed to continue the conversation. Ryson came to a decision. "I am seeking news of a certain Lord Mesmer of Frotz," he said cautiously. "I am told that he is now majestral to the Zoïtie of Gollimaul."

The leperon's thin haunches quivered with tremulous excitement at the mention of this exalted name. "Such is indeed the case, your lordship. His highness Lord Mesmer is one of the grandest of the majestrals."

"He is known, perhaps, for his interest in dinosaurs?"

"Oh yes, your lordship! Even in our humble warrens on Mars, his highness Lord Mesmer is celebrated for the affection he lavishes upon his lovely dinosaurs." The servitor leaned forward and spoke with fervor. "As an exalted visitor from another world, your lordship would not be aware of it, but his highness Lord Mesmer's Zoïtie of Gollimaul has long been associated with dinosaurs."

"How curious. There have been dinosaurs on Earth for a long time, then?"

The leperon tugged at a pendulous earlobe. "My own schooling, of course, is not profound: no more than what I need to carry out my duties. Still, many of my forebears have had the honor of serving the Zoïtie of Gollimaul; some have had the privilege of serving their highnesses the majestrals themselves; tales about their wondrous beasts have been told and retold for thousands of years now—I myself recall them well from my own days as a cub. It is my impression that millions upon millions of years ago dinosaurs once covered the entire planet Earth, long before the days of even their highnesses the Palatines. For reasons unknown they suddenly died out. Then at some time in the recent past, no more, perhaps, than a million years ago, they reappeared, as pets and pastimes for those who comprise the Zoïtie of Gollimaul."

"But if they had died out, how could they reappear?"

"Perhaps from some other planet, your lordship? Brought perhaps by the Zoïtie of Gollimaul? For is not their very zoïdion a stegosaurus rampant?"

Ryson tried to imagine the enormous shuffling bulk of a hump-backed stegosaurus, its spine and tail bristling with armored plates, standing erect on a single foot, but entirely failed. "Lord Mesmer devotes himself exclusively to the cultivation of stegosaurs?"

"By no means, your lordship. I believe that he is occasionally observed riding on the back of one of his domesticated brachiosaurs; and his collection of the more ferocious varieties is occasionally cited by us as a warning to what awaits unruly cubs."

Ryson felt a sudden thrill race along his spine. "The more ferocious varieties—these would include tyrannosaurs?"

"That may well be the name, your lordship, of at least one of them. The great carnivores, of course, being of a menacing disposition, are kept well away from the public, on his highness Lord Mesmer's estate at Tumbling Springs."

"Tumbling Springs. Is that where Lord Mesmer is now?"

"Oh no, your lordship. I should imagine his highness Lord Mesmer to be at the Tinctorian Games, along with his eleven fellow majestrals."

"Ah, the Games! I was forgetting the Games." Ryson made himself comfortable against the counter, leaned forward. "Tell me about the Games."

Ryson had known a variety of cramped quarters aboard a number of spacecraft; never before had he paid for the privilege of clambering into a large fabric-lined drawer in order to spend the night. He stared in astonishment at the coffin-like device that had slid smoothly out of its niche in a gleaming metal wall, one of four hundred such units.

"Our highnesses, in their rightful preoccupation with matters of far greater import, have never concerned themselves with the trivial matter of facilities for encouraging tourism," explained the clerk unnecessarily as he demonstrated to Ryson how to work the drawer's controls to move it back and forth out of the wall. "Nonetheless, at one point several thousand years ago our highnesses must have anticipated the arrival of a substantial number of offworld guests: the arrangement your lordship sees was deemed to be the most practical in attending to the needs of the greatest number in the most economical and least space-consuming fashion."

Ryson made certain that the unit's ventilation system was working satisfactorily, then pulled the blanket around his shoulders, and extinguished the light above his head. He lay in absolute silence and blackness as he tried to make sense of what the leperon servitor had told him. How could the dinosaurs have once roamed all of Earth, millions of years in the past? What was their connection, no matter how tenuous, with the beasts that were native to Stohlson's Redemption? How could they have vanished, only to reappear in the recent past?

Ryson felt his heart beating faster. Tomorrow he would travel to Carayapundy and the 61,644th Tinctorian Games. There he would seek out Lord Mesmer of Frotz, the exalted Majestral of Gollimaul and dinosaur connoisseur.

His nails dug deep into the palms of his clenched fists.

Would it be in Carayapundy that he would at last find the Immaculate Ultim of Aberdown?

CHAPTER 26

Transport between the spaceport on the Tibbitane Plateau and Agu-Agu was a freighter come for the cargo discharged the day before by the *Vagabond Princess*; almost as an afterthought a number of seats had been arranged in a cargo hold: a none too subtle reminder to even the loftiest of outworlders, Ryson decided, of their true status in the eyes of the Terrans.

The freighter lifted smoothly and silently from the otherwise deserted landing field; moments later it had passed though the heavy gray cloud cover that still blanketed the Tibbitane Plateau. The mountains fell below; a yellow sun rose above the horizon to shine brilliantly in the deep purple sky of near-space. There was no sensation of motion; Ryson unavailingly tried to make himself comfortable in the unyielding seat, finally bent to watch the rugged landscape slip past far below.

An hour passed, another. Through occasional breaks in the cloud cover Ryson caught glimpses of barren gray and brown mountains, broad green prairies, dark green forests. Eventually the ship began to sink into a smooth white blanket of clouds that stretched across the horizon. Just before landing on the outskirts of a small town nearly hidden beneath a thick canopy of shade trees Ryson had his first view of the ocean, somber, gray, and white-capped.

Agu-Agu was many thousands of feet lower than the Tibbitane Plateau. In spite of the overcast the air was hot, thick, and damp. By the time Ryson reached the terminal, sweat was already prickling his forehead.

In sharp contrast to the spaceport in the mountains, Agu-Agu was clearly a transportation center serving the convenience of the ruling Terrans: the sky above the broad expanse of fresh white concrete was filled with the traffic of brightly colored aircars and larger commercial airships; here the terminal buildings were light and airy, the temperature inside rigidly controlled; brown-skinned Palatines attired in the twelve distinctive colors of the zoïtiac moved briskly about their affairs, trailed at a respectful distance by clusters of drably uniformed leperons.

Ryson stood with a dozen Palatines on a red marble floor in the center of the main lobby. Most of them were neatly dressed children. At their feet the gleaming marble gave way to an apparently bottomless black well some hundred feet across. Sparkling within the well was the starry splendor of the entire galaxy; inside the star field, rotating with almost imperceptible slowness, floated a thirty-foot relief globe of Earth.

Ryson bent over the well's protective railing. A brilliant pinprick of glowing red on the northeastern shore of a large green continent apparently represented Agu-Agu; the rest of the planet was mostly ocean, shown here as gray, blue, pale turquoise, emerald green. A broad green continent spread across the southern polar region, a cobalt-blue sea across the northern. Except in the immediate neighborhood of the nine or ten distinct land masses large enough to be qualified as continents, islands were sparse in the great planet-girdling ocean. A few scattered chains of bare gray mountains thrust up; otherwise the land surfaces were entirely green. If the colors of this globe were at all accurate, Ryson decided, then the entire planet must be covered by tropical or semi-tropical forests and vegetation.

A pleasant enough world, he judged, even if overly hot and muggy. Perhaps the Terrans were justified in isolating themselves so stringently from the encroachments of the rest of the galaxy . . .

The cluster of children to his left suddenly squealed with glee as a series of brilliant orange lights flickered rapidly across the land surfaces of the globe. Each light seemed to represent the location of a specific city. Every five seconds the lights vanished, to be replaced by others. Ryson cocked his head to eavesdrop on the conversation of the Palatine children. But aside from an occasional merry whoop of triumph, the Terran children were silent; their bodies and faces, however, were curiously taut: indicative perhaps of intense concentration?

Orange lights glowed on the shoreline of each of the southern continents; a boy of twelve dressed in a short tunic of blazing lavender hooted with exhilaration. Ryson considered the possibilities. From their attitudes, the children seemed to be generating the lights. Was this globe a psionically activated map serving the needs of the traveling Palatines?

Idly he put the notion to the test: *Carayapundy*, he thought, framing the word with his lips, and concentrating upon each of its absurd syllables. Instantly, it seemed, the entire globe was glittering with thousands of flashing orange lights. A moment later they changed to red, then blue, yellow, and back to orange. They grew in brightness and intensity, and the cycle was repeated. The colors of the oceans changed to purple, puce, and maroon; the greens of the land masses became a sickly roiling of yellow and orange. The children beside him giggled nervously and uttered sharp cries.

Ryson watched the colorful display a moment later, then turned away. His notion of a geographic aid was clearly wrong; could all this form some artistic pattern easily discernible to those raised in the Terran culture? Whatever the globe's function, he would probably never learn it. He shrugged, and moved across the lobby to a desk from which a leperon was apparently dispensing tickets.

Now he heard sharp cries of outrage and alarm from behind. Three pale leperons stood blinking at the tumultuously mutating colors of the globe in perplexity, while two adult Palatines in flowing red robes expostulated angrily with the cluster of children. From all over the concourse Palatines and leperons were converging swiftly on the dazzling display. Ryson moved on to the ticket counter with a wry smile. Whatever their skin color, children remained the same from one end of the galaxy to the other: this particular group had apparently contrived to cause a spectacular malfunction of the globe; now they were about to reap the painful consequences . . .

Carayapundy was nearly a quarter-way around the world, not far from the deep blue sea that girdled the northern polar regions. The sleek white conveyance that served the Palatines was scheduled to take Ryson to his destination in little more than two hours.

Ryson and sixty Terrans sank into deep leather chairs in a bright airy compartment at midships that was almost entirely transparent. Soft music of an unfamiliar but agreeable tempo whispered from all sides, discreet leperons offered liqueurs, aromatics, pastries, and sweetmeats. The copper-skinned Palatines darted a single startled glance at the outworlder in their midst, then loftily averted their eyes. Except for the star-filled black sky around them and the curvature of the shining globe beneath, Ryson might have thought himself in a particularly luxurious waiting room. But somewhere near the stern of the ship, he knew, several hundred leperons had boarded separately, to sit stolidly on straight benches in a windowless cargo hold. Ryson shrugged: the pallid Martians appeared to far outnumber their brown-skinned lords; if they still chose to submit to serfdom, this was their own affair.

The ship moved swiftly northeast over the Peaceful Ocean, the Barrier Mountains where the sea met the lands of the Zoïtie of Alifan, the vast mosaic of savanna, lakes, and forests that composed the Unchartered Territories. The southern reaches of the Yanatara

Sea glinted in the distance; the curvature of the planet grew less pronounced, the stars faded from a steadily brightening sky, the horizon once again took on its ruler-like straightness. The endless green expanse of the Unchartered Territories fragmented into a dozen subtle shadings of greens, green-blues, and yellow-greens. Moments later the ship settled without perceptible motion upon the landing field of Carayapundy, for nearly a million years the home of the bidecennial Tinctorian Games.

CHAPTER 27

The Games were invariably held during the fourth month of the Bidecennial Year.* To the somnolent lakeside town of Carayapundy came the meticulously chosen hopes of each of Earth's twelve zoïties. Here they congregated for two weeks of ceremony, conviviality, and trials of skill which would inalterably determine the social lot of the planet's twenty-four million Palatines for the ensuing twenty years.

In spite of the Games' transcendant importance, few of Earth's citizens chose to attend in person; preoccupied as they were by their own elaborate private festivities and family groupings, scholarly speculations and recondite studies, vigorous sports and erotic divertissements, it was far more feasible to view the spectacle by holovision in the lush comfort of their own homes. In consequence little more than the contestants themselves and the head of each zoïtie troubled to make the journey.

The site of the Games was two miles to the west of

---

*The Palatine calendar was divided into four equal quarters of thirteen weeks each; the first two months of each quarter consisted of four weeks, or twenty-eight days, the last month of five weeks, or thirty-five days. The year's three hundred and sixty-fifth day was a null known as Remembrance Day, and was inserted between the thirty-fifth of Dyshter and the first of Suaud. Every fourth year a second null known as Requital was observed six months later, between Marree and Vi.

193

Carayapundy, where a cluster of ancient buildings of
dark red brick nestled in a lush parkland among gentle
hills. It was here that Ryson was delivered by individual
aircar a few minutes after his arrival at the landing
field. It was early afternoon; the ninth day of the Games
was already underway. Most of the sixty Palatines who
had accompanied Ryson from Agu-Agu had already
vanished from sight; the neatly tended parkland was
deserted except for leperon gardeners moving unobtru-
sively through the deep shade cast by the elms and
hemlock. Ryson strode swiftly through the trees until
he came to the edge of a natural amphitheater, the
Prismatic Arena.

Twenty-foot-high totems, or zoidïons, of the dozen
competing clans were spaced evenly around the arena's
rim. Below them, each of the twelve sections of the
amphitheater glittered with the colors of its zoïtie.
With a sharp shock of recognition Ryson spied on the
far side of the arena a mottled yellow and green
stegosaurus standing erect on a single hind leg. Beneath
the totem that section of the amphitheater was a dire
black. Ryson's heart beat faster: somewhere in the
sparse crowd dressed in black would be Lord Mesmer
of Frotz, Majestral of Gollimaul.

Ryson stepped forward to make his way toward the
stegosaurus. His way was quickly blocked by three
lanky leperons who respectfully, but firmly, directed
him to a narrow tier of seats reserved for outworlders.
Here a small scattering of tourists in a wide variety of
dress sat in plain white seats. Ryson obediently took his
place among them.

At the bottom of the amphitheater's steeply
pitched walls was a broad round greensward on which a
hundred men and women in short white tunics and
knee-length red boots stood motionlessly in a single
tight cluster, their faces turned up to the cloudless sky.
Around the edge of the intensely green field were a
dozen or more figures in elaborate costumes of yellow
pantaloons, red and orange shirts with billowing

turquoise-blue sleeves, pale green boots, and dark purple headpieces that dangled from the backs of their heads: the first Palatines Ryson had seen wearing clothes of more than a single color.

The hundred contestants clad in white continued to stare upward into the sky. Ryson's eyes followed their gaze. Was that a small gray cloud beginning to form directly above the amphitheater? The cloud grew larger, took tangible shape, began to darken ominously. An excited murmur ran around the amphitheater. The sun passed behind the cloud and the amphitheater was cast into deep shadow. Rain began to fall; Ryson felt a half dozen drops splash against his face. Loud groans of derision rumbled across the arena.

The falling rain came to a miraculous halt in midair a few feet above the rim of the amphitheater as the hundred contestants on the field now spread apart into a broad circle. Water began to gush from the sky in a single narrow cascade, and a bubble-like spheroid quickly took shape at the base of the cascade. When it was twenty feet in diameter, the water feeding it slowed to a trickle, stopped. A soft breeze blew the cloud away from the arena and the sun returned.

As the watery sphere glittered brightly in the sunlight the brightly clad Palatines who stood on the edge of the field now gathered in a single small group. A few minutes later an amplified voice spoke to the arena in Terran; the sparse audience responded by a mixture of moans, cheers, and gibes. The voice spoke again, this time in Versal. "Towering Vermilion, the Zoïtie of Rondyl: imposition of Palatine will upon inchoate nature by the generation of a rain cloud and confinement of its output. Judgement: fourteen points of a possible nineteen. The aspirants will now pass directly to the concomitant category: creative artistry."

Two hours later Ryson's initial curiosity and apprehension had turned to acute boredom and finally outright impatience as he watched the champions of the clan of Rondyl painstakingly manipulate the floating ball of water into a succession of attenuated abstract concepts. None of the shapes signified anything at all to Ryson, but appeared to carry rich emotional and intellectual overtones for the audience of Palatines.

At last the bubble of water took on the discernible shape of a large four-legged animal with an enormous rack of antlers growing from its head. That section of the Prismatic Arena which was denoted by red burst into noisy cheers; the other eleven hooted derisively. The glittering totem floated triumphantly through the air around the circumference of the entire field; at a concealed basin it suddenly began to dissolve like ice melting under a hot sun, the water disappearing neatly through a drain. A few minutes later the judges rendered their decision: twenty-three points of a possible twenty-seven.

Ryson rose to his feet with the rest of the spectators; the yellow sun had sunk into the trees on the nearest hillside; the day's activities appeared to have come to a conclusion. He looked up at the rim of the amphitheater: it was ringed by several hundred officious-looking leperons bowing and curtsying to the passing Palatines. Undoubtedly they would block his way if he tried to cross to that section of the arena which was tinted black. All of the arena's spectators were climbing towards the rim; on the field below stood the contestants and the judges. Ryson glanced quickly to either side, then stepped over a low barrier and into the presence of a dozen purple-clad members of the Zoïtie of Dreymon. None of them hindered him as he marched purposefully down the steps that led to the bottom of the amphitheater.

Five of the garishly clad field judges, three men and two women, stood in a cluster at the base of the steps. Ryson attempted to sidle around them, to no avail. Their eyes turned to him, their eyebrows lifted.

"May we be of some assistance?" asked the elder of the three males with distant courtesy as all five examined him with frank curiosity.

"Perhaps. I have a rendezvous on the far side of the amphitheater. I was kindly directed this way in order to avoid the crowds on the rim."

"Which zoïtie claims your interest?"

"I believe that Gollimaul is the designation."

"Ah! That would be the section in black, then. Who is the person you would visit? I ask only from the merest curiosity: I myself am issue of Gollimaul."

Ryson hesitated, then reluctantly spoke. "A certain Lord Mesmer of Frotz."

"What, Glorious Old Triceratops, Got himself? You have affairs with that old dinosaur?"

"Such is the case. They concern, as a matter of fact, dinosaurs."

The field judge pulled at his chin. "I fear that you will be disappointed: Old Triceratops stalked off yesterday evening in high dudgeon, in protest to the judgement upon his zoïtiemen's rendition of the Dance of the Seven Ridottos."

"Quite scandalous," observed a female judge.

"Entirely outrageous," corrected the youngest of the males. "An insult to the Games, an affront to the integrity of the Thirteenth Majestrality!"

"Phah!" uttered the other female. "What does Old Triceratops know of affronts and sensibilities? In sheer boorishness he far outdistances one of his pet tyrannosaurs in rut!"

"But you say he is no longer here at the Games?" persisted Ryson. "Perhaps you could advise me how I might reach him elsewhere; my business with him is of a certain urgency."

"Hrmph!" The judge who had proclaimed himself issue of the Gollimauls snorted angrily. "Old Triceratops has small truck with the niceties of protocol: what an incalculable catastrophe to an ancient and honorable zoïtie to have him come into the majestrality! He would be far more apt to receive you as a guest had you a twenty-foot tail and armored plates upon your belly. Hum! Let me consider . . . None of his immediate family cared to accompany him here to the Games, and small wonder, I say! Still . . ." He looked thoughtfully into the middle distance. "Yonder stands one of old Got's white-nieces,* or so I believe, young Yveena Soolis. Perhaps she would care to intercede for you."

Ryson scrutinized the near-empty stands, seeking a white face among the hundreds of brown- and copper-skinned Palatines.

"No, no, my good fellow, it's no good seeking her among the brash Gollimauls: there she is at the far end of the field in the same costume as ourselves, indubitably pondering the feeding habits of the bugle-horned duckbill."

---

*In a world in which twenty-four million people were divided into twelve clans, with every clansman theoretically linked genetically to each of his two million kin, the Palatine language was correspondingly rich in precise delineations of even the most subtle and distant of relationships. Milk, or white, cousins, for instance, described those no more than three times removed from the referent; blood, or red, those four to six times removed; heart, or blue, those seven to nine times removed, and so forth.

CHAPTER 28

"Can you create a rain cloud, then shape its output into a twenty-foot bog-stalker moose?"

"No."

"Or dance the Dance of the Seven Ridottos two hundred feet in the air, held there solely by the combined mental efforts of one hundred of your zoïtiemen?"

"I would hesitate to try."

"Or cause molecules of air to jump about in such a manner as to imitate the sound of a gold-toed bassoon in a seventy-four-piece orchestra?"

"This too is beyond me."

"Or turn back by the sole force of your mind the attack of three hundred cherryflames, launched at you simultaneously by the opposing team?"

Ryson shook his head in wry denial. "I'm afraid that I can accomplish none of these marvels."

"Marvels, fah! Childish tricks, fit only for the edification of imbeciles and the mentally decrepit!" Yveena Soolis glared at Ryson with bitter scorn. "What *can* you do, O visitor from the stars?"

Ryson felt himself shrinking back from the blazing anger of this appalling young woman. Even on the *Divine Providence* he had never felt entirely comfortable in the presence of the other sex, especially when they were as young and physically lovely as this Earth girl. But how had he been so inept as to incur such inexplicable wrath? He had hardly done more than introduce himself! His thoughts whirled in confusion, a mixture of uncertainty, chagrin, and anger: any possible approach to Lord Mesmer through his niece must now be ruled out. "What can I do? Very little," he muttered unhappily, preparing to bid her a curt farewell.

"Just another blurg. From a whole *universe* of blurgs." Yveena Soolis glared at him a moment longer, then to Ryson's astonishment stepped forward and linked her blue-sleeved arm through his. The forbidding grimness of her tight-lipped mouth melted into a shy grin. "Well, neither can I," she whispered almost inaudibly. Her mood changed again: she laughed harshly, a short, clipped bark. "Come along then, O blurgy starman; we have an infinity of matters in common to discuss: all those things which you can't do among the stars, and all those which I can't do here on Earth."

Ryson shifted his weight uneasily from one foot to the other in the deepening shadows outside an ivy-covered building of ancient brick that sheltered beneath broad shade trees in a quiet quadrangle of similar buildings. It was here, he supposed, that the contestants in the Games were housed. Ten minutes passed, twenty. Palatines in the various colors of their clans strolled past, along with competitors in their short white uniforms. All of them glanced at the outworlder curiously; a few halted, obviously considered demanding his business, then shrugged and went about their own. Idly Ryson watched a lithe youngster bound effortlessly down the broad steps, her long black hair streaming behind her in the soft evening air. The sight of such carefree winsomeness invoked a sharp pang of wistfulness that startled him by its unexpected poignancy. Ryson turned away, reproaching himself impatiently. Hadn't he far more serious reasons for standing here than staring like a mooncalf at—

A hand tugged at his elbow. "Already regretting your impulsiveness?"

Ryson whirled, looked down at glittering black eyes that had an indefinably exotic cast to their angle, high cheekbones in a face of burnished copper, a long, slim neck as graceful as that of a silvertip cyne floating on the Sleepyhead River in front of Blue Finger Mill.

"I'm afraid I didn't recognize you."

"In these clown's clothes?" she demanded with startling bitterness. "Who else could you take me for?"

Startled by her vehemence, Ryson fell back a step, appraised her from head to toe. He could find nothing clownish about what she wore: a trim white suit whose long sleeves and trousers accentuated her slim grace without concealing her essential femininity. A narrow black band circled her waist, then fell to dangle against her left hip; a broader swath with all the colors of the spectrum ran from her left shoulder across small but distinctive breasts to the swelling of her right hip. Her feet were hidden by dainty white slippers, a ruffle of delicate white lace sat in the middle of her glossy hair, offset by an aromatic white flower tucked above each ear. He essayed a wan smile. "You look fine to me, your clothes as well."

The girl's lips twisted for an instant into a harsh parody of a smile. "On Earth we are taught to scorn those uncouth savages who are so ignorant as to inhabit the rest of the galaxy; it is easy enough to forget that they in turn know little or nothing of our own preposterous customs. How could you possibly know what this white uniform signifies, this wretched rainbow? Or even care? Come: I talk too much about myself. We will dine, and you will tell me of life among the stars, and what has brought you to Earth to see my white-uncle." Now her eyes sparkled with animation, and her curiously mobile face was once again serene, that of a vivacious girl in her late teens. Ryson stared at her with a growing enchantment mingled with indefinable misgiving. Never in all the harsh years since leaving Blue Finger Mill had he encountered so contradictory and so bewildering a creature!

"And you in return will tell me about your own customs?" he suggested.

Her eyes hooded over. "Perhaps. Come."

One course succeeded another, one kind of wine or liqueur followed the other, each of them served with meticulous care by a staff of leperons in dark blue uniforms with a dashing white sash about the midriff. Ryson noticed that the crystal goblets in front of Yveena Soolis seemed to be replenished rather more frequently than his own. He shrugged. In spite of her youth and slight frame, she was undoubtedly accustomed to the wines: let her drink as much as she chose. He himself had come halfway around the galaxy on a mission in which he could not afford to let his senses be lulled—he would not try to match her. Nonetheless, he allowed a leperon servitor to replace a half-empty glass of pale straw-colored wine with another whose tint was a deeper yellow, almost lemon-colored. He sipped cautiously; Yveena Soolis took half of hers in a single swallow. Even in the dim, unfocused light her black eyes somehow glittered like jewels. They fixed Ryson unblinkingly as she raised the glass to her lips. "Tell me about your cluster and this planet Bir," she commanded. "Tell me about this overlord of the galaxy and her palace of justice!"

Ryson nodded obligingly. They sat in the privacy of a small leafy bower fifty feet above the ground, balanced without visible support midway out the enormous limb of a Terran shade tree which Yveena Soolis had identified as a Tonkinese banyan. The chairs were soft and yielding, the tabletop a floating slab of brilliant blue turquoise in which swam a myriad of brightly colored fish. Concealed yellow and orange luminifers cast a soft light across their faces; through the carefully trimmed leaves of the great tree they could look out across the dark waters of Resolution Lake, where lights of nine of the twelve colors of the zoïtiac moved in graceful patterns under the starry sky. Ryson looked across the table at the exotic glowing beauty of Yveena Soolis and felt as if he had wandered into a dream. A servitor riding an impulsion beam drifted silently up through the branches of the tree to set another dish before them as Ryson finished his description of the planet Bir.

"This restaurant must be extremely costly," he ventured.

Yveena Soolis glanced about the bower as if seeing it now for the first time. She shrugged indifferently. "Perhaps: it seems modest enough to me."

"What? You dine like this every evening?"

"You mean with an outworlder as blurgy as I?" Her voice was edged with the weary bitterness which Ryson found so inexplicable in one so young. She extended her glass imperiously to one side, to be instantly refilled by a leperon who darted out of the shadows. "Who else would I dine with, except the company of my fellow blurgs?"

"I don't understand."

"How could you? I don't understand it myself. And yet I am undeniably blurgy, and will be for the rest of my life. A long, long life in the company of other blurgs, every twenty years coming to Carayapundy to impose order upon the antics of the children at play, the intervals between spent tidying up their messes; always, always, *always* in the company of my fellow blurgs!" She blindly gulped the contents of her glass, thrust it out for more.

Ryson's brain seemed half numbed, enveloped by a soft golden haze; through it he became acutely aware of a terrible pain that shone in the eyes of the half-drunk girl. Wondering greatly at his own daring, he saw his hand reaching out to take hers, heard his voice speaking. "I too am blurgy, or so you say. There should be no secrets between blurgs, only frank communion. Tell me."

Her mouth half opened, as if to speak. She shook her head wildly, her long hair snapping from side to side. "I can't," she muttered, "you're an outworlder."

Ryson's fingers tightened gently around hers. "But I'm also blurgy."

Her exotically shaped black eyes glittered in the blue phosphorescent glow of the transparent table, as if they were filling with tears. "I can't," she whispered.

"Perhaps I can help," he said wildly.

"Help? How could you help?"

"I don't know." It must be the wine, he thought; he felt suffused to the point of bursting with the need to comfort this anguished creature, this perfect stranger; to protect her against the unknown demons that held her in thrall, to pull her close against him and hold her in his arms. His hand squeezed hers imploringly. "Tell me."

Yveena Soolis raised her eyes to stare into his. Her pert breasts rose and fell beneath her clinging white suit. Suddenly she threw her hair back over her shoulder with a decisive gesture. "I suppose that you can always be deleted—so what does it matter, after all?" She stumbled to her feet. "But not here," she said. "Come, we'll walk beside the lake."

CHAPTER 29

A little more than a million years earlier a researcher at the Molecular Theater of Theoretical Dance in the now vanished city of Aviar had made an unexpected discovery: the sixteenth hexenary of the antiquark particle called giddy could be minutely, but predictably, manipulated by nothing more than his own intense concentration—so long as he himself was individualized by a solid gold Cedex chronograph on his right wrist, an iodized piece of number-seven emulsion draped about his left shoulder, and a negatively charged swath of raw Bermon silk around his head. Thus was born the psionic augmentor.

Further progress thereupon languished for seventy thousand years as the planet's entire intellectual resources were suddenly diverted to the battle to reverse the atmosphere's inexorably rising temperature. To no avail: the polar icecaps melted, water was released sufficient to raise the level of the oceans by one hundred and thirty feet. The world's population of one and a half billion abandoned their ancient waterfront cities and migrated inland to those lands which remained; the Tinctorian Games, a local divertissement decreed thousands of years earlier by the 64th Soltoon of qu'Iriindi, relocated from Aquidauana to Carayapundy.

Here the Games gradually caught the fancy of the rest of the planet by the introduction of a new area of competition: trial by psionics. The efficacy of psionic augmentors increased rapidly; but the application of psionics to practical matters remained essentially where it had been eighty thousand years earlier. A thousand rigorously coordinated men and women, aided by gigantic mechanical and electronic contrivances, could now roll a yellow and red beachball back and forth across a playing field by the force of their collective minds, but little more. Psionic research had apparently reached an impasse.

While casting about in random directions for means to increase the power of his zoïtie's augmentor for the forthcoming Games of 691,746 OFR, Davourd Dee Doe, Lexicog First, titular of degrees from seventeen institutions of higher learning, inadvertently constructed the first time machine.

"But time travel is impossible," said Ryson, stopping abruptly in their sedate promenade through the powdery white sand that blanketed the edge of Lake Resolution.

He heard Yveena Soolis snicker sardonically in the darkness. "Of *course* time travel is impossible—in all the rest of the galaxy." She hesitated, swaying slightly. "Do you know *why* it's impossible?"

"No."

"Because every time it's invented anywhere else, someone from Earth is sent back in time to *dis*invent it."

"Disinvent it how?"

"A thousand ways, a million! The simplest and most definitive is to delete the inventor before he ever makes his machine: by infecting him with a childhood disease, perhaps, or by deleting his parents, or—" Yveena Soolis hissed angrily. "Oh, use your own imagination!"

Ryson did, aghast at the appalling new vistas that opened before him. His brain whirled with a million fancies, each more horrifying than the last. A tiny corner of it wondered how he could feel so chilled, standing here in the starry brilliance of a tropical evening with a lovely girl so near that he could feel the warmth of her breath against his face? "Is that what you meant earlier?" he asked at last. "When you said that I could always be deleted?"

"Your actual physical entity, I suppose, would not be deleted: merely your memory of our conversation." Yveena Soolis laughed harshly, with a slightly hysterical edge to it, and swayed briefly against him. The stroll through the warm night air had not tempered the effects of her numerous glasses of wine. "Why go to all the trouble of taking more drastic steps simply to expunge the indiscretions of a blurg to a dinosaur rancher from Ambrose? As for myself: no deletion, but a stern chastisement and demotion in grade."

"But—how?"

"How would we delete your memory? A thousand ways exist. But the first principle is always this: the less the timestream is disturbed, the better. So then: wasn't it one of my fellow blurgs, a zoïtieman of the Gollimauls, who directed your attention to me?"

"I think so, yes."

"Well, then. An operative would return a few hours downtime, order the silly blurg to divert your attention elsewhere. We would then have never met; consequently we would not now be standing here discussing forbidden matters."

Another cold chill ran up Ryson's spine as the full implications of her words penetrated: his entire life could be arbitrarily redirected in a single moment— and he would never be aware of it! "Why are these matters forbidden? And to whom?"

"Do you really need to ask?" Yveena Soolis stepped closer to Ryson, so that her shoulder touched his upper arm. Without conscious thought he put his arm around her waist, pulled her closer. "Let's walk on," she said somberly. "It hardly matters if three hours of your memories are deleted, or three hours and fifteen minutes, does it?"

"Do you really think they will?"

"Only if they find out what I've told you."

Ryson laughed harshly. "They're hardly likely to be told by me, now that I know the consequences." His arm tightened against her slender waist. "To have you obliterated from my memories: inconceivable!"

She stopped, swung around on tiptoes to suddenly brush her lips against his cheek. "You're sweet," she murmured, her mood changing mercurially to jaunty merriness. "Worse things than that have happened, you may be sure! Come: we will stroll to the pavilion and I will tell you about some of them."

Excitement at the prospect of time travel ran high; the finest minds of Earth were brought into the project. Within twenty years a practical time machine had been constructed. Scholars, historians, and scientists clamored for its use, along with prophets, monomaniacs, and speculators. One such scholar was Vorbo wan Monchie, a paleontologist long obsessed by the inexplicable abruptness of the disappearance of the dinosaurs two hundred million years before.

At this point no one had ventured downtime more than two million years; wan Monchie's proposal coincided perfectly with the experiments already planned by the machine's developers. An expedition was formed, returned in time to the mid-Triassic. Vorbo wan Monchie and his picked team of microbiologists, geologists, astronomers, taxonomists, paleontologists, and cameramen floated out cautiously into the steaming air of the late Mesozoic. It was well that they had exercised caution: two hours later their aircar brought them to within sight of a discovery fully as stunning as that of the time machine—the Ravagers.

The gigantic and inconceivably hideous aliens had landed their mile-long spaceship on the edge of a vast yellow savanna and set up camp at the base of a smoldering volcano. Three of the thirty-foot-high yellow and blue monsters now frolicked imperviously in a stream of bubbling lava that flowed past their encampment.

As the Palatines watched in stunned disbelief from the shelter of a craggy outcropping of the volcano, a six-legged Ravager came bounding across the plain, threw itself zestfully upon a startled tyrannosaurus rex. Five minutes of titanic struggle ensued; the dead dinosaur was quickly disjointed and its two rear haunches slung jauntily upon the back of the triumphant Ravager. The alien monster returned to camp; in the midst of a circle of similar monsters it cooked its meal over an open fire and avidly devoured the charred flesh and bones of the mightiest killing machine that Earth had ever known.

Half paralyzed with horror, the scientific expedition turned their craft about and returned with hysterical speed to the concealed aperture of their time machine. Moments later they had returned to the safety of 691,766 OFR Palatine Earth. Two days afterwards it was made a capital offense to travel downtime any point earlier than 641,766 OFR. Whoever, or whatever, the terrifying Ravagers were, they must be given no inkling that two hundred million years in their future a civilization existed—and that a means existed of attaining it.

Twenty thousand years passed, thirty. The memory of the Ravagers gradually receded, grew faint, all but disappeared from the consciousness of the Palatines. Work on the time machine continued. In 726,963 OFR three students of philosophical engineering devised a means by which its operation might be linked to a psionic augmentor. By directing their thoughts through the augmentor, a certain number of Palatines could now manipulate time without direct reference to the machine; the genes of these Palatines were scattered at apparent random throughout the nine hundred and eighty million people who now inhabited Earth.

* * *

"So that's why dinosaurs still exist on Earth," said Ryson wonderingly. "They were brought back by time machine!"

Yveena Soolis uttered a complex sound: indicative of disparagement, wistfulness, reluctant admiration. "Actually, by my gigagreat-uncle Lord Leuten of Maul, one of the first of our line to attain the majestrality. As a small boy he became enamored of dinosaurs; as majestral he had access to one of the more powerful time machines. He made surreptitious forays into the past and returned with a collection of dinosaurs. He possessed great wealth and, totally unsuspected, a talent for even greater duplicity. These allowed him to somehow conceal the dinosaurs on his estate in the Calmness. It was only during the confusion attendant to his death that a bevy of famished allosaurs escaped their reserve and devoured an expedition of mushroom pickers and bird watchers from the Ifness Institute: thus was the deception discovered."

"And then?"

"There was an outcry, of course, but too much time had lapsed since the single sighting of the Ravagers; even with the grisly recordings made by wan Monchie the threat had become abstract. And unlike my white-uncle Glorious Old Triceratops, old Leuten was gentle and scholarly, universally esteemed. In spite of the pleas of the Thirteenth, the Duze Majestrals decided to let him lie peacefully in his grave. Otherwise he would have been resurrected at some point downtime, charged with treason against the human race, and brought before a tribune, which would certainly have condemned him to an ignominious end."

"So he got away with it, then?"

"The true reason is seldom voiced. Undoubtedly the determining factor in the minds of the Duze Majestrals was the fear of establishing a dangerous precedent, one that would permit their own private escapades to be monitored and perhaps censured by some future group of majestrals."

Ryson nodded. Before them the glowing lumens of the pavilion glittered through the trees that ringed a small cove. "But if dinosaurs actually originated here on Earth, how did they get to Stohlson's Redemption?"

"Is that the name of the dinosaur planet? I thought you said you were from Ambrose?"

"So I am. A few species of commercial value have recently been exported from Stohlson's Redemption to some of the neighboring systems. But Stohlson's Redemption is where they range freely; it is in fact taken for granted that Stohlson's Redemption is their planet of origin."

"The Duze Majestrals would be pleased to hear you say that: for three-quarters of a million years they have strived to give that impression. When gigagreat-uncle's secret collection came to light, most of them were shipped offworld, to this Stohlson's Redemption of yours. It was distant and uninhabited; the few dinosaurs they allowed to remain with Lord Leuten's heirs could be explained away as having been imported on a whim from their planet of origin on the other side of the galaxy."

Ryson was baffled. "But why go to such trouble?"

Yveena Soolis looked up at him, her face a pallid green in the fairy lights strung along the pavilion and in the towering cypresses that stood guard around it. "You *still* don't understand?"

"I'm only a blurg, remember? And an outworld blurg at that."

"So you are." She squeezed his hand affectionately.

CHAPTER 30

Long before Vorbo wan Monchie's encounter with the Ravagers, the Duze Majestrals had realized that the possession of a time machine could make Earth powerful and secure beyond the dreams of the most despotic of tyrants—as long as no one else in the galaxy possessed one.

The chance encounter with the alien monsters presented an opportune pretext: time travel beyond fifty thousand years into the past was summarily banned, a veil of secrecy was dropped over the machine's very existence. By additional good fortune, Earth was a little-known backwater in an obscure part of the cosmos, its activities of small concern to the rest of the galaxy.

A quarantine was placed around the Sol System; of the few who took notice in the rest of the galaxy none objected. Scores of Palatines were sent first downtime, then on commercial packets throughout the galaxy. Their goal: the eradication of whatever word of Davourd Dee Doe's momentous invention might have reached the tens of thousands of other inhabited worlds. By cunning deletions and alterations, all knowledge of the machine's existence ceased to exist beyond the boundaries of Earth. Thereafter, Palatine operatives ceaselessly scanned the galaxy's scientific journals; any hint of speculation concerning time travel except to condemn it as impossible nonsense led to the ruthless effacement of the offending parties.

A tiresome detail was the presence of Lord Leuten of Maul's archaic beasts in the preserves of the Zoïtie of

Gollimaul. Should an outworlder ever pause to consider the sudden appearance of supposedly extinct dinosaurs on present-day Earth, the existence of a time machine might well be postulated. Measures were therefore taken to ensure that the origin of the beasts was ascribed to the distant planet of Stohlson's Redemption.

Equally important from the majestrals' point of view was the implementation of a policy to insulate Earth from the incessant wars and turmoil that had plagued the galaxy for hundreds of thousands of years. Even the most minor conflicts between armed planets, it was argued, could theoretically escalate to the point of somehow embroiling Earth. The simplest means of nullifying this threat was to eliminate warfare throughout the galaxy.

One hundred thousand dedicated Palatine deletionists and historians were dispatched downtime, then out through the galaxy. They snipped a life here, pruned a royal branch there, exploded a troublesome planet if need be, generally encouraged the development and spread of religious movements of a pacifist bent. For the first time since humanity had overrun the cosmos the galaxy was at peace, its only strife confined to the surface of the individual planets.

Just as the commonweal of the galaxy was evolving rapidly under the tutelage of its secret, if essentially disinterested, rulers, so too on Earth the Palatines themselves were evolving. Already the population of the planet had shrunk to little more than four hundred million. As millennia succeeded millennia the gene which permitted certain Terrans to interact psionically with time became increasingly widespread. Finally, under the forceful leadership of the Marquess of Torhamber, Majestral of Saverhol during the final years of the Age of Debate, a rigorous program of eugenics was implemented.

The two hundred and fifty million Palatines who still had no trace at all of the time gene were abruptly termed non-citizens, and a potential danger to the planet. They were gathered up by their more puissant brothers and cousins and shipped to Mars. This was termed the Great Rebirth. On Mars they were put to profitable employ by terraforming a rust-colored desert into a salubrious garden planet. Using the tool of temporal manipulation, the Palatines began to breed their Martian kin for useful and pleasing traits, most notably: docility, subservience, fidelity of purpose, and lack of ambition.

Two pathetic rebellions organized on Mars were suppressed by time-jumping Palatines with contemptuous ease; an instant after the final deletion downtime, all trace of the aborted uprisings was thereby effaced forever from the minds of the Martian settlers.

The hundred and fifty million Palatines on Earth were patient: for three dozen generations they worked to inculcate the proper attitudes into their rapidly evolving servant caste. Nine hundred and fifty years after the Great Rebirth, the first of its children—long, pallid, apathetic—came to Earth to serve their Palatine masters.

"This ability to travel in time without an actual machine," asked Ryson, "it can only be used on Earth in conjunction with psionic augmentors?"

"Away from Earth the mightiest of the majestrals is indistinguishable from any of the galaxy's blurgs. It would be inconceivably dangerous to let even an augmentor fall into the hands of anyone in the rest of the galaxy. To ensure that this can never happen, individual augmentors no longer exist: a single central augmentor blankets all of Earth. Any of the Palatines can use it at will."

Ryson stared blindly over Yveena Soolis's shoulder, scarcely conscious of the sparkling lights that still glided back and forth across the lake's surface. He shook his head in awe. "Secret rulers of the universe! Time machines! Psionic augmentors! I can see why all of this you would want to keep secret, why you would efface the memory of any offworlder who gained a knowledge of them." His voice now held the same edge of bitterness that had characterized Yveena Soolis's. "So why are you telling me all this? Because after you're through you'll hop back in time and eradicate these last three hours, leaving me standing back there in the amphitheater, wondering what to do next?"

"That, of course, is what I *should* do," said Yveena Soolis coolly. "But that, of course, is also most precisely what I *can't* do." She turned her face to his, her eyes haunted. "Don't you see, I'm a *blurg*!"

The myriad paradoxes generated by time travel had troubled the majestrals since the creation of the first machine. What daunted them most was this:

They were now embarked on a project of almost unimaginable grandeur, that of recharting the lives of the entire human race in accordance with the needs of Earth. Time, events, causalities, eventualities, pasts, presents, and futures—all of these across the billions of stars of the galaxy would be altered hundreds, thousands, even millions of times in the centuries to come. Every human being would eventually be affected—conceivably including the majestrals themselves. What was to prevent an ill-conceived deletion from initiating a chain of events which might inadvertently lead to the deletion or serious alteration of the majestrals themselves?

And how, once the course of events had been altered, would the Majestrality *know* that they had been altered, for would not their own memories now reflect the events of the new past?

And finally, *who* would take the terrible responsibility of deciding exactly which portions of previous history would be pruned and excised? The chaos resulting from hundreds of millions of Palatine time manipulators each rearranging time to best suit their own goals would be unimaginable.

These were the questions that preoccupied the

Duze Majestrals for a full three centuries before the first of Earth's deletionists were ordered out into the galaxy. Two solutions were proposed. The first was the total suppression of the time machine; this was rejected. The second was almost as simple: the creation of the Thirteen Majestrality, or, as it came to be colloquially known, the Thirteenth Majestral.

The idea was simple; it was its implementation which took most of the ensuing three centuries. At last a series of meticulously calibrated time machines working in sequence were activated in a chain of infinitely repeating loops; the result was the creation of a stasis field. Within the confines of this field time remained on its normal inalterable course; anyone and anything within the field was shielded from the consequences of even the most stupendous alterations of the time flow in the outside universe.

Within the stasis bubble, all of history remained constant; here its changes were dispassionately studied and noted by the impartial arbiters of the Thirteenth Majestrality to whom all proposals for altering the fabric of time in even the most minimal way must now be referred. The physical existence of even the lofty Duze Majestrals might be snuffed out at any moment in the course of a misconceived deletion, for no ordinary Palatine, however august, could seek the shelter of the stasis field. But even the most humble provisionary of the Thirteenth Majestrality could sleep soundly, secure in the knowledge that except for the possibility of natural death he would still exist on the morrow.

Originally the Thirteenth Majestral had been composed of twenty-four hundred Palatines encompassing all fields of expertise, drawn equally from the twelve competing zoïties. Over the course of the ensuing millennia the criteria for selection swung wildly in many directions; each had eventually occasioned resentment, dissention, conflict, and new criteria.

An unexpected development following the exodus of the two hundred and fifty million non-bearers of the time gene led to the final adjustment to the workings of the Thirteenth Majestral. To the dismay and shame of a number of Palatines, it was observed that an occasional child was born hopelessly deformed. Bereft of the time gene, he or she would be forever unable to manipulate time. What then would distinguish them from their genetically inferior cousins, the lowly Martian leperons?

In theory several alternatives existed: the children could be deleted, or never conceived. But Palatine etiquette, and the legal code, forbade the use of temporal manipulation in any fashion that might impinge upon the lives of its citizens; permanent exile to Mars was the automatic penalty for infringement of this stricture.

Other alternatives were to send the crippled Palatines to Mars, to join the leperons; to simply ignore their handicap; or to have them join the Thirteenth Majestrality.

The majority of Palatines had now come to view the Thirteenth Majestral with an uneasy resentment; their unique privilege of meddling with time was galling, their total immunity to the consequences even more so. No one denied the Majestrality's utility; but neither did any of the Palatines relish the outrageously lofty status enjoyed by those who were essentially technicians and soulless functionaries. But now its ranks could be maintained, and its social status dramatically reduced, by the simple expedient of stocking it solely with society's cripples, the sorry blurgs.

"So a blurg is anyone who can't manipulate time."

"I am a blurg," confirmed Yveena Soolis. "You are a blurg, everyone in the Thirteenth Majestral is a blurg; except for the Palatines, everyone in the entire galaxy is a blurg."

"And that's why you've told me all these ghastly secrets?"

In the faint light Ryson could see her incline her

head. "I've never met an outworlder before, a cripple just like me. I saw you standing there . . . a *happy* cripple, a cripple who doesn't *know* he's a cripple, who doesn't *care!*" She pulled abruptly away from his arm and turned toward the quietly lapping waters of the lake. "I thought that perhaps by talking with you, by telling you, I could . . ." She threw up her hands despairingly. "I don't *know* what I thought!"

"But this is crazy!" protested Ryson. "You call yourselves blurgs, you torment yourselves for being cripples, and yet you're the most powerful people on the planet! The most powerful people in the entire universe!"

Yveena Soolis shook her head dolefully. "Only an offworlder could say that; here I'm just a blurg."

"But a Thirteenth Majestral!"

"I'm only a third-year provisional. The training is arduous: I have another four years of study before I become a full member."

"And even then—you'll still consider yourself a cripple?"

"Even then," she whispered almost inaudibly. "Because that's what I am, and what I'll be for the rest of my life: a blurg, a genetic failure, inferior stock, forbidden to have children, forced to—"

Ryson stepped across the soft white sand, laid his hands on her shoulders. He spoke with a lightness that sounded forced and strident even to himself. "You don't have to be a majestral, or even a time traveler, to see there's only one thing for you to do: leave Earth, and join me in the outworlds. There we'll be blurgy cripples together, and Ravening Rolaster take the Palatines!"

CHAPTER 31

Lord Mesmer of Frotz, Majestral of Gollimaul, was unable to be reached at any of his seven estates. Vexed, Yveena Soolis placed a second call to Tumbling Springs, the site of his twenty-six-thousand-square-mile dinosaur reserve. This time she harried the lugubrious leperon majordomo until he admitted that his lordship had departed earlier in the day in the company of Lady Belpina Daine to her underwater estate at Yarrawonga Reach beneath the Great Yellow Reef.

"Illicit trysts at his age, with women like that," snorted Yveena Soolis as she replaced the communicator. "Disgusting! I'd as soon mate with a triceratops! I can't think why you want to meet him."

"I've told you: we share a mutual interest in dinosaurs."

"Hmmph. You look terribly grim when you say that. I don't know if I really believe you." With a crooked grin, she tossed her long hair across her bare shoulders, began to pull on the crumpled white suit she had dropped on the floor the night before. "All men are liars: throughout the universe this is a known constant. Well, no matter. We'll have breakfast on the beach; by the time we're finished the aircar will be here."

"Aircar?"

"Didn't you want to see old Got's smelly beasts? What better time to see them than when the doddering triceratops himself is engaged in sweaty amours on the other side of the world? I wheedled Bougo into sending his lordship's Avalion Arrow for us."

"Us? You're coming too?" Ryson's heart leapt up.

"What about your job here, whatever it is you do while people build water sculptures in midair?"

Her laughter had none of the brassy harshness he had heard so often the night before. "Refereeing the Games? I've already called in sick. Let them find another blurg; there are plenty more at Amaranth."

"Amaranth?"

"Where I live, where the Thirteenth Majestral lives. It's on the other side of the world, on the continent of Malangali. The older Strals almost never leave: they live in mortal fear that an unreckoned time change will catch up with them and flick them out of existence. Someday I suppose that I'll be like that. In the meantime, we provisionaries are expendable: we get sent out every twenty years to referee the Games." Some of last night's bitterness had returned to her voice.

"I meant it, you know, when I asked you to—"

"I know. I'll think about it. I don't think they'd let me go, they'd expunge us both. But I'll think about it. Now let's go have breakfast."

The aircar flew steadily south, crossing the lakes and forests of the Unchartered Territories, the broad savannas of the Winnigosis Plain, coming at last to the shallow waters of the Inland Sea. Here the Avalion Arrow dropped swiftly until it was only hundreds of yards above the azure waters. Twenty minutes later soft yellow hills rose up to define the far side of Cosco Bay. The black aircar rose to skim their oak-studded crests, thereby passing into Tumbling Springs, the domain of Lord Mesmer of Frotz.

The interior of the Avalion Arrow was even more sumptuously furnished than the spaceyacht Ryson had expropriated from Baron Bodissey, but for most of the flight his mind had been on other matters. The glossy dark head of Yveena Soolis which rested against his shoulder failed to divert his attention: his eyes were fixed with burning intensity on the fields and woodlands passing slowly beneath the aircar. Ryson felt his body growing taut with anticipation as the Avalion Arrow neared the seat of the Majestral of Gollimaul.

"Look," said Yveena Soolis, pointing to a small green meadow to the southeast of the aircar. "Some of Glorious Old Triceratops' preposterous beasts, chewing on the tops of those palm trees. Could those actually *be* triceratops?"

Ryson leaned forward. "No. That's what we call a devil's mace: look at the spiked armored ball on the end of their tail. That's the mace; they turn around and use it to defend themselves from carnivores."

"Ugh! Who'd want to eat thirty feet of armor plating?"

"Forty hungry feet of teeth and gut, perhaps. Doesn't your uncle have tyrannosaurs on the reserve?"

"Somewhere up on the northwest side. They tend to be obstreperous: thirty or forty years ago they ate an inspector from the humane society. Got swore it was an accident, but since then he keeps them out of the public eye as much as possible."

"What happened to the inspector?"

"For all that Got sneers at the Thirteenth Majestral, this time it saved him from a lot of trouble. An operative was dispatched downtime to keep the inspector from stepping out of her aircar. She returned safely to make her report, never knowing that in another time sequence she was nothing but chewed meat in the belly of a monster."

Ryson shuddered at words that made intolerably vivid the image of his father's own ghastly fate, then stiffened against the couch as a fantastic glimmer of hope suddenly occurred to him. Could Yveena Soolis conceivably intervene with the Thirteenth Majestral in order to undo the—

"More of them," said the girl, pointing to the horizon.

"Brawnies, or diplos, or perhaps even brachiosaurs; they're too far away to tell."

"And that's what you raise in order to eat?" Yveena Soolis wrinkled her nose fastidiously. "Once again: ugh!"

"There's nothing tastier than a carefully grilled brawny steak," fantasized Ryson, recalling his own peculiar meal of ground brawny on the planet Gys. "Seasoned of course with a handful of freshly ground sizzletongue pimentos as they broil . . ."

Yveena Soolis giggled and snuggled closer. "If reciting recipes is your way of tempting me into going offworld—"

"Let's visit the tyrannosaurus preserve," interrupted Ryson brusquely, motivated by powerful emotions he found impossible to precisely define.

"I think that it may actually be forbidden; I've heard that he put up defenses against—"

"—his own personal aircar?"

"There is that, of course. Let me try." She spoke softly in Terran to the air above her head. An equally soft Terran voice replied. A short dialogue ensued. "We're on our way," said Yveena Soolis. "The aircar has assured me that we will not be volatilized as we cross the barrier."

"What matter?" muttered Ryson somberly, his thoughts on his mother, whom he had last seen in the Hall of Durster some twenty years before. "They'd only resurrect us afterward."

"You don't know my uncle Triceratops. Probably he wouldn't bother. Unless it was to punish us for damaging his aircar: then he'd feed us to his beasts."

Ryson turned to look at her grim face. "You mean that seriously?"

Yveena Soolis shrugged. "There have always been stories. Unfaithful leperons, undocumented offworlders, that sort of thing. No one pays much attention to them."

"But they *could* be true?"

"I suppose."

Both of them returned to their own somber

thoughts. Ryson watched the hills and savannas give way to a dense tropical forest. The forest thinned, became scattered woods of deciduous and conifers, alternating with meadows, lakes, and shadowy glades. The sun rose high in the sky. Yveena Soolis spoke to the aircar. A table appeared before them, and shortly thereafter glasses of pale rose crystal, dishes of translucent blue porcelain. Ryson ate with small appetite, his thoughts increasingly dire as he considered Lord Mesmer of Frotz.

A voice spoke within the cabin of the Avalion Arrow. "A warning from Got's barrier," explained Yveena Soolis as the voice spoke a second time, more insistently. "The aircar will override it."

Ahead Ryson could see a brilliantly glowing red line stretching across the horizon. It grew rapidly, became a two-hundred-foot energy barrier of surging red impulses. The Avalion Arrow passed sedately above it, continued toward the northwest.

"Over there," whispered Yveena Soolis in an awed tone as she peered from the far side of the aircar. Ryson slid to her end of the divan. He looked down in time to catch a fleeting glimpse of a pair of tyrannosaurs hunched over a bloody carcass, their monstrous snouts buried in its steaming innards.

"Are you all right?" asked Yveena Soolis with sudden concern, laying her hand on his. "You look awfully . . . strange. And your hand is like ice."

"Too much lunch," said Ryson, forcing a bleak smile. "I'm not used to some of your food. I'm fine now."

"So what do you want to do now? I told the aircar to take us to the center of the tyrannosaurus preserve. I suppose we'll be there shortly; then what?"

What indeed? Ryson's thoughts were a surging turmoil. "How old is your uncle?" he asked abruptly.

"Old Triceratops? I really don't know. Three, four hundred, perhaps. Older? It's possible."

"Everyone on Earth lives that long?"

"To four or five hundred, of course. Don't you?"

Ryson shook his head dolefully, hardly conscious of the question. It was now almost inconceivable that Glorious Old Triceratops was not the copper-skinned grandee who had come to Stohlson's Redemption twenty-two years earlier in the guise of the Immaculate Ultim of Aberdown, bringing death and catastrophe to the Tandryl-Kundórrs: the man who had visited Qymset under the same name some four hundred years earlier. If only he were somewhere here on his estate instead of the other side of the world . . .

Yveena Soolis could introduce them: even barehanded the matter would be settled in an instant . . .

But . . . but . . . Ryson hissed angrily between his teeth. What then of his family, his clan, their fetish? How could they be found, recovered? And what of his own life? How could he conceivably hope to kill one of the twelve rulers of Earth, of the entire *universe*, and make good his escape?

In fact—and now an icy sweat suddenly beaded his forehead—how could he kill this monster *and ensure that he stayed dead*?

He glanced sideways at Yveena Soolis, who was eying him pensively, her lips pursed. *This girl, along with her fellows from the Thirteenth Majestral, could raise the monster from the dead as soon as Ryson's hands left his throat*!

CHAPTER 32

"Yveena Soolis!" The thick Terran voice was like a physical blow as it lashed the quiet of the aircar's salon. The girl started, Ryson's heart thudded in his chest. He knew without being told that this was the voice of the monster he had pursued so long and so far.

Yveena Soolis licked her lips nervously, glanced at Ryson, then tossed her hair over her shoulder with a careless motion. She spoke to the air before her with apparent unconcern, listened to the ponderous reply. She turned to Ryson, rolling her glittering black eyes in mock dismay. "My uncle," she said in Versal. "He has returned earlier than foreseen. He would appreciate the return of his aircar."

"Of course. Please tell him on my behalf that he has already displayed extraordinary kindness in extending his hospitality this far. I look forward to making his acquaintance."

Yveena Soolis smirked facetiously at Ryson's obsequious reply, spoke once more in Terran. "He will be awaiting us at Green Vista." In spite of her apparent disdainful indifference, Ryson thought that her voice sounded peculiarly strained.

The aircar wheeled about, headed south. Ryson and Yveena Soolis sat silently, her hand in his, each absorbed by their own thoughts. The ship crossed a broad blue lake with duckbills feeding on its shores, then floated silently past a herd of iguanodons grazing peacefully, apparently indifferent to the four great

225

tyrannosaurs that strode purposefully across the savanna a few miles beyond.

A forest of dark conifers loomed up on the horizon, the forerunners to a series of low green hills. At the edge of the forest a faint smudge of gray and brown gradually became a small cluster of weatherbeaten wooden buildings. Three lines of white smoke from cooking fires rose straight into a cloudless sky.

"People live *here*, inside a tyrannosaur preserve?" marveled Ryson.

"It does seem a little odd," agreed Yveena Soolis.

As the primitive buildings passed beneath the Avalion Arrow half a dozen faces looked up.

"Those people," said Ryson in a shaky voice. "Are they leperons? Martians? They didn't look pale enough."

"No? To me they looked mostly naked."

"Well? Is *that* usual, naked leperons? Even on a dinosaur preserve?"

Yveena Soolis frowned. "I suppose not. In fact . . . The leperons aren't *slaves*, you know! I know that all you outworlders think of them as slaves, but they're not! They're just dif—"

Ryson squeezed her hand reassuringly. "I believe you. But if they're not slaves, then why were they living so miserably in the middle of a park full of tyrannosaurs?"

"I . . . don't know. It must be some horrid fancy of old Got's."

Ryson stared bleakly at the tops of the passing trees. "Exactly what I meant. Can we have a closer look?"

"You mean go back?"

"Not to land: just to look."

The girl glanced at his pale grim features, then quickly turned away. She spoke softly to the ship. "I hope old Got doesn't find out: I'm sure he'd be furious."

"Then we won't tell him."

The aircar returned to the edge of the forest, came to a smooth halt two hundred yards above the tiny village.

"Can we go lower?"

Yveena Soolis spoke to the aircar and it drifted downward, unnoticed by a cluster of half-naked folk who stood talking earnestly in the deep shadow cast by one of their miserable dwellings. The men were an even brown from long hours in the sun, but it was clearly not the natural color of their skin; the women were mostly the same light tan as Ryson's own skin. His heart thudded in his chest and his vision blurred as he stared down with horror at the three men and a woman whom he clearly recognized as members of the Tandryl-Kundórrs. Even after twenty-two years, that was unmistakably Cousin Histiss, and beside him his second cousin Lagawaw. And there was his once youthful Uncle Volen, and next to him an aged crone who was undoubtedly his great-aunt Ralaminda.

Only the long harsh years of concealing his anguish and hatred from the Jairaben at the Pandow Keep enabled him to keep from crying out in rage and frustration. There, only bare yards below him, was his family and clan, possibly even his mother. But what should have been a glorious moment of the most exultant triumph was only a bitter reminder of his almost total impotence.

For totally devoid of weapons, alone on a planet twenty thousand light-years across the galaxy, how could he possibly hope to destroy a four-hundred-year-old adversary who could travel in time?

Roughly in the center of his estate of Tumbling Springs was Lord Mesmer's principal residence, Green Vista, an aggregation of ancient stone buildings nestled on the side of Mount Dominance. The aircar swooped low across a broad triangle of meadow lands at the confluence of the Wiggleswary and Blue rivers; Ryson absently noticed the presence of a thick herd of armor-

plated stegosaurs. The ship rose to follow the gentle
slope that led to a dense thicket of shade trees halfway
up the hill. Ryson sat tautly on the edge of the divan,
trying to compose his features. The man he had come
to kill was a time traveler, he told himself over and
over, not a mind reader; he could have no reason to
suppose that Ryson was anything other than what he
claimed to be: a dinosaur breeder who had fallen by
chance into the company of his white-niece . . .

The aircar drifted slowly across the leafy tops of
the great oaks and elms of Green Vista. Below them
Ryson could glimpse a dozen or more buildings in the
dappled sunlight. The single open area was a broad
white courtyard between a high-gabled wooden barn
painted an ebony black and three low stone buildings
that to Ryson's eye might have been army barracks—or
a prison compound. A dozen or more aircars, most of
them the same gleaming black, were parked neatly on
the courtyard. The Avalion Arrow settled between
them, came to a halt so smooth it was barely perceptible.

"Well, we're here!" exclaimed Yveena Soolis with
forced gaiety. "Now to introduce you to my uncle and
let you get on about your dinosaurs!"

Knees quivering with tension, Ryson followed the
girl out of the aircar into the blazing heat of early
afternoon. Three figures stepped out of the inky shadows of a covered walkway that snaked beneath the
towering oaks. Yveena Soolis uttered a sharp exclamation of surprise and vexation. "My parents," she muttered to Ryson. "What are *they* doing here?"

The three figures stood ominously silent, staring
stonily at Ryson and Yveena Soolis as they crossed the
sun-dazzled courtyard. Ryson squinted his eyes against
the glare, tried to pull a half smile denoting pleasurable
expectancy to his lips.

Two of the dark silhouettes before him were tall
and lean, a man and a woman: clearly the parents of
Yveena Soolis. The other black shape was short and

thick, with three rigid spikes like the horn of a duckbill projecting from the top of his smooth scalp. There could be no doubt: this was Glorious Old Triceratops, Lord Mesmer of Frotz, Majestral of Gollimaul, secret ruler of the universe.

Ryson performed the most difficult act of his life: he smiled affably, extended his two hands with palms up, thumbs curled inward, in the fashion of Ambrose.

The blood was pounding in his ears. The man before him Kerryl Ryson had last seen standing high in the Hall of Durster in the Pandow Keep, about to impose his terrible judgement upon his father and the clan of Tandryl-Kundórr.

It was the Immaculate Ultim of Aberdown.

CHAPTER 33

"Hello, Mother, hello, Father," said Yveena Soolis in Versal. "What a pleasant surprise. Hello, Uncle Froddy, so kind of you to lend us your aircar. My mother, Lady Veenabon; my father, the Marquime of Coborne; my white-uncle, the Paramount Margrave and Majestral of the Zoïtie of Gollimaul, Lord Mesmer of Frotz. I present: the Honorable Lulmö Häistön, high dignitary of the planet Ambrose."

Ryson inclined his head graciously. "Nothing quite so grand," he said to the heavy silence. "Merely a dinosaur rancher, come to—"

He was interrupted by the angry voice of Lady Veenabon, addressing her daughter in rapid Terran. The girl protested, shrugged her shoulders, became angry in turn. Her father's deeper voice joined the fray. Ryson turned discreetly away and smiled blandly at the man who had murdered his father and enslaved his mother.

The Majestral of Gollimaul returned his gaze with tiny black eyes that glittered in the copper-skinned moon-face that was so indelibly etched upon Ryson's memory. His stout body was attired almost entirely in black: a loosely fitting shirt with flaring sleeves and a high filigree of white lace at the back of his neck; glossy ebòn breeches; dull, scuffed boots that came nearly to his knees. A short leather riding crop dangled from one hand, tapping ominously against a fleshy thigh. His eyes seemed somewhat more deeply set, his skull was now a shiny hairless dome except for the three grotesque spikes of jet-black hair; otherwise he appeared no older than when last glimpsed two decades before.

Yveena Soolis and her parents had retreated into the shade of the walkway to continue their argument; Ryson and the Majestral of Gollimaul remained standing in the sunlight. Could this stout, middle-aged man really be five hundred years old? Ryson asked himself with a mixture of awe and trepidation as he waited for the great gleaming face to make some acknowledgement of his presence.

At last Lord Mesmer sighed. "You raise dinosaurs?" he asked in a ponderous voice that was not entirely hostile. "On Ambrose?"

"Yes, my lord Palatine. Brontosaurs primarily, imported from Gys. They are developing into an important market in—"

"I am not interested in markets," declared Lord Mesmer glacially. "Nor in tradesmen, particularly offworld tradesmen. I am a connoisseur, not a profiteer. You waste my time." He swung his broad stomach around, thrust his own loud voice into the acrimony beneath the walkway. Yveena Soolis instantly turned to loose a furious barrage of words at the majestral, her breasts rising and falling rapidly with emotion. Spent, she took a deep breath and stepped around her uncle to rejoin Ryson in the bright sunlight. Her lips twitched in a rueful grimace.

"They're angry because you're an outworlder."

"So I imagined. I hope I haven't made trouble for you."

She shrugged listlessly. "No more than I can handle." She reached down to take his hand, raise it between her own. She pressed it tightly. "An aircar will take you back to Carayapundy. I . . . I won't be seeing you again . . . at least for now. I . . ."

Ryson looked down at her in dismay, conscious of a sudden emotion of almost overwhelming intensity:

the same feeling of loss he had experienced twenty years before, as he was pulled screaming from the Hall of Durster. "But—"

Her lips tightened in impotent rage. "They've already intervened directly with the Thirteenth: I've been ordered to return to Amaranth."

"But . . . you can come with—"

"But I *can't*! I'm a cripple, don't you see? You're *not* a cripple, because you don't *know* you're one! But I *do*! I *have* to live out my life with cripples—all five hundred years of it!" Her head fell against his chest and her arms tightened around his waist as her body was racked with sobs. "Oh please, I'm so miserable, so—"

"Fah!" snorted Lord Mesmer of Frotz in profound disgust. "Be gone with you, outworlder, and at once, lest I turn you over to my leperons for justly merited chastisement! Fah! Imposing your filthy lechery upon my poor half-witted niece, taking advantage of her child-like innocence, even in the sanctity of my own—"

The angry majestral broke off, as if a sudden thought had occurred to him. "Ha!" Shouldering by Ryson and Yveena Soolis, he marched ponderously across the courtyard to the aircar which had just brought them to Green Vista. Ryson watched him go with a curious indifference, returned his attention to the girl in his arms . . .

Lord Mesmer climbed into the cool opulence of his Avalion Arrow, commanded the wall to seal itself behind him. He glanced around the ornately furnished salon, pursing his fleshy lips as his gaze fell upon the deep plush of the maroon divan, then stomped purposefully to the rear of the small ship. Here he touched a panel; the heavy blue curtain which concealed the entrance to the freshment room slid aside. The door dilated, Lord Mesmer stepped within. He ordered the door partially shut, tugged the curtain across the gap. Crouching slightly now, the Majestral of Gollimaul peered through the narrow slit into the empty salon of his premier aircar.

Ha! The divan was full in view! Nor could anyone spot him from there—particularly if its occupants were engaged in that infamous conduct which his duty as majestral of the zoïtie compelled him to reluctantly seek out and admonish . . .

Lord Mesmer inhaled deeply, closed his eyes in rapt concentration, and in absolute defiance of a thousand millennia of social custom and specific code, illicitly downtimed by two hours.

He opened his eyes, peered cautiously through the curtains. Ah . . . just as expected, there was his poor imbecile niece Yveena Soolis slouched against the divan. To his intense disappointment she was fully clothed, demurely intent upon the passing scenery. As he prepared to uptime by half an hour Lord Mesmer suddenly frowned. There was his niece, all right; but where was the wretched outworlder who was the cause of all this domestic turmoil at Green Vista?

Suddenly uneasy, Lord Mesmer swung sharply around in the small freshment room, his heart thudding in incipient panic. But no, the room was empty except for himself. Sighing softly in relief, he turned back to the slit in the curtains. Could the barbarian for some reason be lying on the floor? With Yveena Soolis sitting fully clothed on the divan? Absurd. Nevertheless, he pushed his head through the curtains far enough to ascertain that such was not the case. Now he subjected the entire salon to the most minute scrutiny. To no avail: aside from his niece the aircar was absolutely empty.

Where could he be?

Lord Mesmer tugged anxiously at one of his three stiff spikes of hair as he reviewed the afternoon's chronology. Uptime, at Green Vista, he had spoken to Yveena Soolis in his aircar approximately an hour and a half earlier. The outlander was clearly in her company at that time: he had distinctly heard them chattering to

one another in Versal. He had ordered the aircar
returned to Green Vista. An hour and fifteen minutes
later the aircar had duly arrived. Yveena Soolis and her
barbarian lover had stepped out, the guilt of their illicit
liaison clearly written across their faces. Then why
wasn't the barbarian in the aircar at this very moment?

Thoroughly perplexed, Lord Mesmer once again
peeked covertly through the curtains. There was
Yveena Soolis, still scrutinizing the scenery. But now
she half turned and spoke aloud.

"Look," said Yveena Soolis, pointing to the transparent side of the aircar. "Some of Glorious Old
Triceratops' preposterous beasts, chewing on the tops
of those palm trees. Could those actually *be* triceratops?"

After a moment of silence she spoke again. "Ugh!
Who'd want to eat thirty feet of armor plating?" She
paused, as if listening to a reply. "Somewhere up on the
northwest side," she continued. "They tend to be
obstreperous: thirty or forty years ago they ate an
inspector from the humane society. Got swore it was an
accident, but since then he keeps them out of the public
eye as much as possible."

Lord Mesmer's eyes widened. There was no doubt
of it: his niece was conducting a one-sided conversation
with an invisible man!

And—now that he considered it—was that a tiny
hint of coruscation, of flickering, a *thickening* in the air
beside her? And . . . yes! The divan was definitely
indented—as if an invisible being were sitting there!

Close now to panic, Lord Mesmer desperately
downtimed another hour. Once again he found Yveena
Soolis conversing with an invisible being. Heart racing,
all thoughts of illicit lechery forgotten, he uptimed to
within fifteen minutes of the moment the Avalion
Arrow would set down in the courtyard at Green Vista.
And still Yveena Soolis was alone!

Lord Mesmer could hear his own stertorous
breathing, feel the blood pounding in his temples. Once

again he uptimed, this time to the moment the aircar settled softly to the surface of his courtyard. Aghast, he crouched concealed in the freshment room as he watched Yveena Soolis step down alone from the aircar. He moved forward into the salon. From there he watched her bickering sharply with her parents, while his own earlier self stood silently to one side of the family quarrel, as if considering yet another person— one who was clearly visible!

The Majestral of Gollimaul staggered across the salon of the aircar and fell heavily onto the divan. "Up!" he ordered the aircar. "Take me up! Then . . . then . . . take me to Lord Zeeder's. With all possible speed! At once, do you hear, at once!"

He suddenly became aware of the grotesque fact that he was screaming uncontrollably at the inanimate mechanism of his own aircar and fell silent. He shook his head in stunned disbelief. Inadvertently, and totally by accident, he had just chanced across the single greatest catastrophe that Earth could envision: a human being whose time-track was non-existent.

He gasped sharply for breath. This . . . this . . . offworld *monster*: it was totally impossible to determine where he had been even a microsecond before!

CHAPTER 34

Ryson and Yveena Soolis watched silently as the *Avalion Arrow* dwindled rapidly in the sky and disappeared. He returned his attention to the lovely girl in his arms, opened his mouth to expostulate. Yveena Soolis forestalled him by placing her lips firmly against his. "I have to go," she murmured.

"But—"

"We'll meet again. Someday, somewhere, somehow. Trust me: I *know* it." She pressed herself hard against his body. "Remember what I do in the Thirteenth Majestral . . ."

A moment later she had pulled herself from his arms and fled across the dazzle of the courtyard. A rectangular black aircar with a small white coat of arms on its side sat some distance from the others. Yveena Soolis disappeared within, and a moment later the small ship rose just beyond treetop level, then shot off toward the east.

Ryson heard a hoarse cry of dismay from behind him. Lady Veenabon and the Marquime of Coborne rushed into the courtyard, gesturing furiously. Ryson surmised that their wayward daughter had compounded her sins by returning to Amaranth in their own aircar. He grinned wryly, stepped forward to incline his head with gravity. "It has been a pleasure meeting you, but now I must go. Mention was made by Lord Mesmer of an aircar to return me to Carayapundy: perhaps you would be good enough to direct me to the most suitable ship and give it the necessary instructions."

Lady Veenabon could only glare in outraged disbelief; the Marquime of Coborne stared in fury, took a menacing step forward. He opened his mouth, gulped a deep, noisy breath, then finally muttered an ungracious phrase in Terran. He jerked his head in the direction of the aircars. Ryson followed the Terran across the courtyard, his mind a seething turmoil of emotions.

Against all odds he had at last found the man he had sought across an entire galaxy—and had stood helpless while he disappeared into the sky. The single-minded obsessions that had defined his life for twenty years were little closer to being realized than before meeting Yveena Soolis. And here he was, forced to return ignominiously to Carayapundy, where he would be even farther from achieving his ends!

Numbly he stepped into the small black aircar which Yveena Soolis' father silently indicated, stared blindly at nothing as it rose up from the courtyard and turned toward the north.

Four agonizing questions tormented him as he helplessly watched the landscape of the vast estate of Tumbling Springs pass beneath: how could he take his revenge against his father's murderer? How could he rescue his mother and clan? How could he restore the Tandryl-Kundórrs' sacred fetish?

And finally, astonishing him with its unexpected intensity: when would he again hold Yveena Soolis in his arms?

Lord Zeeder of Mistane, the nearest of the eleven other exalted Palatines who composed the Duze Majestrals, was not in residence at his mountain estate of White Crests. He was, in fact, Lord Mesmer now ruefully recalled, attending the Tinctorian Games in virtue of his status as head of his zoïtie. And so, of course, were all the others. "No matter," muttered

Lord Mesmer viciously as he brushed past Lord Zeeder's gaunt majordomo and stalked into his private study. "In fact, so much the better. Shortly now, they'll have that . . . that *monster* right beside them in Carayapundy. Let's see what *they* think they can do with him!"

Seething with impatience, he was forced to wait until the close of the day's activities at the site of the Games before trying to contact his fellow majestrals. He passed the time by pulling open Lord Zeeder's drawers and closets, gulping a glass of clear blue ice-liqueur from a six-hundred-year-old bottle hidden in a dark corner. Now he decided to use the opportunity to call the seat of the Thirteenth Majestrality at Amaranth.

Here he demanded the attention of the Intransmutable himself, the wizened Allden Janders. Lord Mesmer snorted in disgust as he waited for Janders to manifest himself. To the rest of his twenty-four million fellow citizens, he knew, the Intransmutable was the revered symbol of the permanence and inviolability of the social order which the Palatines had carefully contrived over the course of a million long years. But to him, Lord Mesmer, the monkey-like Allden Janders was nothing more than the chief cripple in a city of cripples, a collection of sour spillbeers whose sole pleasure in life came from interfering with the rightful activities of their natural superiors.

A lifesize hologram of the Intransmutable, seated as always in his donjonwood chair, appeared in the center of Lord Zeeder's study. The Intransmutable tugged irritably at his insignia of office, an elaborate headpiece of blue, yellow, and turquoise ribbons. "You astonish me, Mesmer," he remarked airily, "taking your ease in Lord Zeeder's privy study. I would have expected to find a majestral of your keenness at the Games, adding your incomparable moral presence to the efforts of your zoïtiemen."

"Fah! Activities for demented children!"

"Such was not your judgement three Games ago when Gollimaul emerged as Preeminent Citrine and for twenty years the rest of us were relentlessly tormented by your strident whistling of 'The March of Vainglorious Yellow'—constantly off-key, I may add."

Lord Mesmer's tiny black eyes glittered with rage. "If *that* set your teeth on edge, you little monkey, wait till you hear of this . . ."

"But this is calamitous!" cried Lady Oänis of Syra when all eleven of the majestrals in Carayapundy had at last been gathered together by holographic image in Lord Zeeder's study. "The rogue must be instantly destroyed!"

"How sublimely you state the obvious," snapped Lord Wishaw of Purlym, whose zoïtie had just been classified dead last in the afternoon's activities. "More pertinent are the questions: how? and when?"

"Yes," agreed Allden Janders the Intransmutable. "These of course are the vital issues. It goes without saying that this . . . monstrous anomaly . . . must be expunged from the timestream before being permitted to set foot on either Mars or Earth, for his presence on either may have already set in motion catastrophic thrusts of causality."

"Then stop dithering, man," shouted Lord Mesmer furiously. "You yourself are only restating the blatantly obvious. Do what must be done: send your operators downtime to the monster's place of birth and delete his ancestors—all of them, back even to the fiftieth generation!"

"Sage advice from Lord Mesmer," acknowledged the Intransmutable placidly. "The problem, however, is this: because of the monster's peculiar ability to apparently exist independently of the timestream, it may well be impossible to trace him back beyond his point of embarkation on the packet which originally brought him to Earth."

"Nothing is impossible to a time traveler!"

"Difficult, then. This Lulmō Häistön claims to come from a planet called Ambrose. We can, of course, send operators downtime and off to the far side of the galaxy to seek out this Ambrose. In the meantime the chain of causality builds inexorably. I suggest that instead of concerning ourselves with ancestors to the fiftieth generation, we consider what immediate steps we can take to delete Lulmō Häistön as soon as feasible."

"On what ship did he arrive?" asked Lady Taum-Shu of Cobbset.

"A packet called the *Vagabond Princess*. According to information forwarded by the authorities at Long Horizon, this Lulmō Häistön was issued a provisionary visa at Cordeopolis on Phorophat Beta. He boarded the ship at Cordeopolis and eventually passed entry procedures on Mars."

"Scandalous!" snapped the Majestral Doyaine, Lord Blaibeck of Phaëtan. "Our procedures must be rigorously intensified!"

The Intransmutable shrugged. "He had adequate identification showing him to be an innocuous rancher from Ambrose. I imagine that he *is* an innocuous rancher from Ambrose, totally unaware of the chaos he creates by his very existence."

"You're saying that he doesn't *know*—"

"How could he? Who else has time travel except ourselves?"

"All very well," said Lord Gaugrich of Greenwood. "But what do you propose that we actually *do*?"

The Intransmutable's eyebrows shot up. "Isn't it obvious? I have consulted our records: we already have an operator in place in Cordeopolis on Phorophat Beta. The *Vagabond Princess* left Cordeopolis four and a half months ago. We will downtime by five months and send a message to Cordeopolis."

"And what will that message say?" demanded Lady Soldot of Quisk.

"It will instruct our local operator to take whatever steps are necessary to ensure that the *Vagabond Princess*—and its complement of passengers—never reaches Mars."

"You mean—sabotage?"

"What else?"

"And this will expunge Lulmö Häistön?"

The Intransmutable stared at Lady Soldot in astonishment. "We know he boarded the ship at Cordeopolis. We know he disembarked at Long Horizon. We will destroy the ship midway between Cordeopolis and Long Horizon, somewhere in N-space. Lulmö Häistön will thereby be expunged. What could be simpler?"

"Very well," said Lord Blaibeck of Phaëtan, exerting his nominal authority as Majestral Doyaine. "We shall vote formally on the proposition."

Polled, the Duze Majestrals were unanimously agreed; authorization was invested in the Intransmutable to delete the existence of Lulmö Häistön, dinosaur rancher from Ambrose.

"Very well then," said Allden Janders. "I will give the order immedi—"

—ately.

Four thousand miles to the northeast Kerryl Ryson stepped naked from the freshment room of the hotel chamber he had engaged in Carayapundy for the night. He was in the act of reaching for his shirt when an inexorable chain of causality was set in motion by the inalterable determination of Allden Janders.

Kerryl Ryson vanished.

At that instant Lord Mesmer of Frotz was supervising the evening feeding of Green Vista's latest household pet, a spiny nodosaur with glittering green and blue scales and beguiling brown eyes.

In Carayapundy, Lord Blaibeck of Phaëtan, Majestral Doyaine, was about to step into his bath.

Lord Zeeder of Mistane and Lady Danzel of Appis had renewed an old acquaintance; now they were strenuously engaged in games far more satisfactory than those they had witnessed that afternoon in the Prismatic Arena.

Lord Gaugrich of Greenwood, Lady Taum-Shu of Cobbset, and Lady Oänis of Syra sat high among the limbs of a banyan tree sipping wine; their discussion concerned Lord Mesmer's unparalleled boorishness in quitting the site of the Games, and possible means of making his absence permanent.

Lady Natchen of Caldo was dining in state with seventeen members of the Sodality for the Appreciation of Oblatic Aesthetics.

Lady Soldot of Quisk was in an aircar on her way to a romantic interlude two thousand miles from Carayapundy.

Lady Laizon of Baurauban was sitting by the shores of Resolution Lake, absorbed by the patterns of ripples as she tossed small pebbles into the quiet waters.

Lord Wishaw of Purlym and Lord Cundee of Cockaloupe had donned golden masks and black body stockings, and were eagerly anticipating the arrival of twelve highly trained leperon acrobats for purposes that were seldom openly discussed among the Palatines.

In Amaranth, on the far side of the world, it was already early morning. Yveena Soolis lay drowsily in the bed provided by the Thirteenth Majestrality and wondered if she would ever see her offworlder Lulmö Häistön again. She smiled wistfully. Surely with all the vast powers of the Thirteenth Majestrality for transforming the flow of time at her disposal, a matter of such trifling import could eventually be arranged . . .

On the other side of Amaranth lay Allden Janders the Intransmutable, now the only other person on Earth who had ever heard of an outworlder named

Lulmō Häistōn. He slept soundly and dreamlessly. Upon awakening he would wonder fleetingly if his instructions to the Majestrality's operator on Phorophat Beta had been carried out, duly scan the record banks for confirmation of the destruction of the *Vagabond Princess*, then turn his attention to more pressing matters.

PART FIVE

CHAPTER 35

"But you say that he was *deleted*!" protested Lady Natchen of Caldo, Majestral of Ingerton, to the Colloquy of the Duze Majestrals now sitting in emergency conclave in the Crystal Tower of the Adamantine Overlook. "You have shown us the record of our last proceedings, the order for the deletion!"

"Of what certainly *appeared* to be his deletion," replied the Intransmutable uneasily. "Once again I have verified the facts: the man known as Lulmö Häistön boarded the *Vagabond Princess* at Phorophat Beta. He did not disembark at any further port of call. The *Vagabond Princess* was lost in N-space. There were no survivors. Lulmö Häistön, therefore, was deleted. You, of course, Lady Natchen, will have no recollection of our previous discussion of this matter. But you have now seen the record of the conclave held in Lord Zeeder's study during the last days of the Tinctorian Games. The outworlder was well and truly deleted: the very fact that your memories of that Colloquy have been obliterated is proof enough that the timestream was significantly altered."

"First you show us a record of the deleted outworlder descending from the *Vagabond Princess* on the Tibbitane Plateau; then you show us a further record of the very same man disembarking from the *Meritorious Repose* at Long Horizon." Her voice rose, hovered on the edge of hysteria. "And there he stands, alive as you or I, on the other side of this very room!"

"But how, may I ask, can we be *positive* that this is

the same person?" demanded Lady Soldot of Quisk. She cocked her head to study the offworld captive immobilized by neuronic grapples between the four leperons. "He seems a common enough type to me, at least for an outworlder. Perhaps all this is merely a simple mistake in identity."

"Easy enough to determine," said the Majestral Doyaine, speaking softly into a communicator. "Whatever his other attributes, he appears to be more or less human." Two leperons entered the Crystal Tower, each of them bearing a small case. They bowed low. Lord Blaibeck gestured at the paralyzed Kerryl Ryson. "Now we shall see if mindflow works as infallibly with Ambrosians as it does with the rest of humanity."

Instrumentation was attached to Ryson's forehead and wrists, a spray shot into the side of his neck. A moment later his glittering green eyes bulged slightly, then glazed and closed. The leperons knelt to examine their instruments. "All is correct: your lordships may proceed."

"What is your name?" asked the Majestral Doyaine of Lulmō Häistön in Versal.

"Kerryl Ryson," was the almost inaudible reply.

"Ha!" cried the Majestral Doyaine, directing a triumphant leer at the pensive Allden Janders. "Already we progress, already we have unearthed what those of the Thirteenth were incapable of discovering! Now then, Kerryl Ryson, what is your planet of origin?"

"I was born on Stohlson's Redemption."

Lord Mesmer of Frotz uttered a startled exclamation. The Majestral Doyaine considered him speculatively for a long moment, then returned his attention to the prisoner.

"Stohlson's Redemption: a peculiar name for a planet. Tell us, Kerryl Ryson, why you have left your home, and why you have come to Earth under the name of Lulmō Häistön."

* * *

Two hours later the interrogation had come to an end. Another spray was directed into Kerryl Ryson's bloodstream and shortly thereafter his eyelids flickered and opened. Now the eyes of eleven of the Duze Majestrals turned to the Majestral of Gollimaul, Lord Mesmer of Frotz, who squirmed uncomfortably in his seat in the center of Lord Blaibeck's crystalline structure.

"It would appear that we have the esteemed Frotz to thank for the circumstances which have led this outworlder to Earth," observed the Majestral Doyaine with deceptive mildness.

"Ha!" crowed Lord Cundee of Cockaloupe gleefully. "A sight to relish: Old Triceratops drowning in a puddle of dinosaur vomit!"

The Majestral Doyaine inclined his head in evident agreement. "Perhaps later during this Colloquy we shall find a moment to focus our attention somewhat more narrowly upon the rather bizarre offworld behavior of Lord Mesmer, particularly in regard to that planet which he appears to consider his private game preserve. For instance: what of the one hundred and forty-six clansmen of this Kerryl Ryson who were carried off into space by our worthy colleague? Where, my dear Frotz, are all of *their* potentially catastrophic genes now to be found?"

Lord Mesmer waved a pudgy hand carelessly. "They were a contentious lot, hardly worth their fodder; none of the slave markets I approached showed any interest. Finally I opened the doors of the cargo hold while in N-space somewhere in the Abilet Cluster. That was twenty years ago: you may seek them out in N-space if their genes continue to interest you."

"But this is deplorable!" cried Lady Taum-Shu of Cobbset. "The despicable behavior of this so-called majestral, even with outworlders, is—"

"Fah!" snorted Lord Mesmer impenitently. "You think to censure me for initiating the events which brought this monster of depravity to Earth?" He snorted a second time. "Think again, O lofty majestrals! You should even now be extending me your unstinting thanks for uncovering such a dire menace to our very existence!"

"It is *you* that the outworlder wishes to kill, not us," pointed out Lord Wishaw acidly. "And, I may add, it's a great pity that—"

"And yet Lord Mesmer's point is a most pertinent one," interrupted the holographic image of the Intransmutable. "It is, I fear, the single most relevant observation that has been made today. Let us consider," he went on, raising a didactic finger, "not just a unique individual bearing whatever quality it is that renders him opaque and impervious to the manipulation of time, but an entire planet of similar beings . . ." His eyes darted to each of the Duze Majestrals in turn. "A planet of such beings could upset in an instant the stability and balance it has taken us a million years to impose upon a chaotic galaxy."

"Impossible!" protested Lord Mesmer, whose mind had already leapt ahead to where the Intransmutable's logic was remorselessly leading.

"Not at all. This planet with the preposterous name apparently circles a young, harsh sun. Solar radiation is fierce; the deserts themselves glow with radioactivity. How many more mutated beings such as this Kerryl Ryson live on Stohlson's Redemption, have already spread out across the galaxy?"

A pensive silence filled the Crystal Tower.

It was broken by a coarse snicker from Lord Mesmer, who had hurriedly contrived a means of diverting the conversation. "And perhaps we already have an incipient one here on Earth—in the very belly of the Thirteenth Majestrality!"

"Whatever can you mean?" wondered the Intransmutable.

"I mean that *you're* the one who saw fit to inform us that my half-witted niece had been seen in the intimate company of this monster from the stars. Just the sort of shameless behavior that one might expect from those of the Thirteenth, I might add!"

"What!" cried Allden Janders, falling back in astonishment. "This is cynicism carried to an extreme beyond my comprehension!"

"There is much that lies beyond your comprehension," retorted Lord Mesmer darkly. "Summon the trollop, I say; let us put the matter to her directly."

The Intransmutable muttered angrily, but turned briefly away from the Colloquy. A few minutes later the image of Yveena Soolis took its place beside that of Allden Janders. "Lord Mesmer of Frotz, your white-niece Yveena Soolis, Provisional Steadfast of the Primary Level."

The Majestral of Gollimaul puffed out his cheeks in spurious welcome. "Yveena, my dear child. I—"

But her dark almond-shaped eyes had already moved past the dozen majestrals to the immobilized offworlder on the far side of the tower. She gasped in shock. "But he's alive! He's—" She swung around to face the Intransmutable. "What . . . what are they doing with . . . that person? What are your intentions?"

The captive's eyes flickered at the sound of the girl's voice, then fixed her unwaveringly.

"So you *do* recognize him then?" demanded Lord Mesmer of Frotz. "He *is* the man with whom you shamefully—"

"He is the man who was brutally deleted six weeks ago, along with nine hundred and forty other living souls!" cried Yveena Soolis passionately. She stepped forward to partially hide the image of the diminutive Intransmutable and with a visible effort composed her features. Her voice was glacial as she spoke directly to her uncle. "I repeat: what are your intentions with regard to this man?"

"Isn't it evident?" asked Lord Mesmer with obvious relish. "The monster must be deleted a second time, this time with utter certainty."

"But how?" demanded Lady Soldot of Quisk. "I repeat: how? Since it now appears that he will have to be physically terminated, not merely deleted by classical expunction, we—"

"What do you mean?" cried Yveena Soolis. She whirled about, her hands lifted, as if to seize the Intransmutable and shake him violently. "I understand none of this! Why have you reanimated this harmless man in order to reexpunge him? Already, I know, you ordered him expunged once before. A shameful act! And now you—"

"It is not *we* who have reanimated him," snapped the Intransmutable testily. "It is he himself who has returned to Earth, surely the most remarkable and unsettling event in our two million years of recorded history! Our earlier efforts at deletion were apparently unavailing; the potential danger which we apprehended six weeks ago and took immediate steps to expunge is now amply proven by his very presence. We are obliged to try other means of deletion."

"But—"

"You were not present at the interrogation of the prisoner," continued Allden Janders drily. "You will, of course, be horrified to learn the sole purpose of this monster's visit to Earth: the assassination of your uncle, Lord Mesmer of Frotz!"

Yveena Soolis's eyes flicked rapidly from the Intransmutable, to the paralyzed Kerryl Ryson, to her scowling white-uncle. "It's a pity then that he hasn't succeeded," she observed coolly. She drew herself up, directed an imperious gesture at the twelve silent majestrals. "Whatever his motives in coming here, surely a human being as unique as this would amply repay the effort of studying him for a few days rather than deleting him out of hand in a moment of unreasoning panic?"

"Not unreasoning panic, my dear child," protested the Majestral Doyaine from high in his curious crystalline artifact, "merely a mature caution joined to a resolute determination."

"There is, nevertheless, much in what the girl says," mused Lord Wishaw of Purlym. "Far better to first determine precisely wherein lies the risk, and then—"

"Totally out of the question!" snapped his longtime rival, Lady Oänis of Syria. "The risk is self-evident, the peril beyond calculation." Her finger trembled with emotion as she pointed it at the uncomprehending prisoner. In a sudden spasm of venomous fury, she continued in Versal so that the captive might now be lashed by her harsh words. "There is no other choice: we must destroy *him* before he destroys *us!*"

"But what then of the world which gave him birth?" asked Lord Gaugrich of Greenwood in the same language. "The Intransmutable has already argued that it may well nourish—"

"It too must be deleted," said Lady Oänis grimly.

"You propose the deletion of an entire world?"

The captive's luminous green eyes widened in shock and he somehow produced a single terrible croak in spite of the neuronic grapples that held him rigid.

"But surely logic demands this course of action?" asked the holographic image of the Intransmutable. "And how many times in the past has the Colloquy already moved to act in such decisive fashion?"

"An entire world?" murmured Yveena Soolis in wonder. "The Thirteenth has already deleted entire *worlds*?"

The Intransmutable shrugged indifferently, his thoughts already clearly elsewhere. "Be still, girl, or I shall banish you from the discussion." He returned his attention to the Duze Majestrals. "What, then, is your decision?"

Twenty minutes later the Colloquy of the Duze Majestrals had determined upon the physical destruction of both the man Kerryl Ryson and of his distant planet. Far too much time had elapsed since the establishment of the original settlers on Stohlson's Redemption to resolve the situation by the manipulation of past time: thousands of years of established history across the entire galaxy might now be catastrophically undone. All natives of Stohlson's Redemption, therefore, wherever they might be found within the galaxy, were to be tracked down and mercilessly terminated by whatever means were at hand. Implementation was to be effectuated within the shortest feasible time. Of the twelve majestrals, only Lord Mesmer of Frotz and Lord Wishaw of Purlym registered their dissent.

"All very well," interjected the Intransmutable from where he sat before his priceless Heitzo tapestry, "but how do you now propose to actually effectuate the destruction of the man Ryson? You are now fully aware of the constraints which limit us."

"We shall have him killed," replied the Majestral Doyaine.

"Excellent. And by whom? You, Lady Danzel, you shall fasten your fingers about his neck and choke the life from him?"

The twelve majestrals squirmed about in their seats, exchanging quizzical glances. For a long pregnant moment no one spoke. At last Lord Mesmer of Frotz cleared his throat with a stentorian note. He spoke with ill-concealed sulkiness. "You mean then to actually carry out this insane notion of destroying this perfectly harmless planet with the peculiar name?"

"Such has been the decision of the Colloquy," said the Intransmutable with a thin smile. "I feel certain that in reaching it they took into careful consideration your scholarly interests in the local fauna."

"Fah! You mock me for my unselfish efforts!" The Majestral of Gollimaul tugged ferociously at his three spikes of hair. "As you are aware, my own interests are diverse; my experience in certain fields is perhaps broader than that of some of my more sedentary fellow majestrals." His cold black eyes turned to meet those of the prisoner Kerryl Ryson, and now they glittered with fury. "You may safely entrust the person of the outworlder to me; I will transport him to Tumbling Springs; there he will be dealt with in a fashion to preclude all uncertainty as to the outcome."

Yveena Soolis gasped sharply. "But Tumbling Springs is where you have your . . ."

"Exactly," replied the Majestral of Gollimaul with a complacent smirk, coolly disregarding his niece to sketch a courteous gesture encompassing his eleven peers. "I hereby invite my fellow majestrals to attend the subsequent festivities in person." He paused for a moment's thought, then patted his own enormous corporation with ponderous sardonicism. "I should say: those of you with stomachs as strong as mine."

Everyone present clearly heard the stifled cry of horror uttered by Yveena Soolis.

CHAPTER 36

None of the Duze Majestrals had availed themselves of Lord Mesmer's invitation. The neuronic grapples that rendered Ryson's legs immobile were
deactivated and he was marched stiffly from the Crystal
Tower by his leperon guards. The holographic image of
Yveena Soolis stood pale and trembling for a further
moment beside that of the Intransmutable, then
abruptly flicked out.

"A flighty creature, prone to ill-considered mis-
chief," observed her white-uncle judiciously. "Nor can
her association with the Thirteenth be said to have
ameliorated her conduct. You must henceforth keep
her under the most stringent personal supervision,"
Lord Mesmer admonished Allden Janders.

The Intransmutable scowled in barely controlled
fury. "The Thirteenth Majestrality has survived a
million years without the benefit of Lord Mesmer's
advice; I imagine that it will be able to do so for the
foreseeable future." He turned his attention to the
other majestrals. "I have already registered my most
adamant opposition to the peremptory personal vengeance which you have seen fit to invest in the persona of
Lord Mesmer. I now repeat it: think carefully upon
your actions!" The Duze Majestrals were silent. Allden
Janders studied them with waspish ill-humor. "So be it.
Kindly make adequate recordings of the proceedings
and send a copy to my archives." His image winked
out.

* * *

Ryson was marched by the leperons to the cargo hold of a bright yellow airship belonging to the Majestral Doyaine. He sat stiffly on a narrow bench against the bulkhead; a moment later the neuronic grapples upon his legs were reactivated. His four guards took their places around him; a fifth positioned himself across the hold, a small hand recorder fixed unwaveringly upon the outworlder. Only Ryson's eyes were capable of movement; they glittered with rage and frustration as they considered the confines of the hold, the ignominy of the recorder, the utter impossibility of escape.

The hatch swung shut, the ship rose smoothly from the landing field. The twenty-seven crystal towers of the Adamantine Outlook fell rapidly away, dwindled to become a flickering glint of prismatic light against the craggy mountains. Ryson sat helplessly, desperately trying to make sense of the incomprehensible events which had brought him to this calamitous pass.

Much of what had just transpired in the chamber of the Duze Majestrals was still mysterious. But what was apparently true—even if beyond the bounds of belief—was that he, Kerryl Ryson, was somehow subtly out of phase with the normal progression of time. The Earthans could travel in time; but they were unable to find his own existence in time past, and equally unable to effect changes upon his past timestream.

Ryson's eyes widened as a sudden thought occurred to him: perhaps it was *this* which had deranged the psionic brains at the Hall of Mercy and Judgement on Bir and caused his otherwise inexplicable exile to the planet Yellowjack!

But no matter . . . What did he recall of the interrogation he had undergone, the snatches of Versal he had overheard? Improbable as it now seemed, another Kerryl Ryson had actually boarded the *Vagabond Princess* on Phorophat Beta and eventually come to Earth. Here his strange temporal anomaly had been discovered and immediately been declared a menace.

Agents were thereupon dispatched into the past to destroy him. But now his temporal anomaly, activated by this threat to his timestream, had come into play; this time it had kept him from boarding the doomed packet.

The time manipulators of Earth believed him dead. Six months later another Kerryl Ryson had disembarked at Long Horizon on Mars and been identified by agents of the Thirteenth Majestrality. As a consequence, *this* Kerryl Ryson was now being carried off to meet a grisly doom at the hands of the very man he had come to Earth to kill!

Ryson's body strained futilely to break the grips of its paralysis; his eyes welled up with the tears of unbearable frustration. Twenty years of his life: a total waste; twenty years of all-consuming hatred and single-minded purpose: all now come to naught! His father stood unavenged, his family enslaved, his clan's fetish unrestored. And very soon now, upon the moment of his own death, the line of Tandryl-Kundórr would cease to exist . . .

The continent of Yuro fell far behind as the airship continued its westward climb above the gray waters of the Landers Ocean. Ryson remained motionless between his guards, his mind a raging turmoil. An hour later the ship reached its apogee on the fringes of space, began its descent over the green continent of Rurca. As the eastern seaboard fell behind, far ahead the sun began to glint on the blue waters of the Inland Sea. The ship dropped down across the vast estate of Tumbling Springs, came to rest upon a grassy landing field ten miles to the northeast of Lord Mesmer's residence of Green Vista. Here was the main depot for the matériel required to run the Majestral of Gollimaul's twenty-six-thousand-square-mile preserve.

The master of Tumbling Springs had arrived a few minutes earlier in his glistening black Avalion Arrow. Now he stood in the shade of the dozen long black warehouses and stables which bordered the landing field, watching with grim satisfaction as the outworlder was marched slowly out of Lord Blaibeck's yellow cargo ship.

Ryson and his guards stood blinking in the bright sunlight of midafternoon as the airship rose silently into the sky and disappeared toward the east. Lord Mesmer gestured at the guards. Ryson shuffled slowly forward, arms held rigidly at his side, his body paralyzed except for his legs.

The Majestral of Gollimaul appraised him coolly. "So you're the bratling responsible for that disgusting incident twenty years ago. I see now that I should have fed you to my lovelies at the time: it would have saved an incalculable amount of trouble." He glanced up at a distant speck in the sky. "Ah, here comes my cargo ship! Now we'll be able to—"

Lord Mesmer grew suddenly thoughtful, his eyes narrowing as he considered the leperon guards surrounding his prisoner. "What do you mean by recording my private conversations?" he demanded angrily. "Give me that thing at once! The Intransmutable only meant you to record when I tell you to! Is that clear?"

"Yes, your lordship," whispered the cowering leperon.

Lord Mesmer jammed the recorder into a voluminous pocket of his baggy black blouse, raised his eyes to the empty blue sky. "Where the devil did that ship go to?" he wondered aloud. He scowled at the sky, gestured at one of the leperons. "Go over to that building there, find out from the foreman why the ship hasn't arrived yet. And the rest of you: back off, go stand over there, can't you see I want some privacy?" The leperons moved away, and Lord Mesmer directed his gaze at Ryson.

"So you've come to Earth to find your family, eh? Well, well, so you shall—first I'll let you watch them fill the bellies of my lovelies, and then your own turn will come." He watched with satisfaction as Ryson quivered at the impact of the words. "Hah! You thought perhaps they'd been dumped in space? Just a small misdirection of the facts to keep the Thirteenth from nosing into affairs that are beyond its grasp. Actually, we'll find them scattered about two hundred miles north of here, laboring cheerfully as gamekeepers in my little tyrannosaur preserve. Not all of them have survived the rigors of tending my lovelies, of course, but I understand there have been a number of births to replace their numbers." Lord Mesmer smiled broadly. "Ah, what a feast it will be for—"

Ryson took one long step forward on legs the leperons had neglected to paralyze and with the accumulated rage of twenty-two years kicked Lord Mesmer just below the rotundity of his ample belly. The five-hundred-year-old Terran uttered a terrible cry of agony and fell forward to the turf. Eyes glittering with exultation, Ryson leapt aside and raised his foot for the awful blow that would crush the majestral's exposed larynx.

Dimly he heard the anguished cries of the leperon guards. Just as his foot began its descent, both his legs went numb and he tumbled helplessly to the ground, his boot brushing the side of the majestral's thick neck.

Ryson lay paralyzed in the grass, raging silently at the fraction of a second that had cost him his vengeance. The five leperons quickly carried the master of Tumbling Springs to the shade of the nearest building. A cluster of Lord Mesmer's own leperons ran out to surround their stricken master, and he was borne tenderly within to the emergency medical facility.

Twenty minutes later the Majestral of Gollimaul emerged pale and trembling, shuffling along in a grotesque crouch. His tiny black eyes found the form of the outworlder lying in the grass where he had fallen. Uttering hoarse cries of fury, Lord Mesmer limped forward to direct a number of feeble kicks upon the inert body. This had no appreciable effect upon the paralyzed Ryson; at last the enraged Palatine fell back panting, his glossy skull beaded by drops of sweat. Still raging, he turned to the three leperon guards who stood

nearby with their neuronic grapples. "Where *is* that
cargo ship? I'll have the persons responsible—"

Even as he spoke, the shadow of a long black ship
enveloped him. Moments later it had settled to the
ground and its cargo hatch was swinging open. "Dump
him in the hold," ordered Lord Mesmer. "Watch him
carefully and . . . where's that other wretched guard?
Well? Including the creature with the recorder, there
were five of you; now I see but four. Well? *Well?*"

The leperons turned puzzled blue eyes to each
other, glanced uneasily around the great black warehouses that surrounded the landing field. "He appears
to be missing, your lordship," murmured one of them
softly.

"Fool! Imbecile! Isn't that what I just said?" Lord
Mesmer raised his fist as if to vent his fury upon the
leperons, then winced at the effort and slowly lowered
his arm. "It must be the fool responsible for failing to
grapple the prisoner. Let him run: soon he'll know what
it means to meet my lovelies at first hand. Well, then,
what are you waiting for? Carry the prisoner to the
ship: he too has a rendezvous with my lovelies."

CHAPTER 37

Yveena Soolis moved with a terrible urgency through the spacious living quarters allotted to the provisionaries in the service of the Thirteenth Majestrality. Her unspeakable uncle could have but a single reason for taking Lulmö Häistön to Tumbling Springs. Unbelievably, he actually meant to feed the beautiful man she had once held in her arms to one of his horrible beasts! And the other majestrals had acquiesced in this unthinkable horror! Even the Intransmutable had failed to stop it!

She raced through an empty dining room and into the gleaming kitchens behind. Three pale leperons huddled together around an elaborate pastry. They eyed her curiously; heedless of their scrutiny Yveena Soolis pulled open drawers and shelves with frantic haste. At last she found what she had come for. She slid three razor-sharp knives of assorted sizes into her shoulder bag and ran breathlessly out the service entrance.

The tiny artificial sun that brought light to Amaranth was high in the sky as she hurried across the shady quadrangle of the Center of Advanced Learning and came to the lacy footbridge that crossed Lake Lewand. *Lake* Lewand! she screamed silently to herself. It was nothing more than a glorified pond, nothing but a carefully tended artifice, just like everything else here in Amaranth! Just like all of the carefully tended cripples of the Thirteenth Majestral, blurgy hothouse flowers, pale imitations of what real men and women were supposed to be!

And now her ghastly uncle was about to kill the only *real* man she had ever met, the only man who had ever treated her as something more than a crippled blurg! Her grip tightened on the shoulder bag as she raced down from the footbridge and approached the aircar compound. Well, let the monster try! Killing people was something at which two could play as easily as one!

An elderly leperon sat dozing at the entrance to the compound. "On the Intransmutable's most urgent private business," she snapped. "He has directed me to use your swiftest aircar."

"At once, my lady. That would be the Gossamer Lightning at the far end of the second row. Let me direct her ladyship to the—"

"You needn't bother, thank you." Yveena Soolis ran lightly down the rows of white aircars, the shoulder bag clutched to her breast. Suddenly she stopped short, darted into the space between two aircars. Leperon servicemen must be at work inside one of them: tools were scattered about the pavement. She glanced around, saw no one, reached down to clasp a rubber-headed mallet and a small metal hammer. Wedging them into her bag, she darted off toward the Gossamer Lightning.

Its panel opened to her command. A moment later she had settled into one of its deep chairs in the salon and was watching the row of aircars glide by as the Gossamer Lightning floated along the path that would bring it to Eternity Falls.

The actual passing of time was of little consequence in Amaranth: the aircar moved with stultifying slowness through the shady paths and past the ancient white buildings of the Thirteenth Majestrality while Yveena Soolis twisted her hands in anguish. At last the single means of entering or leaving Amaranth loomed before her.

A voice reverberated in her mind: *Attention: you are about to exit Amaranth. Have you made your time-check? Have you reviewed the Tree of the Three*

Spreading Branches? Have you integrated the Calculus of the Seven Forlorn Extensions? Have you computated all possible deleterious consequences to your temporal integrity? Be warned: by passing Eternity Falls you risk modification or obliteration to your temporal integrity! Stop and reconsider: have you made your time-check?

The aircar now came to its obligatory two-minute halt just before the great cascade of blue and green water that tumbled in an immense curtain over the entrance to Amaranth. Yveena Soolis sat with clenched fists on the edge of her deep white seat as she waited for the interminable seconds to pass.

How long would it take to reach Tumbling Springs in this supposedly ultrarapid Gossamer Lightning? she asked herself frantically. No one in the Thirteenth was ever in a rush: just what would their fastest flier amount to? Amaranth was on the east coast of Malangali a little north of the equator; already she was at least twenty-five hundred miles further away from Tumbling Springs than her uncle's starting point at the Colloquy of the Duze Majestrals in Schuizze. Suppose that Lord Mesmer got to Tumbling Springs ahead of her . . . suppose . . .

Her heart pounded at the renewed thought of her unspeakable uncle and his even more unspeakable plans. But even so: would she *really* be able to kill him with those horrible knives in her bag, stab his gross body until the hot red blood squirted forth as if from a fountain? She shuddered convulsively. Almost certainly not . . . Never in her life had she held a deadly weapon—nor had anyone else on Earth: arms of any kind had been unknown for nearly a million years now, ever since their final use in the forced exodus of the Great Rebirth.

If only I weren't a blurg! raged Yveena Soolis, if only I were normal! A normal person could have downtimed a million or so years into the barbaric past, returned with some horrendous nuclear disintegrator that would effortlessly—and bloodlessly!—transform her murderous uncle and the rest of the monstrous majestrals into pale drifting clouds of innocuous molecules!

At last the aircar moved slowly forward, began to pass through the carefully contrived image of falling water of Eternity Falls. A moment later it emerged into the natural sunlight that bathed the garden city of Serenity. Here the more venerable members of the Thirteenth Majestrality came to settle for a final century or so of well-merited respite from the rigors of their selfless devotion to the well-being of the planet. Slowly over the millennia an exquisite little town had grown up beneath the lush tropical foliage of central Malangali, a community of subtle refinements and sensibilities, renowned for its absolute tranquility, soaring aesthetics, profound scholarship . . .

Yveena Soolis took little notice of Serenity in the few seconds the aircar hovered beside Eternity Falls before suddenly rising into the sky at a speed she had never before experienced. Within minutes the horizon had become a hazy blue curve, the sky above the aircar the black of outer space. Yveena Soolis sat rigidly in her seat, the shoulder bag clutched tightly against the front of the plain white uniform she wore as a provisionary. She would have to give the knives to Lulmō Häistön, she decided—once she had freed him from his constraints. He was an outworlder, from beyond the borders of civilization; he had come to Earth to kill her uncle; surely he wouldn't scruple about the means.

Yveena Soolis looked deep within herself, once again recalled the pleasures of her brief interlude in the arms of Lulmō Häistön, posed herself a question. This time the answer was easily forthcoming: she would have no qualms at all about using a hammer to smash her uncle or anyone else who tried to stop her from saving Lulmō Häistön . . .

The Gossamer Lightning fell out of the sky in a great parabola that would set it squarely on top of Lord

Mesmer's residence of Green Vista. As the broad landscape of Tumbling Springs rushed to meet her, a panicky thought suddenly occurred to Yveena Soolis: how was she actually going to locate her uncle? And how was she to keep him from first finding her?

"Are there any aircars or airships nearby?" she asked the Gossamer Lightning. "Any, that is, within a fifty-mile radius of our destination, Green Vista?"

"Three, my lady," replied the ship.

"Give me more detail."

"One: a Stalwart cargo, now crossing the southwest perimeter of the delineated radius. It is presently on a course from Fairflower to Maudly. Two: an Avalion Arrow, just now alighting nine point seven miles to the northeast of Green Vista. Its exact course is now uncertain, but it would appear to have originated somewhere in Yuro. Three: a Polaris airship, just now entering the eastern sector at an altitude considerably lower than our own. Its present course will take it precisely to the same spot as the Avalion Arrow."

"And its origin?"

"Almost certainly Schuizze in Yuro."

Yveena Soolis pondered briefly. "Change course to a point fifteen miles northeast of Green Vista. Descend to treetop level, then wait for further instructions."

"As my lady pleases."

Yveena Soolis had examined the rear of the estate's warehouses under high magnification from the cover of a thicket of oaks two miles away. She could see no windows from which she herself might be seen; a moment later the aircar moved at high speed across the rolling meadow until it came to rest in the shadows of a small shed attached to the back of one of the long black warehouses.

Now she peeked cautiously around the corner of the building—just in time to see Lulmō Hãistōn break out of his apparent paralysis and deal her uncle a terrible kick to the midsection. She gasped with astonishment and exaltation, then half cried out in dismay as in turn Lulmö Häistön toppled to the ground under the assault of the leperon guards.

Could he be *dead*? she asked herself, panic-stricken, as she watched the five leperon guards rush the screaming Lord Mesmer towards the very building which concealed her. She pulled her head back around the corner, her heart pounding violently in her chest. Trembling, she moved slowly back to the deep shadows that hid the aircar, let herself fall numbly against its cool side. Dead? The man she had rushed around the world to save, the man—

Suddenly she uttered a half-choked sob of relief. Of course he wasn't dead! How could he possibly have been killed by the leperons? Their only arms were neuronic grapples, low-powered come-alongs issued to certain elite members of the leperon constabulary only in the most extraordinary circumstances. A grapple couldn't kill, it could only—

A leperon guard stepped around the corner of the building, his red kirtle and yellow breeches dazzling in the bright sunlight. He glanced incuriously at the small white aircar, apparently failed to see Yveena Soolis in her white uniform standing paralyzed against its side in the deep black shadows. The leperon swung around to face the warehouse, fumbled with the front of his breeches.

Hardly aware of what she was doing, Yveena Soolis reached into her shoulder bag and brought forth the heavy mallet she had taken in Amaranth. An instant later she had leapt out of the shadows and smashed its black rubber surface against the back of the leperon's neck. The leperon grunted softly and tumbled forward against the building. His mild blue eyes seemed to gaze up at Yveena Soolis in sad reproach. She hit him again, this time on the temple, and his eyes closed.

She stood staring down at the crumpled figure, remotely wondering if she had killed him, more immediately concerned with what she was going to do next.

She looked from the mallet in her hand to the assortment of knives in the open shoulder bag, to a small black instrument attached to the leperon's belt. Was that a communicator of some sort—or his neuronic grapple?

Yveena Soolis carefully set the shoulder bag on the grass behind her. Then hesitantly, warily, the mallet held ready to smash at the slightest movement, she slowly extended her hand toward the small black instrument on the leperon's belt.

CHAPTER 38

The cargo hold in which Ryson lay paralyzed had been used to transport fodder, fertilizer, crops, and in all probability live dinosaurs; so much he could discern from the ripe smell and the accumulated detritus from dozens of years of service. The four leperon guards fixed him unblinkingly with their pale blue eyes as the minutes slowly passed. There was no appreciable sense of motion, no way to judge how long he had been lying here, how much closer he was to his impending doom.

The hatch suddenly opened and sunlight flooded the hold. By straining his eyes to the left Ryson could see the dark trees of a conifer forest, catch a bare glimpse of cloudy sky.

A great voice came through the open hatch: "Men and women of Stohlson's Redemption, rejoice! Your personal redemption is at hand! Your days on Earth are ended, you are to return to your native planet! Cease your activities at once; gather your children and babes and proceed immediately to the ship; do not stop for possessions: all necessities will be provided. Quickly, now, quickly; step lively there, time is of the essence! Recall, moreover, the explosive bands which encircle your necks: these will be activated on all laggards no more than five minutes from now . . ."

Ryson groaned silently in impotent rage. The Immaculate Ultim of Aberdown had profited by his dealings with the Jairaben in more ways than one: he too had adapted their dinosaur bands for human use. Lord Mesmer could be doubly certain that any

Demptionists who heard his great amplified voice would shortly be climbing into the cargo hold, joyfully, heedlessly, unaware that they were about to be carried to their doom.

Helplessly he watched the remnants of his family and clan shuffle up the ramp and look uncertainly about the cargo hold. They were dressed in rags and tatters, but at least they seemed reasonably strong and fit; food did not appear to have been a problem in this semi-tropical game preserve. But their eyes, their faces! How gaunt and weary they were, how defeated and haunted!

Ryson lost count of how many had come aboard: twenty or thirty at least. The very old were too wrinkled and stooped to identify; the children he had never seen; many of the Coober-Weezlers he had never known except as the clan which he was to join by marriage.

Marriage! To a redheaded girl with yellow eyes and a squint . . . How long ago he had forgotten all that! Dalli Weezler . . . the girl he had been fated to marry! It could be argued that all the subsequent years of misery and grief suffered by both their clans had in some part been her responsibility . . .

Ryson strained to move his eyes from one group to the next, seeking Dalli Weezler. That leathery woman there with the naked child clutched to her thin breasts: her tangled hair was a dark auburn, her eyes . . . Impossible! That crone? That half-withered hag? Ryson closed his eyes in agony, tried to blot out this ghastly reality that had eventuated from his fatal gesture of puffing a load of chuzzleneck at the jowls of a strutting tyrant king . . .

The hatch shut, the cargo ship rose without discernible motion into the sky. Ryson listened to a babble of excited voices speaking the half-forgotten language of his childhood. A group of children came over to stare solemnly where he lay in a dark corner on a few wisps of dirty straw. They were joined by a number of adults, three of whom he recognized as cousins; they speculated softly as to his presence, thoughtfully considered the silent leperons and their neuronic grapples. Faces grim, they turned away to cluster around the ship's two small portholes.

Four more times the hatchway opened and additional members of the two clans trooped aboard. Ryson listened to shrill cries of joy and sorrow as families who had been sundered for years or decades were now unexpectedly reunited. But why didn't they rush the four leperon guards with their puny neuronic grapples? he wondered. Surely the indomitable Tandryl-Kundórrs he had last seen charging the neuronic disrupters in the Hall of Durster would never have hesitated; perhaps they had been made overcautious by twenty years of disaster, exile, and privation. And, of course, he told himself bleakly, their normal reactions would have been numbed by the sudden promise of a hope which all of them must have long since abandoned: that they were about to be returned to their far-off home . . .

Once again the ship set down with imperceptible smoothness and the hazy sunlight of late afternoon permeated the hold. This time the great voice of Lord Mesmer conveyed a different message: "Men and women of Stohlson's Redemption: this is the final stop before the transfer to the starship. Here the last of your clan will be joining you; in a few minutes the final journey will begin. Remain quiet and orderly—soon you will be on your way."

One of the leperons raised a communicator to his ear, listened for a moment, then gestured at the others. The grapples on Ryson's legs were deactivated and he was pulled to his feet. The ragged survivors from Stohlson's Redemption fell back to let him pass. Ryson desperately tried to make eye contact with the woman that might be Dalli Weezler, with a number of pitiful crones who might conceivably be his once-beautiful mother. It would be the last time he would ever see them . . .

Surrounded by his guards, Ryson was marched slowly down the ramp and into the ankle-high grass of a broad savanna. Two copses of dark trees could be seen on the distant horizon; the sky was an intense blue, piled high with towering cumulus clouds tinted rose and gold by the late afternoon sun. Ryson was pulled implacably towards the prow of the long black ship. A dozen more natives of Stohlson's Redemption passed him on their way to the cargo hold. Ryson halted, attempted to scrutinize their leathery faces; he was pushed inexorably forward by his guards.

As they came around the prow of the ship Ryson's nostrils were assailed by a familiar smell: the overpowering stench of the great carnivores. A line of towering stone stables stretched before him; their green metal doors were twenty-five feet high. Behind the stables was a cluster of ramshackle buildings; here were the miserable homes of the slaves Lord Mesmer had brought to tend his tyrannosaurs.

Ryson's heart sank as he saw what awaited beyond a flickering blue energy barrier in front of the stables: the largest tyrannosaurus he had ever seen. Even those at the Pandow Keep had seldom surpassed eighteen or nineteen feet in height; this monster was at least four or five feet taller, nearly fifty feet long, and broad in consequence. The black silhouette of the Majestral of Gollimaul was outlined against the translucent blue barrier, his three spikes of hair protruding like eerie horns. The tyrannosaurus tossed his head angrily and roared at Ryson's approach. Lord Mesmer tore his admiring gaze away from the great brown carnivore and turned to the outworlder and his leperon escort. His mouth tightened angrily.

"His legs," ordered the master of Tumbling Springs, and a moment later Ryson felt the familiar numbness in his lower limbs. He swayed briefly, had his balance restored by one of the leperons. "You're certain that this time he can't move?" demanded Lord Mesmer. "Very well, the lot of you go join my leperons in their office: I have a few last words to say in private. And tell my foreman to join me here."

"At once, your lordship."

A broad-shouldered leperon nearly as husky as Ryson trotted out a side door of the stables, bowed low before his master.

"Ah, the good Vaggett," said Lord Mesmer. "Vaggett, I shall be needing you, and all the rest of the station's staff, for a few days' work at Green Vista: exceptional new specimens are arriving. Gather all the personnel of the station immediately; tell them to take sufficient personal effects for three or four days at the most. Then join the outworlders in the ship. There should be one hundred and thirty-three of them; make certain that this tally is correct."

"As your lordship pleases."

Lord Mesmer returned his attention to Ryson, who was staring at him with stony hatred. "Well now!" he muttered somberly. "I fear that this will wrap up the affair of Stohlson's Redemption. Thousands of years of family tradition, hundreds of years of my own efforts, an entire planet—all destroyed because of you and your monomania! And now in addition I have to destroy all of these inconvenient witnesses such as the good Vaggett." Lord Mesmer tugged petulantly at his lower lip. "It *would* be enjoyable to let you watch your family being eaten by my lovelies, *most* enjoyable, but that delightful notion I fear is merely the poet in me coming to the fore." He shook his head regretfully. "No, all the outworlders, all my faithful leperons, everyone who knows of the outworlders, all must now vanish quickly and forever. The middle of the Landers Ocean will be as good a place as any." He patted the side pocket of his voluminous black blouse. "Only the recording of your demise will make its way back to old Blaibeck and the Thirteenth. All their leperons, I fear, will have met with some unfortunate accident. We certainly wouldn't want the Thirteenth poking their noses in my affairs in downtime, would we?"

Lord Mesmer turned back toward the paddock, looked up at the restlessly pacing tyrannosaurus. "A beauty, isn't he? They promised me he would be a big one, and for once the Jairaben told the truth. Would it interest you to know that this is the same lovely that ate your father? Hah! I see that it does." He limped away from the flickering blue barrier that kept the monster at bay, gestured at the leperon escort waiting by the stables to come forward. "But before we throw you in, perhaps we can conceive of some means by which you'll provide a little sport for my lovely: it seems a shame to bring you all this way just to be gobbled up in a few brief seconds." A faint smile tugged at his lips. "And perhaps my lovely niece Yveena would appreciate a recording as well: a last memento, so to speak, of her lover from the stars . . ."

CHAPTER 39

The pale blue energy barrier that enclosed Lord Mesmer's tyrannosaurs had been designed only to keep his monstrous carnivores within their paddock; transparent and semi-resilient, the great carnivores could charge it ferociously, attack it with their six-inch fangs, rake it with their foot-long talons, bounce harmlessly off its surface without damage to themselves or the enclosure.

The far larger barrier that circled the entirety of the majestral's tyrannosaur preserve was a brilliant glowing red: the color universally denoting danger. As the Gossamer Lightning followed Lord Mesmer's black cargo ship from a discreet distance of six miles, it approached the interdicted area at an altitude of three miles; the same warning that Yveena Soolis had heard six weeks earlier was now repeated in the aircar's salon.

Yveena Soolis jumped forward in her seat: she had forgotten this additional nonsense of her uncle's. "The aircar and its occupant are on official business of the Intransmutable," she snapped. "This preempts any and all priorities; adjust your defenses accordingly, and let us through instantly."

"This must first be verified with Amaranth. Halt your craft at once and transmit your specifications."

"Impossible! The matter is urgent! Let me pass!"

"Warning: in twenty seconds your craft will be destroyed. Halt immediately! Warning: in fifteen seconds your craft will be destroyed. Halt immediately! Warning: in ten seconds your—"

"Stop immediately," Yveena Soolis commanded the ship. The aircar came to a halt a mile and a quarter from the deadly barrier. She turned to look down at the glowing red line three miles below. The barrier, she recalled, was only a hundred feet or so high; could it *really* knock her out of the sky at this altitude? She posed the question to the ship.

The ship communicated silently with the entity that directed Lord Mesmer's defenses. "Only the lower part of the barrier is visible to the human spectrum," it replied. "The barrier is a sphere extending to twenty thousand feet; it cannot be penetrated from any point."

"I see," said Yveena Soolis, her thoughts racing wildly at this maddening delay. Lulmō Häistön had just vanished behind an impenetrable barrier; there he would be killed in unspeakable fashion.

What was she to do now?

The enraged tyrannosaurus pawed futilely at its five-foot snout with its two tiny forearms—forearms that were tiny only in comparison to the rest of its monstrous body, thought Ryson as he backed cautiously across the hard dirt of the paddock. Each of the forearms dangling from the almost non-existent shoulders was fully long as his own body, each of the two-fingered hands was armed with a three-inch talon that could rip him to pieces with a single motion.

Ryson hefted the puny eight-foot length of industrial-grade pipe which Lord Mesmer had solemnly tendered him. Unbreakable it might be; it was also far too light to inflict any damage at all to a monster as enormous as this one; nor would its unsharpened one-inch diameter ever be capable of penetrating the armor-like leather of the tyrannosaur's brown skin.

Ryson continued his shuffling movement to the far side of the paddock while the furious beast pawed at the muzzle of transparent tape which the Majestral of Gollimaul had ordered his leperons to wrap around the monstrous snout while the dinosaur had been temporarily immobilized by force beams. His back came to the soft, yielding surface of the pale blue energy barrier; Ryson pushed desperately, hoping against hope that somehow he could force his body through, knowing full well that it was impossible. However many additional minutes of life he had just been granted by the gloating Lord Mesmer, he would surely have to meet his fate within this four-hundred-foot-wide paddock . . .

The setting sun was now at Ryson's back, its last golden rays casting his long black shadow directly at the towering tyrannosaur, simultaneously bathing the monstrous dinosaur with a soft, rosy light. From a corner of his eye Ryson saw that Lord Mesmer and his escort of uniformed leperons had also made their way around the outside of the barrier to stand only a few feet behind him. The majestral's own leperons had all trooped obediently into the maw of the cargo ship—where they too awaited their doom, thought Ryson bitterly.

Without warning, he whirled and thrust the end of the pipe directly at the round coppery face of Lord Mesmer. The barrier yielded easily to his savage thrust, and for a triumphant instant Ryson thought that he might have a measure of vengeance upon the Terran after all. But within a dozen inches the pipe was forced to a halt in Ryson's hands as Lord Mesmer recoiled in panic. Ryson fixed him with his gold-specked eyes. "Wait till I dispatch this beast of yours," he said with absolute certainty. "Then I'll come for you."

Lord Mesmer's eyes widened and he involuntarily fell back another step. Ryson laughed harshly, reluctantly returned his attention to the great beast that so nearly filled the paddock. Snuffling loudly through its muzzle, and tossing its head in vexation, Lord Mesmer's gigantic lovely had finally begun to take notice of the intruder in its pen. Its small red eyes fixed Ryson intently; then slowly, ominously, an enormous paw as long as Ryson's body was lifted ponderously in the air, slapped down heavily against the hard dirt, its three great talons spreading wide.

Half a pace—and already the monster had stepped ten feet closer! The stench of its hot breath engulfed him. Ryson gulped convulsively, tightened his grip on the length of smooth black pipe. He and Sergeant BuDeever had occasionally fought mock battles with stout wooden staffs; what sardonic counsel would that long-dead mentor have for his pupil in his present predicament?

The tyrannosaur suddenly lurched forward with stunning speed, its ghastly head instinctively darting forward to snatch its prey in a decisive crunch of its terrible maw. With a gasp of horror Ryson leapt to his left. Confused by the binding that held its jaws shut, the animal's nose brushed Ryson's hip, plunged straight into the resilient blue barrier. Even in the act of tumbling away Ryson thrust the pipe without conscious thought—deep into the bright red eye of the beast. As he felt it penetrate he pushed with desperate strength, simultaneously trying to rotate its tip within the semi-yielding substance of the tyrannosaur's eye.

The great head snapped back, ripping the pipe from Ryson's grip, then the entire gargantuan body arched up in agony. Ryson rolled frantically across the dusty ground, trying to regain his feet. The roar of his own blood seemed to fill his ears; in spite of it he heard a loud wail of horror and shock: the Majestral of Gollimaul screaming in outrage.

Ryson bounced to his feet, ran swiftly to the far end of the paddock. The doors to the stables: perhaps he could somehow slide one open, wriggle through! His fingers scrabbled desperately across the smooth green metal; panicky glances over his shoulder showed the agonized tyrannosaurus hopping frantically about the far side of the paddock, its tiny hands pawing at the short black shaft projecting from its skewered eye. Its twenty-foot tail lashed fitfully against the side of the barrier where an appalled Lord Mesmer watched in horror.

The door remained immovably shut. Ryson raced to the edge of the next one, twenty-five feet high and thirty feet wide. He put his shoulder to its edge, pushed with superhuman determination. It quivered slightly, refused to move. He ran on to the next.

A terrible roar filled the warm evening air. Ryson's heart thudded in his chest as he whirled about: the monster had finally snapped the bindings of its muzzle; as Ryson watched, the protruding shaft fell from its eye. Blood poured out of the mutilated organ; the beast's red and black tongue snaked out between rows of fearsome teeth to lap at it tentatively. Ryson could hear Lord Mesmer shouting frenziedly. He pushed again at the unyielding door, lost his balance and tumbled headlong to the ground. The movement drew the attention of the monster. It threw back its head to roar a challenge, then lurched forward toward where Ryson lay sprawled in the dust.

Ryson scrambled to his feet, feinted two steps to his right, then ran despairingly to his left. Where was the length of pipe? Perhaps he could use it to—

A great paw thudded into the ground just behind him, a warm cloud of fetid breath engulfed him as the monstrous jaws snapped shut inches above his head. Thick drops of saliva and blood splashed his face as he leapt frantically for the pale blue energy barrier, caromed off it at an angle, and was halfway across the paddock again before the nine-ton tyrannosaurus could halt its enormous momentum and swing the length of its fifty-foot body about.

For a brief moment Ryson's eyes looked directly into those of Lord Mesmer, then he spotted the black length of pipe—lying in the middle of the paddock, almost beneath the enormous rounded belly of the rapidly approaching monster. He could hear the harsh breathing of the great beast as it rushed forward, see its grotesque forearms waving hypnotically . . .

Ryson waited a heart-pounding moment for the carnivore to commit itself in its rush, then broke to his right, sprinted a dozen yards, turned and darted straight for the center of the paddock. As he reached for the length of pipe he could hear Lord Mesmer shriek a warning—to the most murderous killing machine that had ever existed. Gasping, half running, half stumbling, Ryson's fingers closed around the pipe, then he was lurching forward, frantically trying to regain his balance. He glanced over his shoulder—just in time to see the monster pivot with appalling speed. The great green-striped tail lashed the air. Its leathery tip caught Ryson with agonizing pain just below the shoulders, catapulted him across the paddock in a series of tumbling somersaults.

Ryson smashed heavily against a green metal door; dimly he heard the reverberation of a great gong. Head whirling, he half stumbled to his feet; his knees buckled, he collapsed to the ground. With his remaining strength he rolled frantically sideways, just as a foot-long talon crashed into the ground beside him. The enormous shadow of the tyrannosaurus darkened the paddock; the beast bellowed with triumph as it lifted its paw to smash its exhausted prey. Even as he rolled over and over Ryson could see the three cruel talons of the massive paw descending toward him . . .

Yveena Soolis had long since given up counting the minutes that passed with such agonizing slowness. To have kept track of the passing time, to have tried to correlate it with what might have already happened to her lover, would have driven her to madness. Her body was taut with despair, her mind numb with anguish, as the aircar streaked across the wooded savannas and gently rolling hills of Lord Mesmer's vast dinosaur preserve. Suddenly just ahead of her, and closing rapidly, was the glowing red barrier that denoted her uncle's tyrannosaur reserve. Once again Yveena Soolis heard the warning voiced by the barrier. Her lips drew back in a feral snarl. "Faster," she urged the aircar, "faster!"

The Majestral of Gollimaul, Lord Mesmer of Frotz, pushed his round belly deep into the resilient blue barrier in a frenzy of exultation. At last the outworlder lay writhing on the ground, a footstep away from extinction! He watched the great paw come down —and miss! Somehow the outworlder had managed to reverse his course and was now rolling furiously in the other direction! Lord Mesmer's breath caught in his chest and his mouth fell open. What was happening? Once again his lovely had paused to paw at the blood that gushed from its mangled eye. Lord Mesmer could see the outworlder lurching unsteadily to his feet, begin to hobble rapidly along the stable doors.

"Get him!" screamed Lord Mesmer, imploring his beast to action. "Get him now! Don't let him—" His voice trailed off as the carnivore suddenly snorted loudly, then stalked ponderously forward in pursuit of its prey, its great brown and green tail quivering rigidly. The five-foot jaws opened, the massive head bent lower . . .

Ryson felt a sudden gust of warm air on the back of his neck. He glanced over his shoulder, saw the terrible fangs approaching . . .

And fell sprawling to the ground as a half-glimpsed black projectile flashed across his vision and with a meaty thud crashed into the enormous belly of the tyrannosaurus. The impact lifted the nine-ton beast two feet from the ground, then smashed it with appalling force against the rigid metal doors of the stables. Bones snapped and organs ruptured. The great carnivore uttered a single screech of mortal agony, then fell dead in a bloody heap.

CHAPTER 40

Lord Mesmer stood paralyzed in stunned incomprehension as he numbly watched the small black aircar float away from the remains of his beloved dinosaur, then lift straight into the air. Its blunt prow was covered by a horrid mixture of blood and dripping entrails; and it was obvious from the aircar's color that it could only belong to someone in the Zoïtie of Gollimaul . . .

His eyes followed the aircar as it lifted above the fifty-foot blue barrier, hovered momentarily, turned slightly on its axis, then set down on the grass a few feet from where he stood rooted. The four leperon guards backed away in amazement as the side panel slowly dilated open.

A dimly seen figure dressed in white stepped out of the aircar's shadows and gestured with a sweeping motion; the four leperons fell rigidly to the ground.

"But . . . but . . . it's *Yveena*!" croaked her uncle in disbelief. An instant later the rubber-tipped mallet smashed against the side of his head and he lurched back against the barrier. Yveena Soolis stepped forward, brought the mallet around a second time, a third. The rotund body of the Majestral of Gollimaul slumped to the ground, lay motionless. She knelt briefly, looked grimly at the closed eyes. Suddenly she jabbed a finger viciously into the folds of fat that encircled the majestral's neck. Lord Mesmer showed no reaction.

On the other side of the barrier Kerryl Ryson

watched with astonishment akin to Lord Mesmer's as the lovely Terran girl he had glimpsed briefly during his hours of judgement an eternity ago now hurriedly returned to her aircar. It rose briefly into the air, then to his even greater amazement settled in the dust beside him.

The side panel opened. "Hurry," called a woman's voice in Versal, "get in!" Numbly, Ryson climbed into the aircar. The panel shut, the girl spoke briefly, the aircar rose. It settled again beside the still form of Lord Mesmer. "He's still alive," said the girl breathlessly. "Can you lift him up, get him in here?"

Ryson looked deep into her eyes, his mind whirling with a million confused thoughts. What an extraordinarily beautiful woman! he thought irrelevantly. What could her role in all this possibly be? "Best that I kill him immediately," he said brutally, wondering what her reaction would be.

"No! You can't! I mean . . . Quick! Just get him in here and I'll explain! Quickly!"

The girl had just saved his life: no further explanations were necessary. Ryson jumped to the ground, dragged the inert figure of Lord Mesmer by his spikes of hair to the side of the aircar, then awkwardly humped the heavy body onto the floor of the salon.

"He's still unconscious?" asked the girl anxiously when Ryson had rejoined her.

Ryson knelt and briefly examined the majestral. "Yes. It could be for ten minutes—or forever. You never know with blows to the head."

"Best it were forever," said the girl viciously. She leaned forward in her seat, took Ryson's hands in hers. "There must be much that you don't understand," she said tenderly.

"I understand that you saved my life. For the moment that seems entirely adequate."

The girl smiled wanly. "To you I'm a perfect stranger; to me you're . . . well, we have already known each other—rather well, as a matter of fact." Unaccountably she blushed, turned her face away. "Listen," she said earnestly.

At the end of five minutes Ryson could only whisper, "All of this is true?"

"All of this is true," she assured him solemnly.

Ryson cast an uneasy glance at the crumpled figure of Lord Mesmer. "Then whenever he comes to his senses he can downtime a few hours into the past, warn himself about what is about to happen, and so prevent himself from lying here unconscious?"

"It would set up fearful paradoxes of causality, but . . . yes, that is what he could do. And what we must prevent him from doing!"

"And if I simply kill him?"

"If you do so, it has to be done so that the Thirteenth Majestrality can't simply downtime and undo it—and us as well!"

"Tell me again about this Thirteenth Majestrality."

Yveena Soolis spoke rapidly, urgently. When she had finished Ryson tugged pensively at his lower lip while he tried to order his thoughts. Suddenly his eyes turned to the massive black cargo ship on the far side of the stables. "My mother," he murmured urgently. "I've forgotten my mother!"

"Your mother?"

"In that ship—I hope! Along with the rest of my family from Stohlson's Redemption. Your uncle kept them as slaves here on this reserve; he was about to kill them all . . ."

"Yes, that sounds like Uncle Froddy," said Yveena Soolis contemptuously. She stared thoughtfully at the cargo ship. "But this is horrible! As soon as the Duze Majestrals discover the existence of your family they'll—"

"Yes: they're contaminated by the same genes as mine. I've got to get them away from here immediately, away from Earth. Can that cargo ship fly in space?"

"Of course. But only between the planets—it isn't equipped with N-drive."

"But your uncle must have a spaceship somewhere: he came to Stohlson's Redemption in one! It was enormous: he used it to carry away his animals—and my family."

"We could ask his leperons, they'd probably know. But you still don't understand: even if we use it to leave Earth, all the Thirteenth has to do is—"

"I understand perfectly," said Ryson grimly. "We'll take care of the Thirteenth shortly. First let's get my family away from here." He started toward the aircar's door, stopped short. "But before I see them, there's still another matter to attend to . . ."

Yveena Soolis watched in bewilderment as Ryson strode into the stables. One of the great green doors slid open; Ryson stepped out into the paddock of the dead tyrannosaur with a large sledgehammer in his hands. He raised the hammer, brought it down on the monstrous head of the beast. A six-inch fragment of tooth fell to the ground. Ryson discarded the hammer, raised the bloody tooth to wipe it against the dinosaur's leathery skin, then disappeared again into the stables. Yveena Soolis shook her head in dismay and astonishment: was this truly the same Lulmö Häistön she had known barely six weeks before?

With growing anxiety she watched him leave the stables and disappear around the prow of her uncle's cargo ship. Suppose that Uncle Froddy's leperons tried to attack him? Well, he now had the neuronic grapple she had used to stun the four leperons who still lay rigidly in the grass. And any man capable of fighting a tyrannosaurus with his bare hands . . .

She cast an uneasy glance from the mallet in her hands to the comatose form of her uncle on the floor of the aircar. What was *taking* him so long? Suppose her uncle suddenly regained consciousness and downtimed before she could hit him again? Perhaps Lulmō Häistön was right: he should be killed immediately. That, at least, would be one less problem to—

She jumped in surprise as Ryson stepped silently out of the shadows and into the aircar. The grimness of his features seemed marginally softened. "Your mother . . . ?"

"Alive. Not well, but alive. She'll live to return home, to Blue Finger Mill, along with my brothers; the eldest, Alvo, is now the hetman—I've given him the new fetish." A twitch of his lips might have been a wintry smile. "And my fiancée: she too will return home."

"Your fiancée?" repeated Yveena Soolis numbly.

"We were affianced at the age of ten. A small redheaded girl with yellow eyes and a squint. My mother told me that she'd outgrow the squint . . ."

"And has she?"

Ryson nodded. "She still has her red hair. And three children by the man she will marry as soon as they return home."

"Home! You keep saying that they're going *home*!" said Yveena Soolis with a sharp note of exasperation and alarm in her voice. "They're far more likely to suddenly vanish into thin air, along with the two of us!"

"We'll think of some way of dealing with the Majestrality. In the meantime, your uncle is still unconscious, and I've had a discussion with his stable leperons. None of them are eager to be dropped into the Landers Ocean; they too will come to Stohlson's Redemption. They told me that your uncle's spaceship is in an underground hangar about six miles from here. A full crew of leperons lives aboard. Their communicator number is AAAA-7777. I suggest you call them, tell them on behalf of your uncle to prepare for imminent departure with approximately one hundred and forty passengers. We'll include those leperons lying there in the grass, as well; your uncle has a valid point about not leaving awkward witnesses."

"You seem to think of everything," murmured Yveena Soolis, turning to look at the soft blue twilight that had fallen over Tumbling Springs. "And you: you'll be returning to . . . this Stohlson's Redemption?"

Ryson stepped across the salon, gently turned her head around. "What an absurd notion! You saved my life: by the customs of my country I now belong to you, I am yours to command. I have a spaceyacht in orbit around a sun fifty light-years from here. We shall transfer from your uncle's ship to the yacht and then . . ."

"And then?"

Ryson shrugged. "There are hundreds of billions of stars in the galaxy: you will have a wide choice. Someday we may visit Stohlson's Redemption."

"And now you really belong to me? What a curious custom!"

Ryson grinned broadly. "It's a curious world."

Yveena Soolis turned away from the ship's communicator, her face perplexed. "Something very curious is happening: the ship is already prepared, they're only waiting for our arrival to lift off . . ."

"But how can—"

"It can only mean one thing: that someone is playing with time." Yveena Soolis suddenly threw herself into Ryson's arms. "Oh, Lulmō, I'm frightened! I don't want to be suddenly blotted out! Now that I've found you again I don't—"

"Hush," said Ryson, tenderly brushing his lips against her forehead. "Neither of us is going to be blotted out. Give me one more minute to get my family started; then we'll be on our own way."

"On our own way? We're not going with them after all?"

"How can we? If we do, you say that the majestrals will merely send someone downtime to delete us all."

"But they *can't* delete you!"

"But they can delete *you*—and my family?"

"Me: certainly. Your family: probably."

"Then it comes to the same thing. And I won't let them do it."

"But what are you going to do?"

"The only thing I can: go to Amaranth and reason with the majestrals—as Sergeant BuDeever taught me how to reason."

CHAPTER 41

The leperons employed by the Majestral Doyaine to escort Kerryl Ryson had been swiftly gathered up and carried to the cargo ship; the ship had lifted off into a starry sky and disappeared to the north. Now Ryson and Yveena Soolis fled south to Green Vista with as much speed as the aircar allowed. Yveena Soolis sat nervously on the edge of a chair in the forward part of the salon. Ryson sprawled on a soft divan, his left hand fixed immovably around Lord Mesmer's right wrist by a heavy binding of transparent tape. The breathing of the Majestral of Gollimaul had become ragged and stertorous; his eyelids flickered; his limbs thrashed restlessly.

"I think he's about to wake up," warned Ryson. "I urge you to let me kill him. Suppose this notion of yours doesn't work?" He raised his left hand awkwardly, lifting with it the majestral's meaty arm.

"I'm *certain* it will! All of this panic among the majestrals is because you somehow neutralize their ability to manipulate time, at least as it affects you. Now that Uncle Froddy is actually physically attached to you, whatever it is that protects you will prevent him from downtiming, or anything else."

"So we hope. Suppose he simply wakes up and strangles me on the spot?"

Yveena Soolis grinned wanly. "I'd like to see him try! Anyway, if he does wake up, I have the grapple ready to keep him from becoming obstreperous."

"And this other ship we're going to, it's at his home?"

"Hidden in the woods behind. That's why I was almost too late in getting to you: even the Intransmutable's ship couldn't cross his barrier. First I wasted time by going back to the warehouses in order to get his own ship, but it was gone: he must have sent it back to Green Vista. So then I had to go all the way to Green Vista and land in the woods, then sneak out and steal another one of his aircars."

Ryson looked at her admiringly. "All of this for a man you'd only met once?"

Yveena Soolis smiled reminiscently. "It was a memorable once." She quickly sobered and leaned forward as Lord Mesmer's head began to loll restlessly back and forth. He snorted loudly, then began to mutter incoherently. A moment later his eyes opened and focused blurrily on her face. Yveena Soolis raised the neuronic grapple and adjusted it carefully. Lord Mesmer stiffened beside Ryson, with only his chest now moving. "Welcome back, Uncle Froddy," said Yveena Soolis sardonically.

Lord Mesmer's eyes moved rapidly back and forth between Yveena Soolis, the grim-faced Kerryl Ryson, the dark night sky visible outside the aircar. "Where are you taking me?" he muttered at last.

"Wait and see," replied Yveena Soolis ominously.

"Fah! Best you release me at once! Your behavior is incomprehensible! I may be able to plead mitigating circumstances. Otherwise your punishment will be severe, your—"

The girl's fingers moved on the neuronic grapple and Lord Mesmer fell silent. She turned her eyes to Ryson. "We'll be at Green Vista shortly. Have you *really* thought out all the consequences of what you're going to do next?"

"Not really," admitted Ryson with a sigh. "But do you have any better suggestions?"

The Intransmutable's white Gossamer Lightning fled swiftly through the night to meet the rising sun just above the coast of Malangali. Ryson dozed fitfully on the divan, his fingers still attached to the wrist of the rigid Majestral of Gollimaul. The morning sun filled the aircar; Ryson awoke, stared with blurry eyes at the motionless form of the monster he had come halfway around the galaxy to kill. Now they were inseparably attached together: could any irony be greater!

Ryson's thoughts turned to the majestral's great white spaceship that had brought such disaster to his life twenty years before. By now it should be deep in the mysterious regions of N-space, en route with his family for the planet Brynt in the Capella system, the world to which he had dispatched the late Baron Bodissey's spaceyacht from the planet Gys. Ryson yawned convulsively, as much a manifestation of tension as of fatigue. For the moment his family was safe; but in order to ensure their future safety he would now have to keep the most powerful men in the history of the universe from flicking them—and himself—out of existence . . .

Ryson tugged irritably at Lord Mesmer's rigid arm as he struggled to sit up. The only possible solution was to be wrested from the Thirteenth Majestrality; what would he and Yveena Soolis find in the sanctuary of Amaranth?

It was midmorning in eastern Malangali as the Gossamer Lightning settled smoothly over the densely wooded city of Serenity. Lord Mesmer of Frotz lay on the floor, hidden from casual view by a colorful blanket Yveena Soolis had found in a compartment beneath the divan. His left hand concealed beneath the blanket, Ryson peered intently through a side panel.

Only a few bright roofs were visible through the heavy canopy of tropical shade trees that covered Serenity. One hill quickly became more prominent than the others. Trees were sparse on its steep grassy sides; a great waterfall fed from some underground source tumbled across its lower slopes. As the ship dropped lower, the hill loomed ever larger, its carpet-like green slopes far steeper and more regular than any natural hillside. Ryson's eyes narrowed. "But that's a Remnant!" he blurted.

"What is?"

"That hill with the waterfall. They're scattered all over the galaxy, built by the Engineers hundreds of millions of years ago." He stared at the rapidly approaching cascade of water. "Is this the way they originally were, with the waterfall over the entrance? You must have downtimed and—"

Yveena Soolis shook her head in perplexity. "I don't know what you mean. That's just Amaranth. We—"

"Amaranth is inside that waterfall? Inside the Remnant?"

"It's certainly inside *something*. But Eternity Falls is nothing more than an illusion, and—"

"But then you must know who the Engineers are," insisted Ryson, "the Deliverers, as they're sometimes called."

Yveena Soolis shook her head. "When did you say these Remnants were built?"

"No one really knows. Two hundred million years ago, probably."

"Then no one here on Earth would know. I told you: those are the Forbidden Eras; downtiming is strictly forbidden beyond 995,465 BF."*

"These aliens you mentioned, the ones that frightened you out of the Forbidden Eras, how long ago in the past were they discovered?"

"The Ravagers? I don't really know; a couple of hundred million years, I suppose. I tell you: no one here in Amaranth takes much interest in the past; it's always too much with us."

---

*995,465 BF: 995,465 Before Flowering (of the Indomitable Perpetuality). The same date would be 641,766 OFR (Old Fallacious Reckoning).

"Doesn't it seem likely that the Ravagers are the same as the Engineers, the aliens who built the Remnants?"

Yveena Soolis shrugged. "I suppose it's possible. The Ravagers were enormous beings, as big as dinosaurs. I suppose that in consequence they'd build large buildings."

"Such as Remnants . . ." murmured Ryson pensively.

The aircar had halted a hundred yards from Eternity Falls and was now waiting its turn behind four other small white ships to pass beyond the cascading water. Ryson could understand why a black aircar covered with gobbets of mangled dinosaur flesh might have seemed conspicuous in the streets of the genteel town of Serenity.

"Let me get this straight," he said as the aircar slowly moved forward. "All the Palatines, the good citizens of Earth like Uncle Froddy here, can downtime at will with the help of a psionic amplifier."

"Except that they're not really supposed to; and in any case the augmentor won't allow them to go back beyond 995,000 BF."

"But here in Amaranth, time is held in a sort of stasis—it isn't affected by changes outside?"

"Yes. But—"

"And none of you members of the Thirteenth can downtime by yourselves: you have to use a machine to transport you?"

"Yes. But—"

"How far into the past can the machines downtime you?"

"I told you: only as far back as the Forbidden Eras."

"Are you *sure*? *All* of them?"

"Well . . ." Yveena Soolis stared blankly through the panels at the illusions of bright blue skies and distant mountains above the towering trees of the slowly passing community of Amaranth; the aircar was automatically returning to the compound from which it had come. Ryson watched her in an agony of suspense while she tugged thoughtfully at her lower lip. Suddenly she swung around in her chair. "Stop!" she instructed the Gossamer Lightning in Terran. "Take us instead to the Promptuary—the side entrance on Driftwood Stream, and quickly!"

Crime had vanished from Earth a million years before with Davour Dee Doe's invention of the time machine. The last civic disturbances had been recorded during the upheavals of the Age of Debate and the enforced exodus of the Great Rebirth a hundred thousand years later. The occasional rare violence that still flared up in the course of domestic quarrels was subsequently readjusted by the smooth intermediary of the Thirteenth Majestrality, with all memories of the incident completely expunged from the minds of the parties involved. The very concept of personal security, except as it applied to the planet as a whole, had been relegated to the forgotten past, along with such myths as hunger, manual labor, and psychotic behavior. Even the Promptuary, the enormous repository for the eclectic fruits of a million years of research and treasure-collecting, was totally without discernible protection or defenses. "In any case," said Yveena Soolis hopefully, "its only occupants are likely to be a few doddering scholars come to Amaranth from their homes in Serenity."

She directed the aircar through the Promptuary's broad freight entrance overlooking Driftwood Stream and into a cavernous warehouse. Two gaunt leperons looked up from the crates they were lethargically inspecting. "A delivery to the Whispering Gallery of the Arcade of Neo-Purple Revivalism," said Yveena Soolis languidly. "The Promptuarian awaits us there. Which service way do we take?"

"In the aircar, my lady? Without a manifest? His highness the Promptuarian had not foretold us of your most gracious arrival; this is all most—"

"—irregular; I know, I know. I imagine that the Promptuarian has his reasons; undoubtedly he will take careful note of your remarks. Now, then, kindly direct us: the Promptuarian awaits."

A glowing red nimbus materialized in front of the aircar to lead the Gossamer Lightning through the back corridors of the vast building; Yveena Soolis fell back in her seat in relief. "Where are we going?" asked Ryson curiously as one empty passageway slowly succeeded another.

"The Whispering Gallery of the Arcade of Neo-Purple Revivalism. I was here a year or so ago, just after beginning my studies. I think the service area to the rear of the Arcade is just behind the Testimony of Chronos."

"The Testimony of Chronos?"

"The Museum of Time—it's where all the great historical machines are exhibited: Davourd Dee Doe's, Vorbo wan Monchie's, Lord Leuten of Maul's. Some of them have been here almost a million years. But no one ever bothers to come look at them, not even the members of the Thirteenth."

"Except you."

"I came to see Lord Leuten's; that's my gigagreat-forebear who secretly brought the dinosaurs to Tumbling Springs."

"His machine is *here*?"

"At the time of his adventure with the dinosaurs, each of the Duze Majestrals had a machine; after that they were confiscated and destroyed—all except Lord Leuten's, which was deemed to be of historical interest." Yveena Soolis shrugged. "So they brought it here and forgot about it."

Ryson felt his heart racing with excitement. "And you think that it still works?"

"There's no reason for it not to. Why would anyone bother to dismantle it?"

"But after thousands and thousands of years?"

Yveena Soolis shrugged again. "The best way to find out is by trying."

CHAPTER 42

"What are we going to do with *him*?" asked Yveena Soolis distastefully, indicating the inert form of her white-uncle, Lord Mesmer of Frotz.

"Take him with us, of course," said Ryson cheerfully. "He's our expert on dinosaurs, isn't he?"

The Gossamer Lightning was nestled in the vast clutter of an unimaginable miscellany of crates, statues, gliders, stuffed animals, quarter-scale buildings, electronic contrivances, animated waterfalls, and glowing volcanos that crowded an enormous storeroom between the Arcade of Neo-Purple Revivalism and the Testimony of Chronos. The neuronic restraints on Lord Mesmer's legs were released and he was marched stiffly through the shadowy repository out into the Museum of Time.

As Yveena Soolis had predicted, except for its exhibits the cavernous room was entirely empty. Late morning sun streamed through windows thirty feet high that looked upon a gently sloping parkland and a shallow lagoon on which two blue and white sailboats drifted languidly. At the far end of Amaranth, just above the community's thick canopy of trees, Ryson could glimpse the turbulent waters of Eternity Falls apparently cascading from a rocky cliff.

Lord Leuten's machine was at the far side of a broad expanse of polished blue marble, protected from the public by nothing more than a long brass railing. Ryson shook his head in disbelief as he pulled the reluctant Majestral of Gollimaul rapidly across the room: were the children of Earth so totally unlike those of the rest of the galaxy? But for that matter, did these remarkable Earthans even *have* children? Perhaps they all sprang full-grown from laboratory incubators; he would have to ask Yveena Soolis . . .

Lord Leuten's time machine was not readily apparent as such: a small white platform surmounted by a narrow twelve-foot ring of shiny alloy studded with what appeared to be thousands of blue gemstones. At the back of the platform stood a glossy opaque cylinder eight feet wide by ten feet high. Ryson yanked the heavy form of Lord Mesmer over the exhibit's brass railing, through the ring of glittering stones, and onto the platform. Yveena Soolis was already pulling open the bulky hatch on the side of the machine. Ryson pushed the majestral roughly through the hatch without regard for his shins, then clambered after him. Yveena Soolis pulled the hatch to with a dull clang and spun a wheel to dog it shut. A faint murmur of humming machinery suddenly filled the heavy silence. Yveena Soolis looked across Lord Mesmer's shoulder at Ryson in the cramped interior of Lord Leuten's time machine. "Well," she said, "what do we do now?"

The Duze Majestrals of eight hundred thousand years before had not been specialized technicians, trained in the operation of complex time machines; they were imperious rulers whose sole wish was to use their machines with a minimum of difficulty. It took Yveena Soolis thirty-five seconds in front of the unfamiliar controls before the opaque wall in front of them suddenly vanished. Ryson found himself looking out into the sunny room of the Museum of Time. "*Something* seems to be working," said Yveena Soolis, reaching forward to rap her knuckles softly against the invisible barrier that now separated them from the museum. "Now let me see what *this* lever does . . ."

Ryson sat on the edge of one of the tiny compartment's two padded stools while he watched her manipulate one control after the other. Still attached to Ryson's left hand, Lord Mesmer of Frotz stood immobilized against the sealed hatch, his small black eyes darting frantically from side to side. "How long ago did we leave Tumbling Springs?" asked Ryson as he nervously watched a uniformed leperon wander slowly across the blue marble floor of the Museum of Time and out of sight.

"About five hours ago."

"Can you downtime us twelve hours?"

"I can try."

A few minutes later the sunlit room of the Museum of Time was suddenly replaced by a darkened room illuminated only by the feeble glow of a half moon shining through the enormous windows. "We're twelve hours in the past?" whispered Ryson in awestruck wonder.

"So the instruments say."

"You could open the hatch, then, and step out into the past?"

"Certainly. But right now? And why?"

"To find a communicator, and call AAAA-7777: the number of your uncle's spaceship. To tell the crew to prepare for space." Ryson chewed at his lower lip as he strove to focus his thoughts. "And to prepare them for the arrival of two groups of passengers: one group of a hundred and forty, the other—"

"Ah," murmured Yveena Soolis softly. "I begin to see . . ."

The Terran girl trotted swiftly across the moonlit floor, squeezed back through the hatch. "It's done," she said, her voice edged with excitement. "They're preparing for N-space. And now?"

"And now?" Ryson could hear the excitement in his own voice. "And now back to the Forbidden Eras: Lord Mesmer is eager to meet the original dinosaurs at first hand."

A hundred and sixty million years in the past, Ryson and Yveena Soolis stared in dismay into absolute blackness. "It must be night," said Ryson dubiously. "Downtime another twelve hours."

Yveena Soolis made delicate adjustments. "It's *still* night!" she exclaimed nervously. "I don't—" Suddenly she let out her breath in an explosive gasp of relief. She grinned in sickly fashion. "We're forgetting: we're still inside the Remnant. No one bothered to light it in 150,000,000 BF."

"I suppose not. But how do we get out? Is this machine mobile?"

"There are controls that look like an aircar's manual override. But suppose that the entrance is closed? It must be: that's why we don't see any light at all."

Ryson felt a prickle of sweat break out on his forehead. "You mean that we're trapped here inside the Remnant?"

"Didn't you say these things were built two hundred million years ago? Why don't we just downtime *three* hundred million years? That ought to put us out in the open air."

"Or a thousand feet underground," said Ryson, nervously recalling his experience at the Palace of Mercy and Justice.

"You worry too much," said Yveena Soolis with an impatient toss of her head, and she bent over the controls.

Bright sunlight suddenly blinded them. Ryson gasped, and raised his free hand to shield his eyes. Blinking furiously, he saw that the machine now hovered motionlessly fifty feet above the gentle swells of an endless blue ocean. Great yellow and gray clouds hung against a distant horizon. "You're right: I do worry too much," said Ryson with a feeble grin of relief. "Why don't you take us a couple of miles straight ahead to make certain we're out of the Remnant, then uptime fifty million years or so. I think your uncle is becoming anxious to see his dinosaurs."

Fifty million years uptime the ocean had become a swampland whose waving palmettos nearly brushed the bottom of the time machine. Ryson scanned the horizon: there was no sign at all of the glittering hemisphere of an Engineers' Remnant such as he had seen years before on the planet Azure. He gestured to Yveena Soolis; they moved twenty-five million years uptime. The swamp was now a broad savanna that stretched to distant horizons. Far away to the west, just below the late afternoon sun, was the faint outline of purple and gray mountains. As Ryson squinted into the setting sun, he detected faint movement against the mountains. "Can you take us over there?" he asked Yveena Soolis. "Slowly, cautiously . . ."

A vast herd of green and gray iguanodons of a variety Ryson had never before seen browsed tranquilly on the long yellow grass of the savanna. "Lots of fresh meat for the intrepid and resolute hunter," observed Ryson as the machine rose to fly silently above the thousands of twenty-foot beasts. "Over there: a fine little thicket of trees to construct a shelter. Green Vista II, it might be called. And over there? Ah!"

Ryson stared intently into Lord Mesmer's glittering black eyes for a moment, then swung the majestral's rigid body around to face a group of animals that had just sortied forth from behind a low yellow hillock on the apparently flat savanna. "A little closer," he urged Yveena Soolis, "but not too low: we don't know how high those things can jump."

The time machine stopped to hover just above the outstretched heads of two dozen yellow and orange allosaurs. Eighteen feet high and thirty-six feet long, the snarling carnivores hopped and thrashed with frustrated rage as their fangs gnashed the air just below the platform. Ryson turned away from the window to edge past the rigid form of the Majestral of Gollimaul, then carefully opened the hatch. A blast of hot sulfuric air poured into the capsule.

"Are . . . are you going to throw him out, then?" asked Yveena Soolis, trying to conceal her horror. "To *them*?"

Ryson coldly appraised the monster in human guise who had laughingly fed his father to a tyrannosaurus, then turned his somber gaze to the terrifying jaws of the great carnivores all around the machine. His soul writhed in an agony of indecision. "I *have* to," he whispered at last. "This is the moment I've dreamed of for twenty years; it's all that I ever lived for." He stared again into the baleful black eyes of the Majestral of Gollimaul. "There's nothing he more richly deserves. But I can't." Ryson slammed the hatch shut. "Take us back to that cluster of trees."

The machine drifted across the savanna to the dense thicket on the far side of the grazing iguanodons. Ryson prepared to disengage his hand from the majestral's thick wrist, was stopped by a sudden panicky thought. "But he can time travel without a machine! If we leave him here, he can uptime to just before we seized him, then dispose of us at his leisure." He stared bleakly at the paralyzed Lord Mesmer, wondering what dire thoughts could be passing through that alien mind. "So I have to kill him after all." Lord Mesmer blinked frantically. "He should be grateful that my mother and brothers aren't here to supervise the business; they saw my father's end; it would undoubtedly be protracted."

Yveena Soolis shuddered. "Kill him if you like; as you say, there's nothing he deserves more. But if you do decide to leave him here, I can assure you that here he'll stay forever. Even the Palatines need their psionic augmentor to time-hop; and the amplifier simply doesn't function beyond 995,000 BF."

"You're certain?"

"This is the first thing we learn about time-hopping."

"Then I have no further need to be attached to this monster." Ryson took a kitchen knife from Yveena Soolis's shoulder bag and turned to Lord Mesmer, looked him grimly in the eyes. "You should think of your niece often: she has just saved your life—for what it is worth." He cut away the tape that had bound them together, jerked his hand brusquely from the majestral's loathsome flesh. "Set us down at the edge of the woods."

The time machine settled smoothly into the high grass that stretched across the savanna. Once again Ryson sidled past Lord Mesmer and opened the hatch to let in the hot sulfuric air of the Mesozoic. Without further ceremony he tipped the majestral's rigid form through the hatch and onto the machine's white platform. With his foot he rolled the rotund body over and over until it dropped heavily into the grass.

Ryson looked down dispassionately at the partially hidden majestral for a long, bitter moment, then turned to the open hatch. He returned with the three knives purloined from the kitchens of the Thirteenth Majestrality two hundred and twenty-five million years in the future and tossed them into the deep shadows of the woods. "I imagine that you'll always regret giving me that piece of pipe to use against the tyrannosaur," he said. "I wonder if I'll ever come to regret leaving you these knives? Farewell: may your life be long and miserable."

Ryson climbed back into the interior of the time machine, motioned for Yveena Soolis to lift off. When the machine was thirty feet in the air Ryson leaned through the open hatch, directed the neuronic grapple at Lord Mesmer. A moment later the majestral had rolled laboriously to his side and begun to climb awkwardly to his feet. His three black spikes of hair protruded from his skull like the horns of a triceratops; slowly, painfully, he raised his head until his glittering eyes met Ryson's; his mouth opened.

Ryson turned his back on the howls and imprecations and slammed the hatch shut. Rivulets of warm sweat ran down his face. "Uptime," he said to a somber Yveena Soolis. "Another twenty-five million years. Let's find out exactly why the Ravagers frighten the majestrals so much."

CHAPTER 43

The Ravagers were remarkably easy to find. Seventeen million years uptime from where they had left Lord Mesmer of Frotz the time machine reappeared in the shadows of a low mountain range that in the intervening ages had been thrust into existence. Three miles away an enormous blue-gray sphere glittered in the sunlight. Ryson and Yveena Soolis stared in silent awe. The Remnant stormed by Ryson on Azure had been half buried in a desert, its scale difficult to judge; this one stood majestically free, the mighty curve of its mile-and-a-half diameter sunk twenty yards deep in the surrounding bedrock.

Yveena Soolis shook her head in wonder. "Is *that* Amaranth?"

"The top half, at any rate. See that dark spot halfway up the right side? That's the entrance where you've put the waterfall."

"But it's so *enormous*! And just sitting there in the middle of the fields like . . . like a gigantic beachball! What can they possibly use it for?"

Ryson could only shake his head.

"Look!" Yveena Soolis gripped his arm in alarm. "Coming out of the entrance—ships! And in this direction!"

"Didn't you want to ask them to what purpose they put the Remnant?"

Yveena Soolis hissed angrily; a moment later they had jumped a million years uptime.

* * *

Locating the Remnant had been easy; finding the Ravagers in precisely the circumstances that Ryson sought took another seventy-seven hours of time-hopping. Three times they slept on the time machine's platform under starry tropical skies; two hundred and forty times they shuttled back and forth across twenty million years of the Mesozoic, searching, always searching. Ryson pondered the girl's account of Vorbo wan Monchie's encounter with the Ravagers and refused to give up hope. At last, forty thousand years downtime from their first glimpse of the unburied Remnant, and two thousand miles to the northwest, they sighted what Ryson had begun to despair of ever finding: the Ravagers engaged in furious activity with hundreds of thousands of frantic dinosaurs.

Like the sortie of Vorbo wan Monchie which had initially discovered the Ravagers, Ryson and Yveena Soolis were concealed in the purple shadows of a craggy mountain range. Below stretched a vast yellow savanna, mile upon mile of which was covered by the greatest collection of dinosaurs a human being had ever seen. How the Ravagers had ever assembled so colossal a grouping of the enormous beasts Ryson could not imagine.

Side by side, each species apparently segregated from the others by invisible barriers, milled thousands upon thousands of agitated duckbills, allosaurs, iguanodons, brachiosaurs, stegosaurs, ankylosaurs, hypsilophodontids, and titanosaurs. Carnivores, herbivores, long-necked diplodocuses, squatty scelidosaurs, agile bird-like saurornithoides, howling boneheads, roaring megalosaurs, yellow, brown, orange, green, and gray, a hundred varieties of beasts screamed and raged and pawed furiously at the ground. Far across the plain they stretched, until details blurred and Ryson could discern only a seething, multi-colored mass.

Not far below the time machine, in the cool shadows at the base of the mountains, were the Ravagers and their camp, for in spite of the gigantic size of their eight windowless structures an indefinable air of impermanence hung over the small settlement. At the sight of the grotesque aliens Ryson's tongue recoiled in his mouth, and he understood instantly why Vorbo wan Monchie and his party had fled back to Palatine Earth and forever closed the gates of time upon the Forbidden Eras.

Thirty feet high, with six great legs to support their bulk, the yellow and blue monsters had broad, flat faces so hideous that even the hungriest of tyrannosaurs might have paused to reconsider their value as a potential meal. The two or three hundred that Ryson could see moving purposefully from one shiny pale blue building to another bounded with an improbable lightness and grace that made him wonder if they could be entirely substantial in being; surely with that size they must mass as much as the largest brachiosaur; and equally surely no brachiosaur had ever leapt and gamboled with such startling ease!

Two gigantic white spaceships of cylindrical design lay in the grass beyond the cluster of buildings. Another two dozen aircraft, little more than airborne chairs, shuttled their single occupants back and forth across the heads of the milling dinosaurs. Most of these Ravagers seemed equipped with elaborate machinery which to Ryson's inexperienced eye nevertheless suggested recording equipment. Suddenly a great gong-like peal tolled across the plain, clearly audible to Ryson and Yveena Soolis over the time machine's sensors.

The frantic activity of the Ravagers came to a sudden halt; from the side of one of the ships stepped forth two more Ravagers. The blue and yellow markings of their gleaming pelts far outshone those of their more pedestrian fellows; even by the fearful standards set by the Ravagers their facial traits were of an unspeakable ghastliness. The other Ravagers fell back as if in awe, and the couple proceeded like royalty to an awaiting aircar. They disappeared into its interior; a moment later the aircar shot off towards the far end of the sea of howling dinosaurs. Immediately upon their departure the remaining Ravagers returned to their own feverish activities, and another dozen aircars took to the air.

Ryson and Yveena Soolis exchanged quizzical looks. "What on earth can they be doing?" murmured Yveena Soolis.

"The late Baron Bodissey, an anthropologist of repute, would almost surely have said that they are engaged in a religious rite of some nature; it appears to be a universal compulsion."

"But you don't agree."

Ryson shook his head. "Consider all of those recorders flying about, look at—"

He was interrupted by the sudden eruption of a wall of red and orange flames on three sides of the vast corral of dinosaurs. An agonizing shriek of an electronic nature simultaneously seemed to skewer his brain from all directions and leave it battered and quivering. Yveena Soolis slapped a trembling hand to disable the auditory system. Gasping with shock, they looked down upon a plain on which a million panic-stricken dinosaurs were now in concerted motion, bolting forward in mindless flight.

"Look!" cried Ryson with elation. "The greatest stampede in the history of the universe!"

"A stampede? But why?"

"Holographic adventure movies? Look at all of those aircars chasing the dinosaurs from every angle: doesn't that look like recording equipment to you?"

Yveena Soolis blinked, leaned forward, squinted into the distance. The enormous herd of rampaging dinosaurs had already outpaced the flaming savanna grasses by hundreds of yards but showed no signs of abating its mad rush forward. Most of the Ravagers from the camp were also in motion, some of them trotting easily alongside the perimeter of the flames, others darting back and forth above the herd in sudden manic swoops of their aircars. Yveena Soolis turned her almond-shaped eyes to Ryson. "I don't suppose that you're now going to say that all of these vast, inexplicable, totally indestructible spheres that the

Ravagers have left all over the galaxy are actually nothing but their *movie theaters*?"

Ryson grinned. "*I* wasn't. But now that *you* make the suggestion, I feel certain you're right. Perhaps someday some interested member of the Thirteenth Majestrality can ask them . . ." He pointed to the distant horizon. "Can you take us over there, perhaps ten or fifteen minutes downtime, right at the point where all of those monsters are headed?"

While combing through the Mesozoic for the Ravagers, Ryson had had three full days to absorb as much practical knowledge as Yveena Soolis could impart about the functioning of her gigagreat-forebear's time machine. For tiny as the machine was, this was still the same apparatus that her ancestor had used to scoop up and transport hundreds of beasts eighty feet long . . .

"It's the aperture-ring on the front of the platform," explained Yveena Soolis, indicating the frail upright alloy band set with thousands of blue gemstones. "It generates a field up to two hundred yards wide. Anything that enters it is sent uptime and out the ring in the opposite direction."

Ryson ran his hands through his curly brown hair and sighed plaintively. "If I understand you correctly, both we and the machine are right here in the Mesozoic, moving freely about all over the planet; two hundred million years in the future this same machine is still right where we left it, ready to spew out anything we push into it." He sighed a second time. "It doesn't make sense."

"Very little about time-hopping makes sense," agreed Yveena Soolis solemnly.

Now she took them downtime twenty thousand years into a warm Mesozoic drizzle. The same yellow savanna stretched before them, this time devoid of animal life. The machine flew away from the shelter of the mountains and off across the broad plain until Ryson judged they were a mile or so beyond the far end of the great assemblage of dinosaurs. He leaned forward on the edge of his stool, his face gaunt with tension. "Just be ready to get us out of here instantly if we've made a mistake," he advised unnecessarily.

Yveena Soolis scowled and nodded brusquely. Her fingers moved over the controls.

The machine uptimed twenty thousand years—to materialize directly in front of the two garishly colored Ravagers Ryson and Yveena Soolis had last seen flying off in an aircar above the seething mass of dinosaurs.

Now the two hideous aliens came galloping and bounding across the burning savanna in apparently witless panic, their six churning legs a flickering blur of motion. Two hundred yards behind them, gasping and screaming, rushed the vanguard of a million maddened dinosaurs.

A six-ton yellow and green allosaurus surged a few yards ahead of the pack, stumbled slightly, and disappeared forever beneath the feet of the following herd. And now the smaller of the two Ravagers suddenly stumbled in turn, rolling over and over through the savanna grass. The other enormous Ravager instantly spun to a halt, leapt back through the grass. The gigantic form bent over its companion, lifted it tenderly to its feet; the two raced on just before they could be overwhelmed by the rush of dinosaurs.

Inside the time machine, Ryson braced himself against the control panel, heard himself drawing a ragged breath. Ten million tons of living flesh were about to engulf them: if any of Yveena Soolis' calculations had been wrong they would hardly have the time to—

The two terrifying Ravagers loomed up just before the machine, hesitated for a bare instant at seeing the construct for the first time, then leapt powerfully into the air in order to bound high above this strange object in their path.

Ryson jerked his head up just in time to watch the ends of their enormous yellow and blue bodies disappear as if into an invisible hole in the sky. A moment later nine hundred terrified duckbills and allosaurs thundered straight toward the time machine, unable to alter course. Behind them, and to all sides, was a solid wall of howling dinosaurs. Ryson squeezed Yveena Soolis tight in his arms as the duckbills drew near, seemed about to bury them beneath their mottled brown flesh . . .

It was a quiet afternoon in Amaranth—except for Allden Janders the Intransmutable, who had been frantically summoned to the communicator by a provisionary research student deep in the recesses of the Promptuary. If the Intransmutable had understood him correctly, the provisionary was asserting the unthinkable: that one of the time machines exhibited in the Testimony of Chronos was in actual operation!

The Promptuarian had been alerted, a dozen antiquarians and leperon technicians summoned. Now they stood troubled and baffled on the small white platform of Lord Leuten's time machine, staring helplessly at the opaque cylinder of the control room. Six tiny red lights flickered in sequence around its top, while its hatch resisted all efforts to open it.

"It's definitely drawing from the central power grid," said one of the technicians as he consulted a battery of instruments. "In fact, it would seem to have been doing so for three or four days now."

"And no one noticed this, no one thought to notify me?" cried the Intransmutable in a rage. He whirled to confront the trembling Promptuarian. "Incompetent dunderhead! How can you—"

He was interrupted by an antiquarian tugging urgently at his sleeve. "Look—that blue light has just come on . . ."

"What catastrophe does *that* foretell?" demanded Allden Janders harshly of the leperon technicians.

"That . . . that the machine is about . . . about to transmit, O highness," babbled the leperon.

"Transmit?" snapped the Intransmutable. "What could it possibly be trans—"

Two thirty-foot Ravagers materialized in the air

just above his head, alit gracefully on the polished blue-marble floor. As the Intransmutable watched in numb astonishment their momentum carried the great yellow and blue monsters swiftly across the slick flooring and with a shattering crash out through the broad windows of the Promptuary.

Allden Janders staggered backwards in shock, falling into the arms of an aghast leperon, as a heavy cloud of warm damp air with a sharp tang of sulfur settled upon them. A moment later the first of the duckbills came racing through the aperture and out into the hushed silence of the Museum of Time. As they too crashed through the already shattered windows that gave onto the pastoral vista of midafternoon Amaranth, the main body of the stampeding herd began to pour through an opening in time that stretched two hundred yards wide.

In the initial three seconds of their onslaught two hundred and eighty-three duckbills, allosaurs, and megalosaurs had leapt through from the Mesozoic; now the entire east wall of the Promptuary began to buckle. The Intransmutable watched in utter disbelief as a tiny aircar bearing a gigantic Ravager materialized in the air above him, then crashed with a stunning explosion against the top of the distant wall.

Frantic hands pulled the Intransmutable off the platform and into the shelter of a deep wall embrasure just as the upper floors of the Promptuary began to collapse with a deafening roar upon the backs of the streaming monsters. An impenetrable cloud of dust quickly shrouded what had once been the sheltered cloisters of the Testimony of Chronos, but as he was hustled down a shadowy passageway the Intransmutable retained a last vivid image: that of a thousand rampaging monsters and aliens investing the quiet parkland of Amaranth, all of them set on a direct course for Eternity Falls and the tranquil retirement community of Serenity . . .

CHAPTER 44

As the last of the dinosaurs stampeded from the Mesozoic into the far future, accompanied by several score of baffled but resolute Ravager cameramen, second directors, and assistant producers, Yveena Soolis downtimed the machine fifty million years into the past. She and Ryson were weary from near-hysterical laughter at the thought of the chaos that by now must have enveloped all of Amaranth.

"How vexed the Intransmutable must be!" gasped Yveena Soolis, threatening to lapse once again into uncontrollable giggling.

"As well as the rest of the majestrals," agreed Ryson. "Best we be on our way before they think to come looking for us."

"With their city and time machines full of Ravagers? They'll *never* be able to look for us!"

"So we hope," said Ryson drily. He moved to the control panel of Lord Leuten's time machine. "Tumbling Springs is halfway around the world; how long do you think it will take us to reach it from here?"

With Yveena Soolis once again at the controls, the long black warehouses and cargo ship belonging to Lord Mesmer of Frotz came into view a few miles to the southwest. Yveena Soolis consulted the machine's chronograph. "I think they must be just about ready to lift off in order to start collecting your family," she said. "Would you like to downtime a few minutes to watch yourself kicking Uncle Froddy?"

Ryson shook his head. "I've had my revenge; let's

leave well enough alone. I still don't fully understand why you wanted to come back precisely here."

"My compulsion to tidy up loose ends. That leperon I knocked unconscious behind the warehouse: I don't want any of the majestrals or the Thirteenth snooping around in time and coming across him before we have a chance to get to the time machine. Don't forget: at any moment at all we could have been stopped by a few words at that Colloquy in the Crystal Tower. And we still could be!"

Ryson nodded, a knot of tension in the pit of his stomach. "Whatever you think best, then. I'm just anxious to be aboard ship and off in N-space."

Yveena Soolis let her breath out softly. "So am I, my love, so am I."

The time machine had settled down beside the densely wooded mountainside in which the Majestral of Gollimaul concealed his enormous white spacecraft in an underground facility. Yveena Soolis had taken aboard the leperon guard they had collected without incident from the grass at the base of Lord Mesmer's warehouse. Ryson had wanted to bring the time machine aboard, to use in the hunt for the agents the Thirteenth Majestrality had dispatched to effectuate the destruction of Stohlson's Redemption.

Yveena Soolis had objected vigorously. "You'll just have to find some other way to protect your planet! Now that you *know* it's been marked for destruction, that ought to be easy enough!"

"It would be a lot easier if—"

"It will be a lot *safer*—for all of us, *including* your planet—if we wrap the majestrals in so many impenetrable paradoxes that they'll *never* be able to straighten them out!"

"But—"

"Hush, my love. Just do as I tell you."

Ryson nodded and set to work.

* * *

Yveena Soolis consulted the time machine's chronograph. Lord Mesmer's cargo ship bearing his outworld slaves and leperons should be arriving in three or four minutes. As soon as Ryson's family was aboard, the starship would lift into the starry night sky and the sanctuary of N-space.

"You really have a spaceyacht circling a planet in the Capella system?" she asked idly, her thoughts on the beautiful blue world that had given her birth—and that now she would never again see.

"I told you: I'm a wealthy dinosaur rancher."

"So I recall: a certain Lulmō Häistŏn." She straightened up from the control panel, kissed him fleetingly on the cheek. "Your explosives: they'll really destroy this machine?"

"They'll vaporize it, and everything within fifty yards of it. Your uncle maintains an unusual variety of munitions aboard his spaceship."

Yveena Soolis shuddered slightly as she pictured the Museum of Time in the Promptuary. "They'll . . . probably all be standing around, looking at the time machine when . . . when it . . ."

Ryson shrugged callously. "These are the same people who are going to destroy my entire planet—and everyone on it!"

The Earth girl nodded somberly. "I know. I know . . ." She glanced at the chronograph, touched a button, keyed a message into a small viewscreen. "Let's go: the machine will be uptiming in thirty seconds!"

Yveena Soolis was wrong about the risk run by the Intransmutable and the Duze Majestrals. Allden Janders the Intransmutable was cowering under a bed on the far side of Amaranth, while the eleven remaining majestrals were as yet unaware that the sacrosanct premises of the Thirteenth Majestrality had been invested by monstrous dinosaurs and even more hideous aliens.

The only sentient beings in the vicinity of Lord

Leuten's time machine when it exploded deep in the rubble of what had once been the Promptuary were three baffled Ravager cameramen and a second director, all of whom were wondering by what inexplicable course of events they had been brusquely transported from their routine filming of *Prince Saldeman's Quarries* to this outrageously bizarre interior of one of their galaxy-wide chain of theaters . . .*

"I've had a thought," said Ryson to Yveena Soolis as they slipped away unnoticed from the baroque splendor of the starship's banqueting hall towards the equally baroque cabin they had expropriated for themselves. Behind them came the joyous din of the Tandryl-Kundórrs noisily celebrating their first meal in freedom in more than two decades. Somewhere just at the level of perception the mysterious regions of N-space whispered around the ship and at the edges of their minds.

"What's the thought?" asked Yveena Soolis, stifling a yawn. "Now that you belong to me according to the customs of Stohlson's Redemption, shouldn't you first have to ask my permission to think?"

---

*The Ravagers who had come to Mesozoic Earth to film the cubs' adventure classic *Prince Saldeman's Quarries* were unspeakably impressed by the disappearance into thin air of their film's male and female leads, followed by hundreds of thousands of non-sentient cast and several dozen technicians and directors, none of whom was ever seen again. Ravager scientists and philosophers could only conclude that these apparently witless beasts had somehow jumped into another dimension. The Ravagers were both patient and long-lived. Twenty million years of feverish research devoted to the dinosaurs of this obscure planet eventually led to the discovery of the gateway into the fabulous Seventeenth Dimension. Gratefully taking along those dinosaurs which had survived their experiments, the Ravagers left their mundane universe behind and vanished forever into the enigmatic realms of the Seventeenth Dimension.

Ryson slipped his arm around her slender waist. "Remember when I told you about the Contractionites: the people who saved me from the Jairaben on Stohlson's Redemption?"

"The strange people who think they can stop the universe from shrinking?"

"Strange people, but good-hearted. As soon as we get aboard our yacht I'll try contacting them."

"Why would you do that?"

Ryson grinned. "Didn't you have me blow up the time machine to make whatever additional confusion you could for the Thirteenth Majestral?"

"Yes, but—"

"What do you think the level of confusion will rise to with the arrival of three heavily armed warships filled with religious fanatics seeking the crux of the contracting universe?"

"The crux of the contracting universe? But there *is* no—"

Ryson shook his head solemnly. "Of course there is. I've seen it myself, haven't I? It's right where you'd expect it to be: the augmentor that allows your murderous Palatines to uptime and downtime and run the galaxy to suit themselves."

"But . . . if the Contractionites destroy the augmentor—"

"—then we'll *all* be blurgs, and we can stop worrying about suddenly being flicked out of existence." Ryson pulled Yveena Soolis tight, looked down into her shining eyes. "Especially you."